Smoke and M

Also by Leo McNeir

Getaway with Murder (ISBN 0 9524052 6 1)

Death in Little Venice (ISBN 0 9524052 7 X)

Kiss and Tell (ISBN 0 9531742 1 2)

Devil in the Detail (ISBN 0 9524052 2 0)

No Secrets (ISBN 0 9531742 4 7)

Sally Ann's Summer (ISBN 978 0 9531742 5 6)

and published by enigma publishing.

See the author's website: www.leomcneir.com

enigma publishing

PO Box 1901, Milton Keynes, MK19 6DN

First published 2009

The events and characters described in *Smoke and Mirrors* are entirely fictitious, and any apparent resemblance to real people, companies or occurrences is entirely coincidental.

A CIP record for this book is available from the British Library.

ISBN 978-0-9531742-7-0

Prepared by *specialist* publishing services ltd, Montgomery

Printed in Great Britain by Bell & Bain Ltd, Glasgow

Smoke and Mirrors

Leo McNeir

enigma
publishing

The author

Leo McNeir is a linguist and lexicographer and has edited ten dictionaries in fifteen languages in the past decade, the standard works in their field.

Smoke and Mirrors is his seventh novel, following the successful publication of *Getaway with Murder* (2000), *Death in Little Venice* (2001), *Kiss and Tell* (2003), *Devil in the Detail* (2004), *No Secrets* (2006) and *Sally Ann's Summer* (2007).

He lives with cookery writer Cassandra McNeir and their cat, Mog, in a 300-year-old cottage in a Northamptonshire village.

They have a narrowboat on the Grand Union Canal.

Dedication

For Mac and Joyce, Wendy, Deborah and Susan

Prologue

The small convoy of vehicles rolled appropriately along the dual carriageway like a funeral procession. At its head, a police car carried two constables and a uniformed inspector. Next, a police van, the title *Incident Unit* painted on the sides. Behind it, another car. At the rear, a second van, unmarked, dark blue. Anyone familiar with police activity would have identified it immediately as a mortuary van.

They converged on a village in the south of Northamptonshire, not far from the ancient borough of Stony Stratford and the Victorian railway town of Wolverton.

Seven o'clock on a bright mid-summer morning. The sun broke free of cloud cover as the cortege turned off the dual carriageway at a sign indicating Knightly St John. A minute later the leading driver caught sight of the tall square tower of the church, rising up from among the trees. Progress was slow on the narrow, twisting road. It led to a sharp left-hand bend where they passed the first cottages on entering the high street.

Glimpsing houses and cottages of pale limestone under roofs of slate or thatch, they cruised the full length of the street, passing the church on their left and the pub on their right. Just beyond the primary school they turned left and followed the road round in a sweeping curve. The church tower dominated the skyline, the clock face looking down on them like an impassive eye. It registered five past seven as the convoy steered into a modern executive housing estate, known as Martyrs Close, behind the church and came to a halt beside a grass triangle partly covered with bramble bushes, opposite the churchyard's back door.

A man and a woman were chatting together beside the brambles. Seeing the police vehicles arrive, they stopped talking and turned to face their visitors. The man, in overalls and leaning on a shovel, was stocky with thinning cropped grey hair. The woman wore a grey dress and a dog collar. The Reverend Angela Hemingway, vicar of Knightly St John, shook hands with the inspector and introduced Henry Tutt, church groundsman and grave digger.

After examining and photographing the site, the police began unloading equipment. The inspector gave Henry Tutt the go-ahead; he cleared the bramble bushes away with a chainsaw and dragged them into a pile against the churchyard wall. An open-sided tent like a small marquee provided shade for Henry and one of the constables as they dug down into the clay soil. The young officer was amazed at the work rate of the older man who was well into his sixties but dug steadily, flinging the earth onto a pile just outside the tent.

The excavation had attracted the attention of the neighbours, who watched the sombre working party from behind their curtains. The exhumation of a grave engendered a morbid fascination, but no-one wanted to be seen standing in the street gawping at the proceedings.

The diggers had just reached a heavier layer of damp clay, and even Henry had had to slow down, when the door opened in the churchyard wall and a girl stepped through. She was thin and blonde, almost waif-like, wearing a T-shirt and jeans. Nobody paid her any attention, apart from Angela Hemingway who acknowledged her with a nod. The girl held back at first but gradually advanced until she was standing beside the vicar. They exchanged murmured greetings and watched the digging in silence.

Then it happened. Henry thrust his spade into the earth and met resistance. The police officers stared into the hole. Someone remarked that it was not as deep as they had expected. Henry grunted agreement and, alone in the grave, began shovelling more carefully. He took a gardener's trowel from his back pocket and scraped the wet clay into a bucket. To the accompaniment of mutterings from Henry, the grave's contents were gradually revealed. Henry scratched his head and looked over at the vicar, bewildered. Some of the officers dropped to their knees for a closer inspection.

A gesture from Henry summoned Angela closer, and both she and the thin girl advanced to the graveside. Angela gasped and put a hand to her mouth. The girl stared wide-eyed at what lay in the dark damp ground by Henry's muddy boots.

1
Pain

The old pain was still there, even after two years. Marnie pulled out the battered blue folder which she kept in her desk in the office barn. It lay concealed at the back of the bottom drawer and had not been brought out into the light of day since she first put it there the summer before last.

It was a quiet morning, the sun rising through a clear sky, as Marnie carried the folder through the spinney towards the canal. She emerged in sunlight close to the docking area where her narrowboat, *Sally Ann*, was moored. In the galley she prepared coffee and settled in a safari chair at the table in the saloon. Being on *Sally Ann* was somehow comforting.

Even now, she could still only just bear to read the notes and cuttings from that time. Toni Petrie, the Reverend Toni Petrie, had been killed in her own church. Her ministry had lasted barely a month, and even though they outwardly had little in common – Marnie was an agnostic and no church-goer – in that time they had become friends. Marnie had envisaged a friendship that would endure, but it had been cut down, just as Toni had been cut down by the same hand that had almost put an end to Marnie herself.

Toni had been the victim of the same hatred that had caused the death, the *murder*, of the vicar of the parish church of Knightly St John some three and a half centuries earlier in the time of the English Civil Wars. That summer, the brief summer of Toni Petrie, had stirred up ancient conflicts and tensions. And now Marnie feared they were about to be aroused again.

2
Angel of death

'No! I can't believe I'm hearing this. Tell me it isn't true.'

Marnie paused before replying. 'It *is* true, Beth. I'd hardly ring to tell you something *wasn't* true, would I? Think about it.'

'But they can't be *serious*, not after all the trouble there was two years ago.'

Marnie looked over to the window of her office, a small converted barn, its heavy timber doors drawn back in the daytime, revealing tinted glass like a shop front. Across the cobbled yard she could see roses climbing up the walls of three renovated cottages. The old stone farm buildings were bathed in pale summer sunshine, an idyllic peaceful English scene like a *Country Living* calendar.

'Well, they are serious, in fact they've already made a start.'

'Already?'

'This morning. Anne's gone up to have a look. She was half frightened, half bursting with curiosity. In the end the curious side won.'

Beth groaned. 'Oh god. At eighteen, kids aren't nervous about things like that. But Anne really ought to know better. Think how much she was involved in that business with the murder of the vicar, *vicars* I ought to say. I wish they weren't digging all that up again.'

'They've decided to go ahead as a kind of tribute to Toni's memory. You know it was her wish to move Sarah into the churchyard.'

Marnie's eyes strayed to the blue folder that was now lying on her desk. She had read it through that morning. The memory of that other morning when she had chanced upon the grave had come back vividly. Attracted by a doorway in the churchyard wall, half hidden by ivy, she had walked through to discover part of a headstone concealed in a tangle of brambles. It marked the grave of a young woman who had died in 1645.

Why had she been buried *outside* the churchyard? The question had sparked the interest of both Toni Petrie and her predecessor, Randall Hughes. He had just left the parish in an atmosphere of open hostility to become rural dean. Research had revealed that the young woman, Sarah Anne Day, committed suicide out of shame at the part her family had played in the death of the vicar. The Reverend Jonathan Goldsworthy was a royalist sympathiser in the first civil war; the village predominantly supported Parliament.

'I still don't like it, Marnie. You should stop them. You don't know where this will lead.'

'*I* should stop them? Beth, I don't think there was a letter in the post telling me I was now Head of the Church of England, and no messages from anyone in Canterbury as far as I know.'

'Marnie, the Archbishop of Canterbury is based in Lambeth Palace in London.'

'Of course. Perhaps I should just check the answerphone again.'

'You know what I mean.' Beth had a logic all her own. 'I only hope it will all pass over smoothly without unpleasantness, so everyone can get back to a normal life.'

'Normal life in these parts takes some unusual turns.' Marnie spoke from the heart. She had run into one bizarre event after another since leaving London two years earlier to start a new life and a new business. 'Everywhere I go there seem to be bodies lying around.'

Beth agreed. 'True. Let's hope this time things will be different.'

Marnie sighed. 'Well *hardly*, Beth. They're exhuming a *grave*. I think that *might* involve a body. That's the whole *point*. They're going to re-inter that poor girl.'

'What's her name again?'

'Sarah Anne Day.'

'Yes, well you should keep out of it. You don't want to be getting the reputation as an Angel of Death. It might ruin your business. I can't see anyone renting a cottage or barn conversion from you if they think something unpleasant is going to fall out of the closet.'

'I have no intention of going anywhere near the church until the whole matter is finished.'

Out of the corner of her eye Marnie noticed rapid movement in the courtyard. Seconds later Anne appeared breathless in the doorway. She was about to speak when she realised Marnie was on the phone. Panting, she crossed the office and flopped down onto the chair by her desk. 'Look, Beth, I'm going to have to go now. There's a lot to do. I'll call you later.'

After disconnecting, Marnie waited while Anne got her breath back. 'That was a dramatic entrance. What's up?'

Anne's slight chest was heaving. 'You'll never guess what it is.'

'You're right.'

Anne bit her lip. 'They've found a body in the grave.'

'Ah. In that case, you're wrong. That's just what I *was* expecting.'

'Really?'

'It's hardly surprising. A grave's a dead cert for a body, if you see what I mean.'

She had no idea why she was treating everything so lightly. Correction. She knew perfectly well. Anne had already been through enough drama in her young life and, although Marnie was aware of her friend's depth of character, she had no wish to add to her experience in that direction. *Angel of Death*, indeed!

Anne collected herself. 'Sorry. I'm not making much sense, am I? I'll start again. They've dug down into Sarah's grave and found *two* bodies.'

'*Two*?' Marnie frowned. 'How can there be two?'

Anne sat upright in the chair. 'The body on top of the coffin didn't date back to the sixteen hundreds. I heard one of the men say he thought it could be modern. It just looked like muddy bones to me … *horrible*.' She grimaced.

Marnie mulled this over. On one point she was absolutely clear.

'Anne (with an 'e'), we're not going to get involved in this. It's none of our business and we're going to keep well out of it.'

Anne pulled a face. 'Er, that might be difficult.'

Suspicion. 'How might it be difficult?'

'Angela sent me to ask you to come up straight away. She said they'll need a statement from you as you were the person who originally found the grave.'

Marnie was puzzled. 'Why should the church want a statement from me?'

'Not the church, Marnie. The police.'

'The *police?*'

Anne nodded. 'Angela rang Randall, as he's the rural dean. He's coming over too from Brackley. And a detective is on his way. They want you and me to be available … to give evidence.'

Marnie sighed. 'Oh god. Here we go again.'

Marnie drove them to the grave site in deference to Anne's earlier exertions. On the way up the field track that led to the village, she had the foreboding that the finding of the extra body in Sarah's grave was going to unlock further tragedy.

She parked the Land Rover Discovery outside one of the Martyrs Close executive houses and they walked a short distance towards the churchyard wall. The grave's location was easy to spot under the white tent on the grass.

Uniformed police officers were busy beside the tent, cordoning it off with yellow tape. As Marnie and Anne approached, one of the men looked in their direction. He knew them both from previous encounters. Marnie had the reputation of not always being as co-operative as they would have wished, but he had to admit he liked the way she looked. She was thirty or so, fairly tall, slim, with dark shoulder-length wavy hair, clean regular features and an intelligent face. That day her expression was serious.

Beside her, Anne looked young for her age. She could easily have passed for fifteen or sixteen, though he knew she was older. She drove around in a bright red Mini, which he rightly guessed had been a present for her eighteenth birthday. Marnie and Ralph had presented her with it, and the car had become the proverbial pride and joy. Anne was almost as tall as Marnie, with pale skin and a thin boyish figure. Her eyes were bright with curiosity.

The constable stepped forward. Before he could speak, a voice called out from behind him.

'It's all right, officer. Marnie's been asked to come.'

The policeman turned. It was another woman who had spoken. Women seemed to be taking over the world. This one was a vicar, about Marnie's height with a long face that was horsy but not unpleasant.

'I knew that, miss. I was only going to inform Mrs Walker that my colleagues had had to leave the site.'

'Oh.' Marnie stopped in front of the constable. 'Does that mean you want me to go back or wait here?'

'It means we don't need to interview you here and now. I'm sorry for the inconvenience.'

Marnie saw that Angela had been in conversation with another woman, whom she did not recognise. The latter was dressed in a smartly-tailored jacket and slacks, the English rose type, blonde hair in the style of Princess Diana, like so many women at that time. The two of them came closer, while the constable resumed his taping.

Marnie turned to Anne. 'We seem to have had a wasted journey.'

Angela stepped forward. 'Sorry, Marnie. We wanted to stop you before you set off, but I didn't have your number with me.' She indicated her companion. 'I'm not sure if you know Celia, Celia Devere?'

Marnie offered a hand. 'Hallo. Marnie Walker. This is my friend and colleague, Anne Price. Are you involved in the reburial?'

The newcomer seemed uncertain how to answer the question. 'Well, er, not actually. Though I suppose ... You see, we ... we own the land.'

Marnie looked at the triangle, which was no bigger than a small lawn. 'This piece of ground here?'

More hesitation. 'Well, no.' She made a gesture that encompassed the whole area around them. 'All of this, really.'

Angela stepped in. 'Celia's family owns the land on which these houses are built and most of the land around here. They live at the Court.'

Marnie smiled. 'Sorry to be thick, but what court?'

'Knightly Court.' Angela pointed down the street. 'It's the big house beyond the far wall.'

Marnie and Anne followed Angela's finger and noticed for the first time that Martyrs Close ended as a cul-de-sac at a high stone wall.

Angela continued. 'I suppose, technically, your family are lords of the manor, aren't they, Celia?'

'I suppose so.' Celia turned to Marnie. 'You live in the village?'

'Glebe Farm, down by the canal.'

'Of course. I've heard about you. You actually live on a boat, isn't that right?'

'Temporarily. We're renovating the farm. I hope to move into the farmhouse shortly. We don't farm, of course, but we have a few acres of land.'

'My husband's a property developer, but perhaps you knew that. Is that your line of business?'

'Only because most of the buildings at Glebe Farm are ruins, or rather they *were*. I'm an interior designer.'

Celia looked steadily at Marnie. 'How interesting. You have your own company?'

Marnie inclined her head towards Anne. 'Standing beside me. We're what you'd call a close-knit team. Talking of which, we'd better get back to the drawing board.'

'It's been nice meeting you, Marnie.' Celia lowered her voice. 'Angela was just telling me that you originally found the grave here.'

'By chance. I walked through the gate from the churchyard and there it was.'

'You're not a member of the congregation, are you? I don't remember you being involved in the church.'

Marnie had the impression that Celia did not want her to go. 'No,' she said simply.

'I was just wondering.' Celia said, 'how you came to be passing this way on the day you found the grave.'

'I was taking a walk, getting to know the village. We hadn't long moved in.'

'Ah yes, of course. I couldn't imagine why anyone would be searching among the brambles.' Celia held out a hand to Marnie. 'See you again, no doubt.'

She walked over to a car and drove off. Marnie and the others watched her go and strolled along the pavement.

'What did you say her name was, Angela, your Princess Di look-alike?'

'Devere, Celia Devere. Oh yes, I see what you mean about the *look-alike*. It's the hair, I suppose.'

'Same hair, same colouring, same style. Same car too: Audi convertible. It's odd that I've never seen Knightly Court, or even heard of it.'

'Not really, Marnie. You approach it from a road that only leads to their house and grounds. They also have a gate into the churchyard, further round.'

Anne joined in. 'Manor houses usually had their own private entrance, didn't they? Did the Devere family build the church?'

Angela frowned in concentration. 'I don't think they go back that far. Randall will know the history, if you're interested. I think they took over the manor at about the time of Henry VIII, or thereabouts.'

'And her husband's the lord of the manor?'

'Oh no. It's his father, old Marcus Devere, who owns the place. Celia and her husband live in one wing. It's a very big house.'

They arrived at Marnie's car.

'Did the police say who they thought it might be in Sarah's grave? Presumably her coffin is down there as well?'

Angela grimaced. 'It's horrible, Marnie. They found human remains, partly wrapped in some sort of material, resting on top of Sarah's coffin.'

'You saw them?'

Angela's eyes flickered towards Anne. 'Yes, we both did. They couldn't identify the … whoever it was. The body was little more than skin and bones in what looked like a shroud.'

'Well, this has been a wasted journey for me, as it turns out. I expect I'll get back to find the police in their usual parking place in the courtyard.'

'Usual place?' Angela looked puzzled. 'The detective said he had to speak to Henry Tutt in private without delay. He wanted to see all the tools in his shed as a priority.'

Marnie took the car keys from her pocket. 'That figures.'

'He asked if I knew your phone number.'

Marnie laughed. 'I thought the police know it by heart.'

'Do you know this officer then, Marnie?'

'Let me guess, was it Chief Inspector Bartlett or Sergeant Marriner?'

'Neither of those. Let me think. What did he say his name was?' Angela reflected. 'Binns, yes, DS Ian Binns. That's it.'

Anne made a faint snorting sound as if she had suppressed a sneeze. Marnie pulled the car door open.

'That's a new one on me. Binns. Never heard of him. Oh well, a pleasure in store, no doubt.'

On the drive back to Glebe Farm, Marnie heard another odd sound from Anne and glanced across to see her struggling to control her expression.

'Are you laughing, Anne? What's so funny?'

'Binns!' Anne exclaimed. 'It's a good job he works here and not in London.'

Marnie looked totally blank. 'I don't get it.'

'Really not, Marnie? If he were in the Met, he'd be ... Binns of the Yard!' Anne shrieked like a fishwife.

Marnie laughed, relieved that Anne could see the funny side of things. She had the feeling that the euphoria would not last.

Arriving back at Glebe Farm, Marnie turned in to the garage, another small byre at the back of the office barn. She had been muttering to Anne that they had not so far managed to get the week underway, when she spotted a strange car outside the farmhouse.

'We've got a visitor, Anne. No prizes for guessing who it is. And you'll be pleased to see he's parked appropriately, in the yard.'

This time there was no laughter from Anne. The presence of the police conducting an investigation had become a not unfamiliar experience during their time in Knightly St John. Now, the connection with the suicide of Sarah Anne Day in 1645 and the murder of the Rev. Toni Petrie brought back memories that were still raw. Marnie herself had come close to becoming a murder victim. Anne had saved one man's life, and most people in the village had been affected by the events that had led to the death of their vicar two years before.

DS Ian Binns was peering in through the window of the office barn. He looked round when Marnie and Anne turned the corner. Stocky, an inch or two taller than Marnie and a few years older, with thinning short hair, he looked tough. His expression was grim. When he spoke, it came as a surprise.

'Mrs Walker? Marnie Walker?' His tone was quiet. He held up a warrant card. 'I'm Detective Sergeant Binns. Good morning.'

'Good morning.' Marnie's own voice was deep for a woman. 'Would you like coffee?'

'I'd love one, thanks. It's been quite a morning.'

They settled in the office, the detective in the visitor's chair, a steaming mug before him. Anne sat at her desk across the room, clasping a mug in both hands. Marnie took

Binns's acceptance as a good sign. When the police came to call they normally refused, which she took as a measure of their distrust.

'It must have been quite a surprise, finding a second body in the grave.'

'You can say that again.' He took out a notebook. 'I need to ask you a few questions, Mrs Walker. Then in due course I'm going to need a statement.'

'That's fine.'

Binns asked Marnie to describe how she had come to find the grave. While she spoke, he took notes in shorthand.

'So you just saw the headstone by chance.'

'Yes.'

'Do you often go through that gate in the wall?'

'No. That was the first time.'

'You had a particular reason for going there?'

'I'd noticed the gate and wondered where it led. I hadn't long been in the village. I was getting my bearings, getting to know the place.'

'I see. That's odd, isn't it?'

Marnie felt her stomach turn over. She had the feeling she was about to be caught out, though there was no reason why she should be. It had been the story of her relationship with the police; she somehow always managed to give the wrong impression. This was usually exacerbated by DCI Bartlett, who succeeded in twisting whatever she said to her disadvantage.

'Odd?' she repeated.

'Yes. I mean there's no headstone now, is there? What became of it, do you know?'

Marnie relaxed. 'Someone smashed it. Toni and I … that's the previous vicar …'

Binns nodded. 'Toni Petrie, the one who was killed.'

'Yes. We moved the broken pieces to the crypt to protect them from further damage. People have long memories about some things. Toni said she wanted to give the stones sanctuary.'

'A nice thought.'

Marnie was surprised how easy she found it to talk to this detective. 'I suppose the pieces will still be down there. Is it important?'

'Hard to tell at this stage. What I'd like to establish is who smashed the headstone and why? Can you help with either of those questions, Mrs Walker?'

Marnie paused before replying. She had no desire to rake over the conflicts and tensions that had marked her first year in Knightly St John.

'Sergeant Binns, I really don't think that incident can have anything to do with the remains found in Sarah's grave.' Binns began to speak, but Marnie raised a hand to silence him. 'I know you're going to say something like, *we'll be the judge of that* … well of course, I know you have to be thorough. The point is, there was a lot of ill feeling at the time we moved here between the former vicar –'

'Toni Petrie?'

'No. Her predecessor, Randall Hughes. He left under a cloud – arguments about priorities, policies and so on – and his opponents were delighted. Then they found he'd been replaced by a *woman*. Some people didn't like that. Someone from Sarah's family – yes, they're still around – put flowers on her grave and a parishioner took exception to that in a fit of temper.'

'A parishioner with a sledgehammer and an almighty rage,' Binns said slowly.

'Look, Mr Binns, it's all over now. Everything changed with Toni's death. People got back their sense of proportion. Those wounds have healed. Let's not open them up again. This other body, this skeleton, how long has it been in the ground?'

'We don't know that yet.'

'But probably a long time?'

'That's possible.'

'Do you really believe anyone concerned about parish pump matters like the church maintenance fund or the state of the porch would be involved in this burial? It could be ancient.'

'That depends on a lot of factors, Mrs Walker.'

Marnie shook her head. 'Such as a local argument about women priests?'

'Possibly. Who knows? But you're making a big assumption.'

'What assumption?'

'That the smashing of the headstone was about this woman, Sarah Anne Day.'

Marnie made a dismissive gesture. 'What else could it be?'

'People have long memories about some things. You said so yourself. What if the anger that led to the headstone being desecrated was provoked by the *other* body in the grave? Had you thought of that?'

Later that evening Marnie was sitting propped up on pillows in the sleeping cabin on *Thyrsis*, talking on the phone. As usual when Ralph was working away from home, he rang at bedtime for a chat.

Dr Ralph Lombard, visiting Professor of Economic Sciences in the University of Oxford, was one of the country's leading economists. In his early forties, he had been Marnie's lover and partner for most of the time she had lived in the village. Eventually they planned to move into the main house at Glebe Farm and some day they would marry. In the meantime they were temporarily using Ralph's narrowboat, *Thyrsis*, as sleeping quarters and Marnie's boat, *Sally Ann*, moored close by, as their floating dining room.

'So how are things up in the far north?'

'Oh, the life of the external examiner is the usual wild ride.' He chuckled. 'The University of Durham is lovely, of course. Professor Charlborough is rather a pedant, but he's not a bad old stick. More to the point, how are things with you? There was something on the ten o'clock news: remains found in an unmarked grave in a village in Northamptonshire?'

'I'm surprised it made the main news on the BBC.'

'It was just a snippet and I was changing out of my suit, so I missed most of it. This is presumably Sarah's grave?'

Marnie gave him the story. He listened in silence to the end.

'Did this detective ... what did you say he was called ... Binns? Did he have any idea how long the skeleton had been in the ground?'

'Too early to know, but I think it could be very old.'

'Why do you say that, Marnie?'

'Why? Well, don't you?'

'Is there any evidence to support that conclusion?'

'You're sounding like an academic.'

'Could be because I am an academic. So, is there?'

'Ralph, it's a *skeleton*.'

'I understand that. But do you know how long it takes for a body to decompose and become skeletal?'

Marnie reflected. 'I just thought ... I sort of assumed ...' Her voice petered out. 'Do you know, Ralph?'

'Not at all. I think it probably depends on the conditions in the ground, type of soil, humidity, the protection round the body.'

'You're saying you think it could be modern?'

'No. I'm saying that in the absence of more information, more actual *evidence*, we can't determine how old it is.'

'Binns said something strange – oh by the way, Anne calls him *Binns of the Yard*. I thought you'd like to know.'

Ralph laughed. 'She would! What did he say, your Binns of the Yard?'

'He wondered if the smashing of the headstone was not about Sarah Anne Day but to do with the other body.'

'Did he, now? I can see the logic in that.'

'But don't you remember, Ralph, old Mr Fletcher, the farmer, admitted he'd done it on account of Sarah?'

'Yes, and I'm absolutely convinced Mr Fletcher knew nothing about the other body. No one did. Let's hope the police soon identify it.'

'Or establish that it's too old to be identified,' Marnie added.

'Yes. That might be the best outcome. The last thing we want is for all that business to be stirred up again.'

3
Statement

Marnie heard the sound of an engine and opened her eyes in the dark cabin. She felt *Thyrsis* rock gently at her mooring as the boat passed. The portholes were blocked in by padded buttons, but a faint light seeped under the door. Morning had come.

She had passed a restless night, dreaming of a smashed headstone, thatched houses on fire in the civil war, a vicar killed in his own church, parishioners finding his body at the foot of the tower stairs.

One image stayed fixed firmly in her mind more than all others: a girl was kneeling on the floor, cradling the head of a man in her lap. Round his neck was a noose in the form of a leather belt. Angry red bruising showed where it had bitten into his skin. The scene was the office barn at Glebe Farm. The girl was Anne. The man was Randall Hughes, the former vicar who had hanged himself from a hook embedded in the beam across the ceiling. The beam supported the floor of the attic where Anne had her room and slept every night, untroubled by thoughts of hangings.

It was believed that from that same hook Sarah Anne Day had hanged herself at the time of the civil war. She had discovered her family's implication in the death of the royalist vicar, Jonathan Goldsworthy. The anguish had been too much for Sarah to bear, at a time when the whole country was writhing in torment, and Northamptonshire had become the centre of the decisive actions in the first civil war, culminating in the battle of Naseby.

Almost three hundred and fifty years later, further tension had come to Knightly St John with the appointment of Randall Hughes as the new vicar. His opponents argued that he had swept away the traditional forms of worship and placed the upkeep of the church buildings above the needs perceived by the community. He merely regarded himself as 'progressive' and responsible. Replaced by a woman vicar, he saw himself as instrumental in her death and felt the same overpowering remorse as Sarah Anne Day.

Randall's attempt at suicide failed because of the swift action of Anne, helped by the very man who had been one of Randall's main opponents: Albert Fletcher, the old farmer who had sold Glebe Farm to Marnie.

In a state of shock at so much turmoil and tragedy that summer, the village had given itself a good shaking, recovered some of its equilibrium and settled down to normality. Now, with the mystery of an unexpected body being retrieved from Sarah's grave, the whole mixture could bubble up again.

Marnie groaned audibly and was surprised to hear the sound echoed from close by. Seconds later she was joined on the bed by a sturdy black cat. She felt hefty paws kneading the duvet near the pillow and turned her head to find herself looking into deep amber eyes set in a solid round face. The eyes blinked slowly. Dolly snuggled up on the duvet against

Marnie's shoulder and began emitting a slow, quiet purring. It was comforting, but could not dispel Marnie's anxieties for long.

Marnie entered the office barn to start the day and stopped abruptly, gasping with shock. In the middle of the floor Anne was at the top of the aluminium step-ladder, reaching for the hook in the beam.

Anne glanced round. 'Oh great. Glad you're here, Marnie. Can you just hold the ladder steady. It's a bit wobbly up here.'

Marnie rushed forward. 'What are you doing?' She took firm hold with both hands.

'You'll see.'

Marnie looked up, but her view was obscured by Anne, who seemed to be fiddling with something. 'Are you removing the hook?'

Anne ignored the question. 'I'm coming down. Mind I don't tread on you.'

At that moment Marnie became aware of a smell, fresh and fragrant, and for a moment she wondered if Anne was wearing perfume. The girl stepped down onto the floor beside her and looked upwards.

'There. How's that?'

From the hook hung a spray of lavender, its vivid colour brightening the office, its scent enriching the air.

'I should've asked you first, Marnie, but I thought I'd just give it a try to see if it worked. What do you think?'

Marnie stepped back for a better view. 'Well, yes, it looks good.'

'You don't mind the smell? Of course, it'll soon fade, but while it lasts I thought it might be pleasant.'

'I like it.'

'Not too overpowering?'

'No.'

'Great. So is it all right to leave it up there?'

'Fine by me.'

Anne folded the ladder together and took it back to the garage barn. Marnie sat at her desk, gazing up at the lavender, wondering why Anne should suddenly have chosen that time to decorate the office in this way.

When Anne returned, she picked up a bag that Marnie noticed for the first time was lying by the foot of the attic wall-ladder.

'Off to college?'

'Yes. Back at lunchtime, early afternoon at the latest. Do we need any shopping?'

'Not for now. I have to go out later anyway. I'll sort it.'

Anne flashed a smile. 'Bye, then.'

'Anne?'

The girl paused in the doorway.

Marnie glanced briefly up at the lavender. 'Good idea, nice thinking. I understand.'

Anne smiled again and shrugged. 'Thought it might help.'

The door had barely closed behind Anne when the phone rang.

'Walker and Co, good morning.' Marnie automatically pulled a notepad towards her across the desk.

'Is that Marnie Walker?'

'Speaking.'

The voice seemed vaguely familiar.

'This is Celia Devere. We met yesterday at the, er ...'

'In Martyrs Close, yes. What can I do for you?'

'Sorry to phone so early, but I have to go out and there's something I wanted to talk to you about. I hope it's convenient.'

'Absolutely.'

'Somehow, the timing didn't seem appropriate yesterday.'

'Appropriate for what exactly?'

Marnie heard a car pull up outside and guessed that the police had arrived to take her statement. For once she was glad to see them. She wanted the whole business to be over.

'Well,' Celia seemed hesitant. 'I was wondering. Would you be free to meet me, for a chat some time?'

'A chat. About?'

'One or two things, actually.'

Marnie was intrigued. 'Would this concern interior decoration?'

A pause. 'Among other things.'

Marnie reached for the diary. 'Shall we set a date?'

'Can it be soon?'

Marnie thought she detected pleading in her tone. 'If it's urgent I could come round at the end of the working day, say about six or six-thirty?'

'Oh no. No, not then.' Celia spoke in a rush. 'I'd rather see you during the day, when my husband's at work.'

'Celia, I think I ought to tell you that I like to involve both parties when I prepare a project. It removes any causes for misunderstanding later.'

Marnie waited for a reply, aware that someone was hovering outside the office door.

'There won't be a problem about that, Marnie. I just wanted us to have a preliminary chat, just the two of us, to sort a few things out.'

'Okay. What about mid-morning on Thursday?'

'That's ideal.' Celia sounded relieved. 'Ten o'clock?'

'It's in the diary.'

'You know how to reach us?'

'No problem. I'll bring my trusty navigator.'

'I'd rather you came alone, if you don't mind.' Her tone was serious.

'All right, but Anne will have to be involved as things move ahead.'

'Very well.'

After disconnecting, Marnie went to the office door. She opened it to find Angela Hemingway.

'Why didn't you come in?'

'I saw you were on the phone, Marnie. Anyway, I was admiring what you've done to the place. How soon before the house is ready?'

'Good question. Some way to go yet, and I have to earn the money to keep things moving.'

'It's all looking beautiful. I love those climbing roses on the cottages.'

'You haven't come to talk about aesthetics, Angela.'

'No. Have you got a minute?'

It was a fine morning and they opted to go for a stroll. Slowly they walked through the spinney towards the docking area where *Sally Ann* was moored.

'Have the police taken your statement yet, Marnie?'

'Not so far. I've met Sergeant Binns. He seemed all right, but I worry about where all this might lead, this probing into the smashing of the headstone.'

'I feel the same way. He's already had the pieces photographed in the crypt.'

'Has he had them removed?'

'No. He's had the crypt sealed up, wants the forensic people to examine everything. They're arriving later this morning. That's why I came to see you so early.'

Marnie sighed. 'It won't do any good, just cause trouble.'

'I know. I wish there was some way we could counteract it all.'

Marnie grinned. 'Anne's already made a start.'

'Oh?'

'You know the hook in our office where Sarah ...?'

'Yes.'

Marnie stopped walking. 'Let's wait till we get back and I'll show you.'

They emerged from the trees into sunlight and walked alongside *Sally Ann*. Stepping onto the deck, Marnie perched on the stern rail. Angela settled on the lid of the gas bottle container, looking thoughtful.

'You had a reason for coming to see me, Angela. It wasn't just to ask if I'd given my statement or to tell me about the crypt, was it?'

'They've barred us from removing Sarah's coffin.' Angela's tone was flat.

'Who have?'

'The police. They contacted the diocese. The bishop phoned me last night.'

'This is just a temporary thing, surely?'

'Randall thinks our opponents could use this to reopen the whole question of re-interment.'

'Randall's a tough cookie. I don't see him letting anyone get the better of him in this, or in anything else.'

'You're right, Marnie. But the bishop might feel under pressure and he might want to avoid further conflict. Randall may be the rural dean, but he can't countermand the bishop.'

Marnie turned to look across the water. Beyond the canal, fields stretched away to the horizon. Sheep and cows were dotted over a rolling landscape of meadows. A church spire pierced the skyline in the distance, but no other buildings were visible. On the mainline of the canal Ralph's boat, *Thyrsis*, was moored at rightangles to *Sally Ann*, its green and gold paintwork blending harmoniously with the countryside.

Marnie was struggling with her thoughts. As a devout non-believer she was on one level indifferent to where Sarah Anne Day was buried. What difference could it make? The young woman had been dead for more than three centuries. Moving her a short distance into the churchyard seemed irrelevant. On the other hand, she knew it had been Toni Petrie's last wish. For that reason as much as any other, it mattered to Angela and Randall.

And there were other factors. Randall's attempt to kill himself had been a direct and macabre link back to Sarah. Marnie had her own constant reminder of the hatred and conflict that had led to the death of two vicars. Her ribs still ached on occasions. She too had come close to death from the same weapon that had killed Jonathan Goldsworthy. Good reasons for wanting the whole episode in the history of the village to be laid to rest. Reburying Sarah would symbolically achieve that end and draw a line under the entire episode.

Both women sat in the quiet of their thoughts. Marnie broke the silence.

'Yeah. We've got to get her into the churchyard.'

Angela looked up. 'We can only do that with the support of the bishop.'

'Then we'd better make sure we get it.'

'There's something else, Marnie.' Angela looked away.

'Another problem?'

'No. The police let us inspect the coffin to see if it was capable of being moved. The subsoil's very damp down there, and the wood could've been damaged.'

'Was it?'

'Rotten. We'll have to provide a new one. More expense.'

'But –'

'That isn't all, Marnie. There was a brass plaque on the lid with an inscription: *Mors vincit omnia*.'

Marnie frowned. 'My Latin's rather rusty, but that sounds familiar.'

'You're probably thinking of *Love conquers everything*. This quotation has been changed to mean *Death conquers everything*.'

'Is it from the Bible?'

Angela shook her head. 'No. It's one of the Roman poets, Vergil. I checked. So whoever arranged her burial, added the inscription.'

'And whoever that person was, they had a classical education.'

Angela agreed. 'Yes, and felt very bitter about what had happened.'

'Any idea who it might've been? A member of her family?'

'Hard to tell, but not very likely. They were simple country folk. It's a mystery. This whole thing's a mystery. My guess is it might have been the vicar who took over after Goldsworthy.'

'So, unfinished business, passed down through the ages from one vicar to another?'

Angela nodded. 'You could put it like that, though I can't prove it.'

Marnie stood up. 'Come on. We've both got work to do. Why don't I make you a cup of coffee before you go?'

Angela smiled. 'I thought you'd never ask.'

Back in the office barn, waiting for the coffee to filter, Angela admired Anne's spray of lavender.

'It's beautiful. I love the smell. How long has she been planning this?'

Marnie took mugs from the cupboard. 'It was an impulse. I think this is her gesture against the sadness of what happened here. She's determined to make the best of what we have, in everything, even this tragedy.'

Marnie had hoped that someone might come from the police to take her statement during the morning while Anne was at college, but it was not to be. WDC Cathy Lamb arrived in the early afternoon and parked in the slot usually taken by the police on their visits. It had become a private joke between them, but Marnie had learnt it was better not to make jokes about anything where the police were concerned.

Like all her colleagues, Lamb knew of Marnie's reputation for being less than totally open. Unlike them, she believed that Marnie tried to act with the best of intentions. She had been at her bedside in the intensive care unit when Marnie came close to death two years before and suspected that this coloured her judgment.

Anne was telling Marnie about the exhibition of students' work for the college open day when Lamb's car rolled into the courtyard. When Lamb came into the office, Anne was already putting the kettle on. Marnie offered her desk to the young officer for taking notes, and the three of them sat together in businesslike companionship. It took barely fifteen minutes for Lamb to assemble the facts of Marnie's involvement in finding the grave, discovering the smashed headstone and helping to carry the pieces into the crypt.

Lamb read through her notes in silence. 'And since that time you've had nothing further to do with the grave or the pieces of headstone. Is that right, Marnie?'

'Yes, though I did know about the plan to have Sarah reburied in the churchyard. Angela told me.'

'Are you on the PCC?'

'The what?'

'The parochial church council.'

'No. I'm not a church-goer.'

'Yet you're a friend of the vicar?'

'Yes. She doesn't seem to hold it against me.'

Lamb closed her notebook. 'I think I've got everything I need. Thanks, Marnie. I'll drop by some time with the statement for you to sign, unless you're coming into the station for any reason.'

'I wasn't planning to.'

Across the office Anne snorted. Marnie and Lamb looked at her.

'Sorry.' She got up and cleared away the mugs.

Changing the subject, Marnie escorted Lamb to the door. 'How are DCI Bartlett and DS Marriner these days? I was surprised not to see them.'

'They're okay. They lent me their season ticket to your car park.' She winked at Marnie. 'Actually, they're both working on a serious case in Northampton.'

Marnie knew better than to expect any details. 'So this one is just routine?'

Lamb shook her head. 'We never treat any case involving human remains as *just routine*.'

'Even when it's in a seventeenth century grave?'

'We don't know how old it is or how long it's been there. It's all questions at the moment, no answers. The body's being examined by an expert in Oxford.'

'Body? I thought it was just a skeleton.'

'It's a little more than that, but not much.'

'I was hoping you'd have it all wound up very quickly.'

'So were we. I shouldn't be saying this, but we don't even know the cause of death yet.'

'Really? I suppose that must be difficult when you've so little to go on.'

Lamb nodded. 'Early days.'

Marnie and Anne watched the unmarked police car drive out of the courtyard and head up the bumpy field track that led to the village.

'I hope that's an end to our involvement, Anne.'

'Me too.'

'What was that about, when you made a funny noise back then?'

'Sorry about that. It was silly. You know how you can sometimes get the craziest thoughts come into your head when you're faced with something really serious?'

'Go on.'

'Well, when she asked if you might be going to the police station to sign your statement, I suddenly got the idea you were going to say, *over my dead body*.'

They both laughed. Marnie put an arm round her friend's thin shoulders.

'I think that's known as gallows humour, Anne.'

They turned to go back into the office barn as their smiles slowly faded.

4
Smoke without fire

It seemed strange to Marnie, having the place to herself. After the college open day, Anne had gone back to Leighton Buzzard with her parents for a few days at home. On the following morning, Thursday, Marnie breakfasted alone on *Sally Ann*, opened the office and dealt with the post. For once she had to sift through the junk mail and the special offers, slot the bills and receipts into the appropriate trays on Anne's desk and prepare replies to correspondence. It was a reminder, if one was needed, of how much Anne contributed to the smooth running of Walker and Co.

Despite missing her friend's presence, Marnie was glad that Anne was out of the way while the grave remained as a kind of open wound in the village. And it was good for her to have a taste of family life again. Marnie sometimes worried that Anne was becoming too immersed in her work at the office and at college and that she needed to relax more with her parents, brother and friends.

Life in Knightly St John had at times been intense. When Marnie pointed this out to Anne, she had replied that her life was 'enjoyably balanced' between being Marnie's assistant and studying at the college in Northampton. The argument that she was perhaps spending too much time on serious work for a young person of her age was parried by the counter-argument from Anne that she was '*focused*, like you, Marnie.'

Marnie looked up at the spray of lavender suspended from the ceiling beam. It was typical of Anne's positive influence. She seemed to leave her mark wherever she went. College open day had been a revelation, though Marnie should not have been surprised.

Meeting Anne's parents by the college entrance the previous day, the four of them had walked through reception to be confronted immediately by the display of Anne's work. Although she had only completed the first year of the Advanced level course, her project on the Development of Design from the Art and Craft Movement to the Bauhaus had been chosen as the centrepiece of the annual exhibition. While Anne stood quietly aside, her parents had been visibly proud – and not a little surprised – to be approached by the head of the department of art and design. His words had echoed in Marnie's mind for the rest of the day.

'I have to tell you that Anne is without a doubt the most outstanding student I have ever taught.'

When the college principal joined them and added his comments, two patches of pink had spread across Anne's normally pale cheeks like a clown's make-up.

'In my opinion, your daughter's project dossier deserves to be published, not just as a comprehensive guide to the subject, but as a model of what a student can attain by sheer application and thoroughness.'

Afterwards in the car park there had been hugs and a few tears wiped away with laughter. Ray and Jackie Price had thanked Marnie for her encouragement and for supporting Anne's further education.

On the phone that evening, Marnie had narrated the episode to Ralph, who pronounced himself delighted but completely unsurprised. He was sure Anne would 'walk through' her A level exams the following summer and obtain a place at any university or art school of her choosing.

'That girl's got what it takes,' he had said, 'but you're the one who made it happen, Marnie. By your example, she's gained an insight into what can be achieved.'

After they disconnected, Marnie had thought about this for several minutes and was glad in her heart for Anne, though she added to herself, *even if the experience has almost killed her*.

Bringing her thoughts back to that Thursday morning, a glance at the clock told Marnie she had to be on her way. She gathered up a notebook and pens and thrust them into her briefcase. Celia Devere was expecting her at Knightly Court.

As instructed, Marnie parked the Discovery beside the Audi on the drive of Knightly Court. Built of the local stone in a pleasingly symmetrical style, the house was externally a Georgian manor, though Marnie guessed it had much earlier origins behind the façade. Hidden depths, she thought.

Celia Devere walked out onto the drive, wearing a cream silk shirt and light blue jeans, to receive her visitor with a friendly smile. She exuded informality and elegance. Greeting Marnie with a handshake, she showed her through to a morning room at the rear of the house. It overlooked a perfect lawn and herbaceous borders with distant views over the countryside. Crossing the entrance hall, Marnie noted the wallpaper. It was classical in style, but the pattern was washed-out. Faded grandeur, as if the house had grown tired.

Celia poured coffee from an insulated flask into cups of bone china.

'So nice of you to come, Marnie – is it all right if I call you by your Christian name? – I'm sure you must be very busy, and this is rather short notice.'

'I can usually be flexible. A friend of mine once said that being self-employed gave him total freedom … to work seven days a week.'

Celia laughed. 'Please call me Celia, by the way. I expect you're wondering why I asked you to come.'

'You mentioned on the phone that there were one or two things. I can probably guess one of them.'

'Can you?'

Marnie took the notebook from her bag and set it down on the sofa beside her. 'You said interior decoration was one of the matters.'

'Yes.' It was the expected reply, but Marnie had the impression it was of only secondary interest.

'This is a lovely house. Have you lived here long?'

'That depends what you mean.'

Not the expected reply. Marnie thought the question had been unambiguous. She tried to conceal her surprise and sipped coffee waiting for Celia to continue.

'The family's been here for generations.'

'Ah, yes. I meant you personally.'

'We moved into this wing when we returned from our honeymoon. That was six years ago. My father-in-law lives in what he calls his *apartments* at the other end of the house.'

'I see.' Marnie was well aware of the complications that can arise when refurbishing such a house piecemeal.

'I wonder if you do, Marnie. Before we talk about decoration, and other matters, there was something else. Has Rob Cardew been in touch with you?'

'No. I don't think I know a Mr Cardew.'

'He's Dr Cardew, actually, archaeologist. He's running the overall project.'

'Is this about Sarah's grave?'

'No, though I expect he'll be interested in it. You'll have to get him to explain it all, but the local universities are looking at settlements in the area, something to do with land use since the Romans?' She flapped a hand in the air. 'That sort of thing.'

'Why would he want to talk to me about it?'

'They want to dig holes all over the place to investigate what's under the ground.'

'I still don't follow.'

'They want landowners to let them dig on their land.'

'Great. They can come to Glebe Farm and dig us a pond in the garden. You think this Dr Cardew will want to talk to me?'

'Definitely. I'm sure he'll be in touch. When he came here he was eyeing the lawn with interest. I told him not to even *think* about asking.' Celia laughed. 'It's hundreds of years old.'

Marnie boggled. 'Literally?'

'Absolutely. Anyway, where were we? Oh yes, decoration. Dorothy Vane-Henderson said you did the … what do you call it – makeover? … at Hanford Hall. You did a marvellous job, apparently.'

'Is that what you want here, a makeover? This house is rather larger than Hanford Hall. It would take me a while to fit it into our programme.'

Celia stood up and poured more coffee. 'It would just be this wing of the house, at least initially. My father-in-law wouldn't want his part to be touched. He's quite elderly and wouldn't want the fuss.'

'Does he own the house? Sorry, I don't mean to pry, but it is relevant.'

'Questions like that are never simple with these old manor houses, Marnie. Marcus handed the property over to my husband some time ago, one of these schemes to avoid death duty, you know. But it still *feels* like it's his house.'

Marnie was taking notes. 'I only want to establish that we're not going to run into objections when we've reached an advanced stage in the work. That's another reason why I'm keen for your husband to be involved in the project.'

'If you're worried about him paying your fees, there's no need. We have joint accounts and I'll deal with all that side of things. There won't be any problem.'

Marnie felt her cheeks redden. She thought of Anne blushing the previous day and wondered if she now looked like a clown in make-up. 'That wasn't my concern. I believe it's important for all the people affected by the scheme to be comfortable with it. After all, you'll be living with the design for years to come.'

'Yes, and you wouldn't want people going round saying you produced something that one of your customers didn't like. It could be bad for business, I can see that.'

Marnie was beginning to wonder why Celia had not asked her to use the tradesmen's entrance. 'I wasn't thinking of it in those terms. Design can have a major impact on your surroundings and on your life. That's why I'd like your husband to see the eventual proposals and be happy with them.'

'All right, but he has a lot on his mind at the moment.'

'I can understand that. I'm sure he's very busy with his work.'

Celia turned her head to look out through the French windows into the garden.

'It's not just that, Marnie. You see, I know he's having an affair.'

'Oh.' Taken by surprise, Marnie quickly took a sip of coffee. 'You're sure of that, you know the person involved?'

Marnie regretted asking the question; it just somehow slipped out. She regretted it even more when she heard Celia's reply.

'I rather thought, Marnie, that the person involved, as you put it, was … well, you.'

Marnie was caught in the act, the act of putting down her cup. She jumped and missed her aim, dropping the cup on the rim of the saucer, with the effect that cup, saucer and remains of coffee crashed to the floor. More precisely, they landed on the antique Chinese carpet that Marnie knew was worth thousands of pounds.

'I'm *so* sorry.' Marnie bent down to clear up the mess, grateful to have something to do. Her thoughts were in turmoil. 'Nothing's broken, but I'm worried this will leave a stain and –'

'Leave it!' Celia's tone was firm. 'Just … leave it. I'll have it seen to later.'

Reluctantly, Marnie regained her seat, having retrieved the cup and saucer, unbroken. She placed them with maximum care on the side table.

'You took me by surprise there, Celia. But then I expect that was your intention.'

'I must admit your reaction was not as calm as I expected.'

Marnie was astonished. 'What did you expect me to do when confronted by an accusation like that?'

Celia shrugged. 'Deny it, I suppose, unconvincingly.'

'Well of *course*, I deny it.'

'You do?'

'Emphatically.' Marnie paused for reflection. 'You don't really want me to do a design for the house, do you? That was just a pretext. You really got me here to accuse me of …' Marnie shook her head.

'You're seriously denying it?'

'I've just told you I do. Look.' Marnie held up a thumb. 'First, I don't know your husband. I've never set eyes on him.' Her index finger. 'Second, I don't even know his name.' Another finger. 'Third, I've never had an extra-marital affair in my life, nor would I.'

Celia stared at Marnie without speaking for several seconds. 'But I was convinced –'

'Well don't be. Or at least not about *me*.'

More staring from Celia. Marnie gathered up her notepad and reached down for her bag.

'I'd better be going.' She stood up. 'I have work to do.'

From her armchair, Celia made a gesture. 'Please sit down, Marnie.'

Marnie remained standing. 'I don't think there's anything more to be said.'

'I'm afraid there is.'

'If you think –'

'I do think, Marnie. And what I think is, I've made a *terrible* mistake.'

'You certainly have. Let's just forget about it and go our separate ways, shall we?'

'It's not as easy as that.'

'It couldn't be any worse, Celia.'

'It could.'

Marnie sat down slowly on the sofa. 'How could it be worse?' In the absence of a reply, she worked it out for herself. 'You've told someone of your suspicions.'

Celia nodded.

'Your solicitor? Your husband?'

'No. I've, er, told the police.'

Marnie was stunned. 'The *police*? Why? What's it got to do with them?'

Celia suddenly got to her feet and began pacing the floor. 'Oh, I don't know. I was feeling really pissed off about the whole thing. The detective asked me where my husband was. In a fit of peak I said he was probably with his mistress, and they could no doubt find him … at Glebe Farm.'

'Was that all you said?'

'Yes.'

'Well it could be worse. All you've got to do is phone them up – was it Binns? – and tell him you were wrong.'

'It was worse, Marnie.'

'Do you think you could stop walking around like that? It's making me feel unsettled. What do you mean it *was* worse?'

'It was Binns, but he was standing next to Angela Hemingway when I told him.'

'Angela's no gossip.' Marnie pondered. 'When was this?'

'Yesterday.'

'I don't suppose anyone else was in earshot when you were broadcasting this slander about me?'

'No.'

'So by now it's all round the police station.'

Celia sat down. 'I'm sorry, Marnie.'

'Celia, look me in the eye and tell me you know what you said was untrue.'

'I do know it.'

'Then you have to convince the police of that, and Angela. But first you start with Sergeant Binns. Even then, half the force will be muttering, *no smoke without fire*.'

Marnie got up and walked over to a side table. She picked up a cordless phone and took it across to Celia. 'You've got some calls to make.'

Marnie was still fuming on the drive back to Glebe Farm. With Anne away, the messages would be piling up on the answerphone. There were letters to write and financial matters to deal with, quite apart from the actual work of designing schemes for the clients. And now she had wasted half the morning. Typically, Celia had not succeeded in speaking to anyone, but had left urgent messages on their answering machines.

Turning to drive into the garage barn, Marnie saw Angela's old Ford Escort parked by the farmhouse. As she climbed out of the Discovery, she pulled the mobile from her bag and began pressing buttons. Angela gave her a sheepish look as she approached. Marnie waited until she heard ringing tone and handed the phone to Angela.

'Celia has something to tell you. Don't say a word to me until you've had this conversation.'

Angela frowned and took the phone. 'Hallo, Celia? This is Angela. I'm down at Marnie's place. She says you want to talk to me.'

Marnie unlocked the office barn and went in, leaving Angela outside with the mobile. She was taking down messages from the answerphone when Angela walked in and put the mobile on the desk. Marnie finished the last note and pressed the delete button.

'She's explained?'

Angela nodded. 'Have you had lunch, Marnie?'

'Is it that time already? No, I haven't. Celia offered me cyanide soup, but I declined her hospitality.'

'I've got some sandwiches in the car. Have you time for a quick lunch?'

Marnie was puzzled. 'You've brought food?'

'You're always giving me coffee and things. I thought we could have a chat.'

'Ah, you came to have a quiet word about my morals, assuming Celia was right in accusing me?'

Angela looked shocked. 'Absolutely not, Marnie! I told her she was completely off-target when she told me, you know ...'

'I bet the police weren't so charitable. She must've made their day.'

Angela shrugged. 'Binns passed it off without comment. I think he'd only be interested if he thought it had something to do with the remains found in the grave.'

'Don't be so sure of that.'

'What difference would it make to them, anyway?'

'What *difference*? Angela, you should realise that anything like that, any suspicion of illicit relationships is of potential interest to the police. Affairs lead to complications, which can lead to jealousy, conflict, strong passions. Get the picture?'

'I see what you mean.'

'If the police are always hanging round my door it looks bad for me and my company.'

'But if it isn't true, Marnie, nothing can come of it.'

'Don't you see, there's the small matter of my reputation.'

Angela smiled. 'That sounds rather Victorian. I think you're worrying about nothing.'

'It isn't something that only mattered in the past. Ever heard the expression, *mud sticks*? I have a business here. It involves me in going to people's houses, sometimes having to call in at odd times to check details. Do you think any couple would be happy to engage me if they thought I might just try seducing the husband as part of the service? In short, I can't afford to have anything said about me apart from, *Marnie Walker does a great job; I recommend her*.'

'I see, since you put it like that, Marnie ... Well, you know I'd never say a word to anyone.'

Marnie nodded. After a few moments of awkward silence she spoke.

'So, talking of words, you said you wanted a chat. If it wasn't about me as the Scarlet Woman of Knightly St John, what did you have in mind?'

'It was about archaeology, actually.'

'Oh yes. Celia said something about that.'

'Did she mention Dr Cardew? He's the head of the project.'

'I gather he wants to dig some holes in my field. I thought he might've been involved in the grave investigation, if the remains turn out to be ancient.'

'He is interested, but things are still at an early stage. I told him you might be amenable to letting him do some test pits in your field. It seems quite a few people have been reluctant to let him dig up their lawns.'

'I'm not surprised.'

'Oh, don't you like archaeology? I thought you were interested in that sort of thing.'

Marnie let out a long sigh. 'I think people have done too much digging up the past in this village. Sometimes it's best to move on, let the past take care of itself.'

'I know what you mean. Anyway, how about those sandwiches? Shall I fetch them from the car?'

'Sorry, Angela, I don't mean to sound ungrateful, but I seem to have lost my appetite.'

After Angela left, Marnie sat staring ahead of her. There were times when she missed the anonymity of working in London. In a place like Knightly St John you could be too open to public scrutiny. Telling herself to snap out of it and get on with her work, she looked down at the phone messages on the notepad. In fourth place a name stood out: Cardew.

It rang six times before the answerphone cut in. She left a message on the voicemail.

5
Knightly Woods

Marnie's mood had lifted by Friday morning and it improved further with the first phone call of the day. Anne rang the office barn at eight.

'Hiya! Just wanted to make sure you weren't still lying in bed. How's it going?'

'The joint's jumping, as usual. How about you? Got any plans?'

'Coming back tonight.'

'Don't you want to stay home for the weekend?'

'I can't leave you alone in the office that long, Marnie.' She laughed. 'You'd get everything in a mess.'

'Seriously, though. It would give you the chance to see your friends a bit longer.'

'Actually, Marnie, I was wondering … Perhaps my old school friend Danny could come up for the weekend. Would that be okay?'

'Sure. I don't think I know … er, *him*?'

'It's a *her*. Danielle. Danny Sullivan. She's just finished year thirteen at school, did her last A level a week ago. I thought she might like a weekend away in a peaceful, stress-free environment.'

'Let me know if she finds one.'

'What?'

'Nothing. That's great. If the weather's good we'll take her for a tootle on the boat.'

The next call came in at eight-thirty and was less welcome.

'Marnie, it's Celia.'

'Hallo.'

'I'm phoning to apologise. I feel very badly about what I said yesterday.'

'Yes. Did you eventually speak to Binns and put him right?'

'I told him I'd been completely mistaken. In fact, I've just had a word with Constable Lamb as well.'

'You have?'

'She rang about bringing my statement round for me to sign, so I explained I'd been entirely wrong about you. By the way, she's coming to see you too later today.'

'Right. Well, thanks for doing that.'

'Marnie?'

'Yes?'

'You said you thought my invitation here was just a pretext, but I've been thinking. It really would be good to have our wing of the house redecorated. It's all looking so faded. I wondered, would you be interested in doing a project here?'

'You don't have to make it up to me, Celia.'

'I really am very sorry about what I said, truly. I feel quite ashamed. But it would be good to have a makeover, even if only in our wing.'

A pause. 'Let me check out my commitments and see what might be possible.'

'When can we talk about it?'

'After the weekend.'

Celia sounded brighter. 'I'll ring you Monday.'

It had become the season for reconciliation and contrition. Without hesitating, Marnie picked up the phone and dialled the vicarage.

'Angela Hemingway.'

'Hi, Angela. It's Marnie.'

'Hallo, Marnie' There was real warmth in the tone. 'How are you feeling today?'

'Apologetic. I want to say how sorry I am about my churlish behaviour yesterday. It was inexcusable.'

'Not at all. When I thought about it afterwards I realised how you must've been feeling.'

'I turned away a friend who came to be supportive, ex-friend, perhaps.'

'*True* friend, Marnie. And the sandwiches weren't much good I can tell you. I bought them at the garage. Yuck!' She laughed. 'I thought about giving them to the Salvation Army, but decided it might get me unfrocked.'

Marnie laughed. 'Let me make amends. The forecast for tomorrow isn't bad. Ralph's coming home tonight. We're planning a tootle with lunch on the boat. Can you join us?'

'Well ...'

'No sandwiches from the petrol station, I promise.'

'That's a very persuasive argument, Marnie. The thing is, Randall's hoping to come over.'

'Ah, you've already made plans.'

'Can I check with him and get back to you?'

'Of course. Until later, then.'

'Marnie, I'm not sure I said this properly yesterday. I of all people ought to understand how you were feeling. Randall and I have to be so careful about our ... relationship, with me being the vicar and him the rural dean. Imagine how the tongues could wag.'

There was to be no let-up that morning. Marnie had barely started on her latest project when she heard the crunch of tyres on gravel. WDC Cathy Lamb entered the office with a folder under her arm and a smile on her face.

'Come to arrest me for moral turpitude?'

'No danger of that, Marnie.'

'I always knew you were a fair-minded woman.'

'Nope. It's because I couldn't spell it on the charge sheet.'

Marnie read the statement while they drank coffee. It was a clear summary of her involvement with the grave and the headstone, the bare minimum of facts. As Marnie signed the document, Cathy Lamb looked at her speculatively.

'You know who smashed it, don't you, Marnie, or at least you have your suspicions?'

'Maybe. But I wouldn't want to make any unfounded accusations. I've got no proof of anything and I certainly wouldn't speculate about something like that, least of all to the police.'

'Sergeant Binns is wondering if the smashing was connected with the second body. What do you think?'

'If I thought that, I'd tell you. But he's wrong, in my view. Are you any closer to knowing whose body it is that you've found?'

Lamb shook her head. 'The autopsy didn't reveal much, apparently. The pathologist didn't have much to go on. If you know anything, Marnie, anything at all that might help our enquiries, you know you really should tell us.'

Marnie made a cross over her heart and looked Lamb straight in the eye. 'Cathy, I haven't the remotest idea about who the other body might be. And that's the honest truth.'

'Fair enough.'

'So what happens now with the remains?'

'We get a second opinion.'

'What could another pathologist find out that your one missed?'

Lamb shrugged.

Marnie got the picture. 'You're not able to tell me. I shouldn't have asked.'

'You'll probably find out soon enough. Have you heard of Dr Rob Cardew?'

'Cardew? I know the name, in fact we're swapping phone messages at the moment. He's an archaeologist.' Marnie's eyes narrowed. 'Ah, so you do think the remains are ancient.'

'I told you, we don't know. Perhaps another type of expert – like an anthropologist – can give us a lead. Why has Dr Cardew been in touch with you?'

'It seems he wants to dig holes down here. Perhaps he thinks I know where the bodies are buried.'

~~~

Hugh Devere parked his Saab on the driveway beside his wife's convertible and walked through to the terrace at the back of the house. Tall, burly, with dark hair receding from the temples, he wore an expensive pinstriped suit, silk tie and handmade brogues. A leather briefcase completed the image of the city businessman. Celia was where he expected to find her, reclining on a steamer chair, her head cushioned on navy and white striped upholstery. She was wearing shorts and a skinny top, reading a magazine, sunglasses pushed up on top of her hair.

'You're back early. I wasn't expecting you. Are you staying for lunch?'

Hugh kissed the top of her head. 'Yes. I've had enough of bloody meetings for one week. I'm taking the afternoon off.'

'Won't the firm collapse without you?'

'Not after the deal I've pulled off in the past few days. All I want right now is a peaceful weekend with no hassle.'
~~~

'You haven't forgotten we're going out to dinner tonight with the Littlejohns?'

He groaned. 'Are we? Do we have to go?'

'It's Meg's birthday.'

Hugh loosened his tie and sat down heavily with a grunt on the other recliner. 'With the bonus I'll make on this week's deal, we could afford to put in a swimming pool.'

'Could we run to a redecoration of the house, our part of it, at least?'

A pause for reflection. 'Don't see why not.'

'There's an interior designer in the village. I thought I might get her involved.'

'Okay.'

'Thank you, darling.' Celia looked at her husband. 'Have you come across her?'

'Don't think so. Who is it?'

'Her name's Marnie Walker.' Celia watched her husband for a reaction. 'She lives down near the canal, on a boat.'

Hugh looked at his watch. 'Really? Well, I'll leave that side of things to you.' He stood up. 'I'm going to get out of this suit. Fancy going for a walk this afternoon?'

'A walk? Where?'

'Knightly Woods? Should be pleasant up there, nice day like this. Shady trees.'

Celia stretched her long legs. 'Why not?'

Marnie was outside the main house talking to Bob, the foreman builder, when a Land Rover came slowly down the track and pulled off onto the grass at a respectful distance from the farm complex. She forced herself to concentrate on the matter under discussion and listen to what Bob was telling her.

'I know it's less obtrusive, Marnie, but if it was me, well, I'd go for ordinary radiators any time.'

'But underfloor heating is so *good* these days, Bob. I've used it before on other projects.'

'All right, if that's really what you want.'

'Why are you so anti?'

'It's more complicated to install, for a start, so it's pricey, and if you need to get at it for maintenance or a leak … Call me old-fashioned, but –' He stopped abruptly and looked over Marnie's shoulder. 'You expecting someone?'

She turned to see a man walking towards the office barn, turning his head slowly, scanning the surroundings. Marnie muttered at Bob before addressing the newcomer.

'Hallo, can I help you?'

The man stopped. 'My name's Cardew. I'm looking for Mrs Walker.' He smiled. 'I think I've probably found her.'

Cardew was in his thirties, of medium height and build, very tanned, with short brown hair. Black wire-rimmed glasses and a beaky nose gave him an owl-like countenance. He looked the rugged outdoor type in check shirt, faded jeans and walking boots. A brown leather bag was slung over one shoulder. He could have been an early studio prototype for Indiana Jones.

Marnie was surprised when he accepted her offer of a drink and something to eat while they talked. By the time they had reached *Sally Ann*, they were on first name terms and Marnie had learnt he was a research fellow in the Institute of Archaeology and a lecturer at New Melville Hall, Cambridge.

Marnie scrabbled together a simple lunch. While Rob took safari chairs and a picnic table out onto the stern deck, she warmed pitta bread in the oven and mixed tuna with mayonnaise and a squeeze of lemon juice. To complete the filling she shredded a little gem lettuce, chopped some cucumber into cubes and diced half a red pepper. Rob carried the stuffed pittas outside on a tray while Marnie poured designer water into tall tumblers and added ice cubes and a wedge of lime.

In between mouthfuls, Rob pulled a map out of his bag and showed Marnie the area being studied. A brown sunburnt finger traced the extent of the works, extending over several nearby villages. He spoke quietly and calmly but had a gleam in his eyes as he explained the project.

Marnie scrutinised the map. 'So you're looking at how people in these villages changed the landscape over time. That's the idea?'

Rob nodded. 'Settlements. Some of the communities were too scattered to be villages as we now know them, quite isolated units for centuries. It was much more wooded then, of course, mainly oak and elm.'

Marnie extended her gaze over the countryside. 'Even these open meadows and pastures?'

Another nod. 'All this used to be ancient woodland. There are only a few pockets remaining and they're carefully managed. What you see has been man-made, all of it.'

'How long ago?'

'Depends. It was in phases. Some of it was already fields when the Romans came two thousand years ago. It's going on all the time.'

'Even now?'

'The countryside is always undergoing change, Marnie. It's never static. Don't get me started. I could talk field patterns and land usage from now till Christmas.'

Marnie sensed that in his quiet way, he was passionate about the land. He saw it differently from other people and read it like a book or a chart. To Rob Cardew the country was there to be interpreted; it was peopled with the ghosts of past generations.

'And what do you want to do here at Glebe Farm?'

'Just dig a few test pits, well, initially. Then see what we find and what you'd agree to. I can't be more precise until we've got a few holes in the ground.'

'How many?'

'Half a dozen, maybe? It's up to you entirely, Marnie.'

'Actually, I'd have to check with Leonard Fletcher, the farmer. Although it's my land, I let the field to him for grazing.'

Rob checked his notebook. 'He won't be putting any sheep in here until autumn. His flocks are over on Blackbird Close and the Pightle till then.'

'You've done your homework.'

A shrug. 'He told me when I asked him about his fields. It was he who said I should talk to you.'

'Okay. What happens next?'

'We dig a few test pits, one metre square. We record whatever we find – if anything – and fill them in at the end of the day. The turf will go back on top. In a few weeks you'd never know we'd been there. That's the deal.'

'When will this happen?'

'Some time over the next few weeks.'

'What do I need to do?'

'Not a thing. We're self-contained …' That smile again, '… like an army on the move.'

Marnie smiled back. 'Without the same impact, I hope.'

'So do I.'

Hugh had been right about the woods. By the time they had eaten lunch, the afternoon heat was becoming oppressive, and they had been only too glad to drive to Knightly Woods and take one of the footpaths through the trees. Others had had the same idea. They had been walking for barely five minutes when Hugh stopped and scanned the forest.

Celia looked around uneasily. 'What is it, darling?'

'It's like Piccadilly bloody Circus! Just look, people *everywhere*.'

'But it is cool and shady, like you said. You don't want to go back, do you?'

He shook his head. 'I'm not going to be chased out of my own woods by a load of plodders.'

Celia was confused. 'Do we own these woods? I though they were Forestry Commission.'

'They are now. Grandfather had to sell 'em. Death duty years ago. He brought me up here when I was about six or seven, not long before he died. Told me how the government would be stealing my birthright. I still think of them as ours. I'm going to get them back one day.'

'How?'

'Don't worry about it. That's not the problem this afternoon.'

'What is?'

'How to find some peace and quiet without being trampled on by all and sundry. Come on.' He set off up the slope away from the footpath. 'This way.'

'But the path goes down there.'

'Celia, a path doesn't have to have markers and little blue arrows painted on trees to be a path. There've been tracks all over this hill for thousands of years. You just have to know how to find them.'

Celia trailed after her husband, planting her feet – in their calf leather walking boots – carefully on the rough ground. Soon they were on their own. Trusting Hugh's judgment, she relaxed and began to enjoy a feeling of independence, breathing in clean, cool air, fresh with the smells of trees and vegetation. The canopy overhead protected them from the sun's rays and dappled the ground with light and shadow. After ten minutes of steady climbing, she asked for a pause to get her breath.

Hugh pointed. 'Just a bit further. There's open ground ahead. It'll be nice up there.'

Hugh reached it first and sat down on a patch of moss, leaning back against a tree, both legs thrust out in front. Celia caught up with him and perched on a tree stump.

'You knew this clearing was here.'

'I know every part of these woods, practically grew up in them. Even after they were taken over by the Forestry I used to roam about all over. They were felling trees then, coppicing, replanting. That was before they were opened to the public.'

'That was good, wasn't it, darling? Isn't that sort of thing necessary?'

Hugh looked pained. 'They changed the *character* of the place. It had been ancient woodland. The new *owners* marked out footpaths, cleared space for rustic woodland tables.' He emphasised each word with contempt. 'Turned it into a glorified picnic site.' He let out a long sigh.

Celia stood up and walked to the middle of the clearing. With eyes closed she turned her face to the sun and felt its warmth on her cheeks. For the first time she became aware of birdsong. Somewhere far off through the trees a voice called out. A distant dog barked. A motor droned faintly, an aeroplane way beyond the treetops. She breathed in slowly and rhythmically, catching a light whiff of woodsmoke on the air.

'It's funny, isn't it?'

Hugh was watching her. 'What is?'

'You think you're far from everything, *far from the madding crowd*. But things are going on around you all the time. Even here it isn't really silent.'

'I suppose not.'

'Is this one of the spaces they cleared for picnics?' She spoke with her eyes still closed.

'No. This is way off the beaten track.' He pulled his feet up and rested both forearms on his knees, turning his head to look down through the woods. 'This place is a mass of bluebells in the spring.'

'Yet you've never brought me here until now.' There was an edge of reproach in her tone.

'We'll come again. We've missed the bluebells this year, but we'll come back next time they're out.'

'Perhaps there'll be crowds of people here to see them then.'

Hugh shook his head. 'I doubt if anyone comes up here.'

'Someone must've been. They made a fire. There's ash on the ground.'

He turned to see her scuffing the soil with her foot. 'Foresters, I expect.'

'Hugh, are there animals in these woods?'

'Of course. Probably badgers, rabbits of course – they get everywhere – hedgehogs, squirrels, grey ones.'

'Do you get sheep?'

'No.'

'Are you sure?'

'Yes. Why?'

'What's that, then?'

Hugh got up and went to join her. Celia pointed at the ground. 'Doesn't that look like a sheep's skull to you?'

He squatted down. 'Mm … odd …' He reached forward.

Celia exclaimed. 'No! Don't touch it. It looks, I don't know, creepy.'

Hugh ignored her and picked it up. 'It's hardly going to bite.'

'What do you think it is?'

He turned it over in his hands. 'Too small for a sheep, I'd say.'

'A lamb?'

'Surely not up here.' Hugh examined it from all angles. 'Ah … I wonder …'

'You know what it is?'

'Could be a muntjac. Yes, that's possible.'

Celia was dubious. 'I've never seen one.'

'You don't, at least not very often, but they do live round here. They're all over the county in fact, bit of a nuisance. They eat the bark off the young trees.' He turned the skull round again. 'Mm …'

'What?'

'It isn't quite the right shape when you look closely.'

Celia shuddered and backed away. 'I don't want to look closely.'

Hugh held it out in front of him in both hands. 'I know what it is. It's a *goat* skull.'

'A *goat*? Are there wild goats in England, Hugh? Are you sure that's what it is?'

'Yes. You can see the shape of it. Look.'

He held it out to Celia, but she took two steps backwards. 'I don't want –' Her foot caught something and she stumbled.

Hugh seized her by the elbow and dropped the skull. Looking down, they saw where Celia had trodden. Beside her foot another skull lay in the dust, another goat skull. She frowned in disgust.

'What's been going on here? Is this some weird camp or something?'

Hugh studied the ground carefully. '*Weird* is the word.'

Celia stepped back again, distancing herself from the skulls that now lay side by side on the dusty ground. Looking up, she saw that Hugh was staring, his eyes roaming around the place where they stood. A sense of uneasiness came over her.

'What is it, Hugh? You're making me nervous.'

'What's the date today?'

'The *date*? What's that got to do with it?'

He spoke as if talking to himself. 'Mid-summer is around the twenty-second to the twenty-fourth …'

'Mid-summer? What *are* you –'

'That would be the second half of last week. It figures. Yes.'

Celia struggled to comprehend. 'What figures? I wish you'd stop talking in riddles. It's like being out with Yoda.'

'Well, mid-summer's day was last week. So I was just wondering ...'

'What? Tell me!'

'Look around.' He pointed. 'Over there, that's another goat skull. There, and there. You see? Things made of sticks plaited together, like corn dollies. And that's a piece of candle. Not something you'd expect to find in the woods.'

Celia followed where he pointed. 'What does it mean?'

'My guess is, there might have been a sort of mid-summer festival, you know, a kind of pagan thing.'

Celia's mouth fell open. '*Here?* You mean on this spot?'

'Seems like it to me. See? Those objects were laid out in a pattern. Yes. They form a *ring*.' Enlightenment dawned. 'I know what this is. I think it's a *witches' circle*.'

Celia was aghast. 'A *what?*'

Hugh pointed at Celia's feet. 'Yes, I'm sure of it. It *is* a witches' circle. Can't you see? Look, you're standing right in the middle of it.'

Celia's scream startled two wood pigeons from a tree at the edge of the clearing. They took off noisily and carried her cry away with them, down the slope and off through the woods.

~~~~

Marnie walked with Rob Cardew back to his Land Rover, standing in sunlight in the field by the end of the track. He pulled open the door; heat from inside the cab billowed out. Rob winced, hesitating to climb in. He turned to Marnie and shook hands.

'Lunch was an unexpected surprise. Thank you.'

'What do you normally do?'

An owlish smile. 'Forget ... don't notice the time ... go without.'

'Doesn't your wife tell you to be sensible?'

Rob looked at his wedding ring. 'You have an eye for detail. Actually, my wife's as bad as I am. She's an archaeologist, too. We get carried away by our enthusiasm.'

'Will she be involved in your dig here?'

'It depends what we find. She's an osteoarchaeologist, specialises in bones, as the name implies. If we come across any interesting remains ...'

Marnie had a sudden impulse. 'What about the remains in the grave, Sarah Anne Day's grave, the extra occupant?'

'Ah, you know about that. I suppose I shouldn't be surprised. You originally found the grave, didn't you?'

'Yes. Do you know if there have been any results back from Oxford?'

'There I was, trying to be discreet, Marnie, and you probably know more about what's going on than I do.'

'Not necessarily. I know the remains have been examined by someone in Oxford.'
~~~~

Rob nodded. 'Dr Rosemary Goodchild at the Archaeological Materials Laboratory.'

'Presumably this Dr Goodchild is an osteoarchaeologist like your …' She looked at Rob. His expression was impassive. Another impulse, an intuition. 'She is your wife, isn't she?'

The owlish smile again. 'Brilliant. You should've been an archaeologist, Marnie. Attention to detail and the ability to make deductions. It's all detective work.'

'So do you have any results, or do you have to be discreet about that?'

'The tests are still in progress, in fact they've only just begun. I, er …'

'The remains aren't seventeenth century, are they?'

He grinned. 'So you did know.'

Marnie stayed silent and let Rob continue.

'They're testing samples in the lab to determine the age, but I think we're looking at something more modern.'

'Much more modern,' Marnie suggested.

Rob climbed into the Land Rover. 'Could be.'

'Any idea how modern?' Marnie shut the door behind him.

He slid open the window. 'Not for certain, not yet. I wouldn't like to comment without firm evidence.'

'When do you expect to know?'

'It's hard to say. We have to take our turn in the queue at the lab.'

'Will your wife be able to determine the cause of death?'

'I honestly don't know. One thing's for sure, Marnie, when you dig up the past, you never know what you might find.'

She watched the Land Rover climb the field track. That phrase again: *digging up the past*. Tell me about it, she thought.

6
Danny

Marnie yawned and blinked. Saturday morning. She lay in bed with eyes closed, listening to the birds singing, one of the pleasures of country life. Beside her, Ralph was still asleep, breathing steadily, his head inches from hers on the pillow. She crept quietly out of bed, grabbed a shirt and tiptoed along to the bathroom. In the galley she pulled a curtain open with one finger. It promised to be another fine day.

Ralph was on his side facing the wall when she returned and climbed under the duvet to join him. They had hardly spoken when he got home the previous evening. His train had been delayed by faulty points somewhere in the north of England, and it was almost midnight before he had collected his car at the station. Marnie had waited up, though she was flagging after a busy day. When Ralph had finished showering, he reached the sleeping cabin to find Marnie dozing. With great care he had climbed over her, kissed her gently on the head and almost at once they were asleep.

Marnie stretched both arms above her head and lowered them onto the duvet. Ralph stirred.

'What time is it?' His voice was muffled.

'Ten past seven.'

Ralph breathed out, a long audible sigh and turned onto his back.

'Sorry if I woke you.'

In reply he moved over and kissed her.

'Tell me something, Ralph.'

'Mm?'

'When you got home last night …'

'Yes?'

'Was I sensational when we made love?'

'*Unbelievable*.'

'I'm so glad you didn't wake me to tell me so at the time.'

'I'm considerate like that.'

'It's your best quality. Why were you so late?'

'I thought I told you, there was some excuse, a mole ate the points, or something like that.'

'Must be the rutting season. Do they rut, moles?'

'Constantly, they're famous for it. Sometimes causes earthquakes. How was your day?'

'Let's get up and have breakfast and I'll tell you about it.'

Later that morning a red Mini left Leighton Buzzard and headed north, destination Knightly St John. With no moles to disrupt their passage, Anne was able to make good progress in moderate traffic. It was the first time since moving up to work with Marnie that she had had a friend to stay. Beside her in the car, Danny kept up a barrage of questions about her work, her life with Marnie and Ralph, her college course, everything that had happened since Anne had left school two years earlier. Even Anne had been surprised at how much she had packed into that time.

After half an hour they turned off through the field gate at the end of the village high street. Anne drove slowly down the track, carefully avoiding the bumps and tussocks. Danny, a young woman now with school and A levels behind her, looking forward to university, who normally preserved an unruffled exterior, was unable to conceal her excitement. Halfway down the slope the roofs of the farm buildings came into view, mauve-blue Welsh slate over pale honey-coloured limestone.

'Oh *wow*! This is *so cool*.'

Anne parked in the garage barn between Marnie's Discovery and Ralph's Volvo, and they grabbed their hold-alls from the back seat. In the courtyard Danny stopped to take in the scene. Facing them across the way stood a terrace of three cottages, each with a bottle green front door and roses climbing up the facade. Tubs of flowers strategically placed on the cobbles softened the hard surfaces. Adjoining the cottages at rightangles to their right, the farmhouse itself was double-fronted with stone-mullioned windows.

'Who lives here?' Danny asked.

'Two young couples are renting cottages one and two. They're very nice.'

'Who's in number three?'

'Marnie let it to Angela when they sold the old vicarage before she moved into the new one. She's going to let it to another couple but they can't move in until later on, so it's empty for now.'

'And the house?'

'It's not finished yet. There's still a lot to be done inside and the garden's a tip. Marnie wants to get it just right and it's taking longer than she hoped. She and Ralph will live there when it's ready.'

'What about you, Anne?'

She indicated the building to their left. 'Let me show you the office barn.'

'Where you work.'

'And where I live. Come in.'

Dropping her bag inside, Anne went back out to pull open the barn doors, revealing the tinted plate glass window. She beckoned Danny to enter and pointed to a ladder attached to the wall.

'My attic's up there.'

Before she could show Danny the way, the phone started ringing. Anne picked it up on Marnie's desk.

'Walker and Co, good morning.'

Danny waited while Anne took the call. Everything here was a surprise to her. It seemed no time at all since they were schoolgirls together in the classroom, Anne always introverted, constantly worrying about her unemployed father, twice made redundant. Now, here she was with a job, her own car, a place to live, confidently taking a call on the office phone as if she ran the company. The call came to an end.

'Okay, Angela, that's fine. I'll tell Marnie and Ralph. We'll see you later. Bye!'

Anne wrote a quick note on the pad and turned to Danny. 'We'll be going for a tootle.'

'A what?'

'A trip on the boat for lunch.'

'That was a friend?'

Anne nodded and picked up her bag. 'The vicar.'

Danny was amazed. 'You're *friends* with the *vicar*? You use her first name?'

'Yeah. She's bringing her boyfriend.'

'Vicars have *boyfriends*?' Danny had never considered this possibility.

Anne grinned. 'Yes, even the female ones. But seriously, Angela doesn't just have any old boyfriend. This one's the rural dean. You'll like him.'

Danny had never heard of a rural dean before, but it sounded impressive. She looked around the office. A memory stirred.

'Isn't this where …?'

Everyone from Anne's old school had heard the story of Sarah Anne Day's suicide at Glebe Farm. Anne had not been going to mention it, but since Danny had raised the subject, she pointed up at the spray of lavender. She spoke in a matter-of-fact tone.

'Yes. Sarah hanged herself from that hook.'

Danny swallowed and stared upwards with wide eyes. 'And your room is up there, just above the hook?'

'Is that a problem, Danny? It was all a long time ago … 1645 … and she hasn't been back since.'

Danny boggled. 'You mean …?'

'She's not a ghost or anything. If it bothers you, you can sleep on *Sally Ann*.'

'No, no. That's okay.'

'It's up here, then.' Anne climbed the ladder.

Danny put her head through the opening. All thoughts of dead girls hanging by the neck went out of her head at the sight of Anne's room. The whole attic area was her domain, with exposed beams of dark timber against light-coloured plaster, sloping up to the point of the roof. It had no windows save for a narrow glazed slit at one end that let in a single shaft of daylight. Table lamps radiated a jewel-like atmosphere of comfort and intimacy. The double bed in the centre of the attic was covered in a woollen throw of deep blues and greens, a traditional Welsh pattern, with cushions in various colours piled at the head. Oriental rugs were strewn over the floor. There was a hint of something spicy in the air.

'Anne, it's *magic*.'

They had lingered over breakfast on *Sally Ann* and spent a lazy hour or so reading the papers. Marnie looked at her watch.

'I expect Angela will've rung by now about the tootle.'

Ralph looked up from the *Financial Times*. 'There weren't any messages when I called into the office for the papers.'

'Anne should be here soon. She'll let us know. She's bringing a friend back for the weekend, a girl from her old school.'

'Good. Do we need to shop for lunch?'

'No. I did it yesterday after my meeting with Rob Cardew.'

'It seems to be the season for new faces.'

'Mm ...'

Something in Marnie's tone made Ralph lower the newspaper. 'Is there a problem?'

Marnie outlined her conversation with Celia Devere.

Predictably, Ralph was unruffled. 'It's a pretty serious accusation without some evidence to go on.'

'I know. She just seemed to have got it into her head that it was me.'

'But you managed to persuade her she was wrong.'

'Yes. She rang up to apologise, even asked me to do a makeover on their wing of the house.'

'Oh well, it's an ill wind, as they say.'

Marnie looked surprised. 'You think I should do it?'

'Don't you?'

'I did say I'd talk to her about it, but my instincts tell me not to have any more to do with Celia. I think she could be trouble.'

'You think she's probably neurotic.'

'She must be. To be honest, Ralph, I feel torn about this, don't want to turn business away. In my line it's all about word-of-mouth and reputation.'

'I know exactly what you mean.'

'Of course it's the same for you, I realise that, but you're famous all round the world as a leading economist. Your reputation is established. How many people get invited to advise at the White House?'

Ralph grinned. 'Perhaps I could put in a word for Walker and Co, interior designers. I'm sure the Oval Office could use a make-over.'

Marnie laughed. 'That'd be good!'

'Marnie, I know this Celia person seems problematical, but if you keep everything on a businesslike footing, it should work out all right, surely?'

Marnie was still smiling. '*Problematical* ... only an academic would use a word like *problematical* to describe someone.'

'Talking of academics, tell me more about this Cardew. What's he like? What does he have in mind?'

Marnie explained the archaeology project.

'Oh well, that seems harmless enough.'

'Mm ...' That tone again.

'What is it, Marnie? You seem troubled.'

'Something's making me feel unsettled.'

'The archaeology project can't do any harm. They'll dig some test pits, record whatever they find and fill them in again. Nothing to worry about.'

'It's more than that, Ralph. It's the digging up of Sarah's grave, this other body they've unearthed. Rob Cardew said that when you dig up the past you never know what you might find.'

'Like another lot of remains that no-one knew were there. Yes, I see your point.'

'And then there was the accusation by Celia. That's thrown me off balance, too.'

'But none of these things is connected, Marnie. They're just coincidental. Or is that another word only an academic would use?'

Ralph was smiling and Marnie tried to join in, but her thoughts were elsewhere. Suddenly she sat upright.

'We have visitors,' she murmured. 'We'll talk about this later.'

Ralph turned to see Anne emerging from the spinney accompanied by another girl, slightly shorter, with a pleasant face framed by a mop of dark curly hair.

Marnie brightened. 'Let's meet Danny.'

Hugh Devere was accustomed to having breakfast alone during the week, but on Saturday and Sunday mornings he normally shared the table with his wife. On that particular Saturday it was fine enough to eat on the terrace, and it was only when he had finished reading the Sports section of the *Telegraph* that he realised that Celia had not appeared. The *Daily Mail* was lying unopened beside her plate; the silver pot containing her favourite Tiptree *Little Scarlet* Strawberry Conserve was untouched.

He listened in the house for sounds of her stirring. At the foot of the stairs he could not hear the faint hissing from the shower that usually proclaimed Celia was up and about. Outside their bedroom door he put an ear to the panels and heard nothing. Pushing it quietly open, he found the room in darkness, the heavy lined curtains shutting out the morning sun. There was a movement from the bed and the hint of a groan.

'Are you all right, darling?' Hugh spoke in little more than a whisper, bending over the pillow.

'... nasty headache.' The words struggled out.

'I'll fetch you some Disprin.'

He turned away, ignoring the muted protests behind him. In the bathroom he dissolved two tablets in water, swirling the glass to quicken the process. He might have known something like this would happen. After their walk in the woods the previous afternoon, Celia had announced she was too upset to eat and had gone to bed early. He wished he had not pointed out the witches' circle. After six years of marriage he ought to have realised she would be spooked by it.

Any normal person would have been mildly amused at the idea of a gaggle of middle-aged women harmlessly reliving their youth by dressing up in baubles, bangles and beads – or prancing about *starkers*, for all he knew – chanting hippy songs round a camp fire. But not Celia. She was prone to refer to herself as 'highly strung', which meant she would make a drama out of anything remotely unusual. He snorted silently to himself. The *witches* had probably bought the skulls, corn dollies and all their paraphernalia from car boots, jumble sales and junk shops!

Back at the bedside he propped Celia up. She gave in, gulped down the medicine, grimaced and slumped back. Looking down at his wife in the half light coming from the open bathroom door, he had to admit she was a beautiful woman. If only she could act like a grown-up.

'Thank you, darling. You're an angel,' Celia murmured.

He felt guilty, as if she could read his thoughts. 'Can I get you anything?'

'Just let me rest.'

Hugh frowned, thinking, *When did you ever do anything else?* Her eyes opened and he quickly adjusted his expression to one of tender concern.

'I'll come back in half an hour to see how you're feeling.'

'Yes.' The word evolved into a sigh as she closed her eyes and turned her head on the pillow.

Hugh crept across the floor, turning to look back in the doorway. Celia had given a fine performance. She had a natural gift, elevating saintly forbearance almost to an art form.

After breakfast Anne gave Danny a guided tour of Glebe Farm, including the unoccupied cottage number three. They spent a happy half-hour wandering in and out of the buildings and grounds, while Anne outlined the redevelopment plans. At the rear of the main farmhouse they stood facing the 'tip' that was to become a secluded garden.

Danny gave her verdict. 'It looks like a jungle. Our garden was like this when we first moved. Took my dad years to get it straight. Did his back in.'

Anne laughed. 'Marnie's getting a contractor. There'll be a pond over there, a terrace just there, the conservatory here, ooh, lots of features.' She checked her watch. 'Come on. We'd better fetch our things. Time to tootle.'

On their way back to the attic, Danny asked about Angela and Randall.

'What are they like? I've never really met a vicar and a rural wotsit before.'

'Rural *dean*. That's like a sort of … super-vicar, in charge of the other vicars round here. He used to be the vicar in this village.'

'Is he like, you know, ultra God-squad, preachy?' Danny made a face.

'No, not all. He's a bit like Ralph in a way, very intelligent.'

Danny looked uncertain. 'I'm not really used to people like that.'

'Like what?'

'Sort of, like … intellectual?'

'Don't let that put you off. Randall's okay, honestly.'

'And the lady vicar?'

'Oh, Angela's all right. She's fun. Just think of her like a normal person. She's about thirty. Randall's getting on for about forty, I think.'

'So they're quite old.'

Anne grinned. '*Ancient*, but still able to get around without crutches or a Zimmer frame.'

They were in high spirits when they climbed down the wall-ladder, though Danny could not help but look up at the lavender suspended from the hook in the beam. Anne noticed but said nothing. She would never tell Danny that Randall had once tried to hang himself from that same hook two years earlier, in despair following the murder of Toni Petrie. Anne's face clouded. Perhaps the re-opening of Sarah's grave could stir up ancient conflicts and hatred. She shook herself mentally.

'Right,' she exclaimed breezily. 'Roll call. Got your sunhat?'

Danny held up a beach bag. 'Yep. In here.'

'Book to read if we pull over for a sun-bathe?'

'Got it.'

'Bikini for same?'

'On underneath.'

'Sunblock?'

'Ah …'

'You can use mine. Sweatshirt for if it clouds over?'

'All present and correct.'

'Let's go!'

Anne was locking the office barn door when they heard tyres crunching.

Danny swivelled round. 'Ford Escort?'

'That's Angela's. Brace yourself, Danny. You're about to meet a real live vicar and her rural wotsit.'

~~~

It was one of those summer days that boat people dream about: just warm enough for relaxing, just enough sunshine to brighten the landscape without dazzling, just enough clouds to make the sky interesting. Anne and Ralph cast off while Marnie reversed *Sally Ann* out of her docking area. She brought the boat round in mid-channel and pointed her nose north towards Stoke Bruerne, an hour away with plenty of quiet places to tie up for lunch.

At noon they had barely been underway for five minutes when Anne went below and returned to the stern deck with a tray of glasses and a chilled bottle of Aussie Chardonnay. Danny followed her out, carrying a tray with dishes of olives, cashews and pretzels. She had been wondering what could be the attraction of travelling on a canalboat at four miles per hour. Now she was beginning to understand. While serving the nibbles, she noticed that some of the moored boats they passed were not the same design as *Sally Ann*. She remarked on this, commenting that Ralph's boat, *Thyrsis*, also looked somehow different.
~~~

Marnie explained. 'Ralph's boat is a *trad*, a traditional design, with a stern like the original working boats. Most people think that's the most attractive style.'

Danny looked around her. '*Sally Ann*'s got more room out here at the back.'

'That's right. It's called a *cruiser* stern. Boats with this layout were designed for leisure use. It may offend the purist, but it has certain advantages.'

'Which do you prefer?'

'For looks, it's got to be the trad, like *Thyrsis*. But for socialising, the difference is obvious.'

'More space.'

'You've got it. That's why we use *Sally* when we go out for a tootle. There are six of us on board, and we have enough room, just about, to stand on the stern deck. If we'd taken *Thyrsis*, someone would have to be back here steering in splendid isolation, while the rest of us would sit up front, being sociable in the cratch.'

'The *cratch*? Is that what you said?'

'The space in the bows.'

'Funny name!'

Anne handed her friend a glass of wine. 'It comes from the French word, *crèche*.'

'Is that where the children stayed when the boats were travelling?'

Angela and Randall tried to conceal their mirth but Anne laughed.

'That sounds logical, but it's the word for a *manger*. It's where they kept the hay for the horse that pulled the boat along before they had engines.'

Danny sipped her wine. 'There's more to this boating thing than you'd expect, isn't there?'

After half an hour Marnie went below with Ralph, leaving Anne in charge of the helm and their guests. Soon the smell of food in preparation began to waft out. The cool summer fragrance of chopped cucumber blended with the pungent tang of garlic, shortly to be joined by a warm aroma. Something good was in the oven. In the galley, Marnie and Ralph noticed the boat begin to slalom and guessed that Danny was making her first attempt at steering. They heard a shriek from the stern deck before the boat resumed a straight course.

They were approaching Stoke Bruerne bottom lock when Marnie looked out to announce that lunch would be ready in ten minutes. From behind her came the encouraging plop of a cork being extracted from a bottle. Danny handed the tiller back to Anne.

At the point where the river Tove entered the canal like a tributary, Anne slowed the boat and announced that they were going to *wind*. She pronounced it to rhyme with 'tinned'. Danny laughed, thinking it sounded rude until Anne performed the manoeuvre, a three-point turn. For a few minutes they headed back south and tied up opposite a field of sheep, bounded at the water's edge by a row of tall willows. The consensus was to eat out on deck, and Ralph put up a huge creamy parasol while Anne set out folding picnic tables and Randall brought safari chairs up from the saloon.

It was the simplest and most satisfying of meals: a classic *quiche Lorraine*, plus a non-meat version with salmon and broccoli; a mixed salad in vinaigrette; new potatoes with butter and a sprinkling of parsley. The wine was a young red *Côtes du Rhône* from southern France, helped along by glasses of sparkling mineral water.

Danny now fully understood the appeal of boating and wondered why the whole world did not live like this. And Anne had been right about the *God Squad*. Angela acted like, well, a normal woman, and Randall was friendly. Best of all, nobody tried to talk about religion. The closest they came was when Angela mentioned that the old vicarage was up for sale again.

Marnie looked thoughtful as she sipped her wine. 'So what's happening about Sarah? I'm not really up-to-date on how things stand after the latest … developments.'

Danny did not register the connection and thought Marnie was asking about a mutual friend. She was taking a mouthful of quiche when Angela replied.

'There could be real problems with getting her reburied in the churchyard.'

Danny almost choked, and Anne came to the rescue with a glass of water. Gasping, she muttered, 'Sorry, went down the wrong way. Sorry.' She took another sip.

Angela leaned forward and laid a hand on Danny's arm. 'No, I'm sorry. This is all rather distasteful.'

Danny smiled weakly.

Anne explained to her friend. 'Sarah's the one who hanged herself in the office barn.'

Danny grimaced. 'The lavender.'

'Yes. Angela and Randall want her to be reburied – she's outside the church grounds at the moment – and they think that isn't fair.'

'Why is she outside? Do I really want to know?'

Anne tried to sound matter-of-fact. 'She committed suicide when she found out that her family had been involved *indirectly* in the murder of the vicar.'

'That was all a long time ago, right?'

Anne nodded. 'Hundreds of years.'

'So it's all history.'

'Yes, well, almost … sort of …'

Danny looked doubtful. 'I don't get it.'

Randall joined in. 'We know she did what she did when the balance of her mind was disturbed. It could happen to anyone. That's why we want to bring her back into the churchyard. We don't want her to be an outcast any more.'

'Okay. Thanks.'

'We're just wanting to move her a few yards.'

'So no big deal, really,' Danny suggested.

Randall raised both palms upwards. 'Not everyone sees it like that.'

Danny was puzzled again. 'Why not?'

'Well, some people say she might have been a witch.'

Danny's eyes grew wider. 'Could she have been?'

'No, but in the sixteen hundreds a lot of people believed in that kind of thing.'

'How can you be sure she wasn't one?'

Ralph stepped in to try to head off the conversation. 'There's a lot of historical evidence to the contrary.' He thought that sounded anodyne enough to bring matters to an end. 'More wine anyone?'

Randall picked up his glass, turning back to Danny. 'We know for a fact she wasn't a witch. Her grave was aligned west-east – witches were usually north-south – and she was buried with a crucifix in her hands.'

Danny gasped. 'You've looked inside the coffin?'

'Well it was falling apart and in any case, we had to. We needed to be sure we were reinterring the right person.'

Danny felt her past life floating before her eyes, as if she were drowning. They were talking about bodies, coffins and witches as if they were the most commonplace things in the world.

Angela held up her glass for a refill. 'Just a little, please Ralph. I'm driving. We know it is the right person in the coffin, at least we have no reason to doubt that. The brass plate on the lid confirms it, and it's definitely a woman inside. This new development, as you call it, Marnie, could well cause delays, could let our opponents mount a new challenge to the bishop's decision.'

Against her better judgment Danny asked, 'What's this new development?'

'Well, when we began the exhumation, we found there was another body, on *top* of Sarah's coffin.'

Danny had never heard anything so appalling in her life. 'Another body?' she repeated faintly.

Ralph poured himself some more wine and sat down. 'Just a skeleton, surely?'

Randall shook his head. 'Rather more than that, actually. There's also some … the pathologist called it *other tissue* … mainly skin, still attached to the bones in places. The soil in the grave was damp at that depth.'

'I see. How interesting.'

Danny looked at her plate. Small pieces of finely chopped bacon were visible through the cheese topping of the quiche. She wondered what skin – and *other tissue* – looked like after it had been in the ground for a few centuries.

In the background Ralph was still talking. 'Is there any means of identifying the other body?'

'Not yet. That's why it's gone to this specialist lab in Oxford.'

'The Archaeological Materials Laboratory,' Marnie said. 'Quite a mouthful.'

Randall looked surprised. 'Yes, that's right. How did you know that, Marnie?'

'Rob mentioned it, Dr Cardew.'

'What do they expect to find at the lab?' Ralph asked.

Marnie shrugged. 'I think they want to try to put a date on the remains. As for anything else, I'm not sure. We'll have to wait and see what they turn up.' She was anxious to steer the conversation away and turned to Angela. 'On a slightly different tack, what can you tell me about Celia Devere? Until the other day I'd never heard of Knightly Court. Celia's interested in a makeover, just in their wing of the house.'

Anne pricked up her ears.

Angela looked thoughtful. 'Well, you know I don't like to gossip …' Everyone pricked up their ears. '… but it's common knowledge that Celia is Hugh's second wife.'

Marnie smiled. 'That's hardly gossip these days, Angela.'

'No, but I gather there was some sort of scandal about their relationship before they got married.'

'Even that's not uncommon. Were they worried about the family's good name? Are they the local aristocracy?'

'I'm not sure. I bet you know, Randall. You were vicar here for a few years.'

'I think they're what is known as *landed gentry*, not actual lords, but related to some branch of the nobility. They tend to regard themselves as the backbone of Britain. The big house – Knightly Court – is owned by Hugh's father, the Honourable Marcus Devere. He's now old and infirm, lives in one wing with his butler and a housekeeper.'

'Butler?' Marnie could hardly believe her ears.

'Yes, really. He doubles up as chauffeur, though the old man doesn't get out much these days. The butler's wife is the housekeeper.'

Suddenly Anne burst out laughing. 'Oh well, that solves the problem of the body in Sarah's grave.' Everyone stared at her. She grinned. 'The butler did it!'

For a few seconds there was no reaction. Anne thought she had overstepped the mark. 'Sorry. Of course it's a serious matter. I shouldn't joke about it, not really.'

Then Angela giggled, and laughter spread round the stern deck.

Smiling, Marnie stood up. 'Right. There's a little more food left. Danny, what can I get you? Oh, I see you haven't quite finished. Did I give you too much?'

After supper on *Sally Ann* with Marnie and Ralph, the girls went back to the attic and spent an enjoyable hour or two listening to music, chatting and reading magazines. There had been no more talk of bodies, skeletons or witches. It was only when Anne offered Danny the first turn in the shower at the back of the office that they found she had left her bag on the boat. Danny insisted she could go to fetch it while Anne used the shower. Anne quickly set up the camp bed for Danny, as her friend climbed down the wall-ladder.

Rounding the corner of the office barn, Danny hesitated before entering the spinney, regretting that she had declined Anne's offer to go with her. Night had fallen, though away to her right the sky was not yet completely black. She could make out the shape of tree-tops in the darkness. As her eyes adjusted to the gloom, she saw the path into the woods before her and listened for any sound of movement nearby. Perhaps it was not too late to go inside and accept Anne's suggestion. Then she heard something, a steady hissing. The shower. It was too late. Danny took a deep breath and set off.

The walk proved to be less scary than she had expected. The spinney was no dense forest of Disney-like trees with gnarled branches reaching out to snag her clothes and ensnare her. There were no gleaming eyes glinting in the shadows. Ahead of her she could see lights twinkling. Marnie and Ralph were on *Thyrsis*. This was a tranquil, civilised place where friends led interesting and fulfilled lives. Clutching the boat's keys, Danny reached the docking area and walked to the stern doors to let herself in. Flicking on a cabin light she was struck again by the cosiness of the interior. The walls were lined in tongue-and-groove pine, with brass fittings to the curtains that glowed in a red, blue and cream Liberty pattern.

Danny found her bag on the floor beside a chair and made her way out. She was turning the key in the lock when she became aware of a sound behind her, rhythmic and mechanical, the steady beat of an engine, a boat approaching. But when she turned to face it, there was nothing in sight. Danny felt her pulse quicken and took a few short breaths, telling herself to calm down. Reason told her that her night vision had been impaired by the light in the cabin. Even so, it was the strangest feeling. She could hear the engine louder now, though still only a faint murmuring, yet she could not see any other boat. Without further hesitation she withdrew the key from the lock and jumped silently onto the bank, scurrying towards the shelter of the spinney. From among the trees she looked again and this time she saw it.

The boat looked about the same length as *Sally Ann* or *Thyrsis*. All other details were impossible to make out. It seemed to be black or dark grey, the shape camouflaged against the dim background of the fields and trees beyond the canal. She looked towards the stern as it broke clear of *Thyrsis*, but there too she was deceived. The steerer was almost invisible and seemed to be dressed entirely in black. In seconds the strange craft passed noiselessly behind *Sally Ann* and out of view. Danny began breathing normally again. Turning, she hurried back to the office barn and locked the door behind her.

'Everything all right?' Anne called down from the attic. 'Did you find it?'

'Yeah. No problem.'

'Shower's all yours. I've put a towel out for you on the stool with your pyjamas.'

'Thanks.' Danny made a big effort not to look at the hook in the ceiling beam. Sitting at Anne's desk to slip off her shoes, she called over towards the ladder. 'Anne? Can I ask you something about boats?'

'Sure.'

'When you travel at night, are you supposed to put lights on, like a car?'

There was a pause while Anne considered the question. 'I think most people put on running lights, like side lights, a red one on the left, a green one on the right.'

'What about headlights?'

'I'm not sure. We never really do much travelling at night. I think a headlight would show you where you're going, but it might spoil your night vision for what's around you.'

'Yeah. That makes sense.'

By the time Danny had finished downstairs and climbed the ladder, Anne was sitting cross-legged in the middle of the bed feeling the back of her hair.

'It's the one advantage of having fine hair like mine. You can towel it dry in minutes.'

Danny patted her mop of curls. 'Tell me about it.'

'D'you want a drink or anything? There's fizzy water or fruit juice in the fridge downstairs.'

'No, I'm fine. I've put the boat keys on your desk. Is that all right?'

'Sure. What was all that about boats travelling at night?'

'What d'you mean?'

'You asked me about headlights, you know, when you came back from *Sally*.'

'Oh, that was nothing.'

Something in Danny's tone sparked Anne's interest. She might have let it pass, except that her friend hastily knelt down and began fiddling with the sleeping bag on the camp bed. Was she avoiding eye-contact?

'That was a funny question, Danny. I mean, why did you suddenly think of boats using lights?'

'I just did.'

'Did you see a boat going by?'

'Yeah.'

'With no lights on?'

'Yeah.'

'Danny, look. I don't mean to interrogate you, but you seem somehow spooked.'

Danny sat up and looked across at Anne. 'Not really. It's just … I dunno … I've heard some weird things today. Then, I go to fetch my bag and this strange thing happened. This boat came by.'

'What was strange about it?'

'At first, I could hear it coming, but not see it. Peculiar. D'you know what I mean? It was like *there*, but not there.'

'It might've been a generator on another boat. That can sometimes sound like an engine – well, it *is* an engine – but quieter running than most boat diesels.'

'No, Anne, this was a boat. I saw it, sort of, anyway. It went by when I was going into the spinney. It was really weird, black, or very dark all over, no lights on, very slow. Whoever was steering it was, like, the same colour as the boat, all in black.

Danny was no longer looking at Anne but focusing on the images in her head. When Anne spoke, her voice seemed to come from far away.

'A stealth narrowboat.' It was little more than a whisper.

'Yes.' Danny smiled. 'Yes, that's a good way of –' She noticed Anne's expression and stopped. 'What's up?'

'Danny, what else did you see? Did you see its name? Did you get a look at the steerer? What did he look like?'

'I told you, it was all dark, no lights or anything. I could only just make out … no, wait a minute. There was something. When it went by, I think some light came from a window on *Thyrsis*, just for a second, a touch of colour. Yes. I think the steerer may've had blonde hair.'

'Which way was it travelling, north or south?'

'Er ...'

'Left or right as you face the canal?'

'Left.'

Anne's reaction took Danny by surprise. She leapt from the bed, pulled on her trainers and scrambled down the wall-ladder, still in her pyjamas. Anne was out through the office barn door before Danny could speak. Minutes passed while Danny waited. She was on the brink of going off in search of her friend when she heard the door open again and Anne climbed the ladder, panting.

'Sorry about that, Danny.'

Anne flopped onto the bed, breathing heavily. There were twigs in her hair and a thorn stuck in her pyjamas at the shoulder.

'What's going on, Anne? You look as if you've seen a ...'

7
Whizz-bang

Danny knew it was morning. A thin crack of light was showing in the narrow slit that was the attic's window. She rolled onto her back and yawned. Instead of the troubled and restless night she had expected, she had fallen asleep as soon as Anne turned out the lamps. She listened. Through the thick stone walls of the barn no sounds penetrated from outside. More strangely, she could not hear Anne breathing, even though her friend was only a few feet away.

'Anne?' Danny whispered.

Turning sideways she found her watch on the floor and squinted at its face. Just before seven. She had never woken so early. Struggling out of the sleeping bag, she sat up and looked across to the bed. The covers were thrown back; it was empty. In a louder voice she called down through the hatch.

'Anne? Are you there?'

No reply. Danny climbed down the wall-ladder, crossed to the kitchen alcove and switched on the kettle. As it began rattling, she checked out the shower room on the other side. The shower looked as she had left it the night before. She knocked on the door of the loo before entering.

The previous night's conversation came back to her in snatches. At first Anne had been evasive. But when Danny asked outright if she had gone looking for the mysterious boat, Anne had just nodded, pulling a thorn slowly out of her shoulder, gritting her teeth. A tiny bloodstain had spread round the hole in the pyjama top where the thorn had come through. She had begun rubbing it.

'So did you find it?' Danny had asked.

'It had gone too far, at least too far to catch up with in the dark. If it didn't tie up, it could be a couple of miles away by now.'

'Whose boat is it, Anne?'

'Until I see it, I can't know for certain.'

'But?'

'It might belong to someone I know, or rather knew.'

Danny had shown her impatience. 'I guessed that much.'

She had worried that the explanation would be as creepy as the conversation over lunch. Yet when she had pressed Anne, it wasn't so strange after all. If the steerer of the strange boat was the person Anne thought it was, then this was about some boy Anne had known. That was familiar territory. Stories about boyfriends, Danny could handle. Anne really had grown up a lot since she had left school. Perhaps she had even crept out once Danny was asleep to spend the night with the boyfriend on his boat!

Danny washed and climbed up to the attic to dress. Climbing back down, she noticed something different about Anne's desk. From one of the drawers, the corner of a folder was sticking out and had prevented it from closing properly. Danny was pulling the drawer open to push the folder into place, when her attention was drawn to a photograph protruding from under the flap. She slipped it out.

It was a black and white photo, but not an old one. The subject was three black boys, teenagers with dreadlocks, standing beside a child, a little fair-haired girl of about six or seven. One of the boys was holding her hand, and they were all grinning at the camera. What could this be?

Danny drew out more photos. They were a curious mixture: crowds of children in what looked like a playground; children's faces in the windows of buses; parents waving; a mob of skinheads running down an alleyway. Not exactly holiday snaps. Was anything normal these days where Anne was concerned? She turned the photos over. Each one had a number pencilled on the back and several had a caption, 'Summer School', in neat writing. At the bottom of the pile were three pictures of men dressed alike in black shirts and trousers; one had an arm-band in a lighter colour. On the back of those picture the caption was 'New Force'. In the bottom right-hand corner of every photograph were the initials, *DS*.

DS. Danny Sullivan sat staring at her own initials and felt her blood run cold.

Marnie and Ralph did not normally make love in the morning, so that Sunday was an exception. The day had started as usual with Marnie getting up first and using the bathroom. On an impulse she decided to take a shower, which was also not the norm; she tended to shower at night when Ralph was around. It must have been the season for impulses. If it came as a surprise it was not unwelcome, when Marnie was shampooing her hair with eyes shut tight and felt a sudden rush of cool air as the door to the shower opened and quickly closed. She gasped from the cold as she was bumped in the confined space and her back touched the wall tiles.

'Oh, sorry.' A quiet, polite, distinguished voice. 'Is this shower occupied? I couldn't see with all the steam.'

'Could that be why you're having to use your hands to find your way around?' Marnie twisted her face under the showerhead to rinse off the suds.

'Absolutely! What other reason could there be?'

'Of course. Well, just pretend I'm not here. I wouldn't want to spoil your shower.'

'That's very considerate of you, but easier said than done.'

The fact that various parts of their anatomies were colliding in the narrow cubicle only served to underline the point.

'Oops!' Marnie lurched as something clattered to the floor with a splash.

'What's up?'

'I've dropped the shampoo bottle.'

'Is that a problem?'

'I'll have to bend down to pick it up. In this place that's not going to be easy.'

Ralph sighed as if all the worries of the world were on his shoulders. 'Never mind. We'll manage somehow ...'

Danny was in the loft packing her bag for later when she heard a car arriving. She was hovering over the gap in the floor by the wall-ladder when the door to the office barn opened. It closed with a bang followed by a muffled curse.

'*Damn!*'

'Hi Anne.'

'Sorry, Danny. Hope I didn't wake you.

'No, it's okay, I'm up and about. Where've you been, jogging?'

Anne laughed. 'Not likely! Not my kind of thing. Are you ready for breakfast? I've been to fetch some stuff from the boat.'

Danny scrambled down the ladder to find Anne filling the kettle.

'I thought we'd eat here, give Marnie and Ralph a bit of time together. Unless you want a cooked breakfast?'

'No. Not *my* kind of thing. Cornflakes, toast, anything like that'll do. Not really a breakfast person.'

'It's lovely out. We can sit on the bench in the courtyard if you like.'

'Great.'

Danny helped by loading the tray and carrying it outside. The sun was climbing through wispy cloud, birds were singing, the air was warm and fragrant, a perfect morning for breakfast in the open. This was unlike anything Danny had known. Sure, she had eaten in the garden of her parent's house before, but this felt different. Glebe Farm was another world.

The sun reflected off the stone walls of beautiful buildings; the cobbled yard and climbing roses created an atmosphere of peace and calm. It was as if Marnie had fashioned a way of life more like a holiday than the reality that most people knew. But there was something else. Danny had been uneasy ever since she saw the lavender hanging in the office. It was as if there was a sinister presence in this haven, something unmentioned below the surface. There was more to everything than met the eye in this paradise.

Why had Anne taken the car that morning if she was really going to *Sally Ann*? The boat was a one-minute walk away through the spinney. Why had she not given a straight answer to the simple question of where she had been?

Off with his head! It was a swift and accurate beheading. Ralph removed the top from his boiled egg with one tap and one stroke of the knife. Marnie was always impressed by the way he did that. The action coincided with her arrival on the stern deck of *Sally Ann* carrying a teapot and a dish of lemon slices. She put them on the table and kissed Ralph on the cheek before sitting down.

'How's the egg?'

'Perfect, just as I like them, like everything you do.'

Marnie laughed. 'Cupboard love.'

It occurred to them simultaneously that the shower on *Thyrsis* was about the size of a broom cupboard. They were both smiling as Ralph dipped a soldier in his egg and Marnie poured Orange Pekoe through a strainer over three slivers of lemon in her cup.

'It's funny, isn't it? I always have a fancy for lemon tea after we've … had a shower like that.'

Ralph swallowed. 'First thing on Monday I'll phone Fortnum and Mason and order a hundredweight of their best Ceylon FBOP.'

Marnie added a cube of sugar to the golden liquid and watched it sink onto the lemons. 'Ralph, did you hear a car early on this morning?'

'No. But then I never hear anything when I'm asleep.'

'True. I wonder if I dreamt it.'

'Have we any plans for today?'

Marnie slowly stirred the tea and took a sip. 'Mm … that's good. After a start like that I feel like relaxing. How about you?'

'Definitely a day off … busy time ahead. Perhaps a walk and a picnic?'

'What shall we do today?'

Danny finished her toast and marmalade. 'Don't mind. It's nice just being in the country. D'you have a plan?'

Anne folded her napkin. 'Not really. We could just have a lazy day if you like.'

'What about Marnie and Ralph?'

'I thought they might want to be together, just the two of them. Ralph's been away all week and he travels a lot giving lectures, going to meetings, conferences.'

'They're very high-powered. You all are. You have a really full life, don't you?'

'It's fun, couldn't be better. I wouldn't want it any other way.'

Marnie unfolded the local ranger map on the table, and they pored over it. She showed Ralph the location of Knightly Court, both of them wondering why they had never been aware of it before. She tapped the map at a spot to the north-west of the village.

'What about Knightly Woods for our walk? We haven't been there before.'

Ralph bent closer. 'Make a change from the boat. Plenty of footpaths. We could probably find somewhere to picnic.'

Ralph offered to clear up the breakfast things while Marnie checked out the girls. She walked through the spinney, breathing in the smells of the morning. When she reached the edge of the trees, she hesitated. Instead of going straight ahead towards the office barn, she made a detour, skirting round the back to the other cluster of barns.

The garage barn was constructed of stone, open at the front like a car-port, big enough to house four cars. Facing her on the right was Ralph's Volvo, standing beside her Land Rover Discovery. In the left-hand bay Anne's red Mini lined up next to a small car concealed under a dust-cover. This was Marnie's classic pre-war MG, a two-seater built in

1936 and lovingly restored. That morning, her focus was on the Mini.

Marnie walked into the barn, put a hand on the bonnet of the little red car and stood looking thoughtful. It was still warm. This must have been the car she had heard, but where had Anne been going? It had been too early to fetch newspapers; there were no other shops open at that hour on a Sunday; no point in making a special journey for petrol. Still lost in thought, she headed for the office barn. Rounding the corner, she found the girls sitting on the bench in the sunshine. For a fraction of a second Anne's expression registered surprise.

Ralph's version of a day off was to spend only two hours that morning working in his study on *Thyrsis*. The forward section of the interior was equipped as a workspace with desk, computer, printer, bookcases and filing cabinet. Built-in shelving housed a small television, mainly used for monitoring news broadcasts, and a hi-fi unit to provide background music while Ralph sorted statistics. The office chair was supplemented by two small armchairs.

While Ralph dealt with preparations for his next conference trip, Marnie changed into overalls, returned to the garage barn and pulled back the cover from the MG. The sound of the starter motor, followed by the throaty rumbling of the old engine brought the girls running. Marnie reversed out and began inspecting the venerable machine for leaks of oil or fluids. Her late husband, Simon, had devised a special cleaning pad, part duster, part buffer, and Marnie set to, giving the bodywork a thorough rub-down. Danny said it reminded her of grooming the pony she had as a child. Soon the morning sun was glinting off shiny paintwork in British racing green.

With the girls dedicated to hedonism by the waterside, Marnie announced that she and Ralph would be using the MG for their trip to the woods. In reply to an unspoken hint, she took Danny for a ride up the field track and on to the village shop to fetch the papers. Anne stayed behind, digging out sun-beds and towels.

Marnie's pleasure in the morning and the drive in the sports car were dimmed when she parked outside the shop at the same time as Celia Devere came out onto the pavement. In a floral summer dress and looking more like Princess Di than ever, she stopped in her tracks and stared at the MG as Marnie hopped out.

'What a lovely little whizz-bang!' Celia's laughter stopped abruptly; she put a hand to her mouth. 'Sorry. I didn't mean –'

'*Whizz-bang?*' Marnie repeated.

'I meant it as a compliment, honestly Marnie. It's *beautiful*. I've never seen a car like that before, well not close up anyway. I wasn't being rude about it.'

Marnie looked at her car with its antique styling, its soft top folded back, exposed headlamps, sloping wings over chromed wire wheels, twin bucket seats of cream leather and the spare wheel slung on the back of the fuel tank. She smiled.

'Actually, I do see what you mean.'

Celia laughed and put a hand on Marnie's shoulder. 'I'm so glad you're not offended.'

'Of course I'm not. It's not a bad description.'

Celia turned to one side and lowered her voice. 'I'm afraid we got off to a bad start the other day, Marnie. It was all my fault. I bitterly regret that. I hope we can start again with a clean sheet.'

'No problem.'

'Friends?'

'Sure.'

Aware that Danny had climbed out of the car and was standing behind them, Marnie introduced her to Celia who then walked off in the direction of the church, turning round briefly to smile at the car and blow a kiss over her shoulder.

It was a day for Sybarites. In bikinis and sunblock, Danny and Anne reclined on loungers with magazines, chatting about friends from the past, plans for the future. Danny commented that Anne seemed to have her life thoroughly worked out; she knew where she was going because she was already there. Anne's reply was unexpected.

'Nothing's guaranteed. What I have today I might not have tomorrow.'

Danny wondered why Anne was so gloomy when she had everything – and more – that anyone of her age could wish for. She was doing well at college and had a job that gave her a steady income throughout the year. No chasing after jobs on the Christmas post or in burger bars for Anne Price. She had her own car and a great pad. Why not be optimistic?

Surreptitiously Danny watched Anne. Lying there in the sun, she looked like any relaxed eighteen year-old, but there was more under the surface where Anne was concerned. Danny noticed that each time a boat came into earshot, Anne would look up at once until it came into view and then return to her reading.

Suddenly Anne glanced round and caught Danny watching her. 'What's up?'

Danny was flustered. 'What?'

'You had a strange look on your face.'

'I, er …'

Anne swivelled round and sat up. 'Something's bothering you.'

'No.'

'Danny …'

'It's just. I was only thinking …'

'Go on.'

'Nothing really, just well, I suppose it was about your life.'

'What about it?'

'I can see why you're so happy here. It's a sort of *idyllic life*, on the surface.'

'But?'

'Look, don't think I'm being rude or anything, but it comes at a price, doesn't it?'

'How d'you mean?'

'I'm not sure how to say it.'

Anne waited for her friend to continue.

'It just seems a bit strange. I mean, you don't get out a lot, do you? It's as if you've grown up so fast, you've left all your old life behind.'

'I've moved on, that's for sure. But I'm happy here and it's really interesting. I wouldn't want it to be different. I know where I'm going and what I'm doing. Is that too high a price to pay?'

The sound of a boat engine intruded, and Anne's head snapped round. Two children were sitting in the prow wearing life jackets. Anne smiled and waved as they passed.

Danny waved too. She had not intended the conversation to go in this direction and wished she could change the subject.

'Sorry, Anne. I didn't mean to speak out of turn. You've got a good set-up here.'

'Yes, I have, but something's bugging you. Was it that talk of skeletons and graves?'

'No, though that was a bit creepy. It was more about your own life. I don't know how to put it.'

'Try.'

'Oh Anne, I don't know. Maybe I think you concentrate too much on work for someone of our age.'

'Working with Marnie's great, very interesting and fulfilling. How else would I want to spend my time?'

Danny sighed. 'Well, you don't seem to go to parties or have friends of your own age, or do you? I mean, even your boyfriend's some kind of weirdo, prowling the canals at night on a boat like a ghost.'

Anne stared. 'Boyfriend?'

'Anne, I have to be honest. I saw your folder , the photos, the *DS* in the corner.'

'How did you see them?'

'Sticking out of a drawer. That was him, wasn't it? You spent the night with him, didn't you?'

Anne's face reddened. 'How did you ...? There was nothing in the folder –'

'I meant last night. You went out to see him.'

'Danny, I was in the same room as you last night. You know I was.'

'Not when I woke up. You were gone.'

'That was this morning. I got up early. I often do that.'

'So where were you? Look, it's none of my business, I know –'

'I had things to do. They didn't include seeing ... what did you call him? ... a *weirdo, prowling around on a boat like a ghost*.' Anne smiled. 'Danny, I think we've talked too much about ghosts while you've been here. It's not usually like that, honestly. We just get on with our lives.' Anne stood up. 'Right. I'm going to make us a cup of tea.'

Danny managed a smile and reached for the sunblock. 'Good idea.'

Parked under the trees at the edge of the woods, the sporty MG looked like a poster from the 1930s advertising the joys of motoring – *You can be sure of Shell!* Beyond it, Marnie was unselfconsciously creating another period image as she spread the large tartan blanket in dark blue and green on the ground. When Ralph hauled the vintage picnic basket out from the well behind the car seats and they began unpacking it, Marnie pondered the latest conversation she had had with Celia.

She had just dropped Danny back at Glebe Farm after the expedition to the shop and was in the barn loading up the MG when her mobile rang. Celia launched in with no introduction.

'Sorry about this, Marnie, I know it's too silly, but I forgot to mention something when we bumped into each other just now.'

'Oh?'

'I just wanted to check with you about Monday.'

'Monday?'

'Yes. You said we could get together after the weekend, you know, to talk about redecorating the court? And I thought we'd settled on Monday. Only we didn't fix an exact time. Remember?'

Marnie scoured her brain. Had they agreed to meet on Monday or was it less definite than that?

'Er, I don't have my diary with me at present, Celia. Could I ring you tomorrow when I'm in the office?' She hoped that wasn't too subtle a reminder that this was supposed to be a day of rest. 'I'll need to check my commitments.'

'Oh, yes, yes, Marnie. That'll be fine. I didn't mean to interrupt your plans for today. Are you doing something nice?'

'We're going off for an outing, just getting ready to leave, in fact.'

'I won't keep you. Are you going on your boat?'

'Not actually. We're, er, taking the *whizz-bang* for a ride, just a short run up to the woods for a walk and a picnic lunch.'

At that moment Ralph came round the corner carrying the small rucksack they used for the wine. Marnie was waiting for Celia to respond, but found herself listening to air.

'Hallo? Celia, are you there?'

'What woods?' Gone was the bubbly tone. Celia's voice was flat.

'Well, just the local ones, Knightly Woods, you know.' No reply. 'Celia?'

'Yes.'

Marnie had a sudden thought. Perhaps Knightly Woods were privately owned by the Devere family and Celia was trying to think of a tactful way of telling her they would be trespassing.

'The woods aren't private are they, Celia? I mean, there are public footpaths marked on the map.'

'Yes, they are public.' Still the flat tone. 'Though Hugh's family used to own them years ago when he was a boy.'

Marnie was puzzled. 'So it's all right to walk there and have picnics, isn't it?'

'Yes, only you will make sure you don't wander from the marked footpaths, won't you?'

'Why's that?'

'Oh, no reason. It's just better like that, safer.'

'I see.' Marnie didn't see, but she had no wish to continue the conversation. 'Well, I expect you'll be getting ready to go to church.'

'Church?'

'As it's Sunday, I mean. I can hear the bells ringing.'

'I'm not going to church this morning. I had a migraine yesterday, so I'm taking it easy today.'

'I understand.' This time Marnie thought she did understand. Celia's change of tone was due to an after-shock from the migraine. She spoke softly. 'I mustn't keep you. We'll talk tomorrow.'

'Marnie?'

'Yes?'

'You will stay on the public footpaths, won't you?'

'Of course.'

'Promise?'

'Yes.' This was really strange. 'What's this about, Celia?'

Once again she was listening to silence, and this time it was final.

A bright red Mini was cruising the dual carriageway heading south at a steady sixty. Beside Anne, Danny surveyed the interior. The little car looked like new inside and out, and Danny could not help thinking that if it was hers there would be chocolate wrappings on the floor and rubbish on the back seat.

Anne glanced sideways at her friend. 'I know what you're going to say.'

'What?'

'You're going to tell me how lucky I am.'

'You are, but that isn't what I was thinking. Can I borrow the mirror for a minute?'

Anne checked the traffic behind her. 'Sure.'

Danny swivelled the rear-view mirror towards her and began examining her face. 'I think my nose is red.'

Anne laughed. 'You've caught the sun, all right, but I don't think you need worry too much.'

'Really? I'm not so sure. Pity it's not Christmas. I could get a holiday job with Santa as Rudolph.'

They laughed together and Anne readjusted the mirror.

Danny looked at Anne. 'I think you've got some colour, but you're not burnt like me.'

'With my pale skin I have to be careful. That's why I use loads of sunblock. I'll put some more cream on when I get home.'

'You're going home?'

'Yeah, after I've dropped you off.'

'Where's home?'

Anne looked confused. 'Where I live.'

'You mean back at Glebe Farm?'

'Yes. I'll call in to say hallo to Mum and Dad and Richard, but after that I'll drive back to Knightly. I've got work tomorrow.'

Danny watched the countryside going by. It seemed strange that Anne thought of her attic room as home, rather than her parent's house. She knew Anne got on really well with her family and thought there was no conflict about her relationship with Marnie and Ralph. Even so, it struck her as odd that Anne had made the transition to a new way of life and felt at home in an old barn where just below her bedroom a girl had hanged herself.

'I wonder where I'll think of as home once I've gone to university.'

'It'll be different. You'll be in digs or in a hall of residence, going home at the end of each term. I keep all my things in the attic and I live there most of the time.'

'And you've got used to that,' Danny observed. 'Being in the barn, in your attic.'

Anne sensed something unsaid below the surface. 'Danny, I don't believe in ghosts. There aren't any at Glebe Farm. Sarah's not there any more.'

'I can see it doesn't bother you, Anne. It's just somehow, kind of funny, how you talk about her, as if she *is* there, or as if you know her.'

'Not really. I've got my own life to lead. We all have. There's a lot of work, running a company, even a small practice like Marnie's. We don't have time to worry about what's over and done with.'

'Mm …'

'Honestly, Danny, we don't spend our lives digging up the past.'

'No. I suppose not.'

8
Faint

'I think your friend Danny got a bizarre impression of our life here,' Marnie observed at breakfast the next day.

'I know.' Anne pushed the plunger down on the cafetière and brought it to the table in the saloon on *Sally Ann*. 'She must've thought we spoke of little else but witches and dead bodies all the time.'

'I hope it didn't spoil her weekend.'

'Oh no. She enjoyed it right enough, said she'd like to do more boating next time she comes.'

'Good.' Marnie laughed. 'We'll try to act like normal people for a change.'

Ralph joined in. 'At least she didn't actually refer to us as *weirdoes*, as far as I recall.'

Anne stopped laughing and looked thoughtful. Marnie noticed the sudden change.

'What's up, Anne? Are you all right?'

'It's nothing, just something I thought of. Coffee?'

'Thanks.' Marnie let it go.

Ralph pushed his cup forward. 'Anything special happening this week?'

'I'll be chasing the conservatory people if they haven't phoned by midday. Then there's the joy of a meeting with Celia some time.'

Anne looked up from pouring Ralph's coffee. 'And we have to invoice Willards for the next phased payment on the hotel project.'

Ralph took his cup. 'I'm going over to Oxford this morning. Should be back late afternoon.'

Anne was looking serious again. 'What's this meeting with Celia? Is that Mrs Devere? I don't have it in the diary.'

'She wants to talk to me about a redec at the Court, or rather their wing of it.'

'Oh yes, you said something about that the other day. Do you want me to phone her and fix a time?'

Marnie shook her head. 'My guess is, she'll get in first.'

~~~

Anne dropped the morning's junk mail into a cardboard box beside her desk and took the post over to Marnie.

'What's that?'

'One bank statement, two cheques, details of a new range from Farrow and Ball, a couple of letters, this month's *Domus* magazine, notice of an exhibition in Milan, usual stuff.'

'I meant that box over there.'

'I'm collecting waste paper for the bottle bank.'

'Isn't that a contradiction in –' The phone began ringing. Marnie looked up at the
~~~

clock. Nine on the dot. 'I thought as much. It'll be Celia.'

Anne picked up Marnie's phone. 'Walker and Co, good morning. … Who's calling? … One moment, please.'

Mouthing what looked suspiciously like *Smartarse* she passed the phone to Marnie.

'Good morning, Celia.'

Anne went back to her desk. She was looking through the latest design for the renovation of Willard's Grand Junction Hotel near Hemel Hempstead when Marnie disconnected. Anne pulled the diary towards her.

Marnie groaned. 'We're meeting this morning. That's all right, isn't it?'

'Sure. Only we never book meetings for Monday morning. You always say it's your time to get the week launched.'

'I know, but she's very pushy and it'd be good to get her out of the way.'

'What time are you going to see her?'

'She wants to come here.'

'Oh? Won't you want to look at the house while you discuss what she wants doing?'

'I know it's unusual but she said she wanted to meet here and I just agreed. It seemed the easiest thing to do. I expect that's how it is with Celia. She says what she wants and gets her own way.'

'Mm … So what time's she coming?'

'Ten o'clock. I told her I needed to deal with the post and make some phonecalls.'

Anne wrote in the diary. 'Do I give her a job number?'

Marnie smiled wryly. 'I suggest six-six-six.'

'What?'

'The Devil's number.'

Anne looked blank. 'I don't get it.'

'Sorry. I think it's in the Bible, *The Book of Revelation*. It seemed appropriate. We're living through an odd season.'

'You can say that again.'

Marnie's turn to look blank. 'How d'you mean?'

'Oh, nothing.'

'Come on, tell all. I noticed you went quiet at breakfast. What's on your mind?'

Anne leaned forward with her elbows on the desk.

'Danny had to go to *Sally* to get something on Saturday night while I was in the shower. A boat went by that spooked her out.'

'Why? Did it make a noise?'

'No. The opposite. She said it was very quiet, painted so dark it was almost invisible. The steerer was the same, may have had blonde hair.'

Marnie frowned. 'Ah …'

'Danny said he was a … weirdo.'

'You think it might have been …'

'Yes. Donovan.'

'Has he been in touch?'

'No. Not since he went away last summer.'

'Have you tried to –'

'No.'

'Is that where you went in your car early yesterday morning, looking for him?'

Anne's mouth opened, her eyes widened.

'I, er …'

'Where did you go?'

She regained her composure.

'I drove up to Stoke Bruerne. He wouldn't have got much further but he wasn't there, so I walked down to the bottom lock. There was no one about to ask, so I just came back. A wasted journey.'

'So what's brought him back up here, assuming it was him?'

Anne shrugged. 'Dunno.'

Marnie said nothing, but she had a shrewd idea.

Ralph was laying his briefcase on the rear seat of the car when Marnie came round to the garage barn.

'Are you in a hurry, Ralph?'

'Not particularly. The college library's been there for the past five hundred years; it can wait a little longer for my arrival. What's up?'

'Donovan.'

'Oh?'

'He may be in the area, or at least he may have passed through on Saturday night.'

Marnie explained about Danny's sighting. They reflected silently for a few moments on what the reappearance of Donovan Smith might mean.

A year or two older than Anne, half British, half German, he was the son of a late colleague of Ralph's. Both Donovan's parents had been killed in a road accident in South Africa when Donovan was ten years old. He had been with them and had survived the accident. Later he had gone on to start a course at university but had dropped out in the first year and gone travelling on a narrowboat that he had painted battleship grey.

His arrival in Northamptonshire had been timed to coincide with a by-election for the European Parliament. One of the candidates was a leading figure in far-right politics. With a family history of persecution by the Nazis, Donovan was a fierce opponent of extreme nationalism and, when the candidate had been killed, gunned down in the street, he had left suddenly without saying good-bye.

Ralph closed the car door. 'I wonder what could have brought him back here.'

'In a word … Anne.'

'You think she contacted him, Marnie?'

'I'm sure she didn't. We don't know where he lives.'

'But you think he wants to see her again.'

'I'm sure of it.'

'Even though he hasn't been in touch?'

'Typical Donovan. He must know the police would like to question him about … you know.'

'So he drifts up at night and what? Lies low somewhere? Where do you hide a narrowboat?'

'In a secluded spot.' The voice from behind them startled Marnie and Ralph.

Their heads snapped round. Anne was standing at the corner of the office barn.

'There are plenty of them around,' Marnie said. 'He could moor under the trees on the off-side.'

'Yes. That makes sense. He'd be able –' Anne stopped abruptly and put her head on one side, listening. 'Ah, that's what I came to tell you. Celia phoned. She's on her way. She said she hoped you wouldn't mind if she came a few minutes early. She has a hair appointment she'd forgotten about, apparently.'

Marnie made a face as they heard the sound of a car coming down the field track.

'What a surprise.'

Celia looked as if she had just come from a fashion shoot. Not jealous by nature, Marnie found herself irritated by the fact that Celia always seemed to be turned out as if she was on her way to a smart social occasion. That Monday morning was no exception. No one would have guessed she was just popping in for a talk about decor on her way to the hairdresser.

Parking the open-topped Audi, she walked across the courtyard in a pale blue floral summer dress that had never seen a chain store from inside or out. Marnie was waiting for her by the door of the office barn.

'This is *lovely*, Marnie, so … quaint and charming.' She extended a hand palm down, as if expecting Marnie to kiss it. 'I'd love you to show me round. Is this all your property?'

'Yes, but if you don't mind I'd like to get on with our meeting. A busy day.'

'Oh yes. I wouldn't want to be a nuisance.'

Marnie bit her tongue, feeling once again that Celia had wrong-footed her. She turned to open the office door, but Celia put a hand on her arm.

'Do you think we could talk outside? It's such a lovely morning, pity to waste it.'

'I was going to take notes as we talked.'

'Oh.' It was amazing how one syllable could encapsulate so much: disappointment, a rebuff, a challenge to one's position.

Marnie indicated the bench where Anne and Danny had breakfasted at the weekend. 'We could sit here if you'd prefer. I'll fetch my notepad.'

Celia was still standing when Marnie emerged from the office a few seconds later.

'I was wondering, perhaps it would be possible to see your boat? It's down here somewhere, isn't it?'

As they walked through the spinney, Marnie tried hard to contain herself and wondered if even at that stage she could tell Celia she would have to postpone her project because of pressure of work. It was a very tempting thought. What made her hold back was the certainty that Celia would definitely put the word around that Marnie was in some inexpressible way not satisfactory. That would be bad news. Celia was bad news, but it would be better to keep her onside rather than make an enemy of her.

Celia exclaimed in delight when she saw the two boats nestling against the bank, *Sally Ann* in her dock, *Thyrsis* on the mainline. She ushered Celia aboard *Thyrsis*, by far the smarter of the two boats, and led her into Ralph's study. Her client was charmed. They sat in the armchairs while the kettle boiled and Marnie steered Celia towards the project in hand.

It was hard going. Celia had few ideas about the house and seemed to expect Marnie to produce a master plan from her own imagination without any clues.

'I mean, that is what you do, isn't it, Marnie?' She smiled. 'You come up with all sorts of schemes and I choose the one I like best.'

'Well, er, that's one way of doing it, I suppose. I prefer to discuss what a client likes in terms of colours, textures, style, and then I relate it to their house. That's why I like to meet the client in their home. It makes it easier to discuss things if we can look at the rooms, their orientation, the effect of natural light and so on.'

'Oh, but it's wonderful here, don't you think? It's a nice ambience for thinking about beautiful things.' She swept a hand towards the window and the view over the countryside.

Marnie struggled to make Celia focus on what she wanted at Knightly Court. She rapidly came to the conclusion that Celia expected the redecoration just to happen as if someone had waved a magic wand. After half an hour Marnie succeeded in reducing possibilities to two, possibly three, colour schemes.

'Okay, Celia, I think we've got as far as we can this morning.' Marnie gathered her papers together in a gesture of finality. 'I'd offer you another coffee, but I wouldn't want to make you late for your hair appointment.' Marnie hoped that was not too unsubtle.

'Oh, that would be lovely, Marnie.'

When Marnie produced the second cup, Celia gave her a faint smile.

'Sorry if I'm not quite with-it, Marnie. I've not been myself lately.'

'Really?' Marnie tried not to sound uninterested. This woman was making her tread on eggshells.

'Yes, ever since this *graves* thing happened, and everything else going on in my life, of course …'

'Celia, I don't want to seem uncaring, but I like to keep my relationships with clients on a professional basis. I find it better that way.'

Celia got the point. 'Oh, it wasn't the affair I was thinking about. It was the witchcraft.'

Marnie sat up. 'What witchcraft?'

'I wondered if Sarah was buried outside the church because she was a witch.'

Marnie shook her head. 'No. That's absolutely not the case. She was just a young girl who killed herself because she believed her family was linked with the murder of the vicar.'

'Mm …' Celia looked unconvinced. 'That's only part of it, Marnie. There were other things.'

'To do with witchcraft?'

Celia glanced towards the porthole. 'I went for a walk with Hugh – that's my husband – on Friday afternoon. We went to Knightly Woods.'

Marnie could see where this was leading. 'You told me to keep to the marked footpaths.'

'Yes. Hugh knows the woods like the back of his hand and he took me off the path up to a clearing near the top of the hill. We came across some strange things on the ground. Hugh said they were a witches' circle.'

'How old was this circle?'

'Quite recent. The ash looked fresh to me and there were *things*, goat skulls, something like corn dollies, candle stubs, black ones. I thought Hugh was just trying to frighten me, sort of teasing, you know.'

'But you think he was right.'

Celia nodded. 'I asked Rob Cardew if it was true there had been witches in the area.'

'That was all in the past, Celia. Cardew's an archaeologist.'

'I know that, but he told me there was a history of witchcraft in the county, always had been. There were trials, hangings.' She shuddered. 'It was *horrible*, Marnie.'

'But that was then.'

'He said they were still supposed to be around and now I've seen the evidence for myself.'

Celia was away with her thoughts, as if in a dream world of her own. Marnie seized the opportunity to gather her up, leave the boat and walk her back through the spinney. They were almost through it when Celia turned to her.

'Do you think I have too vivid an imagination, Marnie?'

'Well, I –'

'Hugh says I ought to face up to things in a more adult way. I don't think that's fair.'

'Perhaps he just doesn't want you to worry about things that he doesn't see as a problem.'

'Meaning?' Celia's expression had hardened.

'This witchcraft thing in the woods, maybe it was just some kind of … I don't know … mid-summer party or something.'

'And this Sarah Anne Day business.' Celia seemed to be wandering off in her private thoughts again.

Marnie took her by the arm and led her out of the spinney. Celia turned in through the open door of the office barn and sat down. When she spoke again her voice was calm.

'I'm not neurotic, Marnie, and I can face up to things. Do you think I could possibly have a glass of water?'

'Of course. Are you all right?'

'Yes.' It was almost a whisper.

Marnie headed for the kitchen area. 'Would you like sparkling water or still?'

'Anything. The point is, I can't help thinking about that poor girl, Sarah. I keep imagining what it must have been like when they dragged her off to the gallows and hanged her.'

Marnie was squatting down by the fridge and did not see Anne walk in from the courtyard carrying an empty tray. She was only aware of Anne's presence when she heard her speak.

'They didn't.' Anne tried to sound reassuring. 'She hanged herself.'

'Are you sure?'

Anne pointed. 'Yes. She hanged herself from that hook up there, where the lavender is.'

Celia stood up quickly, staring at the ceiling beam. With a stifled exclamation she put a hand to her forehead, stumbled and fell to the ground.

The phone rang three times at Knightly Court before it was answered.

'Hugh Devere.'

'Oh, good morning, this is Angela Hemingway.'

'Morning, Angela. What can I do for you?'

'I was hoping to speak to Celia.'

'Car's not here. She's gone out. Hairdresser's, I think she said. Take a message?'

'It's about the archaeologists. Could you please tell Celia that Rob Cardew has phoned to say –'

'Just a second. Let me find a pen.' He opened a drawer and pulled out the message pad. 'Fire away. Cardew, d'you say?'

'Yes. He's got dates for digging test pits. He wants to –'

'Ah, hang on.' He saw Celia's car through the window, coming up the drive. 'Here she is now. You can tell her yourself. I'll call her to the phone.'

Hugh went outside and immediately realised that something was wrong. A woman was getting out of the driver's seat of the Audi, but it was not his wife. He rushed forward.

'I say, what's going on?'

The stranger went round to the passenger's side and opened the door to help Celia climb out. Hugh was aware of another car, a red Mini, following on behind.

'What's happened?'

By now Celia was standing unsteadily, being supported by the other woman.

'Mr Devere?'

'Yes. Who are you?'

'My name's Marnie Walker. I've brought Celia –'

'Why are you driving her car?'

'She had a dizzy spell in my office, so I offered to drive her home.'

Hugh looked bewildered. 'What office? Aren't you the hairdresser?'

'No. Look, I think we ought get her inside, don't you?'

'Oh yes. Yes, of course.'

Celia had been watching this exchange with interest.

'I'll be all right. I just need to lie down.' Her voice was weak. 'I would've phoned you, but I didn't know you'd be here.'

Marnie led Celia, holding her by the arm, while Hugh walked beside them.

'Had to call in for some papers on my way to a –' He stopped abruptly. 'Phone! *Damn!* The vicar's on the phone, hanging on for you.'

Celia looked round. Anne had now joined them and was hovering near her elbow. 'Perhaps Anne could take it. Say I'll ring her back.'

Hugh pointed. 'Phone's in that room on the left.'

Anne needed no further prompting and dashed into the house. Marnie and Hugh escorted Celia through to the morning room and settled her on a sofa by the window overlooking the terrace.

When Celia was comfortable, Hugh held out a hand to Marnie. 'Very kind of you to do all this. Hugh Devere. Good to meet you. Sorry if I was a bit short back there. Rather a shock, seeing Celia like that.'

'Quite understandable. We didn't think anyone would be here, but Celia insisted on coming home.'

'Like I said, I just came to pick up –' He looked at his watch. 'Oh hell. Sorry. I mean, I've got this meeting with a client and –'

'I'm fine, Hugh. Really, I am. You go to your meeting. Marnie's here. I'll be all right.'

Surreptitiously Marnie glanced down at her own watch, but said nothing.

Hugh hesitated. 'I'm sure you have your own affairs to attend to, Miss …er …'

'Marnie Walker.'

'Marnie, right. Celia was in your office, you said?'

'We were discussing –'

Everyone looked round as Anne came into the room.

'You talked to the vicar?' Celia spoke as if she was addressing a maid.

Anne stared back and briefly considered dropping a curtsy. 'I gave her your message.'

'Did she say anything?'

Anne looked quickly at Marnie. 'Dr Cardew wants to start test pits in a few days' time. He's given Angela a schedule for the village.'

'Anything else?'

Anne looked uncertain. 'Well, there was one other thing, but I'm not sure if …' She looked again at Marnie.

'What is it?' Celia sounded insistent.

'It's about the grave.'

'Go on,' Hugh prompted.

'Perhaps I could tell Marnie afterwards?'

'If it concerns the grave, it concerns us.' Hugh's tone was firm.

Celia looked annoyed. 'There's no need to keep things from me, Anne. I didn't faint in the office, if that's what you're thinking. I just stood up too quickly and came over dizzy, that's all.'

'Faint?' Hugh repeated.

Celia ignored him. 'What about the grave?'

'Angela has heard from the police. They've had results back about the other body. Apparently they're now sure it was put there recently –'

'But I thought it was just a skeleton!' Hugh blustered.

'How recently?' Marnie asked.

'Angela didn't say, but the police are now treating it as a case of murder.'

Ralph's meetings went on longer than expected and it was nearly seven before he got back from Oxford that evening. He looked in on the office barn and found Anne writing at her computer and Marnie standing by the photocopier.

'What's this?' Ralph's expression was mock horror. 'When I coom 'ome from 'ard day at t'pit, I expect me dinner steamin' on t'table and a fresh pair o' clogs warmin' by t'fire.'

Marnie crossed the office. 'You can get knotted for a start.' She put her arms round Ralph's shoulders and kissed him on the lips.

Ralph winked at Anne who was grinning at them from her desk. 'See? Oos Northerners know 'ow to turn a woman on.'

'It's the thought of those clogs that does it. On the other hand, north London doesn't really count, Ralph.' Marnie turned back to the photocopier. 'So, you've obviously had a better day than we have. How was it at the coal face of All Saints College?'

'Fine. What was wrong with your day?'

Marnie looked at the wall clock. 'Gawd! Is that the time? If you want to eat this evening it would be quicker to tell you what was right.'

Ralph considered this briefly. 'Okay, how's this for a plan?'

By the time he was back from the Indian take-away the office was shut up, the table was laid and candles were burning in the saloon on *Sally Ann*. Over a selection of Korma and Madras dishes, Marnie outlined the Monday highlights. Her narration lasted throughout most of the meal.

'All in all, it's been a day I'd rather forget. Oh, and I meant to tell you: the police want to question me again about my statement. So your suggestion, my darling, about getting a take-away was perfect. I'd cheerfully go out and buy you those clogs any time.'

'And warm them for me by the fire?'

'Absolutely.'

'Getting back to your story, presumably Celia didn't take the news about the second body very well?'

'Understatement. In fact, both she and Hugh seemed pretty stunned by the news.'

'How old are these unexpected remains, did they say?'

'When I phoned the station I got put through to Cathy Lamb. She told me they'd probably been in the ground about fifty years.'

Anne got up to clear the table. 'Well, at least they can't pin that one on you.'

Marnie looked sceptical. 'They'll probably try.'

9
Marcus Devere

Marnie was at her desk soon after seven on Tuesday, determined to get the week back on track.

Anne came down the wall-ladder in pyjamas, yawning. 'You're keen.'

'Good morning, O Wondrous Fair One. Did I disturb you?'

'Not really. I've been awake for a while.'

'Something bothering you?' *As if I couldn't guess*, Marnie thought.

'I was wondering about … Donovan.'

'What about him?'

'Oh, you know, what he's doing up here, if he *was* up here. That kind of thing. Don't worry about it. I don't want to stop you getting on. All right if I use the shower?'

'Go ahead.'

Anne stretched both arms in the air and yawned again. 'Are we up against a deadline or something?'

'Not exactly. It's catch-up time after Celia's total disruption of yesterday.'

Anne was back in the office, showered and breakfasted, in little over half an hour. She immediately got to grips with the filing before settling down to study Marnie's designs for a canalside pub. It was her favourite activity and she made notes on each drawing for discussion later in the day. When the post was delivered at eight-thirty, she leapt into action and had the junk mail junked and the rest of the items sorted before Marnie had even noticed its arrival.

On the other side of the office Marnie was working on the Grand Junction Hotel scheme, completely absorbed in the decor of the main entrance and reception area. She was engaged on one of her trademark murals when the phone rang. It was nine o'clock exactly. Marnie and Anne traded looks across the room. The call was what they both feared.

'Good morning, Celia. How are you today?'

'Much better, Marnie. That's why I'm phoning, to thank you for taking such good care of me yesterday.'

'Don't mention it.'

'I'm very sorry to have taken up so much of your time like that. I must have been the most *awful* nuisance.'

'Absolutely dreadful, pain in the neck.' Time stood still. The line was silent. At her desk, Anne's jaw dropped, before Marnie added, 'Only kidding! I'm sorry you didn't feel well. Hope you're much better now.' She sounded sincere.

Celia tinkled a girlish laugh down the phone. 'Marnie, you're *terrible*! But I am, thanks, much better.'

'Great. What can I do for you? I hope you're not chasing up the design for your makeover.'

'Not at all. As long as you've got it to me by ten o'clock, that's fine.' Marnie hesitated before Celia added, 'My turn to be kidding! No, that's all it was, Marnie. Just to thank you for yesterday. Now, I'll let you get on. I'll not darken your doorway again. Bye!'

Marnie sat looking at the phone after hanging up.

'Was she all right?' Anne asked.

'Mm … Tell me I'm getting paranoid –'

'You're getting –'

'But I doubt that's the last we'll hear from Celia today.'

'She has an amazing talent for getting under your skin, Marnie.'

'If she phones again, I'll be very tempted to tell her to get stuffed, and no kidding.'

Shortly after ten, Marnie took the tray of mid-morning refreshments out to the builders working in the farmhouse. There were details to discuss with Bob, the foreman, and she was in need of a break from sitting at the desk. Perhaps her absence was fortunate. Anne took Celia's call.

'She's out of the office at the moment, Mrs Devere.'

'Will she be long?'

'Hard to say. She's in a meeting. Can I help?'

'I don't think so.'

'I've got the schemes for your project on my drawing board at the moment, if you wanted to talk about them.'

'Really?' A long pause. 'I thought … I *assumed* Marnie would be dealing with them *personally*.'

'We work together on all the projects.'

'I see.'

'Marnie's the principal designer, of course, but I assist her.'

'Actually, that's not why I rang, but I will want to talk to her about that.'

'Can I give her a message?'

Marnie came back into the office, saw Anne's expression and mouthed *Celia?* Anne nodded. Marnie walked to her desk, pointed at herself and the phone.

'Oh, one moment, Mrs Devere. Marnie's just come back. I'll put you through.'

Marnie picked up the phone. 'Celia, hi.'

'I'm glad I caught you, Marnie. Are you free later today?'

'Today? Diary's chocablock, I'm afraid.'

'But you do take a break for lunch, I assume?'

Marnie grimaced. Anne reached for the diary.

At twenty minutes to one Anne reminded Marnie about her appointment. Muttering under her breath, Marnie made a quick note on a file and disappeared in the direction of the washroom. She returned a few minutes later, hair brushed and with a hint of *Diorissimo* in the air, to collect her bag and notepad. Anne had placed a folder on her desk.

'What's this?'

'The file – such as it is – on the Knightly Court job, just in case Celia raises it.'

Marnie picked it up, looked thoughtful and placed it firmly back on the desk. 'She said we were meeting Rob Cardew to talk about the dig. I'm going to keep her to that.'

Anne frowned. 'Er …'

'What is it?'

'We don't have any photos on file. To get them would mean *another* visit.'

Marnie considered this. 'Perhaps I should take –'

'The Polaroid's in your bag.'

Mouthing *smartarse*, Marnie walked to the door. Pushing it open, she turned to look back at Anne and smiled. 'Thanks. You're in charge.'

'Don't tell Celia.'

Rob Cardew's Land Rover was already parked in front of the house when Marnie arrived. Approaching the front door she found a yellow Post-it note stuck beside the bell pull:

Marnie - we're on the rear terrace. C

It was a charming scene. A buffet lunch had been laid out on a round table under a cream parasol beside the lawn that seemed to have been manicured for the occasion. With much kissing on cheeks, Marnie was invited to take a seat. Four chairs were set around the table, two of them occupied by Celia and Rob Cardew, the other so far vacant. Celia explained that Angela was on her way over from a meeting with the Archdeacon and would be joining them as soon as she could.

They began eating, and Marnie opted for a glass of *Perrier* water, while Rob joined Celia in a spritzer. When Marnie complimented Celia on the food, the hostess made a nonchalant gesture.

'Good old *M & S*! I popped into town this morning after we spoke on the phone.'

When Angela arrived, Marnie thought she looked stressed, but said nothing. A spritzer soon revived her, and they began talking about Rob's plans for the site investigations. He flipped open a notebook.

The students would begin digging test pits in the coming few days. There would be about two dozen of them, plus occasional visiting archaeologists and academics, including a few specialists from further afield. Angela and Celia listened attentively, as if being briefed for the first time, but Marnie became convinced something had changed. She said so.

'Rob, forgive me if I'm mistaken, but haven't we been over all this before? Is there something you're not telling us?'

The archaeologist grinned, white teeth in a suntanned face. 'You're too perceptive, Marnie. I might've known *you'd* have spotted it.'

Celia looked perturbed. 'Spotted what?'

It occurred to Marnie that Celia was unaccustomed to having someone else as the centre of attention, especially in her own surroundings, especially another woman.

'There's been a development, hasn't there?' Marnie said.

Rob consulted his notes. 'We'll be a slightly bigger group than originally planned, about another dozen people in all. We'll still be camping on Mr Fletcher's field with our own shower and toilet blocks, but it would be useful if I could find somewhere as a kind of base camp.'

'What does that involve?' Celia was determined to take back the initiative. She was the hostess, after all.

'One possibility is to put up a couple of tents. We have some large ones, army style, ex-scouting. One would be the site office, the other for dealing with finds.'

Celia glanced at the lawn and frowned. 'Where would you want to put these tents?'

'Well …'

Marnie interjected. 'You said that was one possibility, Rob. What else might you have in mind?'

'I did wonder. An ideal base for us would be something like a barn, for example.'

Celia spread both hands, palms upward. 'We don't have anything like that at the Court. Have you tried Mr Fletcher?'

'I haven't, actually.' Rob's eyes swivelled towards Marnie. 'I was thinking about somewhere nearer to the action.'

Marnie took the hint. 'Which one do you have in mind?'

'You have one or two small barns behind your garage.'

'Take your pick. Come and have a look some time.'

'Er …'

Marnie smiled. 'You've already got your eye on one, haven't you?'

Rob nodded. 'I don't suppose you have running water nearby?'

'On the corner of the garage barn there's a stand-pipe.'

'Power?'

'We could run an extension cable out there.'

'So you're all set up then, Rob.' Celia sounded cool.

Marnie folded her arms and sat back. 'Not quite. I think there's more.'

'Have you been discussing this with Rob, Marnie?'

'Not until now.'

'Then how do you know Rob has more to tell us?'

Marnie shrugged. 'I get the feeling there's more to this meeting than just telling us about timing that we already knew and a request to use an old barn for a couple of weeks.'

Rob was looking down at his notes when he replied. 'There'll probably be an extra group coming. They'll be around for a while, depending on how their dig goes.'

'*Their* dig?' Celia looked puzzled. 'Is this a *separate* dig?'

'It's a kind of dig within a dig.'

'What will they be looking for?'

While Rob consulted his file, Marnie spoke in a low voice. 'This is connected with Sarah, isn't it?'

'In a way, yes.' When Rob looked up, his smile was meant to be reassuring. 'If they come they'll be looking for the graves of … witches.'

'*Witches?*' Celia looked stunned.

'But we know *Sarah* wasn't a witch,' Angela protested.

Rob raised a hand. 'Of course. Well, at least that's always been the assumption.'

'Then why are they coming here?' Celia was growing agitated. 'And who invited them?'

Rob looked pained. 'There's nothing sinister about it, Celia. We network amongst ourselves. We meet at conferences, read specialist journals –'

'About witches?' Celia looked horrified.

'About archaeology. My professor mentioned our excavation plans for the summer to another professor. Someone from the group phoned me up and asked if they could join in with us. It went on from there.'

'And you didn't think you ought to ask our permission?' Celia's voice had turned from cool to frosty.

Rob looked blank.

'Can I ask something?' Marnie the mediator. 'Will it make any difference to the dig that you've planned? Presumably they won't be digging holes willy-nilly all over the place looking for buried witches?'

'No. Some of them are historians; they'll be researching in the County Archives. The others will be field archaeologists like my students, like me. They'll be using geophysics and aerial surveys to examine the area around the church and look at other possible sites.'

'So it won't seem any different, as far as we're concerned?'

'No, but as far as my excavations are concerned they'll bring more resources into play, which could be useful to all our work.'

Celia was quiet. Angela was lost in her thoughts. Marnie wondered if she was alone in spotting an implication in what Rob had just said.

'Rob, is there still something you've not told us?'

The owlish grin. 'What makes you say that, Marnie?'

'I have the feeling there's more to come.'

'Why?' Celia looked worried at being left behind. 'What are you getting at, Marnie? Is there something you know that I don't?'

'Not really.' She turned to Rob.

He glanced at his notes. 'I'm not sure there's any more I can say at the moment. I must stress that there's nothing definite.'

Celia looked accusingly at Marnie. Angela sat back like a poker player who has thrown in her hand. Marnie was intrigued, but she didn't like this game of cat and mouse.

'Rob, I think you ought to be frank with us.' She smiled. 'If you want your archaeologists to have the use of my barn, my water supply, my electricity, plus I could even offer them exclusive use of an outside loo at the back of the farmhouse.'

Rob laughed. 'I wondered if you had an ace up your sleeve, Marnie!'

Celia leaned forward. 'Can someone please tell me –'

'Give us a clue, Rob,' Marnie said quietly.

'Well, I shouldn't really comment until things are definite, but there's no hiding place where you're concerned, is there?'

The women waited.

'All right, let me just say this. Have you ever been on television?' Rob looked at his watch. 'Now I really must be going. Thank you for a lovely lunch, Celia. Don't worry about the dig. I'll be in touch. Everything will be fine, I promise you.'

As Rob vanished round the corner of the house, Marnie sipped her water wondering, *have you ever been on television?* What was that about?

Celia stood up. 'I'll make coffee.'

'Not for me, thanks.' Marnie reached down for her bag. 'I'll have to be getting back to the office.'

'You'll have some, Angela?'

'That would be nice, if you've got time.'

Marnie stood up, noticing the extra weight of the camera in her bag. 'Oh, do you think I could take some photos, Celia?'

'A memento of a rather peculiar lunch?'

'No. Some shots of the house for the redecoration project. A few interiors plus one or two from the outside?'

'I thought you were anxious to dash off.'

'This will save me making a special visit later.'

'Whatever. Go ahead.'

'Thanks.'

'Tell me something, Marnie. Do you know what Rob was talking about just then, that business about television?'

'I haven't a clue.' Marnie was emphatic.

'But you seemed to know he was holding something back.'

A shrug. 'I just couldn't imagine that some other group would have so many more resources than he did. Geophysics? Aerial surveys? Where would all that come from? It seemed a lot to me, so I thought he wasn't telling us everything. That's all it was.'

'I thought it was very clever of you, Marnie.' Angela was looking up from her seat, admiringly.

'Just guesswork. Thanks for lunch, Celia. I'll be in touch.'

Marnie was glad to get away and spent the next five minutes going through Celia and Hugh's wing taking photographs for the file. Her last image was a shot across the entrance hall. As she lined it up through the viewfinder, a voice startled her.

'I'm sorry, madam, the house isn't open to the public.'

Before she could react, another voice, louder and more authoritative, cut in. 'That's all right, Robert. This lady is a guest.'

Marnie looked round to see a middle-aged man in a cream linen jacket standing in the doorway behind her. He was now looking over to his right. Marnie followed his gaze. In another doorway stood a much older man, with white hair and moustache, leaning on a stick. The first man inclined his head, turned and left the hall.

'I'm sorry,' Marnie began. 'Celia agreed to my taking some photos for the file.'

The old man advanced slowly. 'How do you do?'

'Hallo.'

The man stopped. 'Your generation never replies to that enquiry. It's odd how things have changed.'

'Enquiry?' Marnie wondered if she had missed something.

'How do you do?'

She got the point. 'Very well, thank you. How do you do?'

'As well as could be hoped, thank you. I'm sorry my man confronted you like that.'

The old man was a little taller than Marnie and spoke in an accent that many would describe as *posh*.

'That's all right. Thank you for coming to the rescue.'

'I saw you with Celia and your other friends on the terrace. I'm sure you have a good reason for taking your photographs.'

It did not seem to be a question, but Marnie thought she should explain.

'I'm doing a redecoration project for Celia and Hugh. The photos are part of my records for the job, to help with the design process. My name is Marnie Walker, by the way.'

'Devere, Marcus Devere. Delighted to meet you.' His grip, as they shook hands, was firm and cool. 'Please don't let me stop you taking your photos.'

'That was the last one, actually. I'm just leaving.'

Devere looked confused. 'Celia isn't here to show you out?'

'We've already said good-bye.'

The old man frowned. 'Then perhaps you'll permit me to escort you to your car.'

'Oh, that's really not –'

'Of course. I insist.' They walked at his pace out through the front door onto the drive. 'I knew you weren't one of the archaeologists.'

'No. I'm an interior designer.'

'If you'll permit me to say so, you're much too smart to be an archaeologist. Scruffy bunch.' He was smiling. 'I suppose it's because they spend their time scratching about in the dirt.'

Marnie laughed. 'I hadn't thought of it like that. But then, I don't really know any archaeologists, only Dr Cardew.'

Devere opened the door of the Discovery and stood aside.

'Thank you, Mr Devere. It's been nice meeting you.'

'My pleasure.' He looked pensive. 'Are you involved in these excavations?'

'Peripherally. It all sounds very interesting.' Marnie climbed in, shut the door and pressed a button.

The old man was frowning as the window slid down. 'Do you think so? Digging up the past. I hope we don't come to regret it.'

Ralph arrived in the office barn shortly before five for coffee. It had become a favourite part of his routine when he had spent most of the day shut away in his study on *Thyrsis* working on a book, an article, a lecture or a paper. Anne would take the day's correspondence up to the post box at around four-thirty and call in at the village shop for any supplies they needed. On her return she would make coffee, and the three of them would have a break before settling down for a final work stint leading up to their evening meal on *Sally Ann* at seven.

On that Tuesday afternoon Ralph walked in to find only Anne sorting out mugs in the kitchen area.

'Marnie gone out again?'

Anne looked round. 'She's been down at the boat for the past hour or so. I think she's making something for supper.'

'Oh ...'

They both knew what that meant.

'Something bothering her?'

Anne poured coffee. 'She's been mulling something over ever since she got back from her meeting at the Court.'

'Then we'll soon find out how serious it is.'

Anne agreed. The yardstick would be the novelty of the meal. If something was really worrying Marnie, the food would be experimental, a dish she had not previously made. She tended to cook as relaxation for a troubled mind.

Marnie removed a tureen from the fridge and put it on the galley workbench. The table was too small for her to place it in the middle to dish up, and she ladled the soup into bowls which Anne set out on their placemats.

Ralph leaned forward to sniff. 'This looks interesting. I don't remember having this before.'

'A recipe I saw in a magazine. I thought I'd try it out.'

'An experiment?'

'Sort of.'

'Asparagus?' Anne suggested, setting out bowls of croutons, chopped spring onions and diced cucumber.

'That's right, with onions, celery, *crème fraîche* and chives. I was going to add chervil, but I thought that might be overdoing it. What do you think?'

Ralph tried a first spoonful. 'Mm, yes. More to the point, what were *you* thinking?'

A wry smile from Marnie. 'It's amazing to be so transparent … myself, I mean, not the soup.'

'Delicious,' Ralph commented. 'Both, of course.'

Marnie laughed. 'If there's a compliment in there, I think it's the most obscure I've ever received.'

'So what's been bothering you?' Ralph persisted.

Marnie's smile faded. 'The more I get involved with Celia …'

'Warning bells?'

'Mm. I've met that type before. I bet she started off as a pretty little girl who worked out early on how to get what she wanted.'

'Is that so unusual, Marnie?'

'Maybe not, but it's odd if in adult life you still think the world revolves around you.'

'The Lady of the Manor,' Anne said quietly.

'Very much so, except … How can I put it?'

Ralph scooped cucumber into his bowl. 'Her attitudes are not just self-centred but appear somehow childish?'

'Exactly. You know what? She virtually told Rob Cardew he had no right to run his dig the way he wanted without asking *her* permission.'

'On her land, you mean?'

'No, just in general.'

'Must've been a misunderstanding, surely.'

'I don't think so. She was miffed that he wanted to set up his HQ down here in one of the barns, but *really* upset when he said one group would be looking for witch graves.'

'That's a new development.'

'Angela knew she was like that. I could tell. She went very quiet and kept right out of the conversation, even though the dig is as much to do with the church as anything else.'

'You mean the witch aspect?'

'Yes. That's the part that Celia doesn't like. I even wonder if she really wants Sarah to be reburied in the churchyard at all. The whole thing spooks her out. She's too jumpy to cope with it all.'

'Look how she fainted when we told her about Sarah's hanging herself in the barn,' Anne said.

'Quite. And I'm sure they know this up at the Court. She's got them all worried about her. I met her father-in-law today, nice old boy, very courteous, charming old-fashioned manners. Even he seemed bothered by the dig. That phrase again, *digging up the past*.'

10
Holbeach Man

Ralph was wondering if Marnie had a point. It was eight-thirty on Wednesday morning and he was driving his twelve year-old Volvo up the field track. The going was firm, and the big car wallowed doggedly over the tussocks of grass and the ruts worn in the ground by the passage of vehicles. On a fine, dry summer's morning it was an easy climb, but in less clement seasons the field resembled an auto-cross circuit. On days like that he slithered and slewed about, going up or down.

Marnie's solution had been to buy a four-wheel drive, and she had suggested that he might do the same. She had opted for the infamous 'Chelsea tractor'. The Discovery met all her needs and, most importantly, could negotiate the field track in any weather without complaint or hesitation. But Ralph could not really imagine himself driving such a machine. It seemed somehow too … *hearty* for his character. It would feel like wearing a rough tweed jacket and plus-fours. On the other hand, there was nothing hearty about Marnie to whom he had just said good-bye for the day before setting off for Oxford. By now she would be in the shower and, smiling to himself, he tried to put that vision out of his mind as he reached the top gate.

His smile vanished abruptly as, to his great surprise, he almost collided head-on with a Land Rover that was turning into the field as he was passing through the gateway to leave it. Both vehicles braked sharply to a halt. A head looked out from the Land Rover's window.

'Sorry about that. Are you all right?'

Ralph wound his window down. 'Fine, fine. I wasn't expecting anyone to be coming through here at this time.'

'Nor I.'

'Are you wanting Glebe Farm?'

'Yes.'

'Then I'll get out of your way.'

With a friendly nod, Ralph drove past the Land Rover and turned into the road, noticing in passing that there was some sort of inscription on the side of the driver's door. He caught the words 'University', 'Archaeology' and 'Cambridge' and spotted a small flag attached to the top of the radio aerial. He also noticed that there was a queue of two other cars behind the leader.

Rounding the corner before the village pub, Ralph pulled over and pressed buttons on his mobile phone. Marnie answered after several rings. Ralph came straight to the point.

'Are you presentable, darling?'

'Well, I'm naked and dripping water. I leave it to you to decide.'

'Then you might like to think of becoming clothed and dry – in the reverse order, obviously. You've got visitors.'

'Anne's in the office. She can meet them. Who are they?'

'Archaeologists from Cambridge.'

'Oh?'

'You weren't expecting them?'

'Not today, as far as I recall. I'd better go. See you later.'

Resuming his journey, Ralph realised that something about the Land Rover was bothering him, but he could not think what it was. He was on the dual carriageway heading west when he remembered. The flag on the aerial did not quite go together with the prestigious name of Cambridge University. As far as he had been able to see, it looked suspiciously like a skull and cross-bones.

Anne was busy sorting the post when she thought she heard traffic noises. Glebe Farm was one of the quietest places in the world; every extraneous sound seemed magnified. She listened carefully. A car. Who could it be? No one was expected at this hour of the day.

Muttering that there was one way to find out, Anne got up and walked outside. She found the convoy parking at the back of the garage barn and reached into her pocket for the mobile. Marnie's number was engaged. The visitors were four men, clustered in muted conversation at the entrance to one of the barns.

'Hallo. You're the archaeologists. You must be Dr Cardew.' From Marnie's description, he was unmistakeable. 'I'm Anne Price, Marnie's assistant.'

Rob made the introductions. His colleagues looked like students, not much older than she was. Amid the jumble of names, one of the men was described as the site director. In his early twenties, he had a crew cut and piercing brown eyes. When she shook hands with all four of them, Anne was surprised at how hard their skin felt, like manual labourers.

'Did you know we were going to be using this barn as a base during the dig?' Rob asked.

Anne pointed inside. 'There's an extension cable over there. You can plug it in to the garage barn. That's this building behind us. It'll give you four socket outlets. Will that be enough?'

'Ideal.'

'Good. Marnie said you wanted a water supply. I've rigged up a hose from the pipe on the near corner of the garage barn, just there. But if you need it for tea and coffee, I can provide that when I do drinks for our builders.'

Rob grinned. 'There'll be upwards of twenty or so of us working down here at any one time.'

'Oh.' Anne reflected on this. 'I think they have an urn in the church hall. I'll ask Angela if we can borrow it for your stay. Do you need anything else?'

'No, thanks. We've got all our own stuff.'

Rob indicated the cars. They were packed to the roofs with all manner of equipment. Anne could see plastic buckets of yellow and black stacked together, shovels, crates, boxes and bags.

'What about tables and chairs, that sort of thing?'

'We have our own and we'll be ferrying more stuff down in the minibus. We've just come to set up base before the team arrives.'

'When will that be?'

'Tuesday.'

'I'll put it in the diary. If there's anything you need, let me know.'

The young men began unloading the cars and laying out the equipment in the barn. Anne was impressed at how orderly they were. Everything was lined up in neat rows. Although they were casually dressed in T-shirts, jeans and working boots and joked as they went about their tasks, they worked like a team and looked like professionals. Rob took a business card from his back pocket and gave it to Anne. As she tucked it into her shirt pocket, she noticed the flag on the Land Rover's radio aerial.

'Is that a joke?'

'Why do you say that?'

'It looks a bit like a Jolly Roger, only in different colours.'

The small flag was divided diagonally into two triangles. The top was light blue, the bottom half brown. In the middle was a skull. On closer inspection it was not the figurative type as shown on the traditional pirate flag, but a more accurate image in three-quarters view.

Rob explained. 'The light blue section represents the university's colour. The brown is usually reckoned to signify the ground, where we dig.'

Anne pointed at the skull. 'And who's your friend?'

'He …' Rob paused, as if for dramatic effect. '… is none other than Holbeach Man.'

'Really?'

'You've never heard of him?'

'Sorry.'

'When he was dug up in a field in East Anglia in 1837, his were the earliest known human remains in Britain. That was roughly the time when archaeology started.'

'So he was important and famous.'

'Certainly was.'

The sound of approaching footsteps made them both turn as Marnie arrived quickly on the scene.

'I didn't realise you were coming today, Rob.' She was slightly breathless, her hair still damp from the shower.

'We're the advance guard, Marnie, setting up camp. Anne seems to have everything organised for us already.'

'Just the four of you then, is it?'

'Yes, for today.'

'And Holbeach Man,' Anne added.

'He's coming on later, is he?'

Anne laughed and turned to go back to the office.

Marnie looked at Rob, puzzled. 'What did I say?'

Nine o'clock came and went, with Marnie and Anne staring at their phones like characters in a Hitchcock film, waiting for them to ring with Celia's daily call.

'Must be something we said.' Marnie grinned at Anne.

'She must've taken the hint.'

'Not that one.'

'Marnie, are you ready to go over those plans for the hotel yet?'

'Sure. Coffee time?'

'Okay. Talking of which, d'you think the archaeologists will still be –' Anne stopped and turned her head towards the door.

'What is it?'

Anne's expression was inscrutable. 'Marnie, when we're talking about our projects, don't forget the multi-storey carpark.'

Marnie registered total bewilderment. 'Multi-storey …? What are you talking about?'

'I mean the one we're obviously going to need here for all the visitors we're getting.'

As Anne spoke, Marnie caught the first sound of a car. 'You must have radar instead of ears. I wonder who it could be. Rob Cardew coming round?'

Anne shook her head. 'It's not a diesel.'

'Who then, Cleverclogs?'

'The hot money must be on Celia.'

'Of course. Silly me for not expecting her.'

But they were wrong. The unmarked grey police Cavalier rolled into its customary parking slot and WDC Cathy Lamb trod the familiar path to the office barn door.

Anne left Marnie in conversation with Cathy Lamb and went back to the archaeologists. They had transformed their HQ barn into a fully functioning base camp. At the rear, under a pair of spotlights, a trestle table had been set up with crates, buckets and boxes stacked beside it and a tray filled with marker pens and find-bags at one end.

A similar table stood at rightangles to it along the side wall. On this one there were plans and notebooks, laptops, cameras and large sheets of squared paper. The furnishing was completed by a number of safari chairs. Someone had tacked an Ordnance Survey map of the area to the wall over the table. It was covered in a sheet of cellophane and dotted with coloured discs, circles and inscriptions.

Against the wall on the opposite side they had lined up several wheelbarrows, from one of which protruded a dozen or more shovels like a quiver of arrows. Anne was impressed with the purposefulness of it all and found it hard to believe they had packed so much equipment into their vehicles.

The barn had taken on an almost military air, like the field headquarters of a regiment at the front line. The only difference was that the men who were gathered in a group talking quietly together looked like anything but members of the armed forces. Noticing Anne's arrival, they turned and nodded in her direction and accepted her offer of refreshments.

On the way back to the office barn she pulled out her mobile and rang Angela to ask about the loan of the hot water urn. Returning ten minutes later with a tray of drinks, Anne was able to announce that the urn would be in place later that day. Leaving the tray for a few moments, she took the visitors round to the farmhouse and showed them the loo in the garden. It was Victorian with the original workings, but it was airy and functional and Anne made a mental note to get the builders to give it two coats of white emulsion before the weekend. She would let the archaeologists know they were not the only people to be well organised.

Marnie realised that Anne was keeping out of the way while she went over her statement with Cathy Lamb. The conversation was amicable – the two women had after all known each other for a couple of years and had experienced hard times together – but Marnie was on her guard, wary of saying anything that could be misconstrued. She knew that behind the relaxed atmosphere of their meeting, the detective was keen to find out anything she could that would reveal the identity of the person who had smashed Sarah Anne Day's headstone two years earlier. Marnie stuck to her guns. She refused to speculate on something for which she had no evidence, and Cathy Lamb eventually gave up prodding her.

'I know I don't have to remind you, Marnie, that withholding evidence – especially if it turns out to be important – could be regarded as a serious matter.'

'I know that. But you're not asking me for evidence. There isn't any. You're asking me to try to *guess* what might have happened and for what reason. How could I know what someone else might have been thinking? I'm not a mind-reader. To say any more than I've already told you would be nothing but conjecture. It's not on, Cathy.'

'Fair enough. But I've also got a job to –'

Cathy stopped as Anne looked in.

'Sorry to interrupt. Look, there are things we need from the supermarket. Now might be a good time to go, so I'll leave you to it, unless you want me for anything?'

Marnie got in first. 'No. You go along, Anne. I expect you've got your list.'

Anne's lists were a standing joke in their household. She produced a small notebook from her back pocket and waved it before ducking out of the door. Sitting in the car she had a sudden thought and pulled out a pencil. How much toilet paper would an army of archaeologists need in a fortnight? She added *loo rolls – bumper pack* to her list and set off.

Marnie was grateful for the next interruption when Rob Cardew stuck his head round the door. He recognised Cathy Lamb and from the body language he inferred that she was not conducting an interrogation. The two women smiled to see him.

'Have you got everything you need, Rob?'

'We're fine, Marnie. The barn is just right, we've got power and water laid on, and Anne seems to have all our basic needs met: urn, loo. What more could anyone desire?'

'You're excavating down here?' Lamb sounded surprised.

'Initially just a few test pits. Then we'll take it from there. I'm assuming our equipment and things will be safe in the barn, Marnie?'

'I've no reason to suspect they might not be, but you won't go leaving anything valuable around, will you … computers and such?'

'No.'

Lamb closed her notebook. 'You'll be keeping the barn securely locked, no doubt?'

Marnie shrugged. 'That might be difficult.'

'As a police officer I should advise you at least to get a padlock fitted.'

'Like I said, that might be difficult. The barn doesn't have any doors.'

Lamb frowned. 'Your funeral. Talking of which …' She turned to Rob. 'Are you doing anything up at the grave site?'

Rob glanced fleetingly at Marnie. 'Not as such.'

Lamb seemed to ponder what his reply might mean. Marnie explained.

'Rob's wife is involved in examining the *modern* remains in the laboratory.'

'I see. What about the coffin?'

Rob shook his head. 'That's not archaeology. It's being treated as a burial, not our scene.'

'Oh?'

Marnie interjected again. 'There are discussions going on in the diocese about whether Sarah should be moved into the churchyard.'

'So has everything come to a halt up there?'

This time Rob did not hesitate in replying. 'Not quite. I think you'll be getting the results back from the lab very soon.'

'What will they show?' Lamb flipped open the notebook.

After a brief pause Rob said, 'I mustn't pre-empt things, but I think you might be in for a few surprises.'

Anne emptied the bags from the supermarket trolley into the Mini's small boot. The bumper pack of toilet rolls was so big it occupied most of the back seat. Fastening her safety belt, she sat thinking before turning the ignition key. An idea had been forming as she rolled the trolley up and down the aisles, and in her mind's eye she was plotting a circuitous route home. The itinerary would cross the canal at every point possible on the way back from the supermarket to Glebe Farm.

In Blisworth, looking over the parapet of the bridge, she realised that such a village was too built-up, had too many residents and visitors, was too accessible. If Donovan really had returned and was still in the area, he would have chosen a more remote location if he did not want to be seen.

The next crossing point was in Stoke Bruerne, and she drove on without stopping. Threading her way through the narrow country lane that led to the main road, she turned right and accelerated over the lock bridge with barely a glance at the water.

In minutes she was standing on another bridge by a canalside pub looking down at boats moored on either side of the road. It was hopeless. The pub was popular, attracting frequent traffic tying up at the end of its garden, and there were permanent moorings in both directions. Anne turned and rested her back against the parapet. There were no other crossing places before Cosgrove, which meant there were a few miles of relatively secluded countryside going north and south. The words *wild goose chase* came to mind.

'Don't worry, love, it may never happen.'

Anne had not noticed the man crossing the road, laden down with all the paraphernalia needed for angling. He put his bag down to adjust a collection of long tubes slung over one shoulder. Anne smiled faintly.

'Stood you up, has he? That's a shame. Now if I was twenty years younger …' He winked but seemed to be friendly rather than lascivious.

Anne had an idea. 'Do you come here often?' She laughed when she realised what she had said.

The angler joined in. 'That's supposed to be my line.'

'Sorry. Start again. I just wondered if you fished here regularly.'

'I'm on shifts, so it varies. I'm off this afternoon, not much point sitting at home when my wife's at work, so I get down here when I can.'

'Were you here at the weekend?'

'Sunday morning. She likes me out of the way when she's cooking.'

'I don't suppose … No, it's too improbable.'

'What is?'

Anne shook her head. 'I'm looking for a boat belonging to a friend of mine. I think he may have come through over the weekend.'

'There were hardly any boats passing when I was here Sunday morning. What's the boat like?'

'It looks a bit unusual, painted dark grey, with a black hull.'

'I can assure you that no boat fitting that description came past here on Sunday morning.'

'I thought not. It was just a longshot, but –'

'That doesn't mean it wasn't here at all.' The angler was smiling. 'Now, if you'd asked me if I'd seen a boat like that when I came out of the pub on *Saturday night* …'

Marnie needed a break from the drawing board later that morning, so she went round to see what Rob Cardew and his team had done in the HQ barn. Like Anne, she was impressed with the purposeful appearance of the place and was sure the equipment would be safe, though Cathy Lamb's warning was echoing in her mind. It was curious how people's views varied. Marnie saw the barn as rural vernacular architecture; to Rob Cardew it was a useful space; Cathy Lamb regarded it as a security risk.

Marnie could hear the phone ringing before she reached the office barn. She picked it up just before the answering machine cut in, thankful that it was Angela and not Celia.

'Anne asked if you could borrow the urn from the church hall for the archaeologists, Marnie.'

'So I gather.'

'I've checked with the clerk to the PCC and she says it's available if you want it, so could you send Anne up and I'll hand it over. I'm going to the church in about five minutes. I could meet her there.'

'She's out at the moment, actually.'

'Oh well, we can fix another time. I just thought as I was –'

'No. Now will be fine. I'll come. Nice to have a break.'

Marnie spotted Angela's car outside the church hall as she drew up. Inside, the vicar was wiping the urn over with a cloth.

'There you are, Marnie. I think that's presentable. You just turn the switch here to the temperature you want. It's got a thermostat. Easy.'

'Great. We'll make an appropriate contribution for the loan.'

'That's nice. The church needs all the help it can get.'

'Angela, don't mind me saying this, but when you arrived at Celia's yesterday, you looked rather drawn.'

'Not surprising. I'd just come from a meeting with the Archdeacon.'

'Would that be the Archdeacon, your *brother in Christ*?' Marnie thought that sounded sharper than she had intended. 'Sorry. That was –'

'I know what you meant, Marnie. The theory is sound. But the old codger …' She smiled ruefully. 'That's my *old codger in Christ*, as you might say, he ambushed me.'

Marnie was alarmed. 'What did he do?'

'Oh, not like that. I meant he brought up the subject of Sarah's reburial. We were supposed to be discussing interfaith relationships and the development of the lay ministry.'

'But he sprang Sarah on you?'

'Yes. He'd just mentioned that part of his role was to promote growth in numbers and said it sent out the wrong messages if we kept getting publicity for reburying someone that most people thought was a witch.'

'But she had nothing to do with –'

'I know, I know. But the Archdeacon said that was what the public thought of her.'

'I don't see how he can lay that at your door.'

'He thinks I'm an easy target, that's how. He knows he wouldn't get away with that if Randall was there. He wouldn't stand any nonsense.'

Marnie grinned. 'I wouldn't be surprised if Randall ended up as Archbishop of Canterbury one day.'

Angela laughed. 'I hope *not*.'

'Why not?'

'He's just the sort who'd get bumped off for being awkward, like Thomas Becket!'

Marnie picked up the urn, surprised at how light it was. 'All this because of the Archdeacon. I'm sure you'll win him round in the end. He can't be as bad as all that.'

'Believe me, Marnie, he has as much charm as Genghis Khan.'

Marnie looked at her distorted reflection in the urn's shiny surface. 'How apt. Didn't Genghis Khan bump off his enemies by throwing them into vats of boiling water?'

Angela managed to shudder and laugh at the same time, as Marnie headed for the door.

Anne rang Marnie but there was no reply and she left a message on the answerphone to say she would be getting back a little later than expected. She had an extra call to make.

That sector of the canal wound its way along a contour line between open rolling fields. The towpath was gravelled, firm and dry, but tall weeds sprouted at the waterside and Anne was on her guard to avoid stinging nettles. After walking for half a mile she stopped believing that she would find Donovan's boat round the next bend. She checked her watch and gave herself ten more minutes before turning back.

Almost immediately she saw it. At first the boat looked like a shadow under the trees, tucked in among clumps of bushes that spilled out over the water on the far side. The sight of it made her pulse quicken. There could be no mistake. Danny had been right. This was Donovan's *stealth boat*. Anne walked along the path, all the while staring across the canal. At the prow was the enigmatic name, X O 2, in stencilled characters. It had taken Ralph's insightful brain to work out its meaning, and even he might not have solved the conundrum had he not been attending a conference in Barcelona at the time.

The name had been adopted by Donovan when he had dropped out of a university course that had not met his expectations. The boat was his way of dropping out, even if only temporarily. The number two in Spanish was *dos*. The name spelt *Exodos*, the Greek word for *way out* or *exit*. It was a strange, convoluted kind of name, but then Donovan was not your ordinary Joe.

Anne looked up and down the path. It was deserted. She cupped her hands round her mouth and called out.

'Donovan!'

She waited. Nestling there in the undergrowth, the boat had an abandoned air. Was Donovan out? Could he be on his way to see her at Glebe Farm? Might he already be there, sitting in the office with Marnie, coffee mug in hand, reminiscing about old times?

'Donovan!' Louder this time.

The curtains over the portholes and windows were closed, mid-grey material in the dark grey paintwork. Anne moved a few paces to her left, straining to see if there was a bicycle on the roof. Donovan had used one for local journeys when he had been in the area the year before, a *Muddy Fox*, a classic mountain bike in yellow with black paw prints on the frame. He liked classics. That bike had been sacrificed when he had had to leave Northampton in a hurry. Questions were being asked about the shooting of the prominent politician of the extreme right wing.

'Donovan!'

There was no bicycle as far as Anne could make out. What to do? If she gave up now, she might miss him. On the other hand she could hardly spend the rest of the day loitering on the towpath. She tried phoning the office again, but there was still no reply. Where was Marnie?

Anne walked a few paces. This was all very unsatisfactory. Absentmindedly, she kicked at some loose stones in the compacted gravel. A glance across at the boat. A glance down at the gravel.

Anne scraped up a few stones, weighing them in her hand, asking herself if this was really a good idea. How would she feel if someone threw stones at *Sally Ann* or *Thyrsis*, even with the best of intentions? She knelt down and tugged at a clump of earth and grass. It broke loose and she examined it for stones. Without further questioning, she drew back her hand and hurled the clod over the water. It hit the topside of *X O 2* with a satisfying thud. She waited. No response or reaction. No angry boat-owner leaping out on deck with an irate cry of '*What the hell d'you think you're doing?*'

Kneeling again, she assembled a collection of the smallest stones until she had a fistful. Trying a different technique this time, she swung back underarm and let the tiny pebbles fly. They came down on the boat with a sound like hailstones on a tin roof. Anne dusted her hands together. She had given it her best shot – her last shot – and it was time to go home.

Wondering what else she could do, Anne began walking slowly away. She turned her head as if to say good-bye to the boat and saw a face framed in a window.

Celia was the last person Marnie wanted to see as she came out of the village shop. She had nipped in for a tin of soup and emerged onto the pavement as Celia was passing her car.

'No *whizz-bang* today, Marnie?'

'No what? Oh, the MG. No, not today. I came up to collect an urn from Angela. I thought the Disco was more suitable.'

The colour visibly drained from Celia's face and, for a few seconds, Marnie thought she was going to pass out again. When Celia spoke, her voice was low and husky.

'An *urn*? My goodness! Whose ashes are they, Marnie?'

'Ashes? I don't know what you –' Comprehension. 'Oh, no, not that kind of urn, one for heating water, for making tea.'

It was extraordinary how the colour rushed back into Celia's face. She blushed with embarrassment and put fingertips to her mouth.

'Oh, too *silly*! When you said an *urn*, then Angela, I just thought …' She laughed. 'You must think me a *complete fool*.'

'Not at all.'

'Do I take it you're getting ready for some kind of event down at Glebe Farm?'

'The archaeologists. They're due after the weekend. You remember Rob said they'd be coming soon. We're preparing for the onslaught.'

'Of course.'

'Talking of onslaughts, I'd better be getting back to the office. Anne's out and I've got a *mountain* of work to get through.'

'Including Knightly Court, I hope.'

'Absolutely. I got some useful photos yesterday on my way out.'

'And made rather a conquest too, I gather.' A coquettish smile.

'Oh?'

'My father-in-law was quite taken with you, Marnie.'

'He was very charming, insisted on escorting me to the car. It was like meeting someone from another age.'

'I suppose that's what he is, in a way. He's the only one left now from that generation of the family.'

'So presumably Hugh is the last one to bear the family name?'

A cloud passed over Celia's face. 'Not exactly. There are the boys.'

'I didn't know. Are they at boarding school?'

'No. Hugh has two sons. They live with their mother in Canada.'

'Sorry. I didn't realise.'

'I'm Hugh's second wife.'

'I see.' Marnie really didn't want this conversation, especially not in the high street. 'Anyway, your father-in-law was very courteous. It was nice to meet him. I hope he'll like my scheme when he sees it.'

'He only inherited the Court because his older brother was killed in the war, you know.'

'Really?'

Celia nodded. 'He was quite the hero, apparently, on special missions or something. Intelligence service, behind enemy lines, all that sort of thing. He was the family's blue-eyed boy. They doted on him. Come and see.'

Celia began walking towards the church. Marnie looked at her watch.

'Just for a minute then. I really must get –'

'It won't take more than a second.'

The war memorial stood inside the churchyard close to the gate, on the right of the footpath. Marnie must have walked past it many times, but she had never paid it much attention before. Under a tall stone cross, the names of the fallen from both world wars were listed on separate panels, some of the families familiar to Marnie: Fletcher, Stubbs, Tarry, Tutt. Celia pointed at a separate block of granite on which a longer inscription was carved.

Sacred to the memory of Roland Devere, Major, MC, DSO
Special Operations Executive
1909 – 1944

~~~~

'That smells good!' Anne walked awkwardly across the office to the kitchen area, two carrier bags in her right hand, the bumper pack of toilet rolls under her left arm. 'Is that some left in the pan?'
~~~~

'Executive power lunch.' Marnie got up and relieved Anne of the bumper pack. 'Tinned tomato soup and a slice of toast.'

'Bliss! Put it on my expense account.'

Marnie eyed the toilet rolls. 'Upset tummy?'

Anne grinned. 'They're for the archaeologists. 'I've shown them the outside loo behind the farmhouse. They won't be in the way, going there.'

Marnie dropped a slice of bread in the toaster and relit the burner under the saucepan. 'You were longer than I expected.'

'Did you hear my message?'

'Yes. What was the *extra call* you had to make?'

'Let me sort out executive power lunch – I think I'll have mine in a mug – and I'll tell you all about it.'

After a mouthful of soup and a bite of toast, Anne began her story …

For several seconds Anne had stood gazing across the canal at the dark grey boat. The face at the window stared back momentarily and disappeared. Noiselessly the stern doors swung outwards and a young man came up on deck, standing half-hidden among the bushes. In black T-shirt and jeans, he was slightly built with short blonde hair. He turned abruptly towards the stern, checked himself, glanced back at Anne, smiled briefly and resumed the task of untying the stern mooring rope. While Anne looked on, he started the engine and slipped along the gunwale to unfasten the bow rope. Pushing off with the pole, Donovan reversed out of his hiding place and brought *X O 2* to the near bank where Anne took a rope and helped make her fast.

They sat in the saloon in the monochrome interior, facing each other in the dining unit. The shades of grey, black and white were relieved only by the colours of book spines on the shelves, many of them German. The boat was roughly the same size as *Sally Ann* and *Thyrsis*, but there the similarity ended. This craft had an altogether different atmosphere. It felt like being in a submarine, a purposeful travelling machine unlike any other boat Anne had ever known.

'What brings you back?'

'You've no need to ask that.'

'But why now? It's been almost a year.' There was no hint of reproach in Anne's tone.

'It was safer that way for you and Marnie and the others, for everyone who'd been in contact with me.'

'And for you, too?'

'For me, too.'

'So you think by now the police will have stopped looking for the person who …?'

Donovan shook his head. 'A murder investigation never ends, not until the police have found the perpetrator. The case is never closed.'

'You think they suspect you?'

'I think …' Donovan looked towards the window as if wondering whether the boat might be stormed at any minute. 'I think they're looking for someone like me, but someone in a far right organisation.'

'You mean someone who dresses like a blackshirt and who might live in a U-boat?' Anne glanced over at the shelves by the window. They contained three pre-war Leica cameras, and on the wall beside them were photos of silver German racing cars from the Hitler time, one of them bearing a swastika symbol. 'Smart move, coming back.'

'According to the press, the police are acting on the assumption that Brandon's death was the result of an *internal* power struggle, one faction trying to gain supremacy over the others.'

'What about your racing car photos? Wouldn't that swastika be seen as incriminating?'

Donovan shrugged. 'They were taken by a great-uncle I never knew, who was *disappeared* by the Nazis.'

'I rest my case.'

'I had to see you again, Anne.' Donovan spoke simply. 'The boat was the best way to get here.'

'So you were going to contact me?'

'Yes. Once I knew I could do that without causing you problems. I've been reading the papers, monitoring local radio, keeping an eye on you.'

'Really?'

He counted on his fingers. 'You've been up to look at the grave by the church wall. There's been a girl staying with you. Marnie took her for a run in her old sports car. You've installed archaeologists in one of the barns.'

'You have been spying on us.'

'Keeping watch.'

'In preparation for a visit?'

'That *was* the plan.'

'But not now?'

'I've got family coming over from Germany. I need to get back to London. It's all a bit sudden.'

'When were you planning to leave?'

'Tonight.'

'On the evening tide?'

He returned her smile. 'Something like that. I've been resting so that I could travel through the night.'

'And now I've disturbed you.'

'Doesn't matter.'

Anne looked thoughtful. 'Do you have to do that?'

'How else would I get back?'

'There could be another way.'

'So he's changed his plans?' Marnie took another slice of bread from the toaster for Anne.

'Yeah. I was surprised he agreed when I suggested an alternative.'

'When will it happen?' Marnie put the toast on Anne's plate and lowered her head to whisper in her ear. 'Under cover of darkness?'

Anne pulled a face at her. 'I don't think you're taking this seriously, Marnie.'

'I don't mean to mock, but I'm sure the police aren't searching for Donovan in connection with Brandon's murder, or anything else.'

'Donovan says you can never drop your guard. You must always be vigilant.'

Marnie flopped into her chair. 'Don't you think this is all a bit exaggerated?'

'You think Donovan likes being a *man of mystery*, that he's a fantasist?'

'I'm not being unkind, but … perhaps … just a little.'

Anne nibbled the toast. 'Mm …'

'So tell me about your alternative plan.'

'He comes here. I drive him to the station. He gets the train to London and goes home by tube.'

'Brilliant, Anne!' Marnie rocked with laughter. 'No one but a genius of deception would've thought of anything so *dastardly cunning*.'

Anne's expression remained deadly serious. 'You sink zat vill fool ze enemy, comrade?'

Ralph returned mid-afternoon as Marnie and Anne were leaving the office. On the way through the spinney Anne told him about her meeting with Donovan and explained the plan for getting him back to London. They stood on the bank between *Sally Ann* and *Thyrsis*.

'Where will he leave his boat?' Ralph asked.

Anne pointed. 'Over there, I suppose, opposite *Thyrsis*, same as before.'

'Mm …'

'What's the matter?' Marnie wondered if Ralph had spotted a flaw in the scheme.

'He's no fool, you know. If he thinks there's some sort of risk in being noticed, he may well be right.'

'By the police?'

'Who knows? By anyone.'

'You go along with all this, Ralph?'

'I'm not sure I'm *going along* with anything. I don't normally accept conspiracy theory, but I remember how on-the-ball Donovan was in that business with the far right last year.'

Anne looked worried. 'You don't think it's a good idea bringing his boat here?'

'It's rather conspicuous. *You* described it as looking like a U-boat.'

Marnie walked over to *Sally Ann*. 'What if we put X O 2 here, in the docking area?'

'For how long?' Ralph said.

'Until Donovan can get back up here to move it. Just a short while.'

Anne was still frowning. 'But if it's going to be at risk here, what difference will it make moving it into *Sally*'s dock? It would be just as conspicuous.'

Ralph nodded. Marnie pulled out her mobile and began pressing buttons.

'I think I've got his mobile number entered in here.'

'Whose?'

'Here it is ... Cardew.'

~~~~

Marnie was beginning to think there was a conspiracy to thwart her every goal in life. All her efforts to get on with work were frustrated by other events. Celia Devere seemed to impose on her whenever she felt like it. The call to Rob Cardew had produced nothing. He didn't have a tent large enough to cover a 45-foot narrowboat. That good idea had bitten the dust.

She and Anne had returned to the office to try to get on with some work before the next interruption. They expected Donovan very soon, in fact he should have covered the short distance a while ago. Anne put the kettle on to make tea.

'I think your idea about covering *X O 2* with a tent was a good one, Marnie.'

'So did I. The trouble is, Rob didn't have any spares. Also he pointed out that his tents wouldn't reach that far. We'd need one big enough for a jamboree! Never mind, we'll just have to –'

'Jamboree!' Anne shouted, her face filled with animation. 'What about *him*, you know, that scout man?'

The previous summer the scouts had been their allies in the struggle against the far right. The local scout leader had been a stalwart of the resistance. Marnie searched her memory for his name.

'Roberts. Greg Roberts.'

She grabbed her filofax and flipped it open at the address section. Reaching for the phone, she stopped suddenly.

'What's up?'

'It's a bit hypocritical of me to complain about interruptions to *my* work and then phone Greg at *his* office.'

'He can only tell you to get knotted, Marnie.'

'I suppose so. Quite appropriate for a scout leader.'

Marnie picked up the phone. A secretary put her through. After clarifying who she was, Marnie came straight to her request. Could he lend her a large tent, big enough to cover a 45-foot boat?

'Tricky one, Marnie. This time of year all our tents are either in use already or about to be used. A busy time for the movement.'

'I should've thought of that. Sorry to bother you at work, Greg.'

'No problem. In fact, hang on a sec.' The phone went dead. Seconds later he came back on the line. 'Forty-five feet, you said? I think I can help you. Where do you need it?'

'Here, at home, Glebe Farm. That's in Knightly St John.'

'I know it. And when do you want it?'

'Well ...'

'I thought so. Leave it with me. I'll ring you back.'

Marnie looked up to tell Anne the good news and found they had a visitor in the
~~~~

office. At first, she didn't recognise him. The young man was wearing a sunshine yellow T-shirt, light khaki chinos, white trainers and a pale blue baseball cap in support of Manchester City football club. He was carrying a blue denim duffle bag.

'Blimey! Donovan, is that *you?*'

⁂

They drank tea together. It was like old times. The previous summer, they had doubted Donovan's allegiance until he had proved beyond doubt that he was on their side. Now, he was the one in need of help. Marnie outlined how they were aiming to conceal *X O 2* until he could come back to fetch it. He liked the plan.

Their conversation was interrupted by a call from Greg Roberts. One of his firm's vans would be at Glebe Farm by the end of the afternoon. As Marnie was speaking, Donovan thought of a drawback.

'If this is a tent, how will we be able to put it up? Surely the boat will be in the way of the poles.'

Marnie relayed that thought to Greg. His reply surprised her.

'It's not a tent, Marnie. It's a tarpaulin, the kind fitted on lorry trailers. We have a spare one from a trailer that was wrecked in an accident. It's the only thing I could think of that would be long enough. You'll have to drape it over the boat like a car cover. I'm sending a box of tent pegs. That'll do the trick.'

⁂

As Anne drove Donovan to the station, the duffle bag lay on the back seat of the Mini. Anne glanced over her shoulder at it.

'You haven't got a Luger or anything like that in there, have you?'

Donovan laughed. 'No! I don't routinely go around armed to the teeth, you know.'

'I did wonder. When d'you think you'll be back?'

'That depends on how long my duties as host keep me at home.'

'You said you had family coming from Germany?'

'Yes, probably for about a week. I'll ring you.'

'The new gear suits you, makes a change from black or grey.'

'I paid a quick visit to my tailor.'

'Oh yeah?'

'Got a taxi into town, went to a supermarket, got a taxi back.'

'A supermarket?'

'Everyone's anonymous in a supermarket, Anne. Choose the most bored-looking checkout operator, pay cash and get out. It's as if you'd never been there.'

'You take all this concealment thing really seriously, don't you?'

Donovan reached up and put a hand over the rear-view mirror. 'How long has the big black Mercedes been following us?'

Anne was deadpan. 'That's amazing. It must be magic. Last time I looked – a few seconds ago – it was a little blue Nissan Micra.'

11
Tattoo

On Thursday morning nine o'clock came and went with no call from Celia. Marnie and Anne worked through with only a few business calls until mid-morning when Angela phoned.

'Have I caught you at a good time?'

'Sure. Anne's just made coffee. D'you want to join us?'

'Love to, but I've got a meeting in ten minutes. Look, Marnie, there's something I want to tell you. I found out by accident – sort of – and I don't want to break any confidence, but, could I see you a bit later on?'

'I'm here all day.'

'I'm not sure when I'll be back exactly. Then Randall might be coming over some time this afternoon.'

They juggled diaries for a while before agreeing to meet for a drink at six.

Ralph returned from his latest meeting in Oxford in time to help prepare for Glebe Farm's social event of the evening. While Anne mixed a jug of Pimm's in the galley on *Sally Ann*, he put up the parasol over the table on the bank. It was a mild, still evening, punctuated by the occasional bleating of sheep from far-off.

Angela had sounded edgy on the phone that morning, and Marnie suspected that she and Randall would not be bearing good news. It was time to lighten everyone up. Marnie had asked Anne to prepare a rose-bowl of blooms cut from the bushes growing semi-wild in the farmhouse garden. Around this she set out long-drink glasses and matt black Japanese side dishes. Into these Anne tipped macadamia nuts, pretzels and olives stuffed with anchovies and pimento. The Pimm's, in a Dartington glass jug, took pride of place. Anne added a festive touch of her own, leaving the tiny blue borage flowers with the leaves nestling among the sliced fruit and cubes of ice.

But it was not the table that immediately caught Angela and Randall's attention when they came through the spinney.

'What's happened to *Sally Ann?*' Angela asked. A huge tarpaulin covered the boat in the dock from end to end. 'Is there a problem?'

'That isn't *Sally*,' Marnie said. 'She's over there, alongside *Thyrsis*.'

'But why?'

'We're looking after Donovan's boat for a few days. He doesn't want it known that he's here.'

'Oh?'

'He has his reasons. Come on, let's have something to drink. I'm gasping.'

When they were settled round the table they drank to a successful dig and waited for

Angela to reveal her news. Marnie gave her an opening.

'Any joy with the Archdeacon?'

It was Randall who responded. 'Huh! That old fossil!'

Marnie grinned. 'Is this Christian charity in action?'

'He wouldn't know Christian charity if it bit him on the bum.'

This official pronouncement from the rural dean of Brackley provoked laughter round the table.

Even Randall smiled at the thought. 'Well, he's such an old stick-in-the-mud. He seems to be against *everything* that's new. He opposes women in the priesthood, though he knows it's not acceptable to say so these days. He opposes gays in the priesthood, though he's what the newspapers used to call a *confirmed bachelor*.'

'Confirmed as a nine-bob note?' Ralph suggested, grinning.

This official pronouncement from the visiting professor of economics at Oxford University and Fellow of All Saints College brought out more laughter.

'Got it in one, Ralph.'

'But that isn't what's bugging you, is it?' Marnie steered the conversation back to Angela.

'Well it does bug me, of course it does,' Angela sounded weary. 'But we're used to his attitudes on most things. No, it's the Sarah question that's getting us down. He's trying to manipulate the body-in-the-grave situation to prevent us from moving Sarah. If he has his way, she'll be stuck outside the church wall forever.'

Marnie failed to see where this was leading. 'But surely you've known this all along. He opposed it from the start and only gave in when he was over-ridden by the bishop. Isn't that how it was?'

'That's right.'

'So what's new that you wanted to talk about?'

Angela glanced quickly at Randall. 'I sort of overheard something, a conversation.'

'Yes?'

Randall stepped in. 'It was something confidential.'

Marnie got the point. 'And you don't think Angela should be talking about the affairs of the church with outsiders like us.'

'It wasn't about the church, not directly. It was police business.'

'The body-in-the-grave police business?'

'Yes.'

Angela suddenly reddened and began speaking in a rush. 'Randall, I know what you said on the way down, but this concerns all of us one way or another. It's going to come out anyway, and it's not as if what happened has anything to do with us, not remotely.'

Ralph raised a hand. 'Look, you don't have to tell us anything if it makes you uncomfortable, Angela. We're just enjoying a drink together on a summer's evening. If whatever it is is going to come out sooner or later, then that's fine. Unless it's a threat to us – in which case it would be nice to be forewarned – we can wait until the time comes.'

Angela sipped her Pimm's. When she spoke again her voice was calm. 'Cathy Lamb came to see me yesterday, just after she'd talked to you, Marnie. She wanted to go over the points in my statement as well, such as it was. While she was at the vicarage, Rob Cardew called in to tell me how things were going with the dig preparations. I'd more or less finished with Cathy and I offered him tea. When I came back from the kitchen he was telling Cathy about the analysis done in the laboratory on the remains in the grave.'

'By his wife?' Marnie said.

'Yes. He said you'd somehow guessed she was involved. He thought that was very clever of you, Marnie. He told Cathy that the report on the findings had been sent to the police. The body was confirmed as being in the ground for over fifty years. It was a male, young to middle-aged, too badly decomposed to indicate how he'd died.'

'Then why were the remains buried in Sarah's grave?' Marnie looked at the others for an answer.

She was surprised that Anne spoke first. 'Who knew the grave was even there?'

'Good question, Anne,' Ralph said. 'The houses in Martyrs Close were built when … the seventies … eighties? What was the land before?'

Marnie looked at Angela. 'Didn't Celia say the land was owned by her husband's family?'

'That's right. I've no idea what was there before they built the estate. Do you know, Randall?'

'Not really, never thought about it. Long before my time here.'

Another question from Anne. 'The gate in the churchyard wall, why was it put there?'

Blank looks all round. Randall spoke tentatively.

'The owners of Knightly Court have their own gate further round, and a direct path from it that only they would use, leading round to the west entrance of the church.'

'Is it still in use?' Ralph asked.

'Oh yes. That's how they go to church every Sunday.'

'So could the other gate have been provided for their estate workers? There would've been a lot of them in times past, and they would all have been expected to go to church.'

'It's possible, yes, more than likely.'

Ralph shifted in his seat. 'Sarah's grave was marked by a small headstone, the one that got smashed. Would the estate workers have seen the grave every time they passed by?'

Randall frowned. 'Not sure what you're getting at, Ralph.'

'What I mean is, was it visible as a constant reminder that she was buried there, or was it hidden by the brambles all the time and perhaps only known to certain people?'

'Such as?'

Ralph shrugged. 'Who knows?'

Randall shook his head. 'No idea. This raises more questions every time we look at it.'

Ralph agreed. 'And we're still no closer to knowing who was put in Sarah's grave. We've got no indications about that.'

'Apart from the tattoo.' Angela spoke quietly.

'Tattoo?' Marnie echoed. 'What sort of tattoo?'

'It's very indistinct, according to Dr Goodchild, even under a microscope.'

'What form does it take? I mean, is it a picture, a design, an inscription?'

Angela looked thoughtful. 'Rob said it was too small and unclear to be certain.'

'Will they be able to find out more than that?'

'He said the equipment in the lab at Oxford was state-of-the-art, though they might consider getting a second opinion.'

Ralph sat back in his chair. 'What sort of people have tattoos?'

'Sailors are famous for them,' Anne suggested.

'That's right,' Marnie agreed. 'And canalboat people, too.'

12
Celebrity

The post had only just arrived on Friday morning when Marnie walked over to Anne's desk and put a file down in front of her. The label on the cover read: Knightly Court. Anne opened it to find the initial designs for the redecoration.

She was surprised on two counts. The first was that Marnie had produced it so quickly. She was always a fast worker, believing that good design came from seizing the moment of inspiration, but she rarely progressed from first briefing to options schemes in just a few days. Marnie had accelerated the Knightly Court project to the top of the list.

The second was that Marnie asked her to examine the proposals and give her a reaction straightaway.

'What's the deadline for showing her the designs, Marnie?'

'I'm going to beat her to it. I want to phone at nine o'clock – one minute to nine, to be precise – and arrange to go and see her as soon as she can squeeze me into the diary.'

Anne was puzzled. 'What makes you think –'

'She'll start chasing me if I don't get in first. I want this job out of the way as quickly as possible. Something tells me that once we've got the archaeologists here, everything will be disrupted.'

'But I thought they were just –'

'Trust me, Anne. Nothing in life is ever as simple as it seems.'

Anne smiled. 'Perhaps we ought to call them the *anarchists* instead of *archaeologists*.'

Marnie nodded. 'And it's easier to spell.'

Anne opened the file, amazed at how much detail Marnie had produced in such a short time. There were two schemes, both including Celia's favourite colour, blue. One was based on variations of blue with pink and white or off-white tones, the other used blue with tones in the range from pale primrose to apricot.

At two minutes to nine she checked the phone number for the Court and picked up the handset. The minute hand on the office clock clicked once and Marnie pressed the green button. Celia answered immediately.

'Oh, Marnie, you must be psychic! I was going to phone you.'

'What a coincidence, Celia. Amazing. I was wondering if we could meet.'

Anne had the diary open and was grinning when Marnie disconnected. 'What time, Cleverclogs?'

Marnie's Discovery came to a halt on the drive of Knightly Court at ten-thirty precisely. Celia came out to meet her and they strolled round to the terrace.

Celia concentrated hard and made quiet murmurings of approval while Marnie showed her the sample wallpapers, emulsion colours and materials in each portfolio. For half an hour they studied the plans. Celia seemed less interested in the costs and waved a dismissive hand over the columns of figures. Marnie pointed out that there were several thousand pounds involved and perhaps Celia would like to check the budget with Hugh before they went any further. Again, Celia merely shrugged.

'Hugh said we could do it. He knew it wouldn't come cheap.'

'Nevertheless, Celia, I think –'

'Marnie, we aren't short. It's not going to be a problem.'

Marnie had seen it happen before. She had known marriages break up for lesser sums than she had produced for this project. Celia may have been right. Perhaps they were loaded. But Marnie allowed no exceptions.

'Celia, let me tell you what happens next. I'm going to leave these schemes with you to show to your husband, including the cost estimates. You get back to me when you know which proposal, if any, you want to proceed with. I'll also want you to confirm acceptance of the cost implications. Once you've done that, there'll be a contract to sign, and I'll be able to move on to the next step.'

Celia blinked a few times. 'Is that how you always work, Marnie?'

'Always. It keeps everything clear and simple. Dorothy Vane-Henderson at Hanford Hall had no problems when we followed the same procedures.'

'Very well, then. That's what we'll do.'

Marnie had an afterthought. 'Perhaps it might be wise to include your father-in-law in the discussions about the design, in view of the impact on his home.'

'The house belongs to Hugh and me now, Marnie.'

'But the entrance hall is used by him and I'd like to know that he's happy with the decor. Also, we mustn't forget there'll be tradespeople coming in and out for a few weeks while the work's in progress.'

Celia sat in silence. Marnie decided she had made her point. She took a sip from her cup and waited. Celia's eventual reply surprised her.

'That makes sense. I think you ought to talk to him yourself, Marnie, since you were such a hit with him.' She got up and walked towards the French windows. 'Stay there and I'll see if he's around.'

There has been friction between them, Marnie thought. She wondered if he had made the mistake, in Celia's eyes, of not being captivated enough by her looks? Did he see her as a gold-digger?

Marnie was still mulling over the possibilities when Celia returned. Standing behind her was the man Marnie had seen in the hall on her last visit.

'This is Mr Devere's butler, Marnie. He'll take you through.' She held out her hand, palm down. 'I'll get back to you soon about this.'

Marnie gathered up the files and followed the butler through the house. It was as much as she could do not to laugh. She had never been escorted by a butler before and did not think such people were still around.

She was shown into a morning room where Mr Devere was already standing, waiting for her. He was wearing a suit and tie. They took their seats at a Victorian mahogany round table and Marnie went through the proposals for the second time. The old man paid careful attention, and Marnie went into particular detail about the main hall.

When she reached the end of her description, Mr Devere looked at her.

'You've worked quickly on these designs, Mrs Walker. Frankly, I think they're both excellent. I slightly prefer the one with the apricot tones, as you call it, but either would look wonderful in the house.'

'I'm so glad you like them. Thank you.'

'If I were a younger man, I'd be asking you to do something similar in my part of the house, but I think it's rather late for that now.'

'It's very charming as it is, actually.' Marnie hoped that didn't sound patronising.

A wrinkled smile. 'Faded gentility, I think you'd call it.' He laughed. 'Rather like me, perhaps, though I don't lay claim to the *charm*.'

He stood up shakily and Marnie took his elbow to steady him. They walked to the door and out onto the drive as they had done before.

'Do you watch those programmes on television, Mrs Walker, the ones where people have their homes redecorated by their neighbours?'

'Er, no. I don't get much time to do that. In fact, my own television set is still packed away since I moved up from London two years ago.'

'The programmes are *dreadful*. The people just *guess* what the others might like. It's the opposite of what you do.'

'I do it professionally, Mr Devere. It's how I earn my living.'

'Yes, but you're not like those other people, the so-called experts, who foist their ideas on the ones I call the *victims*. You know the sort of programmes I mean? Some smooth-talking trendy imposes all manner of ghastly gimmicks on some unsuspecting soul who just thought it would be a good idea to get on television. Some of them end up in tears. Then the so-called *designer* shrugs and says he or she will be back next week to *help* some other wretch.'

Marnie was taken aback by this quietly-spoken tirade. She laughed gently.

'No, I'm not a *celebrity* designer. I just aim to make my clients happy.'

Mr Devere rested against the bonnet of the Discovery. It was the perfect height for his elbow.

'Celebrity designer.' A wry smile. 'That's the key word these days, isn't it? *Celebrity* this, *celebrity* that. The world's upside down.'

'In what sense?'

'No disrespect to you, Mrs Walker, you're a true professional, but all this *celebrity* business. It's the people who used to be the servant classes who rule these days.'

'I'm not quite sure I follow.'

'Think of the people who used to be minstrels or jesters. They're now pop stars or comedians, earning huge sums on television. People who used to be hidden away in the kitchen are now *celebrity chefs*, world famous, with their own television shows and chains of restaurants. They're far wealthier than the people they cook for. And half of them sound like foul-mouthed barrow boys.'

'I see.'

'And there are celebrity *gardeners*. More TV shows. We used to have six gardeners and under-gardeners here when I was a boy, and there were dozens of them in my father's day before the Great War. Who ever heard of a *celebrity gardener*?'

Marnie hesitated to disagree with the old man in full flight. 'Capability Brown, John Kent, Gertrude Jekyll?' she suggested.

'Ah now, yes, they were celebrities in their day. But they were like you, Mrs Walker, *experts*, who *planned* what was to be done. The gardeners planted the trees and laid out the beds. *That's* the difference. Anyone can dig the soil. The great landscapers were both artists and botanists combined, people of genius.'

Marnie suddenly saw a way of changing the subject. 'Talking of landscaping, Mr Devere, may I ask you something about Martyrs Close?' She turned and looked towards the church some distance away, its tower rising above the trees near where the executive housing estate was situated, out of sight. 'It's beyond that high wall, isn't it? Can you remember what was there before the houses were built?'

'Trees. A spinney between the Court and the village.'

'And you sold it for housing?'

'No. My father leased the land to a developer. That was over twenty years ago. He had no choice.' The old man frowned. 'Now, if you will excuse me …'

They shook hands and Marnie drove off. On the way home she wondered if Mr Devere regarded his daughter-in-law as an example of the lower orders who had risen above their station, thanks to having *celebrity* looks. *The world's upside down*. Perhaps the old boy had a point.

As Marnie swung round the corner to the garage barn, she caught sight of Rob Cardew's Land Rover parked outside his 'base camp'. She climbed out of her car and met Rob coming towards her. He looked more animated than usual.

'Marnie, can you spare me a minute or two?'

'Sure. Come round to the office.'

'I was wondering if we could have a word in private.'

Marnie stopped. 'This concerns the body in the grave?'

'Indirectly.'

'There's nothing you can tell me that you can't say in front of Anne.' She smiled. 'Sorry, that sounds like a cliché. What's on your mind, Rob?'

'I hinted the other day about television.'

'Don't tell me you're about to become a celebrity archaeologist.'

'A what?'

'Sorry, private joke. Do go on.'

'Actually, you're not too wide of the mark. Have you heard of *Timeline*?'

'I don't think so.'

'It's an archaeology programme on television.'

'I think you ought to come round to the office.' Marnie led the way. 'If things are going to get more complicated here, I want Anne to know what's happening.'

When the three of them were settled in the office barn, Marnie asked Rob to explain.

'The *Timeline* people are interested in the Knightly developments.'

'Surely the police won't let them anywhere near Sarah's grave,' Marnie said. 'They're treating it as a potential crime scene.'

Rob shook his head. 'It's not the grave they're interested in, Marnie. It's what else is going on round here.'

'Your settlements study, you mean?'

'No. *Timeline* is interested in witches.'

Marnie looked bewildered. 'Where did they come in? I mean, I don't recall anyone talking about *witches*, except of course to make the point that Sarah *wasn't* one.'

'There are certain areas of the country where witchcraft has played an important part in history, Marnie, and in many cases continues to this day.'

'What are we talking about, Rob?'

Rob took a deep breath. 'Well –'

'The potted version will do,' Marnie interjected.'

Rob flashed his owlish grin. 'Rather than the three-hour lecture? Right. There are various levels to this. Historically, you could say witches were a kind of invention by the church. That might be controversial, but some would argue it was a way of combating heretics, pagans, superstition, dissenters in general. Okay?'

Marnie and Anne nodded. Rob continued.

'You could say there were three main strands to this. The church was after the ones who were out-and-out devil worshippers. They were seen as a threat to the authority of the Pope, or the head of the church after the Reformation. It was the same idea.'

'And this kind of thing went on round here?'

'Oh yes. Northamptonshire was well known for it. Other counties included Essex, Sussex, Norfolk, Lancashire. They all had famous covens, not to mention the towns and villages around London.'

'I can't imagine devil worship in Northamptonshire,' Marnie muttered, looking incredulous. 'Black magic here? Seems impossible. What did it involve?'

'They were accused of invoking the devil, evil spirits, child sacrifice, the black arts, various lewd practices.'

'The black arts,' Marnie repeated. 'It all sounds like smoke and mirrors to me. What were the other levels you mentioned?'

'The saddest one was probably the persecution of the mentally ill. In those times – we're mainly talking about the sixteenth and seventeenth centuries here – people who suffered from certain conditions: depression, epilepsy, what we might now call paranoia, all sorts of phobias. They were regarded as being possessed by the devil.'

'I think we can guess what treatment the church authorities prescribed for dealing with such people.'

Rob nodded, his face grim. 'Quite. Then you have the group known these days as the *wise women.*'

'Were they the *white witches?*' Anne asked.

'Some called them that. They were in touch with the old ways, the pagan traditions, observing the ancient festivals that went with the change of the seasons.'

'The winter festival of light,' Marnie observed. 'The coming of spring, the harvest festival, the kind of things taken over by the church.'

Rob grinned again. 'Absolutely, but I don't think Randall would quite see it like that.'

'So how will this affect us, this *Timeline* thing?'

Rob paused for reflection. 'They'll be around for just a few days initially, checking out different sites.'

'Here?'

'And around the village.'

'What makes them think they'll find traces of witches?' Anne asked.

'Their historians have been researching the area. They've got some ideas about where to look.'

Marnie frowned. 'Don't tell me …'

Rob shrugged.

When Marnie walked with Rob out to his car, she waited until they were round the corner before she began asking more questions.

'Are you keen on having the *Timeline* people here when your own dig's in progress?'

'I think I mentioned to you before, they bring huge resources, Marnie. They could help us quite a bit.'

'I didn't want to get too specific in front of Anne, but do you think they'll find witch graves at Glebe Farm?'

'Barny seems to think so.'

'Barny?'

'You've never heard of Barny Guthrie, Professor Barnard Guthrie?'

Blank looks from Marnie. 'Nope.'

'He's one of the best-known archaeologists in the country. Used to be at Leeds. Built one of the best archaeology departments virtually from scratch. Retired at fifty about ten years ago. Spends all his time on research now, writing books, doing television.'

'A celebrity archaeologist,' Marnie muttered.

Rob nodded. 'If there is such a thing, he's it.'

They reached the Land Rover.

'I always seem to be walking you to your car, Rob. Why don't you check with your wife and see if you can find a date in the diary to come for a meal some time soon?'

'Thank you, Marnie. I'll get back to you on that.'

'Good. I heard, by the way, from Angela about the tattoo.'

'Yes.'

'Is it confidential?'

The grin. 'Not any more, it seems.'

'Seriously.'

'The police aren't going public on it, not yet, anyway.'

'You don't know what it depicts?'

'I've only seen photographs. It's little more than a blur. You'd need a very powerful microscope to see it properly. The imaging team at the Oxford lab are the bee's knees and it's with them at the moment. Whether they can make it clearer, we'll have to wait and see.'

Anne was putting the phone down when Marnie walked back into the office.

'Don't tell me, Anne. That was Celia. She wants a different scheme altogether, orange and purple stripes in the hall to spite her father-in-law.'

Anne pulled a face. 'Don't be ridiculous. Stripes are out this season. She wants polka dots, but you got the colours right.'

Marnie flopped into her chair. 'Break it to me gently. What did she want?'

'It wasn't Celia, actually. It was Donovan.'

'Oh?'

'He wanted a chat.'

'Good.'

'He said he might come up at the weekend.'

'To take his boat? I thought he had visitors.'

'They're moving on tomorrow morning, going to Worcester. He said he wanted to get the boat away as soon as he could.'

Marnie looked thoughtful. 'Why the hurry? What's bothering him?'

'Dunno, but something is.'

13
Uschi

In the office on Saturday morning two pairs of eyes focused on the phone as the second hand climbed towards the top of the clock face. When nine o'clock came and went Marnie and Anne grinned at each other across the room.

'Why do you think she always phones on the dot of nine?' Anne asked.

Marnie inclined her head to one side. 'I've been thinking about that. I reckon she thinks the office opens or the switchboard starts up –'

'You mean me?'

'I suppose so. That we're open for business from o-nine-hundred.'

'And she wants to get in before anyone else can?'

'Probably. Talking of time …'

'He said he'd ring to let me know. I expect his relatives will go off after breakfast and he'll come up then.'

'How's he travelling?'

'Didn't say.'

'Did you invite him to have lunch or dinner or whatever?'

'I said he should eat with us, yes. That's all right, isn't it?'

'It's fine. I expect we'll have enough notice to kill the fatted calf –'

'Ugh!' the vegetarian exclaimed.

'Fatted aubergine.' Marnie corrected herself.

But there was no call that morning. By lunchtime they were faced with a decision and opted for a sandwich in the office. The main meal of the day would be dinner. Mid-afternoon Marnie and Anne were discussing a menu. It was the nearest they came to a plan.

'Anne, it's three o'clock. I think you should phone Donovan. Surely he'll be on his way by now.'

Anne dialled the number and listened while the phone rang somewhere in the outskirts of London. There was no reply and no answerphone. She checked the address book for a mobile number. This time no ringing tone.

The person you are phoning is not available. Please try later.

Anne sat with both elbows on the desk, chin resting on her knuckles. If he was driving up he would probably have his mobile switched off, she thought, but he was more likely to be coming by train, in which case …

Marnie came over and perched on the corner of the desk. 'This doesn't strike me as being like Donovan.'

'No?'

'No. I know he likes to drift in like a shadow –'

'A man of mystery?'

'Maybe. But he's not unreliable or inconsiderate. What do you think, Anne?'

'I don't know what to think, whether to start worrying or what.'

❧❧❧❧ ❧❧❧❧

Ralph arrived in the office as usual at five and declared he had had enough of analysing statistics for one day and wondered if anyone else felt like a spritzer. The reaction was less than sparkling.

'Have I said the wrong thing? Have I inadvertently stumbled into a gathering of Temperance Anonymous?'

'We still haven't heard from Donovan,' Marnie said flatly.

'Have you tried ringing him?'

'Every half hour since three.'

'That's odd. Did he just assume he was coming for dinner, perhaps?'

'We didn't actually talk about dinner.' Anne's tone was as flat as Marnie's.

They tried ringing again and then gave up. They would just have to be patient.

❧❧❧❧ ❧❧❧❧

Early on Sunday morning Anne took a shower, leaving the bathroom door open in case the phone rang in the office. She had set the alarm for seven but was up earlier. Convinced that something was seriously wrong, she grabbed a quick cup of coffee and a slice of toast while checking Donovan's address with the Greater London road atlas. She knew only that he lived in the Uxbridge area. When she found his street it seemed to be a short cul-de-sac in a quiet corner with the canal just an inch away on the page.

Anne left a note on Marnie's desk, telling her where she was going. With luck she would be phoning from London before Marnie knew she had gone.

❧❧❧❧ ❧❧❧❧

It was unusual for Anne to miss breakfast so Marnie walked through the spinney to the office barn while Ralph was laying the table on *Sally Ann*. The first sign of a change in routine was the faint whiff of coffee and toast in the air. Marnie was calling up the wall-ladder when the note on the desk caught her eye.

Off to see Donovan – couldn't wait around any longer. Back soon. Anne

There was no time on the message and Marnie had not heard the car leave. She would give it until nine o'clock and then try Anne's mobile. In the meantime she would worry.

❧❧❧❧ ❧❧❧❧

Anne pulled into a bus lay-by to check the map. She located Donovan's street, memorised the last part of the route and pulled out in light traffic. Leaving the main road, she turned down a typical London suburban street of yellow-brick Victorian and Edwardian houses and threaded her way through until she saw the cul-de-sac sign. There were trees lining the roads in that neighbourhood and the houses were well-kept, with window boxes and hanging baskets in abundance. The word 'gentrified' came to mind, and both sides of all the streets were crammed with cars. Anne wondered where she would be able to park.

Reading off the numbers, she found Donovan's house at the end. It was an unusual property. To reach it she drove through an arch into a cobbled yard. Facing her was a double garage with black doors. What could this place have been? The house itself was set back on the right, double fronted, facing across the yard. There were no flowers in sight, but the house had a simple uncluttered appearance that was pleasing to the eye.

In the quiet of a Sunday morning it did not look under threat or in danger, but Anne felt uneasy when she got out of the car. Pocketing the keys, she pushed the driver's door noiselessly together and walked over to the house, her trainers silent on the cobbles.

There were no curtains visible at the windows, and the house wore a neutral expression, impassive and closed. On the glossy black door the number 20 gleamed in brass, with a brass letter-box and at the side a brass bell-push. Anne hesitated to ring the bell. She noticed a round handle and reached down to touch it. The door opened inwards without a sound and Anne had the indefinable feeling that she was not alone. Somewhere, in some distant corner of the building, she imagined she heard a scraping of metal.

The idea that she was intruding into Donovan's private space made her uncomfortable, but she had come this far, concerned for his well-being, and she was not going to turn back now. Caution guided her steps through from the small hall to the kitchen at the back beyond the stairs. It took Anne less than a minute to discover that the ground floor rooms were deserted. Everywhere was tidy, though a pile of bedding folded on an armchair in the living room looked curiously discordant.

Anne climbed the stairs slowly, hoping to avoid creaks, her heart thumping. This was crazy, she thought. *What am I doing here?* At the top of the stairs she found herself on a landing with doors facing her on three sides. One was half open, revealing a small bedroom overlooking the front of the house. It was as she was turning that she heard footsteps coming from an adjoining room.

Anne started as the door to the rear room opened. Framed in the doorway stood a young woman of about Anne's own age. Over her shoulder she had hung a towel. Apart from that she was naked. For a few seconds they eyed each other. Of the two of them, Anne was the more nervous.

'I … I was … I thought … Donovan …'

The other girl frowned, then seemed to understand.

'Oh yes. This is his bedroom. He didn't tell me.' She seemed to be trying to find the right words but was otherwise composed, apparently unflustered by her nakedness.

'Sorry. I've made a terrible mistake.' Anne turned to go.

'No. I'll call him.'

'Please don't.'

Anne went down the stairs, planting her feet carefully, her head in turmoil. She had made a complete fool of herself. In the background she heard the girl calling after her, but Anne did not take in what was said. She left by the front door and dropped the car keys as she tugged them from her pocket. Pulling the car door firmly shut, she realised the courtyard was too narrow to perform an easy turning manoeuvre. Taking deep breaths to calm herself, she started the engine, looked over her shoulder and began slowly reversing up the street.

At the end of the cul-de-sac she eased round the corner and began driving forwards. Retracing her route, she approached the main road and pulled to the side to compose herself before joining it. It had been a stupid idea. Donovan had simply forgotten that he was supposed to be coming up to see her and had not spared her a thought.

She was stunned and disappointed and angry and shocked. She could not believe her judgment had been so poor. She felt vulnerable, wounded and exposed. Knowing that she was in no state to drive, she turned off the engine and waited while her pulse slowed and her breathing settled, leaning back against the headrest with her eyes closed.

When she opened them, a red double-decker bus was passing. Normal life was going on in the world outside her mind. It was time to go home. With a firm hand she started the engine, signalled and rejoined the traffic on the main road, looking for signs back to the motorway. Crossing to the far lane, she failed to notice the black car pulling over to follow her.

Marnie let the phone ring several times before hanging up. No reply probably meant Anne was driving. It occurred to Marnie that she had only a sketchy idea of where Donovan lived. His details were not held in the office address book or computer, only in Anne's personal filofax.

Ralph was in his study on *Thyrsis*. Feeling unable to settle, Marnie walked through the spinney to talk to him. It was a warm still morning and promised a fine summer's day for the tootle they had planned for that afternoon.

'Are you worried about her, Marnie?'

'Only because she seems unsettled by his non-communication. Also, I don't know how long she's been gone.'

'How far is it to his place?'

'That's another thing. I don't have his address. I seem to remember it was somewhere in London, but ...' She shrugged.

Ralph opened a drawer and rummaged around at the back. 'I may have it ... could be here somewhere.'

'Why would you have Donovan's address?'

'If I do have it – and it's far from certain – it'll be filed under his father's name, from the time we were colleagues.'

'But that was at Oxford.'

'Yes, but we kept in touch after he left. He went to Reading but couldn't get a full-time post there. I recall he spent half the week at that university and the other half lecturing at one of the London University colleges. I'm sure he got a place on the western side of London, handy for travelling in both directions. Yes, here we are. If Donovan kept on his parents' house, it was here.'

He passed an old address book to Marnie. She took it and read the entry for Dr William Donovan Smith.

'This is probably near the Uxbridge Boat Centre.'

'You know it?'

'After what I've spent there over the years, I think I practically own shares in the place.'

Anne drove steadily, concentrating on keeping to the speed limit as a way of blotting out what had happened. She gave all her attention to the road, using it as a stabilising influence, driving by the book, remembering all the instructions she had received as a learner. Every gear change was precise, every action methodical and purposeful. Before changing lanes or turning, she consulted the rear-view mirror and signalled in good time. It was in one such manoeuvre that she first became aware of a distinctive black shape a few cars behind her.

Anne took the left hand filter lane off the North Circular Road to approach the M1 motorway and looked back to see if the other car followed. There it was. She wondered for how long she had been aware of its presence, but could not be certain. It looked like a VW Beetle and there were now few of that old model left on the road.

She accelerated quickly up to seventy. The black car fell back. Anne was wondering whether she was imagining things and what she should do next – how fast could old Beetles go compared with her Mini? – when the car drew closer and flashed its headlights.

Anne jumped, gripping the steering wheel tightly. There could be no mistake. It was definitely following her. She speeded up and took the little car to eighty. The Beetle dropped back but flashed again. He was not going to be deterred. They came to a road sign: services one mile ahead. Another flash of headlights from the VW, and this time the driver put on the left-hand indicators. They blinked three times. A signal? At the half-mile sign the VW flashed again, followed by three more blinks.

Anne's mind was racing. Should she risk stopping? Absolutely not! It would be crazy, she thought. But then what if it followed her all the way until she left the motorway? He could run her off the road in a secluded spot in the country, if his intentions were hostile. She had only a few more seconds to make up her mind. The three hundred yards board came up. At the motorway service area there would at least be plenty of people around. The two hundred yards board. If he tried to cause her trouble she could go to the security people. At the one hundred yards board she saw the Beetle indicating continuously. She slowed, flicked on the indicators and pulled onto the slip road.

Turning into the car park, Anne drove round to the entrance of the main building. She found the perfect slot just a few spaces from the front doors where people were milling about. Soon, the Beetle rumbled round the corner and reversed into a space almost opposite the Mini. Anne undid her seat belt, ready to make a run for it. She sat and waited. At the first hint of trouble she would be off like a hare spotting a whippet.

The window on the driver's side of the Beetle slid down and a face appeared. It was Donovan. He waved to Anne to come over. She was incensed. *What a nerve!* She shook her head indignantly. There was a pause while Anne waited for Donovan to make the next move, though she was beginning to think that something was not quite right. She heard Marnie's voice in her head.

... he's not unreliable or inconsiderate ...

What was going on? Anne asked herself. Donovan looked out again, this time holding something in his hand. Anne looked on in bewilderment as he began swinging his arm back and forth. At the third swing he released whatever he had been holding and let it fly towards her. She froze.

The object landed with a faint jingling sound on the ground near her car door. She wound down the window and saw a set of keys, the largest one bearing the familiar VW logo. It was a strange, unexpected thing to do. The pursuer had presented Anne with his means of following her. It could be a trick, she realised. But why do such a thing?

Anne got out of the car, still wary, and picked up the keys. Donovan stayed where he was. She walked slowly across the road and stopped near the front of the Beetle.

'What's going on, Donovan?'

His head protruded from the window. 'You've misunderstood everything completely.'

'Really?' Unconvinced.

'Yes, actually, really and completely.'

'You didn't turn up when we expected you. You didn't get in touch. I find a naked girl in your bedroom and you follow me like it's some gangster movie. Which bit of that did I misunderstand, Donovan?'

'All of it. I'm surprised you have to ask.'

Anne was flabbergasted by his bare-faced cheek. 'Then I'll be interested to hear the true version.'

He counted on his fingers. 'I couldn't turn up for a good reason. I didn't have the means of contacting you. I can explain about Uschi. And I wasn't following you. I was driving up to see you at home when I spotted you ahead of me. It took a while to catch up with you.'

Anne stared at him without speaking.

'Look, I'm twisting my neck here. Come and sit in the car.'

Anne did not move.

'Please.'

'I can hear you well enough from where I'm standing.'

'All right.' Donovan pushed the door open. 'Give me a hand.'

Anne could see pain written in his features as he struggled to swing round in the seat. She moved forward, still acting cautiously but slowly, becoming convinced that something was wrong.

'Anne, if you'll hold the door firmly, I can pull myself out.'

She looked into the car. Donovan's left foot was encased in dressings.

'Stop! What have you done?'

'Had a stupid accident. You'll have to help me if you want me to climb out.'

'No. Stay where you are. I'll come round.'

When they were both inside the car, Donovan gave his explanation.

'I was carrying a suitcase downstairs for my aunt. God knows why she has to bring so much luggage. I stumbled and fell from about halfway down. The case landed on my left ankle and bruised it rather badly. That's why I wasn't able to come up to you yesterday.'

'But you didn't phone. We were worried. That's why I came down this morning.'

'I was stuck waiting in casualty all morning, didn't have my mobile or your number. Next they took me off for an X-ray and then – '

Anne frowned. 'Oh god, I had no idea.'

'They gave me something to help me sleep and let me out last night, on condition I had someone around in case I needed help. Uschi did try to phone you earlier this morning. There was no reply so she left a message.'

Anne had a sudden image of an attractive young woman … attractive *naked* young woman … emerging from Donovan's bedroom.

'My aunt and uncle had to go on to Worcester for the funeral –'

'Funeral?'

'My uncle's cousin. So Uschi volunteered to stay behind. She didn't really want to go to the funeral anyway and –'

'*Uschi*? What kind of name is that?'

Donovan had pronounced it to rhyme with *whooshy*. 'It's German, short for Ursula.' He pronounced it like *oor-zoo-la*.

'So she's a relative, a cousin?'

'Yes, a first cousin. She's the closest I have to a sister.'

'She was in your bedroom.'

'Sure. She used my room and I slept downstairs on the sofa where she'd been the night before.'

Anne recalled an image, a pile of bedding on an armchair.

Donovan pointed at his leg. 'No way I could get upstairs like this.'

'She wasn't wearing anything. I just blundered up there and invaded her privacy. Funny, she didn't seem all that bothered about being … undressed.'

Donovan shrugged. 'German girls aren't the same as Brits in that way.' He smiled. 'You saw her upstairs … *undressed*, as you put it … and you thought …' He laughed, then stopped abruptly, wincing and gritting his teeth.

'What else would I think? Though really, I had no right to be in your house like that and –'

'For the record, Anne, the last time I saw Uschi without clothes on, we must have been about three years old. Okay?'

Marnie went back to the office to check the answerphone. Damn! Someone had left a message while she had been with Ralph. She pressed the button beside the red light.

'Hallo. This is a message for Anne. Nicki has … no, I mean *Donovan* has damaged his foot and was not able to come to see you yesterday. He asked me to phone you because he was falling asleep with the drugs. He will phone you today when he is awake. Goodbye.'

Marnie was puzzled. Nicki alias Donovan? Drugs? And who was that girl? Why was she passing on messages from Donovan? She seemed to have a slight foreign accent.

Marnie tried Anne's mobile again. She disconnected when the voicemail message cut in. Where was Anne? Why was she not in touch?

As the two cars came to a halt in the cobbled yard at Donovan's house, Uschi came out carrying crutches. She helped Donovan ease himself out of the driving seat, and Anne could hear her obviously admonishing him in German.

They had driven back in convoy, this time with the black Beetle leading. Anne was trying hard to give all her attention to driving, but Donovan's explanation kept coming into her mind. She examined it from all angles and concluded that it was plausible. He had no reason to lie to her, especially now that they were going back to his house where Uschi – *Uschi?* – would be waiting for them.

What would Anne call her? Somehow she couldn't imagine herself calling anyone *Uschi*. It was the kind of name you gave to a pet poodle or a fat pony at the riding stables. Anne had never actually been riding, but that did not negate her opinion on the subject of names.

Now she was faced with *Uschi* for the second time. Donovan made the introductions.

'Anne, this is my cousin, Ursula. This is Anne, a friend.'

Anne managed a smile. 'Nice to meet you, Ursula.' She was amused to hear herself calling the girl by her name in the German way.

'I've made tea,' Ursula said casually. 'Shall we go in?'

Both young women moved to help Donovan but he shrugged them away and hobbled unaided on his crutches into the house.

Anne had stayed for lunch and was pleased that Donovan had remembered she ate no meat. Ursula soon became *Uschi* as Anne prepared the meal with her in the kitchen after making a quick phonecall to Marnie. They ate in the small paved yard at the back of the house.

On the drive back to Glebe Farm Anne's head was filled with pleasant memories. She had apologised to Uschi for barging in when she was about to take a shower, and the matter was forgotten. It had been a strangely tiring day and Anne retired to her attic, leaving Marnie and Ralph to their tootle without her.

The story of her visit to Donovan's house would keep for another time.

14
Donovan

Anne awoke refreshed on Monday and was surprised to find she had slept for over nine hours. It was just after seven when she climbed down the wall-ladder and padded to the shower. Inevitably her thoughts strayed to Uschi and their first encounter the day before.

After lunch in Donovan's yard Uschi had insisted on doing the dishes while Donovan showed Anne round the house. She noticed that when Uschi spoke to her cousin in German she seemed to call him *Nicki*, and when they were alone together Anne remarked on this.

Donovan explained that his first name was in fact Nikolaus after his maternal grandfather, the great professor, persecuted by the Nazis before the war. Donovan Smith was in fact the family surname, and that was what he used while growing up in Britain.

Donovan's home was comfortably furnished with a mixture of antiques and modern pieces which Anne thought might be mainly early Habitat. The walls were emulsioned in white throughout, giving it a cottage-like appearance, and the floors were varnished woodblock with rugs. There were book-cases everywhere, filled with volumes in English and German. Despite this, the house felt as tidy and uncluttered as Donovan's boat.

Uschi called out that coffee would be ready in five minutes.

Under his breath Donovan murmured, 'She may not look it, but Uschi's a bit of a *Hausfrau*.'

Anne looked pointedly around the living room. 'She's not the only one.'

Donovan smiled. 'Come on. I want to show you my inner sanctum before *Mutti* drags us in.'

Anne repeated the name. It rhymed with *sooty*. '*Mutti*? Would that be like *mummy*, by any chance?'

'You guessed.'

Anne took the keys to the side door of the garage building while Donovan hovered on his crutches. She pushed the door open, expecting the usual array of equipment, shelves filled with grimy cans and old oil stains on the floor. Following Donovan's instructions, she located the light switch. Several fluorescent tubes flickered and blinked into life. What confronted her was unlike any garage she had ever seen before.

Like the house, the walls were painted white and the interior was divided into stalls. Anne turned to see Donovan smiling in the doorway behind her.

'It started life as a stable. I think the house originally belonged to a greengrocer. This was where they kept a pony or two and the cart they used for market.'

There were two stalls occupying half the width of the garage and half the depth. The clear space nearest to them was obviously where the VW was housed. The first stall was occupied by a motorcycle. Its black fuel tank and blue-and-white BMW badges gleamed under the bright lighting. A ground sheet was spread out on the floor beneath it, and parts of the engine lay in an ordered row alongside the machine. In the further stall a dust cover like the one Marnie used to protect her old MG sports car, protected another vehicle.

More than anything, it was the cleanliness that had surprised Anne. The garage was spotless, orderly and dust-free. It hardly even smelt like a garage. On the walls, tin plaques from a bygone age advertised Continental tyres, Bosch spark plugs, *Benzin* Aral and Castrol oil. One wall was lined with shelves holding boxes of tools, spare parts, canisters, ramps and jacks. A locker stood in one corner beside a metal chest of drawers, each identified by a printed label.

'This is where you were when I arrived, isn't it? I heard a metallic sound when I went into the house.'

'I was tidying up. I'd been in here when my aunt was packing. I'd left tools lying around when I went to bring her luggage downstairs.'

'All these are yours.'

'They belonged to my father, his relaxation from academic work. He was good with mechanical things, enjoyed tinkering. Bought the BMW new in '54, so it's over forty years old. I try to keep it the way he would've liked.'

'And the Beetle?'

'1971. The family car for years. It needs some repairs, but gets about okay. Not as nippy as your Mini.'

'But the boat ... *X O 2* ... that wasn't theirs.'

'No. I bought that and did it up myself.'

'You made a good job of –'

From outside they heard Uschi calling. '*Kaffee*! I mean, coffee!'

Donovan performed an awkward turn on his crutches and hobbled out, leaving Anne to switch off the lights and lock up. Walking across the yard, she wondered about Donovan's future.

'Have you got any further with your plans?' she asked.

'What made you suddenly think of that?'

'Maybe you mentioning your father tinkering with machines as a change from university work. You dropped out of college, didn't you? Will you be going back?'

'I've got a place on a course here in London. Media studies.'

Anne was surprised. People usually described that as a non-subject.

'Oh?'

'You're thinking that doesn't sound like a worthwhile thing to do.'

'I didn't say that.'

'You did, actually, but not in words. It's one of the subjects that gets the highest number of people into jobs. Did you know that? It isn't just writing essays on trends in daytime television or studying the socio-economic backgrounds of the people who read tabloid newspapers.'

'Donovan, I didn't –'

'The course I've found includes a lot of technical modules. That's why I chose it.'

'Where will it lead, assuming you get to be in the highest number of people finding jobs?'

Donovan stopped. For some seconds he seemed to be considering his reply or, it occurred to Anne, considering whether she had the right to an answer.

'At the moment I'm thinking … technical, creative, perhaps something like film editing.'

Anne thought over their conversation while she showered that Monday morning. She was getting to know Donovan Smith, but he was becoming no less of an enigma. It had been a strange meeting, and the strangest part had been when she said goodbye. He had come out to see her off, and she had complimented him on his immaculate collection of machines in the garage. Instead of looking pleased, his features had clouded over.

'I'd rather have my parents than a collection of old machinery.'

'I'm sorry, I –'

'Listen, Anne. You think I'm over-cautious about the far-right people, but I know they're still after me.'

The sudden change of direction took Anne by surprise.

'They know who you are?'

'I'm not sure, but I can't assume anything, can't afford to take risks, for myself or my friends.'

'Don't you think you're being –'

'Anne, listen to me. You don't know these people. They're *very* dangerous.'

'But I thought all that Nazi business was over long ago.'

Donovan reached out and held Anne by the shoulders, still balancing on his crutches. She thought he was going to kiss her, but his expression was grim.

'You saw what happened last year in Northampton. They're always there, biding their time, waiting for their opportunity to come. Be aware. Be watchful.'

There was a real Monday morning feeling when they breakfasted on *Sally Ann*. Raindrops were drumming on the roof and streaking the windows. Looking out at the spattered surface of the canal, Ralph announced that he would like to spend the morning finishing some work in his study. That suited Marnie, who had plenty to deal with in the office. They noticed that Anne was quieter than usual and when she said she would catch up on some reading in her room, neither of them made any comment.

It took Marnie an hour to achieve her goals for the morning and when she put the kettle on she called up to the attic. Anne accepted the offer of coffee and Marnie took it up to her. There were no books or magazines open when Marnie put the mug on the bedside table. Anne was lying on her back.

'You okay?'

'I'm surprised you need to ask, Marnie.' Anne sat up with a wry smile. 'That's the kind of reply Donovan would give. Sorry.'

‘Want to talk about what’s on your mind? As if I couldn’t guess.’ Marnie grinned and sat on the bed. ‘I’m doing it now.’

Anne gave an account of her visit, including finding Uschi *undressed* upstairs, the pursuit up the motorway, Donovan’s house, the guided tour and his warning about the Nazis.

‘Do you think he’s exaggerating all that, Marnie, building it up to more than it really is?’

‘Who knows?’

‘It seems to me he’s not told me everything he knows about that business.’

‘Have you ever asked him about what happened to Garth Brandon?’

Anne shook her head. ‘Somehow it’s not the kind of thing you can really say, is it? Oh, by the way, Donovan, did you in fact shoot Brandon dead in the street that day?’

‘But that’s what you think, isn’t it?’

Anne looked perplexed. ‘I think that would be … *incredible*. If he really did do it, I wouldn’t know what to think. And Donovan has never talked about it with me. I’m sure he doesn’t think I’d have the right to pass judgment on him.’

‘I suppose not.’

‘He told me to be aware and be watchful. But of what, Marnie? What am I ever likely to see down here? No one just happens to be passing our door.’

‘I think, Anne, on balance he’s just being careful. He’s known some pretty awful things in his life: the accident that killed his parents, the persecution of his mother’s family by the Nazis in Germany, the disappearance of some of his relatives at that time. It’s no wonder he sees the world differently from us.’

As Marnie was speaking, the atmosphere in the attic gradually changed. A single shaft of sunlight fell across the floor. They turned their heads towards the window-slit.

‘Hey, it’s stopped raining. Anne (with an ‘e’), I think we should wrap up what we’re doing and go for a tootle on good old *Sally*.’

‘But it’s a normal working day,’ Anne protested.

‘I don’t care. It’s our last free day before the diggers arrive. We’ll do a picnic lunch. And I’ve got some scones in the freezer. If I thaw them out we can have a cream tea on board this afternoon. How does that grab you?’

It grabbed Anne very well and Marnie walked briskly through the spinney to put the plan to Ralph. Stepping round the puddles, she thought of Donovan and his worries. Was he making too much of everything? Was that just his nature or did he know more than he was saying?

Be aware and be watchful.

But of what, Donovan? And what was it that Anne had said?

No one just happens to be passing our door.

Marnie thought back to the diary she had checked over that morning. The dig would begin on Tuesday. There would be plenty of people passing their door. Coming out of the trees, Marnie turned towards *Thyrsis*. Two narrowboats were gliding by. People passing their door. Maybe Donovan had a point.

15
Contract

Tuesday began calmly like a normal working day, but that was not to last long. While Marnie worked on the design for the Willard Brewery hotel, Anne produced an invoice with a covering letter for Marnie to sign. It went out with the postman at eight-thirty, and Anne spent the next half-hour dealing with correspondence. At nine o'clock, everything happened at once.

Marnie and Anne heard vehicles arriving, doors slamming, voices calling out nearby. The army of archaeologists had arrived. Simultaneously, the phone began ringing. Inevitably, it was Celia Devere.

'I've been thinking about your designs, Marnie and, yes, before you ask, I've talked them over with Hugh. It was just as I said. He wasn't the teeniest bit concerned about your costings and he left the choice of colour scheme to me. I'd like the blue, pink and white design.'

'Scheme A, that's fine. Would you like any changes of detail anywhere?'

'No. I want it just as you've drawn it up.'

At that moment the door to the office opened and Rob Cardew walked in, accompanied by two other men. Marnie recognised them from the previous week. Seeing Marnie on the phone, they stopped just inside the door. Anne got up and went over, leading them outside to talk.

Marnie resumed her conversation with Celia.

'Sorry, visitors. I think the dig is about to begin. Where were we?'

'The scheme?'

'No changes, you said. Fine.'

'When can you start work, Marnie?'

'That depends. I'll need to check availability of materials, finalise some measurements on site. In the meantime I'll get you a contract letter and –'

'*Contract*? How long is all that going to take? Hugh's always dealing with contracts. He says solicitors take forever to reply to *everything*. They're the bane of his life.'

'Celia, this is just a letter plus a listing of the works to confirm that we've got all your needs covered. It's a standard form of wording. We issue it ourselves.'

'When will I get it?'

'We'll post it tonight.'

'Couldn't you drop it in?'

Marnie counted up to ten, breathing slowly. 'We've got rather a lot on our plates today, Celia. Please leave it with me and –'

'Better still, why don't I pop down later and collect it?'

'Well –'

'You said you'd have it ready today. I could save you the bother of putting it in the letter box.'

Marnie tried not to sigh. 'All right.'

'Great. And I can see what the archaeologists are doing at the same time. Two birds with one stone.'

Celia sounded overjoyed. The world was doing what she wanted. Everything was in its place in the universe. There was little doubt what was located at its centre.

Marnie went out to the courtyard, but the visitors had left and Anne had presumably gone with them. Everyone was at the HQ barn, which was now bustling with activity. Rob Cardew was addressing a crowd of people, many of them young women, most of them wearing jeans, skinny tops and working boots. One group was getting ready to set off, gathering up equipment under the direction of a young man with a crew cut. He detached himself from the group and approached Marnie.

'Hallo. Remember me? Dick Blackwood?' He delivered a hearty handshake and exuded enthusiasm, like Rob Cardew. 'I'm going to be site director here.'

'Not Rob?'

'He's head of the project overall. I'll be running the show in Knightly St John.'

Another young man joined them, another face that looked vaguely familiar. Dick indicated him with a gesture of the head. 'You remember Eddy? He'll be doing levels this morning.'

Eddy flashed a smile at Marnie before turning to Dick. 'How are we labelling this job?'

'Call it KGF: Knightly Glebe Farm.'

'KGF it is. We'll get up to the church, use that marker in the yard as our reference point. See you later!'

'You don't waste any time,' Marnie commented.

Dick grinned. 'Hit the ground running, that's my motto.'

'Is there anything you need from us, Dick?'

'You're spoiling us already. We're used to more primitive conditions. We've got a solid dry base camp, plus water, power and a real loo. The girls are particularly grateful for that. There's only one other thing we need now.'

'If we've got it, you can have it.'

'All we need now is some finds, Marnie. Then we'll be really happy.'

Anne pinned a note to the corkboard in the office kitchen area, a rough timetable for the dig.

09.00 – arrive on site – daily briefing	13.00 – lunch break (1 hour)
09.30 – work begins	16.00 – afternoon break (30 mins)
11.00 – morning break (30 mins)	18.00 – finish

She had caused much amusement when Rob Cardew introduced her to the team in his first briefing session.

'I'd like to introduce Anne, Anne Price. It's thanks to her that we have all these facilities.' There was a ragged round of applause. 'Anything you wish to say to us, Anne?'

'Hi! I am the most important person on site.' She kept her expression serious. A few quizzical eyebrows were raised. 'I am … the tea-girl.' There were whoops and whistles. 'If you need any supplies or have any problems, you can contact me any time in the office over there. Good luck!'

Neither Anne nor Marnie had any interruptions from the archaeologists that morning. Anne went out at ten-thirty to check that the urn was switched on and working properly. At eleven Dick Blackwood ordered them to down tools for their first break. To Anne the process was a revelation. She had expected the students simply to leave everything *in situ* and return to the HQ barn for refreshment.

Instead, the diggers assembled all their equipment and brought it with them from the test pit sites scattered over the hillside. Beside the building they formed a line of wheelbarrows like the starting grid for a race. Behind them they grouped the rubber buckets in a neat formation. Shovels formed another line-up, mattocks another, sieves yet another. These students were no dirt rats. Dick Blackwood made a quick tour of inspection, pronounced himself content and tipped one of the wheelbarrows down onto its handles to use as a seat.

From a shoulder-bag Anne produced Tupperware boxes of biscuits that she opened and laid on the ground in the centre of the group.

'Help yourselves! Not home-made, I'm afraid, but we hope you'll like them.'

The students made appreciative noises and converged on the boxes. Dick climbed out of his wheelbarrow and walked over to Anne, his expression stern as he looked her in the eye.

'This is completely out of order.' His expression lightened. 'Got any custard creams?'

Anne hit him playfully on the chest. He smiled at her.

'For several of the students, this is their first excavation. You'll be a hard act to follow. This is a dig they'll remember for a long time.'

Celia Devere had dressed for the occasion. When she parked the open-topped Audi in the courtyard, it was soon after two o'clock. The dig had just restarted. From her desk Anne watched Celia advancing on the office across the cobbles, looking like the female lead for *Jewel of the Nile*.

In safari shirt and matching skin-tight khaki trousers, with boots of brown kid leather almost to the knee, the ensemble was completed with a fawn silk head-scarf that swept back over her shoulder, plus retro sunglasses.

'She's missing the ivory cigarette holder,' Anne observed.

Marnie looked up, saw Celia and smiled across at Anne. Celia made her entrance.

'Hallo, Marnie. I wasn't sure if you'd be pleased to see me, but that smile says it all. Hallo, Anne.'

Anne was glad she had dealt with the contract letter as one of her first jobs that morning. It would have galled her to be caught out by Celia making an earlier than expected appearance. Anne stood up, went over to Marnie's desk and set down a large envelope before heading for the door.

'I'd better go and make sure they've turned the urn off. They left it almost to boil dry this morning.'

Marnie handed the envelope to Celia. 'You might like to read this while you're here in case anything needs clarifying.'

As Anne went through the door she could hear Celia's mock protests.

'What, all that? Oh Marnie, if I'd realised you'd be producing such a big document I wouldn't have asked you for it so soon. I had no idea.'

From the envelope she pulled out a two-page covering letter, an itemised budget, a statement of fees, plus cash-flow of payments and a room-by-room schedule of works. There were two complete sets of the papers, both to be countersigned: one client copy, one for the office file.

'Isn't there something missing from all this, Marnie?'

'Such as?'

'A start date, a timetable.'

Marnie pointed at the bundle. 'Last paragraph, second page of the top letter.'

Celia scanned it. '... *timing to be agreed on acceptance of the contract* ... Yes, I see.' She held out a hand. 'Do you have a pen I could borrow?'

'A pen?'

'Of course. I'll sign now and we can agree when the work can start.' She beamed.

Marnie breathed in slowly. 'You'll see that both you and your husband need to sign it and frankly, Celia, I think it would be wise to spend a little time studying the schedules for each area. There's a lot of work involved. I wouldn't want any misunderstandings.'

Celia frowned. 'But I thought we'd been through everything already.'

'Even so. I've worked more quickly than usual on this project.'

Celia reread the letter. 'Ah, I understand.'

'Good.'

'You want a cheque for the first payment on signature, a thousand pounds. Is that what this is about?'

Marnie flushed. 'No. That's our standard practice. It covers the briefing process, site visits, the initial design, sketch scheme, the preparation of schedules, costings, everything up to contract preparation and acceptance.'

'It sounds a lot when you put it like that, Marnie.'

'It's a fair amount of work and it all takes time.'

'And you did all that in just a couple of days. A thousand pounds, that's not a bad day rate.'

Celia spoke casually but the words hit Marnie full in the face. She dug deep into her reserves of professionalism to keep calm. She wanted to throw Celia out of the office and tell her what to do with her project.

'As I said, Celia, usually I'm able to spend more time on each aspect.'

'I'm not blaming you, Marnie. It's quite normal. Solicitors do it all the time. They take ages to produce anything. It creates an impression, so much work to be done.'

'A lot of thinking goes into design work. The client is paying a designer to use their experience and training.'

'I find it really interesting talking to you, Marnie. You make me see things I'd never known about before.'

Marnie was unsure how to take that. Was Celia being ironic? She concluded that Celia was incapable of subtlety.

'I really would like you to go through those papers carefully with your husband, Celia. There may be things you'd want to change, and now's the time to do so. Later on, it could lead to increased costs, lengthen the contract period, cause disruption.'

'And when I bring the contract back – with the cheque, of course – you'll be able to give me a start date?'

'Within a day or two. We'll need to check availability and place orders.' Marnie smiled. 'No doubt you'll be on the doorstep when we open the office tomorrow morning?'

Celia's demeanour changed abruptly as if someone had thrown a switch.

'Not tomorrow, Marnie.'

'Oh?' Marnie was wary. 'Is something happening?'

'Good question. Hugh won't be coming back tonight. He's *supposed* to be away on business, a meeting with clients in Norwich.'

Marnie saw a no-go area looming. 'Okay. As soon as you can get the contract to me, I'll set things in motion. I take it you'll want me to find decorators and curtain-makers? I have a list of reliable local –'

'I know he's having an affair, Marnie. I recognise the signs. He has to be away overnight and forgets to mention which hotel he'll be staying in. The diary never leaves his briefcase. He's got one of those *Psion* organiser things, electronic, with a secret password.'

'That doesn't prove –'

'Believe me, Marnie. I know Hugh.'

'Do you have any actual evidence?' *What am I saying?* Marnie bit her tongue.

'What sort of evidence?'

'Anything other than just suspicion?'

Celia turned and walked over to the window, looking across the courtyard to the cottages.

'It's so charming here. Life seems calm, peaceful. There's nothing to disturb the serenity. Yes, that's the word. *Serenity*.'

Marnie was grateful for the sudden change of direction. Now was not the time, she thought, to remind Celia that she was standing in an office where Sarah Anne Day had hanged herself, Randall Hughes had tried to commit suicide, and that they were surrounded by teams of archaeologists, swarming all over the property attempting to dig up the remains of dead witches.

16
Scrapbook

True to her word, Celia Devere was not on the doorstep on Wednesday morning. Instead, when Marnie arrived from breakfast to open the office, she found Rob Cardew leaning against the doorpost, scribbling a note.

'Ah, there you are, Marnie.' He crumpled the paper together and put it in his pocket. 'Got time for a quick word?'

Marnie opened up, switched on her computer and offered Rob a seat.

'So, how's it going? Probably too early to tell?'

Rob pulled a notebook from his top pocket and flipped it open. 'I've got a few things on the list, so let's start there. The results of the first day's geophys and test pits haven't revealed anything significant.'

'Would you expect results right away?'

'Usually, especially when we've got so many people deployed over an area like this.'

'So you're disappointed?'

'No. But it would be helpful if we could widen the hunt, perhaps work nearer to the property?'

'Okay. As long as you don't impede the builders or stop us getting in and out.'

'That's great, Marnie. Next item. The *Timeline* people want to come over this week for an initial visit and discussion.'

'How many will there be?'

Rob counted on his fingers. 'Director, assistant producer, researcher, site manager, Dick, me and, er, would you be available, Marnie?'

'When is this?'

'Friday afternoon?'

'If you really think you need me.'

'Would there be, er, any chance of somewhere quiet for us to meet? The HQ barn is abuzz with activity.'

'I'd like to keep the office clear for Anne at least to continue working. What about *Sally Ann*? If it's fine we could sit out on deck. If not, there's the saloon at a pinch.'

'Perfect.'

'Anything else you need?'

Rob consulted his notes. 'Just one other thing for now. You mentioned that you'd like us to come for dinner one evening.'

Marnie grabbed the diary. 'Great.'

'I realise it's probably too short notice, but Rosemary and I could be free this coming weekend.'

'Saturday?'

'Sure.'

'Let's go for it.'

As Rob stood up and left, Anne returned from her morning check-up at the HQ barn. She remarked that Marnie seemed thoughtful.

'Any problems with the dig?'

'They haven't found anything so far, but they've only just begun.'

'So what's bothering you, Marnie?'

'Maybe it's my imagination ...'

'But?'

'Why do I always get the impression with Rob Cardew that he knows more than he's telling?'

Anne had a surprise phone call in the office that afternoon. She had been round at the HQ barn again. One of the girls had reported in feeling dizzy. The wall thermometer was reading in the upper thirties. Anne had spread a picnic blanket out in the spinney and had left the girl lying in the shade to cool off. She was filling trays for ice cubes in the office fridge when her mobile began warbling.

'Danny, hi!'

'Am I interrupting your work?'

'That's okay. Marnie loosens the chains from time to time. How's things?'

'I've been going over stuff for the new course and I'm getting a bit bored. It's too hot to sit around reading.'

'D'you want to come up here?'

'Could I?'

'No probs.'

'There's a coach to Milton Keynes on Saturday morning.'

'Give me the ETA and I'll pick you up.'

Minutes later Anne was crossing the courtyard on her way to cottage number three when the mobile trilled again.

'Hi! Having second thoughts?'

Silence.

'Hallo?'

'It's Donovan.'

'Ah, I thought ... Never mind. How's you?'

'Coming on.'

'*Mutti* still looking after you?'

A chuckle. 'Could say that. What about you?'

'Slogging on, as usual.'

'You were expecting someone else when I rang.'

'My friend Danny's coming up for the weekend.'

'And you were worried that he'd changed his mind?'

'*She* … Danielle, school friend.'

'Right. Look, I'm still not up to travelling, but I'm weaning myself off the crutches. Could you keep an eye on the boat for maybe another week?'

'Donovan, you're not going to be fit enough to run a boat in a week, especially for a solo run down to London. Unless … how good a crew member would Uschi make?'

'Is a joke, *ja*? She's a great nursemaid, but not in the running for Tugboat Annie.'

'Pardon?' Mock offended. '*Tugboat Annie*? Would that be me, by any chance?'

'Oh, I hadn't thought of … I mean, I didn't mean …' Laughter.

'So what did you mean?'

'You know what I meant.'

'You want to know if the boat's all right. That's why you phoned?'

'Partly. How's the dig going?'

'Never a dull moment. I've never seen so many people around us at any one time.'

'Strangers?' No laughter in the voice now.

'I'm getting to know them. They're mostly students, nice people.'

A pause. 'Anne, make sure you know them all by sight and be aware of any newcomers who turn up.'

'But there'll be –'

'I'm serious, Anne. Maybe I should try to get up for the boat. Perhaps Uschi could crew.'

'You're worrying about nothing, Donovan. Everything's fine.'

Anne had a surprise for the diggers at afternoon break. As they gathered, weary and sweating at the HQ barn, she asked Dick if she could address the team. They fell silent as she stood in front of them.

'I told you I was the most important person on site as tea-girl. Well, I've been promoted. I am now officially water-girl too.' She indicated a large cardboard box on the floor in the middle of the barn. 'You'll find loads of ice cubes in Tupperware boxes and there are bottles of chilled water.' Groans of ecstasy from the audience. 'And some fruit squashes of different flavours. Help yourselves.'

Somebody called for three cheers, while Dick offered to resign at once and put Anne in charge of the dig, the project and the universe as a whole. She graciously accepted all three posts.

'Oh, one other thing. Do you think I could take a photo of each of you to remember you all by? Something for the Glebe Farm scrapbook?'

After the break, she wandered about the test pits for half an hour, snapping Polaroids and noting names. Back in the office she produced a wall chart of all the photographs and pinned it up on the corkboard in the kitchen area.

Marnie looked up from her drawing board and wandered over to take a closer look. 'That's nice. What gave you that idea?'

'Oh, just something Donovan said.'

17
Paranoia

In the days that followed, a hot summer settled in, with temperatures in the upper thirties. The records showed that the daily haul of archaeological results amounted to some sherds of pottery, a few traces of small buildings and on average one student flaked out with heatstroke. Anne left the picnic rug permanently laid out in a cool part of the spinney with a flask of chilled water and a flannel in a plastic container. Here the diggers could flop down whenever necessary. It became known as the *crash pad*.

Anne began using the freezer boxes in every fridge – the office kitchen, the vacant cottage, the boats – to produce ice cubes round the clock. On her way to *Sally Ann* and *Thyrsis* to retrieve that morning's harvest, she saw movement around X O 2. Ducking behind a tree, she positioned herself to gain the best view. There was no doubt about it, a man was taking a more than passing interest in Donovan's boat, peering under the tarpaulin.

What could she do? All the possibilities raced through Anne's mind. Confront the stranger? Brilliant idea. What if he turned out to be a neo-Nazi thug hell-bent on revenge for the death of his leader? Call the police? A sure guarantee that the newcomer would prove to be a boat enthusiast, a harmless anorak intrigued by the boat's unusual appearance. Call Marnie? The next day's headlines would announce the murder of *two* women by a neo-Nazi thug hell-bent … Yeah, yeah, fine.

Then she remembered Ralph, sitting innocently in his study on *Thyrsis*, probably writing words of wisdom to avert the next financial disaster somewhere in the world. What if he decided to get some fresh air and walked into the neo-Nazi …? Ugh!

Retreating into the spinney, Anne tugged the mobile from her jeans pocket. She heard it ring twice.

'Ralph Lombard.'

She half-whispered into the phone. 'Ralph, it's Anne. Listen. There's a man poking about on X O 2. I don't know what he wants, but –'

'I do.'

'You do? What?'

'Coffee with milk and two sugars.'

'Eh?'

'He's the local BW patrol officer, just checking the registration sticker on the boat. He knocked on the door and asked permission to move the tarpaulin. I agreed and offered him a cuppa.'

Anne leaned back against a tree and sighed. *Blimey, Donovan, you're making me as paranoid as you are.*

On Thursday evening Marnie was locking the office barn when Anne came round the corner carrying a large circular sieve, like a cartwheel with a mesh bottom.

'What's this? An important find? A mate for Holbeach Man, perhaps?'

As Anne came nearer, it was clear that the tray was not transporting bones.

'Marnie, would you mind if I ran these mugs through the dishwasher overnight? They do rinse them out, but they're getting pretty stained.'

'How many have you got there?'

'I make it twenty-eight.'

'And I bet you know all the diggers by name.'

'Not quite, but give me another day or two. There should be room for this lot in the machine if that's okay with you.'

'Go ahead.'

Minutes later they were walking through the spinney. Marnie chuckled.

'It was like something out of the *Famous Five*.'

'What was?'

'You, hiding in the trees, alerting Ralph to the dangers of the BW man on his rounds.'

A wry smile from Anne. 'I felt such an *idiot* ... *milk and two sugars* ... would you believe it?'

'What was the outcome, actually? Did Ralph say?'

'The man asked Ralph whose boat it was. He said it belonged to a friend. What was his name? Smith.'

'Ha!'

'Quite. Anyway, he rang the office, gave the registration number and they confirmed the boat owner was a D. Smith, permanent mooring in London, licence fee fully paid.'

'Did he say anything about him staying there, in the docking area?'

'I didn't ask.'

Ralph supplied the answer when they were sitting together over supper on the boat.

'I asked if *X O 2* would be all right there for a while. Apparently there's no technical reason why it can't stay, but only for the fourteen days allowed along this section. He asked why we didn't just tie it up on the towpath side.'

Anne looked concerned. 'He can't make us do that, can he?'

The question seemed to surprise Ralph. 'He didn't press the point.'

'What did you say?' Marnie asked.

'Well, just that we were looking after the boat as our friend had injured his foot and couldn't get up to collect it. It was more convenient to keep it near us, easier to run the boat's engine and keep the batteries charged up.'

'So, no hassling us for another week,' Marnie observed.

'Oh, I don't think BW will mind if it's a little longer, given the circumstances. They're not monsters.'

Marnie snorted. 'Good.'

Ralph continued. 'I think he found *X O 2* interesting, unusual, not like other boats.'

'It's certainly different.'

'There were a few people looking at it yesterday afternoon, actually.'

Anne sat up. 'What kind of people?'

'I think they were from the dig. They looked like students.'

Donovan rang Anne that evening. She had been sitting out in the courtyard reading a book on Le Corbusier and was putting on lights in her attic when the mobile warbled.

'You'd be proud of me,' she announced.

'Any particular reason?' Donovan asked.

'I've taken Polaroids of the diggers and I'm nearly able to call them all by name.'

'They're all students?'

'Mostly. There are three older people here, too.'

'But you're sure they're part of the group?'

'Yes. They're sort of *hobby* archaeologists. They've worked with Rob Cardew for about ten years on a big dig in Somerset, near Glastonbury.'

'The Avalon project?'

'You've heard of it?'

'It's famous.'

'They call themselves *amateurs*, but they go on that dig every year and they know a *huge* amount. The students ask them questions.'

'And you've got Polaroids of everyone?'

'*Ja, Mutti.*' Anne laughed. 'Though I'm thinking of calling them *Paranoids*.'

On Friday morning the office phone rang at quarter to nine. Dreading that it might be Celia, Marnie took the call.

'Walker and Co, good morning.'

'G'day. How're yer doin'?'

A woman's voice. An Australian accent. More accurately, everyone's idea of a stage Aussie accent.

'Beth? What are you –'

'Good on yer.' If anything, the accent had become stronger. 'It's me, yer long-lost sister from down under.'

'Beth, you live in Chiswick. Have you been drinking?'

The voice reverted to normal.

'Well, I might as well be living in the outback. I thought you said you'd be in touch.' Reproach.

'Sorry. Too much going on. How are things, Beth?'

'We're okay. Tell me your news and I'll tell you something.'

'We're working hard, as usual. The dig has started in the village. They've set up base camp here in one of the barns. What else is there?'

'You've got *Timeline* coming.'

'How could you possibly know that?'

'Aha!'

'Tell me, Beth.'

'Simple, my dear Watson.'

'*Elementary*.'

'Oh yes, that, too. A chum of Paul's at UCL is in the archaeology department. Rufus Maitland. He's one of the programme's advisers.'

'Right. They're coming here today for a planning meeting.'

'And you'll be there?'

'They've invited me.'

Silence at the other end of the line.

'Beth? You still there?'

'Yeah.'

'You're not going to lapse into Aussie again, are you?'

'Er no, no, I'm not.'

Marnie waited. 'What is it, Beth? Are you all right?'

'What have they told you, Marnie?' The tone was serious.

'Nothing really. Beth, is this a –'

'Not a wind-up, Marnie. Listen, what are you expecting them to do?'

'Talk about the dig, dates, timing, people. Why?'

'Have they told you about the programme?'

'Yeah. It's about witchcraft, persecution, that kind of thing.'

'I meant *Timeline* itself.'

'What about it?'

'Look, Marnie, Paul's friend Rufus said they're in trouble. *Timeline*'s been running for over ten years. Some people think it's due for retirement. When it first started they thought they might go with it for a couple of series and then move on to something else. The formula was a success, so it kept going.'

'So what's the problem?'

'You know what the academic world's like, Marnie, all civilised on the surface, all sniping, jealousies and back-biting underneath.'

'Where does *Timeline* fit in?'

'It's been hugely successful, so it's got a lot of enemies. Only in the academic world they call them *detractors*.'

'How does that affect us here?'

'It's complicated, so I may not have it right. You know what I'm like about details.'

'In a nutshell, Beth.'

'A lot of university archaeologists disparage *Timeline*'s methods on the grounds that they *popularise* archaeology, give the impression it can be treated like a garden makeover show or a glossy magazine article.'

'You think the Cambridge people here are like that?'

'I don't know. But the university people like to get *Timeline* associated with their own projects because they have seriously big budgets. That's what Rufus told Paul, anyway.'

Marnie heard an echo of Rob Cardew: *They bring huge resources, Marnie.*

'There's no great harm in that, is there?'

'There's something else, something very odd.'

'Go on.'

'Have they hinted at anything?'

'Not to me. What kind of thing?'

'I dunno. This Rufus character wouldn't be drawn, but Paul got the impression there was something going on in the background.'

'What could it be? Are we into university politics here?'

A pause. 'Funny isn't it, Marnie? You and I have both ended up with university men. We both know how academics love gossip –'

'Ralph doesn't go in for –'

'I know, neither does Paul, really, but he hears things.'

'We're going round in circles, Beth.'

Celia rang one minute after Marnie ended her call with Beth. She sounded cool.

'I've been trying to ring you since nine o'clock, Marnie.'

Marnie let it ride. Anyone else complaining about a delay of seven minutes would have strained her nerves, but not now. Clichés involving water and ducks' backs flitted across her mind.

'What can I do for you, Celia?'

'I've – I mean, *we've* – signed your contract letter. I just wanted to tell you that I'm going to pop down with it. I'm bringing my diary, too. I want to discuss timings with you, thought I'd check you were in the office before I set off. I didn't want a wasted journey.'

'Er, I've got rather a lot on today, actually.'

'Oh.' That tone again. 'I thought we'd agreed that I'd let you have the letter – with your cheque for a thousand pounds – and then we'd put a date in the diary.'

'That's not quite what we agreed –'

'You're not going back on that are you, Marnie?'

'Of course not.' Marnie had an image of Celia: a Victorian child with golden ringlets, wearing a white frock, stamping her foot, threatening to *thkweam* and *thkweam* till she was *thick*. The thought made her smile. 'I just need to make a few phonecalls to sort out materials and people.'

Celia heard the smile in the voice and interpreted it as Marnie coming round to her way of looking at things. 'That's super. I'll be with you in a trice.'

'No, hang on a minute.'

'What's the matter?'

'I've got to finalise some measurements before I can go any further.'

'Oh, but you –'

'If I came up now, I could do that and you could give me the letter.'

'Super!'

When Anne returned to the office from her routine visit to the HQ barn, she was surprised to find Marnie gathering papers and files together. Two minutes later they were driving up the field track in the Discovery, with Anne checking her bag for tape measure, camera, notepad and pens.

Knightly Court looked wonderful, the morning sun brightening the mellow stonework, picking out the colours in the flowerbeds, the shadows of trees reaching across the lawn. Celia led her visitors onto the terrace and they sat at the table under the parasol. A sprinkler was at work in the middle of the lawn, its soft swishing a background accompaniment to their conversation.

Taking the envelope from Celia, Marnie took in the garden view.

'Mm, I could get used to this.'

A half-smile from Celia, barely a movement of the lips.

'It comes at a price.'

Marnie rapidly opened the envelope and examined the contents. Attached to the letter – signed by Celia and Hugh – was a cheque bearing Hugh's signature. With barely a glance at it, Marnie slipped it out from under the paperclip and passed it to Anne, who fixed it on her clipboard.

'No changes?' Marnie said.

'I told you there were none when we spoke.'

'That's fine. People do sometimes have second thoughts.'

Marnie passed the papers to Anne who looked at the signature page and slotted them back in the envelope. She made a note on her pad. Celia watched her closely, one hand resting on a diary. She began opening it.

'So.'

Marnie stood up. 'Thank you, Celia. As I said, we'd like to take some final measurements. There's no need for us to disturb you further this morning.'

'But –'

'I'll then order all the materials today, which will give me a timeframe so that I can talk to the people who'll carry out the work and get things started.'

'When will that be?'

'The start? Depending on these various factors, I'd say, within the next two weeks.'

'I see.'

'Is that a problem, Celia?'

'No, as long as you can keep them to that. In my experience, things always over-run. I mean, look at your property. You've been there a couple of years and it's still not finished.'

'Work like that has to be phased over time.' Marnie resented having to explain herself to Celia. It obviously hadn't occurred to Celia that work like that also had to be paid for. 'Anyway,' She held out her hand, 'we'd better get on.'

Measuring up took almost an hour, as Marnie and Anne moved from room to room, double-checking dimensions and noting the measurements against Marnie's originals. They guessed that Celia would be on the terrace and Marnie was wondering whether to return to take her leave when old Mr Devere appeared in the hall.

'Good morning, Mr Devere. As you see, we're making progress.'

'Delighted to hear it.' He glanced at Anne.

'May I introduce my assistant, Anne Price.'

'Marcus Devere. How do you do, young lady?'

'How do you do, sir?'

As he shook hands with the girl, Marnie thought she detected approval in his expression.

He spoke again to Marnie. 'Do you have everything you need?'

'Yes, thank you. We've been finalising measurements. Anne has re-checked all my figures, just to be on the safe side.'

'My daughter-in-law showed me the specification you'd prepared. Very thorough, impressive. You like to do things properly.'

'It's important.'

'She told me you'd insisted that I be shown the document.'

'*Insisted*? It was rather a *suggestion* to a client. As the entrance hall is included in the brief, it would impinge on you and you'll be affected by the works. I'm sure Celia would've shown you the details without my prompting.'

They began walking slowly across the hall.

'Some would say the older generation have – what's the expression? – passed their sell-by date?'

Marnie began to protest. 'Oh, I –'

'They certainly do think that. And it's curious, really. Why do people discriminate against the elderly? Doesn't it occur to them that they're going to be old themselves one day?'

Marnie had never thought about it like that. She had scarcely thought about old age at all. Anne was walking beside her and she tried without success to imagine Anne as an old woman. It was impossible. Age, like accidents, happened to other people.

'Mr Devere, I'm sure Celia wanted to make sure you were happy with the project.'

The old man seemed not to have heard and continued with his theme. 'I can understand people having prejudice against someone different – that's the nature of discrimination, after all. Protestants against Catholics; Nazis against Jews; Shiites against Sunnis. You can do that when you're never going to be one of them. But to show contempt for the elderly is very short-sighted. Some things cannot be changed.'

'I suppose not.'

'You see, it comes to us all in the end, at least … nearly all.'

Anne knew she had scored a hit when the location manager stopped in his tracks and spread his arms wide.

'Look at this!' he declared. 'Whoever set this scene up ought to take over my job.' He turned to Marnie. 'Would I be right in guessing?'

Marnie shook her head and pointed at Anne. 'Her idea. Nothing to do with me.'

The TV production team had arrived in two Range Rovers and immediately been led by Rob Cardew to the canalside for the meeting. Rob knew they rarely stayed in one place for very long and he was anxious to get started.

Anne had set up the octagonal garden table on the bank beside *Sally Ann* under the cream parasol. On the table she had placed a glass vase filled with mixed roses picked from the farmhouse garden. Beside them stood two bowls and a jug, all of Dartington glass. One was filled with dark red cherries, the other contained a small mountain of strawberries. The jug held iced coffee. Places were set with bowls and tall glasses. In the afternoon heat, the master stroke was a pedestal fan borrowed from the office and set up a short distance away to keep the air moving.

Once iced coffee had been served, they got down to business. With complete frankness the producer, Crispin Wade, declared that the previous two shoots had been disappointing. In coming to Knightly St John they were hoping to find something with a *wow* factor.

The location manager, Roger Minton, asked if there had been any other discoveries in the area similar to Sarah Anne Day's grave. Marnie could think of none. The conversation roamed round the possibilities of sites relating to witchcraft ancient and modern and, while the others were speaking, Marnie began to feel increasingly uneasy about how far the TV people would go in looking for their *wow* factor. The opportunity to voice her unease came when they asked if she had personally heard rumours or talk about witches.

'Not at all. It's not a hot topic in the fleshpots of downtown Knightly St John.'

Crispin leaned forward, smiling. 'We need evidence of witches, Marnie. Surely you have some local knowledge?'

'Well, when I was last down at the coven …' She smiled back. 'Seriously, Crispin, I've been here two years and I've never heard anyone mention …' Her voice faded. Toni Petrie had once explained that burials outside the churchyard were not uncommon for women accused of witchcraft. Marnie became aware that all eyes were trained on her.

'What did you hear, Marnie?' It was the first time that Suzi Fraser-Jones, the assistant producer, had spoken.

'Oh, nothing. I think someone once made a joke about witches being burnt at the stake –'

'Hanged.' Adam Lewisham, the programme researcher, interrupted her. 'Witches weren't usually burnt at the stake in England, Marnie. Popular misconception. Witches were hanged.'

Marnie put a hand to her throat. 'Oh, I thought they –'

'No. That was usual in Scotland, not England. Here they were hanged, apart from the ones that were drowned.'

Marnie grimaced. She noticed that Anne was looking down at the table.

'I didn't realise ...'

'Not many people do. English witches were hanged, like Sarah Anne Day.'

Marnie shook her head. 'No, she wasn't. She hanged *herself*.'

'Do you have irrefutable evidence of that?' Lewisham spoke quietly.

Marnie's head was swimming. Evidence? What did they have? 'I'm not sure. But everyone knows –'

'Evidence, Marnie. We have to have firm evidence, keep an open mind.'

Marnie raced through her memories of what they knew, what had been said at the time of the discovery of Sarah's grave, but it was Anne who spoke first.

'Do you have firm evidence, then, Mr Lewisham, that Sarah was hanged as a witch?'

Lewisham smiled at Anne. 'We're beavering away.'

'That's very interesting. How do you do that, exactly?'

Crispin Wade answered her. 'It's what makes *Timeline* different. Unlike most other archaeological programmes, we don't concentrate on just one dig at a time. We take a subject and investigate it wherever the theme takes us. We have historians on the team who produce background details based on archive material from many sources.'

Anne looked wide-eyed with admiration. 'And your many sources are providing evidence that Sarah was hanged as a witch?'

Wade looked at Lewisham. 'As Adam said, we're carrying out research.'

'We had someone doing research for us about the Civil War.' Anne's tone was matter-of-fact.

'Who was that?' Lewisham's tone was encouraging.

'Just a friend of Ralph's. What was his name, Marnie?'

'Fellheimer.'

Silence. Lewisham frowned.

'*Fellheimer*. Guy Fellheimer? Oxford?'

'That's him.'

Crispin Wade sat back and folded his arms. 'You'll want to check that out, Adam.'

Lewisham nodded and made a note. 'I think he's at All Souls.'

'All *Saints* College,' Anne corrected. 'Like Ralph.'

Suzi reminded the team about their time constraints, and Dick Blackwood led them off to visit the test pits. Rob Cardew stayed behind.

'Thank you both for that. The people on the Glebe Farm dig are being spoilt.'

Far from looking pleased, Marnie's expression was serious.

'Rob, do you think they'll find evidence of witches here?'

'Yes, I do. They're confident they will.'

'But not Sarah,' Anne said as she stood up and began clearing the table. 'Guy Fellheimer produced her father's will and other papers. Sarah was not a witch. That's a fact, evidence.'

Rob turned to Marnie. 'What's bothering you about this?'

'I'm worried they'll do harm to the village.'

'How?'

'By stirring everything up again. You don't know what it was like when we first came here. Toni got killed. She'd only been vicar for a month. And if it hadn't been for Anne, someone else would've died.'

'But you're satisfied that Professor Fellheimer had proof that Sarah Anne Day wasn't a witch.'

'Absolutely.'

'Then don't worry. *Timeline* may have its detractors, but if they find no evidence they won't try and invent any.'

Rob stood up and began piling plates together. Anne took them from him and carried them off to the galley. Marnie was watching Rob carefully.

'Are you telling us everything, Rob?' She spoke softly.

'Why do you ask?' He looked momentarily evasive.

'Whenever you talk about archaeology, you light up. But when it comes to Sarah's grave, you go quiet. Tell me it's my imagination.'

'The, er, remains are largely outside my scope, but ...'

'You know about them from your wife.'

'Yes.'

'Is it just that you're privy to information that the police want kept confidential? If that's it, then fine. I can understand that. I don't want to pry into things that are none of –'

'There's more, Marnie, something else.'

'Oh?'

Rob frowned. 'I've no idea what it is. That's the truth.'

'But Rosemary knows?'

'That's what's odd. She knows something's going on, but no one will talk to her.'

'Then how does she know?'

A shrug. 'People turn up at the lab, ask questions.'

'Police?'

'Apparently.'

'Seems reasonable. They have to investigate.'

'She brought some papers home to work on the other night, as usual. Next day, one of the officers gave her a rollicking. Not allowed to remove anything at any time.'

Marnie's turn to shrug. 'Forensic evidence, Rob. Wouldn't you expect that?'

'Marnie, no one was there when she put the papers in her briefcase. She was the last person to leave the lab. No one was there when she replaced them in the file. She's always the first person in the lab next morning. So how could anyone know she'd taken them home? What do you make of that?'

18
Arrested

Anne's first sight of Danny came when she spotted the pink hold-all at the entrance to the bus station. She swerved in and threw the passenger door open, tilting the front seat forward in one deft movement. As Danny pulled the door shut, Anne accelerated away like a racing car leaving the pits.

'Sorry to keep you waiting, Danny.' She spoke breathlessly. 'I seem to be behind with everything this morning.'

'No worries.'

'We had an *enormous* post and there were things that just *had* to be dealt with at once.'

'Relax.'

'It's just that with only two of us in the office, there's always –'

'Anne, take it easy. It's Saturday. Remember Saturdays? The weekend?'

Anne breathed out audibly and loosened up her shoulders. 'You're right.'

'I've been looking forward to a nice weekend in the country with a tootle on the boat, a few laughs –'

'And a visit to the supermarket in Stony Stratford,' Anne added.

'Especially that.'

'I've got to pick up a few things for Marnie. Just a slight detour. Sorry.'

'Anne, anything's gotta be better than the week I've just had. It was *so-o-o boring*, sitting at home reading. I think uni's gonna be hard work.'

Anne swung the Mini off the roundabout at the end of the by-pass and headed for Stony Stratford. They were approaching the town when they saw a white van parked on the grass verge, its darkened glass rear windows facing towards them.

'Looks like someone's broken down,' Anne observed. 'Hope they're with the AA.'

'Nah, it's a speed trap. Look how everyone's putting their brakes on.'

Anne passed the van well within the speed limit and saw the writing on the side of the bodywork: *Police Road Safety Unit.*

'My dad says it's all a big con,' Danny said. 'Just to make money from speeding fines.'

'Oh, look.' Anne pointed ahead.

A grey Cavalier was coming quickly towards them. Anne flicked a stalk on the side of the steering wheel and waved.

Danny swivelled her head as the car shot past. 'Someone you know?'

'I'm pretty sure that was Cathy Lamb's car.'

'Whose?'

'She's a detective.'

'I thought it was a man driving.'

'Really? I could've –' Anne stopped in mid-flow.

'What is it?'

Anne was looking in the rear-view mirror. 'Uh-oh.' Her expression was puzzled as she began slowing down.

Marnie enjoyed her Saturday morning ritual. She donned white overalls, removed the cover from the MG and reversed it out of the garage barn. Going through the maintenance checks made a pleasant contrast with her normal work at the drawing board. Oil, water, battery, tyres. She loved the car's antique styling, the flowing wings, the exposed chrome headlamps and the smells of old leather and warm engine.

Whizz-bang indeed! Celia's description had been outrageous, but perhaps not too unkind or inappropriate.

The little sports car burbled up the field track, dark green bodywork shining after its weekly rub-down. Marnie wanted to take it for a long run on country byways to feel the breeze in her hair and delight in the growl of the exhaust note, but not on that Saturday. She had to content herself with a short trip to the village shop followed by a brief sortie along the dual carriageway just to clear away the cobwebs and give the machinery an airing.

Returning home down the track, she caught sight in the mirrors of a car pulling in through the field entrance. It looked familiar. Marnie left the MG to cool down in the garage.

She turned the corner into the courtyard, expecting to find Cathy Lamb waiting for her. Marnie hoped their conversation would be brief. When she saw her visitor, she stopped abruptly.

'Good morning, Mrs Walker.'

'Mr Bartlett. This is a surprise.'

Detective Chief Inspector Bartlett was a sturdy man around six feet tall, in his forties, with dark hair. He did not looked happy.

'What brings you here this fine morning, a development with the grave site?'

'That's being dealt with by DS Binns. I'm here about Anne.'

Marnie gasped. 'Is she all right? Has there been an –'

'She's cited me as a witness, apparently.'

'A witness to what? What's happened?'

'It appears that –' He turned his head. 'Hang on. I think we're both about to get an answer to your question.'

The red Mini pulled up behind the unmarked grey police Cavalier and Anne stepped out. Danny climbed out on the other side. They both looked sheepish.

After greetings and introductions, they went into the office. Marnie offered Bartlett a seat and asked Danny if she would make coffee while they spoke.

'So what's this all about?' Marnie asked Bartlett.

The detective asked Anne to explain.

'It's a silly misunderstanding, Marnie.'

'About what?'

'I sort of got arrested.'

'*Arrested*? What on earth for?'

Bartlett interrupted. 'That's not strictly correct. Anne was stopped by a police motorcyclist working in conjunction with a road safety camera team.'

Marnie was incredulous. '*You, speeding*? I don't believe it.'

'Not for speeding,' Bartlett corrected. 'For signalling to an oncoming vehicle that a speed check was ahead of it.'

'Is that a crime?'

'It can be regarded as an offence, seeking to impede the police in their work.'

'But I didn't,' Anne protested weakly.

'You deny flashing your headlights at me and making a gesture?'

'No.'

'Does anyone take sugar?' Danny called from the kitchen area.

'Two spoons for Mr Bartlett,' Anne replied.

Bartlett opened his mouth, hesitated, then closed it.

Marnie looked across at Anne. 'You don't deny doing what Mr Bartlett said? But you just said you didn't do it. I'm getting lost here.'

'Marnie, we were on the way to Stony Stratford. There was this van parked on the verge. Danny said it was a speed trap. Everyone was slowing down. After we passed it I saw this car coming towards us. I flipped the headlights and waved. Then this police motorbike came tearing up behind us with its lights flashing.'

'Exactly.' Bartlett folded his arms. 'If that isn't an admission of guilt, what is it? What did you think you were doing, Anne?'

Danny placed a cup in front of Bartlett on Marnie's desk. 'Waving at someone called Cathy Lamb,' she said quietly.

Bartlett looked up at her. 'Cathy Lamb? What's she got to do with it?'

Danny shrugged. 'That's what Anne said at the time. I saw her wave at this car, asked her who it was. She said, *Cathy Lamb*.'

Anne nodded. 'That's right. I was sure it was Cathy's grey Cavalier, going really fast, just like Cathy drives. That's probably why I was mistaken. It was well over the speed limit.'

Bartlett cleared his throat. 'Well, I don't know about that.'

'Oh it was.' Danny was emphatic. 'It was *really* moving. But I saw there was a man at the wheel and said so. When the speed cop pulled us over, Anne said to him that perhaps DCI Bartlett would back up what she said.'

'It was just a friendly wave.' Anne sounded deflated.

Bartlett sipped his coffee. 'Yes, well …'

'A misunderstanding, like Anne said?' Marnie suggested.

'Possibly.'

'Of course, Inspector, I'm sure there was a good reason why you were driving so fast.'

Marnie looked at him expectantly. 'We're really sorry to have held you up like this.'

'I'll speak to Highways.' Bartlett drained his cup and stood up. 'Thank you for the coffee.'

'A pleasure. Nice to see you again.'

They split forces for the rest of the morning. Ralph needed to finish a chapter in the book he was writing. Marnie had more loose ends to tidy up. Anne offered Danny a choice.

'Anything I want, that I *really really* want?'

Anne grimaced. 'If you promise to leave out the *Spice Girls* impression.'

'How about a nice quiet walk by the canal, then a spot of sunbathing by the water?'

'Couldn't have put it better myself.'

They wandered through the spinney. The sun was warming the air, even in the shade of the trees. When they emerged, Danny pointed ahead.

'What's happened to your boat?'

'That's not *Sally Ann*. She's over there, alongside *Thyrsis*.'

'Then what's this, and why's it covered up?'

'It belongs to a friend. We're looking after it for him. Come and see.'

Anne pulled aside part of the cover to reveal dark grey paintwork. Danny stared for some seconds before enlightenment dawned.

'This is ... could it be ... is it ... you know ...?'

'Yes. It's the one you saw that night. You see, it's just a normal boat.'

'Then why have you hidden it under a tarpaulin?'

Anne smiled, trying to look reassuring. 'It's not *hidden*. It's being *stored*. This is just to keep the elements off.'

'Can I have a look round it?'

It would be a good way of dispelling Danny's concerns, Anne thought. Then she recalled the interior. Under the darkness of the tarpaulin, the inside would seem more like a U-boat than ever. Then there were the books and all the other German things on board, including the photo of the old racing car with the swastika markings.

'It's locked.' Anne's tone was emphatic.

'Your *friend* didn't leave you a key?'

'I'd have to check with Marnie. Come on, I thought you wanted a quiet walk.'

Anne was turning to go when her mobile rang. She pulled it out and checked the screen.

'Donovan?' Danny read the name over Anne's shoulder. 'Aren't you going to answer it?'

'I'll ring him later.' Anne turned off the phone.

'Is Donovan the, er, weirdo? Sorry. Out of order. But is that him?'

'Yeah. He's probably just calling to check the boat's still nice and spooky.'

Anne moved to step off the deck, but Danny took hold of her arm. 'But don't you think that is kind of ... *spooky*? He should ring like, when we're actually standing on his boat?'

'I think I'd call that a coincidence, Danny.'

'Will Donovan … your boyfriend … be coming round later? I'd like to meet him.'

'He is *not* my boyfriend.'

Danny gave Anne an I-wasn't-born-yesterday look. 'If you say so. But is this *non-boyfriend* coming round?'

'No. He's injured his foot. He had an accident. Fell downstairs.'

Danny opened her eyes wide. 'Down the wall-ladder from your bedroom?'

'No! He had the accident in London, where he lives.'

'So he won't be coming up here.'

'Correct. Now let's go for that quiet walk you were so keen on. Okay?'

'What are we doing this evening, then?'

'I thought we'd dress up as witches, pop down to the coven, pull a couple of warlocks.'

Danny rolled her eyes.

Anne grinned. 'Sorry. Out of order. We've got people coming to dinner.'

'Who is it this time, Archbishop of Canterbury?'

'Just two archaeologists: the one in charge of the excavations and his wife.'

Danny considered this. 'The talk won't be too gruesome, I hope.'

Anne took her friend's arm and squeezed it.

'Just a friendly social get-together with nice people.'

'Great.'

Danny lay on her front on the sunlounger, watching Anne through half-closed eyelids. Her friend was slipping a T-shirt over her bikini and draping a towel over her legs. Her pale skin was turning a light shade of pink.

'You okay?'

Anne smiled. 'I'm starting to look like a pork sausage. Get you anything?'

'I'm fine.' Danny shifted onto her back and opened the bottle of suntan oil. She began languidly rubbing it on her arms and shoulders. 'You were going to phone your, er, Donovan. Remember?'

'Right.' Anne did not want a discussion about *non-boyfriends*. Without hesitation she picked up the mobile and pressed buttons.

'Ursula Brandt.'

'Hi, Uschi. It's Anne.'

'Oh, yes. Hallo. I will fetch Nicki … Donovan. One moment.'

Danny made a face and mouthed *Uschi?*

Sotto voce. 'His cousin. She's staying to help look after – Oh, hi! How's your foot coming along?'

'Slowly. I'm trying to get around without crutches as much as I can.'

'Good. And you've still got Uschi taking care of you.'

'You could call it that.'

'It was as much as I could do not to call her *Mutti*.'

'Same goes for me. It's scary. I tried ringing you this morning.'

'I know. That's why I'm phoning.' Anne saw Danny perk up. 'Were you concerned about the boat?'

'Just thinking of you.'

'Good. Well, the boat's fine.'

'Somebody with you?'

'I was showing it to my friend Danny. She's here for the weekend.'

'She came up before, didn't she?'

'Uh-huh. So how long can Uschi stay?'

'A few more days, then she'll be going home to Germany.'

'That should see you over the worst.'

'Anne, listen. You will be careful? I don't like *X O 2* being there any longer than necessary. I'll come and collect her as soon as I'm mobile.'

'No need to rush.'

'Try and stop me.'

'I wouldn't want to.'

After Anne disconnected, Danny grinned at her over the top of her sunglasses and began applying suntan oil to her legs. She hummed quietly to herself.

Anne smiled back. 'What?'

Danny's apprehension about intellectual visitors vanished as soon as she met Rosemary Goodchild. Rob's wife was small, dark and vivacious, with curly hair, dressed casually in black trousers and a white silk shirt.

While Marnie helped Rosemary try out steering the boat during the tootle, Danny cornered Anne in the galley, assembling the tray of drinks.

'She really is a doctor?'

'She's got a PhD or a DPhil in archaeology. Dr Rosemary Goodchild. Why d'you ask?'

'She just seems, sort of like, *normal*.'

'Not weird or scary like most of our friends, you mean?'

'Yeah. No! You know what I mean. Your other friends are somehow, well …'

'But she isn't.'

'That's right.'

Neither did she turn out to have much aptitude for steering a narrowboat. Under Rosemary's guidance, *Sally Ann* performed a slalom several hundred yards long before she handed the tiller back to Marnie, laughing at her own inadequacy.

Returning from the tootle, they took their places at the table on the bank. Danny found herself seated beside Rosemary. When Ralph came over from *Sally Ann* carrying bottles and a corkscrew, he paused before putting the wine on the table.

'Good lord, you two could be sisters.'

Danny and Rosemary laughed in harmony.

'That's just what I'd been thinking,' Danny said.

Rosemary seemed delighted at the comparison. 'I think that's a little unflattering to you, Danny. I must be at least ten years older.'

'But you really do have a doctorate and work at Oxford, at the uni?'

'Yes, I do. That's how I met Rob.'

Rob was now passing glasses of wine round the table. 'We met at a dig in a ruined abbey in the Vale of Evesham.'

'How romantic!' Danny exclaimed.

'It was.' He beamed. 'We'd dug up a mass grave and Rosemary – she was working for her doctorate at the time – studies on bone deterioration due to various types of wasting disease – diagnosed that we'd found victims of the Black Death.'

Danny's radiant smiled faltered. Rosemary put a hand on her arm.

'It was easy, really. It was either that or we'd found a leper colony graveyard, but there was no record of a –'

'Red, white or rosé?' Marnie interjected.

'Oh, red, please. Sorry. Mustn't talk shop. But you know what we archaeologists are like, once we get going.'

'Still, it must have been a lovely spot.' Danny seemed determined to rally. 'The Vale of Evesham sounds beautiful.'

'It was. We were doing rescue archaeology, recording the site before a primary school was built next to it.'

Danny was smiling again. 'That's nice. Do you have children, Rosemary?'

Rosemary grinned and winked at Danny. 'Working on it.'

The conversation moved easily on throughout the meal, with Anne and Danny talking about their own plans for the future, Marnie and Ralph describing their busy lives, Ralph's travels, his house in Oxfordshire, Marnie explaining how she came to Knightly St John and her programme for developing Glebe Farm.

'You're a woman of property, Marnie,' Rob observed. 'It must be good to feel settled like that.'

'What about you, Rob? Where do you and Rosemary call home?'

'A small terraced house in Oxford, off Richmond Road. You know that area?'

'Of course.' Ralph was pouring the last of the wine. 'Very nice part of town.'

'Rather far for commuting to Cambridge though, isn't it, Rob?' Marnie asked.

'That's the academic's dilemma. You see, Marnie, we aren't guaranteed security of tenure these days.'

'How d'you mean?'

Rob shrugged. 'I'm on a three-year contract at New Melville Hall, and when the project ends in two years' time, I'm out of a job.'

'And you, Rosemary?'

'Annual contract, renewable. Not a bad arrangement. The lab gets a steady stream of work from outside which keeps us going. Plus we occasionally get involved in things like the grave site here, though that's coming to an end now, of course.'

'Rosemary's submitted her report,' Rob added.

'What was it you found, exactly?' Danny asked casually.

Marnie tried to head her off. 'I think that's probably confidential, isn't it? More wine, Rosemary?'

Rosemary held out her glass. 'Well, I expect you'll hear about it soon enough. You know the remains in Sarah's grave were those of a man who'd been murdered.'

Marnie was pouring red wine. 'Yes, we've known that for some time. Help yourself to salad.'

'Thanks. It was interesting. We found tiny traces of morphine, or more accurately metabolites of morphine, in what little preserved tissue there was. This could have been contained in a substance like, say, laudanum. It's hard to tell. The traces were very small.'

Danny had now given up. Marnie was still trying to follow.

'Metabolites?'

'When a substance has disappeared, it leaves behind something that indicates it had been there. That's a metabolite.'

'I see, and presumably they would indicate some kind of sedative?'

'Yes.'

'Which means?'

'By itself, not a lot. But if you take into account that the hyoid was fractured, well, the evidence is pretty clear.' Rosemary sipped her wine.

'The *hyoid?*' Marnie looked baffled. 'Sorry, I hadn't realised I was quite so ignorant.'

Rob pointed at his throat. 'Little bone in the shape of a U, roughly here.'

Time to move on, Marnie thought. 'I see. Now, whose glass needs topping up?'

Danny was fingering her throat. 'So he broke his neck while taking sleeping tablets?'

Rosemary laughed again. 'Even Sherlock would have problems proving that!'

'What does it prove, then?'

Rosemary took another sip. 'Well, I suppose it looks as if he was drugged then strangled or garrotted.'

Everyone fell silent. Marnie wondered what was the difference between strangling and garrotting, but realised she didn't really want to know.

'Could there be any other explanation?' Ralph asked quietly. 'Could the bone have been damaged during burial or by movement of the skeleton when it was disturbed?'

'Unlikely. The hyoid is well protected, at the base of the tongue. No, I think we have a fair idea of how death occurred here. I've seen this kind of thing before.'

'You've done a lot of work for the police?'

'No, never. But I'm familiar with such things from sacrificial sites I've worked on in Europe and South America.'

'Are you saying these bones could be ancient, that they were already in the ground when Sarah was buried and perhaps just placed back on top of her coffin afterwards?'

'No. We know the bones aren't *very* old. That's not in doubt.'

Marnie was puzzled. 'But you said they were like sacrificial remains?'

'It wasn't uncommon for sacrificial victims to be drugged before they were killed.'

'How horrible!' Danny had found her voice again.

Rosemary touched her arm. 'The whole business was horrible. But in an odd kind of way, it also indicates those primitive people weren't so uncivilised as you might have imagined.'

Danny looked aghast. 'They weren't?'

'Sedating the victims probably made them unaware of what was happening. And strangling can be a very quick death. Joan of Arc, for example, was probably strangled by an executioner who jumped up onto the faggots behind her while others were setting light to them to burn her at the stake. It's all a question of –'

The table shook as Danny leapt to her feet and raced off towards the spinney, a hand covering her mouth. Anne was the first to react. She pushed back her chair, stumbled over it and set off in pursuit.

There was silence in the air as Danny turned over in bed. She blinked and a wall came into focus: varnished pine, tongued and grooved. She took a deep breath, tried to unscramble her brain and yawned.

From near her feet came a gentle warbling sound. She stiffened as something moved on the bed. A furry face peered into her own, black, with long dark whiskers and deep amber eyes. Danny stroked the thick-pile fur and soft velvety ears.

'Dolly,' she croaked. 'What are you doing here? Where *is* here?'

'Hi.'

A quiet, cheerful voice from close by. Anne was standing in her pyjamas, beside the bed in the sleeping cabin.

'You're on *Sally Ann*. We put you to bed yesterday evening. You've been asleep for ages.'

'What time is it?'

'Gone six. Do you remember what happened?'

'Don't think I want to, but you'd better tell me.'

Anne sat on the bed. 'You, er, threw up, behind one of the trees in the spinney. No way we could hoist you up to the attic, so Ralph carried you back here, gave you some brandy to settle your stomach.'

Danny realised she was only wearing bra and pants. Anne continued.

'Marnie and I got you out of your things. They were a bit messed up. You just fell asleep and that was that. I stayed on board to keep an eye on you.'

Danny groaned. 'God, how embarrassing.'

'Don't worry. We put your clothes in the washing machine and tumble dryer. They're good as new.'

Danny smiled weakly. 'Always so practical. Anne, you can cope with anything. Me, I'm useless.'

'Rubbish! These specialists, they've got used to all the horrible details. It's nothing to them.'

'They do strike me as a bit obsessive. D'you think all academics are like that about their subjects?'

'Ralph isn't, but then he works in a different field. Hard to get obsessive about theories and statistics, I suppose.'

Danny yawned again. 'Got anything planned for today?'

Anne smiled. 'No plans at all.'

'No visitors?'

'Nope. We'll just take it easy. A lazy day.'

By the time Anne drove the Mini to the bus station that evening, Danny had recovered her composure. A restful day of sunbathing and reading magazines had done wonders for her tan and her peace of mind. As she turned onto the dual carriageway, Anne glanced at her friend.

'You okay?'

'Great. It's been really nice.'

Anne laughed. 'Not exactly the quiet weekend in the country you'd hoped for.'

'Today's been lovely, and the rest of the visit has been really good for my studying.'

'How d'you work that out?'

'Well, as soon as I arrived we practically got arrested by the Highway patrol. Then the high point at dinner was a romantic first meeting in a mass grave from the Black Death or possibly a leper colony. After that it went slightly downhill. I learnt about bones in the neck that break when you get strangled, followed by an explanation of how it was a kindness to be garrotted while being burnt at the stake. At that point I threw up and passed out.'

'And that helps with your studies?' Anne sounded dubious.

'Sure. It'll be a pleasant relaxation to get back to those boring books.'

19
Memorial

On Monday morning Anne used a spare lump of stone from the farmhouse building site to prop the office door wide open. A new week was underway, and the weather forecast promised a scorcher. Marnie arrived just before eight carrying the pedestal fan, which she set up in the kitchen area.

She spent half the morning on the phone ordering paint, wallpaper and curtain material and talking to the decorators and curtain-makers selected for the Knightly Court job. All the boxes on her organisation chart were filled in by the time Anne put the kettle on, and the computer screen looked like a completed crossword puzzle.

She reached for the phone as Anne set a cup down on the desk. Instead of the usual coffee it contained a golden liquid with two slices of lemon floating on the surface. She looked up at Anne.

'Russian tea?'

'Waitrose, actually, but that's the general idea. Thought it'd make a change in this weather.'

'Good thinking, Batman.'

Marnie dialled a now familiar number and heard Celia's voice in a rather stilted tone on the answering machine.

We regret we are unavailable at this time. Please leave your name and phone number after the beep and we will return your call at the earliest opportunity.

Marnie complied and hung up. She took a sip of the lemon tea.

'*Wonderful.* Just what I needed.'

'No joy with Celia?'

'No.' Marnie sounded thoughtful.

'What's up?'

'I was just wondering what your answerphone message tells the world about you.'

Anne pondered. 'Ours just says we're not here and please leave a message. Businesslike, I suppose. What does Celia say, or is it the butler?' Anne changed to a deeper tone, her enunciation worthy of Noël Coward. 'Her ladyship regrets she is unable to grant you audience. Please leave your details and her people will contact your people forthwith.'

Marnie was deadpan. 'Ah, you've heard her message, then.'

Anne hooted. 'There's probably someone writing a doctorate about answerphone messages at this very moment.'

Marnie agreed. 'Probably. Someone doing Media Studies, I expect.'

Anne's turn to look thoughtful. 'Marnie, did you know …?'

'What?'

'Oh, never mind.'

When the sun climbed to its highest point of the day, Anne took a five-litre bottle of water from the office fridge and lugged it round to the excavations. Her first stop was at the crash pad, where two girls were flopped out in the shade. She gave each of them a drink and splashed chilled water onto the flannel in its container.

On the sloping field, little clusters of students were dotted here and there, digging, sieving, recording. Anne went from group to group and was greeted like a guardian angel. With each test pit she visited, she became increasingly doubtful about the value of what they were achieving.

'I don't get it,' she said to three girls who paused in their labours to gulp down the cold water. 'Surely you won't find anything much here. No one would build on a slope like this, would they?'

One of the girls wiped her forehead, leaving a streak of dirt in the sweat. 'Pit nine had some finds this morning.' She pointed up the field. 'Stonework, some kind of structure.'

'What was it?'

The girl shook her head. 'Not sure yet, a shepherd's hut, or maybe lambing pens?'

'Made of stone?'

The girl shrugged. 'It's the local building material. They used what was around.'

'So you'd say that was a good result?'

Another girl joined in. 'It'll probably indicate farming patterns hereabouts.'

'When?' Anne asked. 'Hundreds of years ago?'

'Possibly thousands. We've found bits of Roman pottery. Maybe someone like you was up here, Anne, bringing an amphora of water to the peasants.'

They laughed together, each of them trying to imagine the scene.

'Romans,' Anne muttered. 'You must be very excited to find Roman things.'

The first girl made a face. 'Nah. We want medieval. That's our period.'

'But wouldn't –'

A cry rang out from somewhere below them. Anne turned and looked down towards the barns.

'Thank goodness,' one of the girls said. 'Lunch break.'

'What did he call out?' Anne asked.

'*Clear up your loose.*'

'What's that mean?'

'Time to tidy up the pit before break. And Dick means it. He's a real stickler.'

All over the hillside Anne saw the students gather up their equipment and begin heading down for lunch, some pushing wheelbarrows, others with mattocks or picks slung over their shoulders. A medieval army on the move.

Marnie and Anne had a sandwich lunch in the office, neither wanting to stray too far from the fan. The thick stone walls of the little barn were great insulation against the heat, and they pulled the barn doors almost closed to keep out the sun.

Anne filled trays for ice cubes and slid them into the freezer box in the fridge before pouring two tall glasses of sparkling water and adding ice and a slice of lemon to each.

'I don't envy them out there in the field in this weather,' Marnie commented.

'They're not. They've all moved into the spinney for their lunch break. They look like a gathering of Robin Hood and his merry men out there under the trees.'

Marnie took a long sip of her *designer water*. 'Merry *girls* mostly, in our case. They seem like a hardy bunch, too. They don't give up, out in all weathers.'

'One of the girls was sick in the spinney. They just buried it, gave her some water and left her on the crash pad to recover.'

'Blimey, I wonder what her parents would think. This archaeology lark's a tough old business.'

Anne agreed. 'Not as romantic as it seems, all this digging up the past.'

'Digging up the past.' Marnie repeated. 'Old Mr Devere said that just the other day.'

'It's a common enough expression,' Anne said.

'I know, but you get the impression with him that in this village it's *his* past they're digging up.'

'I know what you mean. It's *his* past, *his* history, *his* family.'

'They've been here for centuries, apparently.'

'How many?'

'Not sure.'

'Were they here at the time of Sarah in the civil war?'

'I expect so. Talking of wars, Celia showed me the memorial in the churchyard the other day. There's a special stone commemorating Mr Devere's brother, Roland. He was some kind of war hero, apparently.'

'I've never really noticed it. I'll have a look next time I go by.'

Shortly after four-thirty Anne was puffing up the field track on the post run. Halfway up, she turned and looked back at the cluster of buildings. With the angle of the slope, only Glebe Farm's rooftops were visible among the trees. The afternoon sun was producing a heat haze. Combined with the scorched yellow grass, it made this English countryside resemble the South African *veldt*. At the end of their tea break the archaeologists were fanning out to their test pits. They conjured up visions of the early *vortrekkers* advancing to claim the land.

Anne regretted not taking the car, but she wanted some exercise away from the desk.

On the way back from the shop, she turned in at the churchyard gate and immediately found the war memorial beside the path. The numbers who had died in the Great War horrified her. Most of the young men from the village must have perished in the fighting, she thought. She began counting the names, but soon gave up. It was too depressing. The inscription read like a litany of clichés:

... for King and Country ... for our tomorrow they gave their today ... dulce et decorum est pro patria mori ...

Anne moved back into the shade of a yew tree. Only one name on the main list recorded the dead from the Second World War. There would have been plenty of room to include Roland Devere, but he had been given his own special stone tablet. Anne wondered why.

'Paying your respects, Anne?'

The voice made her jump. She turned to see George Stubbs standing behind her. Despite the heat he was wearing his usual tweeds, plus a flat cap and a tie. About sixty, stockily built with a podgy face and bulbous nose, his family had lived in Knightly St John for generations. His butcher's business had thrived, and he lived in one of the finest houses in the village. Anne saw his Range Rover parked at the kerb behind him.

'Sorry if I startled you. Lost in your thoughts, eh?'

'Good afternoon, Mr Stubbs.'

'George, please. We've been friends a long time, after all.'

Anne smiled, knowing that once she got beyond his tendency to look at her as if sizing up a joint of meat, he wasn't really a bad sort.

'I was just thinking how awful that so many men from the village had been killed.'

'Ah, yes, tragic.'

Anne realised there were two members at least of George's own family included in the roll of honour. She guessed there might be other relatives listed with different surnames.

'I was wondering … Roland Devere.' She pointed at the stone. 'Why does he have his own marker?'

'Can't you guess?'

'Because he was a hero?'

'He was, though that's always been very hush-hush.'

'Why?'

'Some things are never talked about, even to this day. Special operations, behind enemy lines.' He tapped the side of his fleshy nose.

'Then why did he get that separate stone?'

'The Devere family paid for the memorial. Simple as that.'

'Is it known where these men are buried?'

'Some, not all of them. That's the nature of war, Anne.'

On her way back to Glebe Farm Anne could not lift the melancholy that had descended on her. It was as if the sun had baked it into her mind. She was turning in at the field gate when her mobile rang. It was Danny, thanking her for the weekend.

'Not interrupting your work, am I, Anne?'

'Just on my way back from posting letters.'

'Lovely day, isn't it?'

'Gorgeous.'

Anne did her best to sound cheerful. Probably not a good idea, she thought, to tell Danny she had just been reading the names of the dead.

Ten minutes after Anne arrived back at the office, Celia Devere walked in.

'Hope you don't mind me barging in like this, Marnie. I got your phone message. Just thought I'd see how things were coming along and have a look at the dig.'

Marnie knew her day's work was over. She stood up and went outside with Celia. In the HQ barn they found Dick Blackwood and a group of students poring over a plan on the side table. He showed no inclination to interrupt their talk for visitors, even for Celia Devere. She made no effort to hide her disappointment, but allowed Marnie to lead her away. The archaeologists in the test pits were too hot for talking and continued their excavations after a perfunctory nod as the women passed by.

They strolled back and found shelter from the sun under a tree at the edge of the field.

'Have they actually found anything, Marnie?' Celia sounded tetchy. 'Anything at all?'

'Some stonework, I believe.'

'Really.' Unimpressed. 'I think this whole witches thing is *ghastly*.'

'They're not looking for witches, Celia. Evidence of settlements, remember?'

'Well, they're part of it all. I don't care what they say.'

'The *Timeline* people are looking at the witchcraft angle,' Marnie reminded her. 'Although I rather wonder what they expect to find down here. What Glebe Farm has to do with witchcraft I really don't know.'

Celia turned to look Marnie in the eye. 'It is here, you know. It's all around us.'

'Witchcraft?' Marnie was astonished. 'Are you serious?'

'Am I laughing?'

'What do you mean, all around us?'

'Up in Knightly Woods. I told you about the walk I had with Hugh a couple of weeks ago when we found that witches' circle.' She grimaced and shuddered.

'Are you really sure that's what it was?'

'Marnie, there were goat skulls, bones, straw effigies, black candle stubs. There'd been a fire. I told you about it.'

'That doesn't mean –'

'It was *horrible*, Marnie. Everything in my life is horrible at the moment: the witches, the body in the grave, the awful reburial, my husband having an affair, just about everything else.'

'Oh, Celia.'

'Sorry, I didn't mean you and the redecoration scheme, of course not. That's the one bright thing in my life right now.'

Before Marnie could reply, they saw Ralph's Volvo lumbering down the track, stirring up dust in its wake.

'Celia, this is Ralph, my partner. I'd like you to meet him and then perhaps you might join us for an aperitif before you go home? Have you got time?'

If Marnie was honest with herself, she hoped Celia would decline the offer, but she had made it out of a genuine desire to cheer up her client.

'Oh, I couldn't *possibly* impose on you.'

Minutes later, after introductions had been made, they were drinking spritzers by the canal. Uncharacteristically, Anne did not join the party but remained behind, dealing with *urgent business* in the office barn. Celia made no mention of *X O 2*. She had her own concerns and probably assumed that boats under tarpaulins were a regular feature of waterways life.

Ralph made a gallant attempt to lift the atmosphere. 'I gather you're having wonderful things done to Knightly Court, Celia. I know Marnie's really excited about the designs.'

'Yes, they are … wonderful.'

Celia's tone held little enthusiasm.

Ralph was not to be deterred. 'Are the archaeologists digging test pits up at the Court?'

'No.'

'Really? I thought that's where it all started.'

'They've lost interest in us, except for the grave, of course. And that seems to have come to a standstill.'

'No further progress?'

Celia gave a short impatient sigh. 'I told Sergeant Binns I wanted it all sorted out without any more delays.'

Surprise, surprise, Marnie thought. She sipped her drink.

'He's rather in the hands of the laboratory people, isn't he?' Ralph persisted.

'That's what he *says*. But the truth is, the police haven't a *clue*. And they're still banging on about Sarah being a *witch*.'

'We have evidence to show that she wasn't.'

'Yes. Angela told me. And I tried to tell Binns that she wasn't, but he just won't listen. Why can't people just get on and *do* things? I wish they were all like you, Marnie.'

Marnie choked on her spritzer. Ralph intervened.

'Look, why don't I get my colleague Guy Fellheimer to talk to Binns – and the *Timeline* people – and give them access to his original material? That will knock any suggestion that Sarah was a witch firmly on the head.'

Celia looked appealingly at Ralph, blue eyes wide and earnest. 'Could you, Ralph? Would you do that for me? I'd be so grateful.'

20
Missing

It was Thursday before Ralph had the chance to speak with Guy Fellheimer. They sat in Fellheimer's study in his set of rooms on the ground floor of All Saints' College, in the corner of Old Quad, looking across to the cloister. The room was panelled in dark oak, much of it lined from floor to low ceiling with bookshelves that contained a lifetime's scholarship. A cool place on a hot day.

'Simplest thing in the world, Ralph.' Fellheimer stretched his long legs. 'I published an article in *Modern History* last year based on the research we carried out at Knightly St John. Everything about the will written by Sarah Anne Day's father is in the public domain. I can let you have a copy. That'll settle the matter.'

'And there's no possible room for an alternative interpretation?'

'None. Sarah was not a witch. She was not hanged but committed suicide while under severe emotional stress. You can tell anyone who wants to know, and if they have doubts, they can talk to me. That should satisfy the archdeacon, the police, anyone who's interested.'

'Thank you, Guy.'

'But that's not the point here, is it?'

'You think there's something else going on.'

'I do, Ralph, and so do you.'

'*Timeline*,' Ralph said simply.

'Quite. They say their programme is about – what do they call it? – *Witchcraft, Ancient and Modern*. That's supposed to give it a suitably ecclesiastical tone, no doubt, a kind of *clerical soundbite*.'

'But you don't think so.'

'Look. All these media types like nothing more than to talk about their programmes. Mention *this* project and ... silence.'

'It is curious.'

'To say the least. I'm no medievalist, but I'm pretty convinced they aren't interested in – no – they aren't *just* interested in witches. That isn't to say they couldn't make a reasonably interesting programme about witches. There's the ritual angle, paganism, persecution by the Church – they probably invented the idea of witchcraft anyway as a weapon against heresy – and then you've got all the gory aspects: the trials, the torture, the ordeals, the floggings, the burnings, the hangings. Add to that the superstitions, the ghost stories, the legends, Devil worship. What more could they want, to cram into a one-hour slot on a Wednesday night when there's no snooker on the telly.'

Ralph threw his head back and laughed. Long, thin, ascetic Guy Fellheimer, fifty-something Fellow of All Saints College, Professor of Modern History in the University of

Oxford, seemed the last person to know either about snooker or the viewing habits of ordinary people.

'So why the wall of silence, Guy?'

Fellheimer steepled his long fingers, his expression bordering on distaste.

'This isn't about witches. I think that's a smokescreen.'

Ralph nodded slowly. 'The other remains in Sarah's grave.'

'What else could it be? What do you know about them, Ralph?'

'I gather they're modern, modern in the usual sense, not the historical sense. The body seems to have been in the ground around half a century.'

'Quite recent, then. Not my period. Might be worth asking locally if anyone went missing at about that time.'

'That's presumably a police matter, Guy, a missing persons enquiry, suspicious circumstances, all that sort of thing.'

Fellheimer shook his head. 'That wouldn't explain why *Timeline* are interested or why no one wants to talk about it.'

'Something deeper, you think.'

'It has to be.' Fellheimer went over to his desk and began typing at the computer. 'Yes, here he is ... chap I know, Fellow at Pembroke. We play chess together. He's ex-army intelligence, specialises in military history.'

'There's nothing to suggest this is a military matter, Guy.'

'No, but he was involved in a *Timeline* programme on coastal defences from Martello towers to the early use of radar.'

'He has contacts inside *Timeline*.'

'Correct. And also, he'll have insights into the period in question. He published a rather good book on espionage, based on his doctoral research: *The Fifth Column in World War Two*.' Fellheimer scribbled a note. 'I'll give him a ring and get back to you.'

The two men left Fellheimer's rooms and walked across the quadrangle that had been built around 1450. They headed for a pub down the road that was almost as old.

The senior common room at University College London was not the place for a quiet private conversation, so Paul had arranged to meet his friend for a pub lunch in Bloomsbury at noon, before the main rush started. Beth had promised Marnie that her husband would try to find out more of the background to *Timeline*. Dr Paul Sutton and Dr Rufus Maitland found a corner table away from the entrance and ordered beer and sandwiches.

Paul began with a casual question about Maitland's latest research project: *the despoiling of the monasteries: Henry VIII's disposal of their wealth following the Reformation in England, 1536-1547*. He had finished one pint of beer, a large ham salad baguette and a packet of ready-salted crisps before Maitland seemed to pause for breath.

When Maitland finally made a start on his baguette, Paul got a word in. 'My sister-in-law's got a load of archaeologists up at her place at the moment, something to do with settlements.'

A nod. 'You mentioned it before. Cambridge, isn't it?'

'Some chap called Cardew.'

'Rob Cardew. Very sound, knows his stuff, all right. Only problem with him is, he's rather obsessive about it all.'

'Really? There's a surprise.'

'Wife's in the same line, too. She's at Oxford.'

'Marnie tells me your *Timeline* chums are coming to descend on her at any minute.'

Maitland paused briefly before biting into the baguette. He chewed steadfastly on, as if his digestion depended on it. Paul was undeterred.

'Are you involved in that programme, Rufus? You're one of their consultants, aren't you?'

Maitland took a large swig of beer. 'Indirectly.' He stared into his glass.

Paul waited. Eventually he spoke. 'I've never really understood where this witchcraft thing came from. To me it's all –'

Maitland turned his gaze on Paul with an extraordinary intensity of expression.

'Rufus, what's going on? I know there's something. I can't imagine what can be so compelling about a load of superstitious old hags dancing round –'

'It's not about witchcraft.' Maitland had lowered his voice.

'Then what is it that's got your knickers in a twist?'

Maitland shook his head imperceptibly.

Paul was not going to be deterred. 'Is it to do with the body in the grave on top of the coffin?'

'What do you know about that, Paul?'

'Only what Beth's heard from Marnie, and she doesn't know much.'

Maitland was not making eye contact and seemed to be lost in reverie. More chewing, more beer. After an age had passed he looked up at Paul.

'Your sister-in-law would be well advised to keep out of the way.'

'Why?'

'That's just it, I'm not in the loop on this one.'

'Then why are you giving me the gypsy's warning? You must know something, Rufus. You're the consultant. You must have *some* idea what's going on.'

Maitland pushed the plate away and drained his beer. 'It started off quite simply, the way these things do. One enquiry leads to another. You begin with one question, you end up somewhere else, sometimes quite different. You never know what's going to emerge when you dig up the past.'

'That's what happened when they dug up the grave and found those remains?'

'Yes. They carried out tests –'

'Who did?'

'This lab in Oxford, where Cardew's wife works. They called in some experts, then some more, then … nothing. Suddenly doors were slamming in faces.'

'Why?'

Maitland shrugged.

'Rufus, you said it began simply. What did you mean by that?'

'I can't tell you anything more, Paul.'

'You've been warned off?'

'In a way.'

'Who by?'

Maitland looked at his watch. 'I've got to get back.'

'Who warned you off? What had your colleagues discovered? You can at least tell me about the start of it all, if it was just simple, as you put it.'

Maitland smiled. 'It reminded me of the old poem, you know, the one about the stairs.'

'You're talking in riddles.'

'I suppose it is like a kind of riddle. You must know the one:

As I was walking up the stair
I met a man who wasn't there.
He wasn't there again today.
I wish, I wish he'd stay away.'

Anne was up in the attic settling one of the students on her bed when the office phone rang. Marnie took the call and listened carefully while Ralph outlined his conversation with Fellheimer.

'I can see why the idea has persisted that Sarah was a witch. These old myths hang around – sorry – and just won't go away.'

'But Ralph, if Guy makes his findings available to the *Timeline* people, surely that will be an end of it.'

'Probably, though you can never be sure.'

'Well that's some progress at least. Thanks. So, what time will you be back this evening?'

'Hang on, Marnie, there's something else. Guy thinks there's something going on in the background, to do with the remains in Sarah's grave.'

'Such as?'

'He's not sure. It's more a question of what *isn't* being said.'

'I don't follow.'

'No one wants to talk about it. Guy finds that suspicious.'

'Is that it?'

'Not quite. He's got a friend who has links with *Timeline*, consulted on one of their programmes. Guy's going to do a little digging of his own to see what he might uncover.'

'You know, Ralph, I'm wondering if we might be reading too much into this. Could it be nothing more than academic jealousy?'

Ralph laughed. 'What a surprise! That's always a possibility, of course. Oh, there was one other thing. Guy wondered if anyone went missing around the time the remains were put in the grave. That would be roughly from the thirties to the fifties.'

'Surely the police will've checked that.'

'Have they said anything about it?'

'Not to my knowledge.'

'Might be interesting to find out.'

Anne came down the wall-ladder a minute or two later. 'Any more of this and I'll be putting in for a nurse's uniform. We'll have to change the name of the place to Glebe Casualty Clearing Station. She's the third one to conk out today. I reckon it's cooler up in my room than outside on the crash pad.'

'Mm ...'

Anne lowered her voice. 'I think she might have more than just heat exhaustion, that one. I've got more than a slight suspicion she's got a hangover.'

Anne looked across at Marnie, who was staring into space.

'Marnie? You all right? Don't say you're going to pass out.'

Marnie looked up as if she had not heard what Anne was saying. 'What? Er, no.'

'You sure?'

'Anne, did the police say anything about missing persons?'

'The remains in the grave, you mean? I think Cathy Lamb did say they were looking into that. First thing they'd check, I imagine.'

Marnie reached for the phone. 'Angela, hi it's Marnie. I want to ask you something.'

'Sure.'

'Do you know if the police have run a check on missing persons from the time the body was buried in Sarah's grave?'

'Yes. They were talking about it some time ago.'

'Do you know what they found out?'

'They've not actually said, but Binns probably wouldn't have told me anyway.'

'No, I suppose not.'

'Cathy Lamb did mention that such occurrences were quite rare in Northamptonshire, people going missing and turning up dead.'

'Oh well, just a thought.'

'Have you tried asking any of the older people, like George Stubbs?'

'George? Surely he'd be too young to remember that far back.'

'He was born in the thirties, a child in the forties, grew up in the fifties. He might have heard things.'

At four-thirty Anne climbed down the wall-ladder and went to her desk to gather up the day's letters for posting. She nodded significantly towards the attic.

'She's still sleeping it off.'

Marnie put down her pencil. 'Fancy a run out in the MG?'

'On a Thursday tea-time?'

'Ideal weather for it.'

'You're on.'

After pausing briefly by the post-box for Anne to drop off the letters, Marnie accelerated up the high street. She was still only in third gear when she gave a hand signal, braked and turned into the drive of one of the finest houses in the village. Passing the name board, *The Old Farm House*, she pulled up at the end of the long drive by a perfect herbaceous border, blipped the throttle and switched off the engine. The classic car looked as if it had been made to stand in front of the creamy stone façade.

Marnie climbed out and Anne followed, looking puzzled.

'This is the run out, calling on Mr Stubbs?'

'Yep.'

'Are you sure he's at home?'

'I checked while you were up in the loft doing your Florence Nightingale bit.'

Marnie pressed the brass button of the bell. They waited in silence, breathing in the perfume from a deep red rose climbing round the doorway. Mrs Stubbs invited them inside and led them through to a large, square living room with double French windows opening into a conservatory. Anne glanced sideways towards the open door of the kitchen. She could see half the Aga, shining in cream enamel with bright chromed lids.

'George will be down in a minute, Marnie. He's upstairs washing his hands, been doing some weeding. You know how it is at this time of year. The garden's an absolute wilderness.'

Marnie could not suppress a smile. 'I think we could show you a real wilderness, Sheila. I haven't even got started on the Glebe Farm garden yet.' She raised a hand towards the windows. 'Look at your view. Magnificent.'

Across the diagonally striped lawn, the view was dominated by a further herbaceous border, swathes of colour glowing in the sunshine, the tops of fruit trees visible beyond.

'You'll get there, my dear, you'll get there.' George Stubbs entered the room. In country check shirt and flannel trousers secured round his substantial girth by a leather belt, he was pink in the face from his exertions. 'I know you want to do it all properly, and that's the only way to get things right. You've transformed the place already. Bloody marvellous. Oh! Pardon my French.'

Sheila invited her visitors to sit down. Anne almost sighed with pleasure as she sank into the deep cushions of a blue and white chintz-covered sofa.

'May I offer you tea while you have your chat with George? Would you like to stay in here or sit outside?'

'Cooler in here,' George said, planting himself heavily in an armchair. 'Tea would be wonderful, dear. I bet Marnie and Anne would appreciate that Lapsang Souchong we had delivered.'

When his wife left the room, George turned to Marnie with a smile. 'You said you wanted to talk about the other body in Sarah's grave. So, how can I help?'

'One of Ralph's colleagues wondered if anyone had gone missing about the time the body was placed there. I don't know if you've heard whether the police have come to any conclusions on that?'

George shook his head. 'They questioned me about it, of course, and a number of other people too. Frankly, my dear, I don't think they've got anywhere with those enquiries. I'll tell you what I told them. To the best of my knowledge there's never been a missing person unaccounted for in this neck of the woods.'

'That's what I thought you'd say, George.'

'Well, I've lived here all my life and I'm sure I'd know, or I would've heard something in the last sixty years. People talk. You know what it's like in a village.'

'I did wonder about asking Albert Fletcher. Being older than you, his memory might go back further.'

George raised his palms. 'True. But I think he'll say the same thing. Though there was his brother, of course.'

Marnie sat up straight. 'His brother?'

George nodded. 'Arthur. He went missing.'

'The name on the war memorial,' Anne said quietly. 'Arthur Fletcher, Corporal.'

'That's right. We looked at it the other day, didn't we Anne?'

Marnie relaxed again. 'But he was killed in the war.'

'The inscription was *Killed or Missing in Action*,' Anne said.

'That's the same thing, isn't it?'

'Pretty much,' George agreed. 'People go off to war, don't come back, are never seen again. It's very hard on their families, never getting the chance to say good-bye.'

'Oh sorry, George, thoughtless of me.' Marnie looked pained. 'He must've been related to you. Albert Fletcher is your cousin, isn't he?'

'Yes. His father and my mother were first cousins, so I think that makes us second cousins. And Arthur, too, though I've no firm memories of him. He was a good bit older than me. I was only three when the war broke out. He joined up straight away in '39. That's practically the last I remember of him.'

'He was lost early on?'

'Not really. He came back on leave occasionally. Then that last time he came home for a short leave. Don't know if I actually saw him. Went back to war and soon afterwards we heard from the big house that he was *missing in action*.'

'The big house?' Marnie repeated.

'Arthur was an under-gardener at the Court.'

'Why did *they* tell the family? Didn't the authorities send a telegram direct?'

'Arthur lived in the servants' quarters up at the Court. That was his address, so they sent it there. Old Quentin Devere went personally to Arthur's parents to give them the news. Very good of him. Some landowners would've just sent a boy along with a message.'

'I see. A sad business.'

George gazed out towards the garden for a few moments. 'Strange, really …'

'What is?'

'So many men were lost in the first war, only those two in the second.'

'Roland,' Anne murmured. 'With his own personal war memorial.'

'Yes. Though no one would begrudge him that. They say it broke the old man's heart when he was posted as missing in action. That was behind enemy lines, of course.'

'He was highly decorated,' Anne said.

'Oh yes. He was the older son, father doted on him. A fine young man, as well as a war hero.'

'Were there any others in the family of that generation?' Marnie asked.

'No, just the two boys.'

'What did Marcus do in the war?'

'Not sure, to be honest. Never really heard anyone talk about it. But then, people lived more privately in those days. Families like the Deveres were somewhat distant.'

On the way home, Marnie banished thoughts of wars and the dead by taking to minor roads. The little sports car was in its element, burbling along country byways that had hardly changed since the time it was first built. Marnie laughed out loud, causing Anne to look at her.

'What's that for?'

'Just occurred to me.' Marnie raised her voice above the sound of the engine and the road noise. 'The MG is almost exactly the same age as George Stubbs.'

'Blimey!'

'Quite. Rather an antique!'

'Which one?'

'Both!'

They laughed cheerfully together. Marnie was glad not to be dwelling on the gloomy subjects that seemed to be dominating their lives that summer. It was good to be out in the country, feeling the taut suspension keeping the car firmly under control in the twisty bends, the faint warm smell from the engine and the rush of the air blowing through their hair.

Anne had thrown her head back in exultation, but turned again to look at Marnie.

'I *love* their house. It's brilliant! Did you see the Aga in the kitchen?'

'Of course.'

'I bet you'll make Glebe Farm just as nice. Will you get an Aga?'

Marnie made a face. 'D'you know what those things cost?'

'Arm and a leg?'

'Both arms and both legs.'

Anne grimaced. 'But they are beautiful, perfect for a country house.'

'Tell me about it.' Marnie smiled.

Anne knew Marnie was trying to imagine the kitchen at Glebe Farm, perhaps with a tiled floor, a Welsh dresser and an Aga as the gleaming centrepiece.

'Are you and Ralph going to have children, Marnie? Oh sorry, don't know why I said that. It just slipped out. None of my business.'

'Thinking of families gathered round the kitchen table for tea on chilly afternoons, warmed by the Aga?'

'I suppose that's what it was. Forget I spoke.'

'I think it's got to be one thing at a time, Anne. That's the answer to your question.'

'Right. What colour Aga will you have?'

Marnie laughed. 'I told you, one thing at a time.'

'Sorry.'

They drove on for a few miles before Marnie took a turning that led back to Knightly St John. The engine was singing in the warm air as Marnie glanced briefly at Anne.

'Maybe dark red or deep blue?'

Anne grinned. 'That's what I'd have. Hard to choose between them.'

Marnie relaxed at the wheel. Rounding a bend, the top of the church tower came fleetingly into view as they approached Knightly St John. In her mind's eye she saw Knightly Court somewhere beyond the church and tried not to imagine the Devere family in times past, gathered round the tea table, the parents with their two boys who would grow to manhood in a war that only one of them would survive.

Marnie parked the MG in the garage barn and went back to her desk, while Anne hauled the heavy five-litre water bottle from the fridge and set off on her regular mission. The red light was flashing on the answerphone. Three messages: two routine, one family.

'Hi, Beth. How's things?'

'Listen. Paul saw Rufus Maitland in college today.'

'Rufus Maitland?'

'I told you about him. Consultant on *Timeline*. Paul mentioned the dig at your place, said he knew *Timeline* were coming to film there.'

'This is the guy who thinks the dig isn't what it seems?'

'That's the one.'

'What did Paul find out?'

'That's just it. As soon as Paul broached the subject, Rufus clammed up.'

'So you rang to tell me Paul's friend said nothing?'

'Look, Marnie, Paul knew Rufus was *dying* to tell him something, but couldn't.'

'Didn't he say anything at all?'

'He did drop a kind of hint.' Beth recited the poem about the man on the stairs, who wasn't there.

Marnie pondered this for a few seconds. 'What does it mean?'

'Well, it must be about a ghost, mustn't it?'

'Obviously, but why did Paul's friend say it? What was the point?'

'I haven't the ghost of a chance of working it out.'

Beth laughed at her joke. Marnie sat in silence.

Anne came back lugging the half-empty water bottle, muttering that there must be an easier way of carrying it around, to find Marnie holding the phone. By her expression, she was waiting for someone to answer.

'He should still be there,' Marnie said, biting her lip. 'Oh, Ralph, hi, it's me. Are you still in college? Listen. There's something I want to tell you.'

Ralph knocked twice on the dark oak door and was admitted by Fellheimer. Leading Ralph into his study, he handed him a copy of the journal containing the article about Sarah Anne Day and her father's will, firm evidence that she had not been a witch. They took their places in the chairs they had occupied that morning and Ralph outlined what had been learnt during the day.

'So no missing persons,' Fellheimer said.

'Not as far as they know.'

'Unsolved murders?'

'I'm not sure how far that can be pursued, Guy.'

'No. I don't think I know any tame criminologists.' He made a note on his pad. 'I'll make a few enquiries.'

'There was one other thing. Do you know Rufus Maitland?'

A pause. 'Know the name, may have seen him at a conference, possibly. UCL?'

'That's him. Archaeologist.'

'What's his connection? The mystery remains are supposed to be modern. Maitland's a medievalist, I think.'

'He advises on *Timeline*.'

'Ah, *that* connection.'

'He had a chat with Marnie's brother-in-law today. Wouldn't say anything specific, but he recited a poem.'

Fellheimer raised an eyebrow. 'A poem?'

Ralph rehearsed it under Fellheimer's quizzical gaze. 'Would you mind saying it again, Ralph.'

Ralph repeated it while Fellheimer listened, arms folded, eyes closed. At the end of the poem, Ralph waited while the Sheldonian Professor of Modern History brought his considerable intellect to bear on a piece of cryptic verse. He sat motionless, breathing steadily as if he had fallen asleep. After a time a smile spread slowly across his features and he opened his eyes.

'Of course, yes. It's quite obvious when you think about it.'

21
The man who wasn't there

On Friday morning Ralph knew it was partly a pretext when Marnie asked if she could join him for his morning walk. She said she needed some exercise and promised not to slow him down. They left Anne preparing breakfast and headed for the towpath. Ralph went on ahead, setting a strong pace. After five minutes of power walking Marnie realised her excuse was based on reality. She really was in need of exercise and was making a mental note to join a health club when Ralph slowed suddenly and spoke over his shoulder.

'Do you think she does fret about things, needs protecting?'

Marnie stumbled, trying not to crash into Ralph's back. 'Where did that come from?'

'You wanted to come on the walk to talk to me about something – I can guess what – and you didn't want Anne to hear. Is she so delicate she needs to be cocooned from everything?'

'I wanted to sleep on what you told me, what Guy Fellheimer had said. It seemed so improbable a theory, and yet you seemed to agree with him.'

'To the extent that it's a viable theory based on what we know at present, yes. Why not?' Ralph regained speed. 'We haven't much else to go on.'

'The man who wasn't there.'

'And the man who never was,' Ralph added.

'You think – or rather Guy thinks – Rufus Maitland was hinting at a connection.'

'What else could it be?'

'It could be a lot of things. He might've been thinking of ghosts or evil spirits, witches summoning up demons, black magic, er …' She had to pause to draw breath.

'Ghoulies and ghosties and long-leggedy beasties and things that go bump in the night,' Ralph contributed.

'It's not impossible.' Marnie managed to sound defensive and unconvinced at the same time.

'Probable impossible or possible improbable?'

Marnie's brain began overheating, in common with the rest of her. 'Look, Ralph, I know I promised not to slow you down, but –'

Ralph stopped abruptly, spun round and caught Marnie in his arms as she cannoned into his chest. He kissed her lightly on the lips. 'Come on, let's go back.'

Without the need to swing their arms, they were able to walk along together, holding hands.

'Ralph, tell me more about this man who wasn't there, I mean this man who never was.'

'Guy thinks it's worth exploring, as a possibility, at least. The point is, there seems to be a move on at the moment to get to the bottom of it all. Guy thinks Maitland knows something he's heard through his contacts with *Timeline*. They're being very secretive about it because they don't want the story to be leaked.'

'They need something big to keep themselves in the forefront,' Marnie said.

'Exactly. They've been criticised for being past their sell-by date. A revelation of this sort could breathe new life into the programme.'

'But if they just let it be known that they were onto something, wouldn't that stake out their claim, make it their territory, whet everyone's appetite?'

'I've been wondering about that. Perhaps they just want to spring a surprise, get the *wow* factor, as you might put it.'

'But, Ralph, they must know that's never going to happen. They won't be able to keep it a secret. They can't expect they'll be broadcasting the programme to a stunned audience. It's not like a daring new fashion kept under wraps – literally – like a new dress by Vivienne Westwood or John Galliano. Media people work on different programmes. They talk. Academics gossip. They drop hints, like Rufus Maitland has.'

'You're quite right, of course. There must be more to it.'

'But what? The story's fifty years old. How could it possibly be important now, after all this time?'

'It must have wider implications, Marnie.'

They crossed the canal bridge and walked along to *Sally Ann*, skirting round *X O 2* in the docking area. Anne came out on the stern deck to meet them.

'Well, did you have a good walk?'

'Fine.'

'Did you talk about whatever it was you didn't want me to hear?'

Ralph laughed. 'I'm going to have a quick shower while you bring Anne up to speed.'

Anne poured two mugs of coffee, set them down on the table in the saloon on *Sally Ann* and took her seat. Marnie sat opposite.

'Are you sitting comfortably?'

Anne nodded.

'Then I'll begin.'

Marnie began with Rufus Maitland talking to Paul in the pub and recited the poem about the man who wasn't there. She explained about the *Timeline* people trying to keep the lid on all information relating to the programme they were preparing.

'Okay so far?'

Anne had been concentrating hard. 'This has to do with which dig, the settlements one down here, or Sarah's grave? I don't quite get the connection.'

'I know how you feel. It's complicated, and I haven't even started to explain it all yet. Basically, *Timeline* are looking into witchcraft, so they're searching for evidence of witches down *here* and linking that with Sarah up *there*.'

'But we know for a fact that Sarah wasn't –'

'Okay, okay. But that's the connection. Ralph told Guy Fellheimer about the programme and the poem, and he came up with a theory linking the two together.'

Anne looked blank. 'How did he do that?'

Marnie breathed out audibly. 'He put two and two together and made five and three quarters.'

'That's why he's professor of history.'

'Probably.'

'So what's his theory?'

'He thinks it has to do with the Man Who Never Was.'

'The man on the stairs? But that's just a –'

'No, someone quite different, from the war.'

'Something to do with Roland Devere and the war memorial in the churchyard?'

'No. It's somehow to do with the grave. It seems rather obscure, but there was an incident in the war involving invasion plans being found on a body. Have you ever heard of that?'

Anne shook her head. 'Don't think so. We didn't do it at school, and I don't read military stuff.'

'There was a film about it – *The Man Who Never Was* – based on a true story. Here's the potted version, as told to Ralph by Fellheimer. The Germans occupied most of Europe, but the allies held North Africa and thought they could invade Europe from the south. Logically, it seems that meant attacking Italy via Sicily, so the Germans based huge forces there. The allies wanted to make them think they were going to attack through Greece or Sardinia. Okay so far?'

'Yep. To distract them.'

'Right. Someone came up with an idea to let secret invasion plans – false ones, obviously – fall into the hands of the enemy. So they got a man who'd died, invented a false identity for him, dressed him up in uniform and made it look as if he'd been killed in a plane crash in the sea off Spain. When his body was found on the beach, he had these plans on him and basically, it worked. The Germans pulled a lot of their forces out of Sicily and then the allies invaded it.'

'Couldn't the Germans have struck back at the allies in Sicily?'

'I think they thought it was just a tactical diversion. By the time they realised it was the real invasion, it was too late.'

'What happened to the man who never was, the body washed up in Spain?'

'He was buried in the local cemetery, apparently.'

Anne sat thinking, sipping her coffee. Eventually she spoke.

'It was a brilliant plan and a good story, but –'

'I know what you're going to say, Anne. What's it got to do with a village in Northamptonshire?'

'Yes. And if the man was buried in Spain, what's that got to do with the body in Sarah's grave?'

Marnie looked defeated. 'I know. I can't see it at all.'

'What does Ralph think?'

'He's open-minded about the whole thing. Since it's Guy Fellheimer's theory …' She shrugged.

'Ralph thinks Professor Fellheimer's such a brain-box, he ought at least to give him the benefit of the doubt?'

'I think that's a fair summary.'

'Well, I know I'm not in their league, but I really don't get it.'

Ralph arrived a few minutes later just as Marnie was pulling toast out from under the grill. Anne voiced her misgivings about the theory when they took their places at the table. Ralph gave her his full attention as if listening to a student reading an essay. When she finished, he hesitated before replying.

'You make a fair point, Anne, but there may be something you're missing. I believe Guy was – how do people put it these days? – thinking outside the box, thinking laterally. You see, it may be that the body in the grave is *loosely connected* with the man who never was, without actually *being* the man who never was, because that person – who of course did exist – is somewhere else. Therefore it isn't so much the *physical* presence that Guy is thinking about, as some other kind of relationship that connects the man who never was with the remains that we actually have. You see?'

Ralph reached for the marmalade, unaware of the exchange of baffled glances between Marnie and Anne. He was spooning marmalade out of the jar when Marnie began quietly chuckling. He looked up as Anne snorted. Within seconds Marnie and Anne were wiping their eyes, laughing helplessly and rocking in their chairs.

'What is it?' he asked innocently.

Marnie was the first to be able to speak.

'Well, I'm glad we got that little matter cleared up.'

Anne was in the loo when her mobile began ringing. With a sigh, she fumbled in her jeans pocket and pressed the green button.

'Hi, it's me.'

'Hi, Donovan. How are you? How's the foot?'

'Getting better.'

'Good. Well, your boat's okay and –'

'I didn't ring up about the boat. I wanted to talk to *you*.'

'Oh, yes. What about?'

'I suddenly just wanted to know how you were, what you were doing, *exactly* what you were doing. Tell me what you're wearing, where you are, at this precise moment. I want to see you in my imagination.'

Anne looked around her in the loo. 'Er, I'm in the office barn, er, light blue jeans, pink T-shirt. What was that sound in the background?'

'It's Uschi, laughing. She's watching a video.'

'At eight-thirty in the morning?'

'It's to help improve her English. She watches them a lot. Anyway, what were you saying?'

'I heard something funny this morning. Do you know the poem about the man on the stairs who wasn't there?'

'*He wasn't there again today, I wish to god he'd go away?*'

'That's the one, more or less. And have you ever heard of the man who never was?'

'Is this a conversation or are we playing trivial pursuit?'

'I'm serious. Have you?'

'Vaguely.'

'What does that mean?'

'I saw the film on TV ages ago, though I don't know how accurate it was, probably not very. Why?'

'It's been mentioned in connection with the archaeologists coming. I'll tell you about it when I see you. Any idea when that will be?'

'I'll try to make it soon.'

'Good. Look, I'd better go now.'

'Sure. I expect you're busy running the office, as usual, taking big decisions.'

'Something like that.'

Even after discarding the junk mail, the post was heavier than usual that Friday morning. Anne was sorting it into heaps – invoices, enquiries, banking – while Marnie started on her list of phone calls. The first was to Angela Hemingway.

'I've got some good news for you. Ralph spoke to his colleague, the one who did the research two years ago. You shouldn't have any problem convincing even the archdeacon that Sarah wasn't a witch.'

'Thanks, Marnie, but it may be too late. The bishop has sent for me. I'm just leaving now to go to Peterborough. I think he's going to tell me we can't move Sarah. The archdeacon has – I quote from the bishop's letter – *raised significant doubts as to the appropriateness of this action at the present time*.'

'It's a delaying tactic.'

'I know, but it's a very effective way of stopping us from going ahead, and it may take years before we get another chance. The church grinds exceeding slow.'

'Don't let it grind you down, Angela. Is the bishop open to persuasion?'

'He's basically on our side, but we have only someone's word to go on and –'

'What if you produced written proof from an unimpeachable source, a professor of history at Oxford?'

'Fellheimer?'

'That's the one. Ralph got the article that was published in the journal. It's here on my desk. You could take it with you.'

'I'm running late already but I'll –'

'Why don't I send Anne up with it? She can be with you in a few minutes.'

Anne was on her feet without any prompting and heading for the door with the journal when she turned, crossed to the photocopier and set to work. Marnie ended her call.

'You're copying it?'

Anne spoke without looking round. 'The bishop will probably want to keep the original for a while, and he's not the only one who needs to see it. I'm doing copies for our file, Binns and *Timeline*.'

Pulling out of Angela's road after delivering the journal, Anne had to wait while a small convoy of vans processed down the high street. She tagged on behind them and was surprised when they turned in through the field gate and took the track down to Glebe Farm. They formed up behind the HQ barn, where Dick Blackwood directed them. Anne drove past and went straight to the office after parking the Mini.

'We've got visitors, Marnie.'

'Who are they?'

'Archaeologists, I think. Dick's dealing with them.'

They went round to meet the newcomers and found them unloading equipment from the vans. Dick went over to Marnie as soon as she and Anne turned the corner.

'Sorry about this, Marnie. These are riggers from *Timeline*. Apparently, they want to set up cameras.'

'What, now? Today? I thought they weren't coming till next week.'

'They're not here to film. These are what they call *surveillance*.'

'Security cameras?'

'No. They stay in place to record everything that goes on. That's here and at all their various digs. They're remote controlled, just send back images for use whenever the producers want to show what's happening around the country.'

'Will they need a power supply?'

'That's just it. We can't let them share ours; we need it for our own stuff.'

'How many cameras?'

'Four, I think.'

Marnie looked at Anne, who shook her head. 'We haven't got any more extension cables.'

'I doubt that'd be a problem,' Dick said. 'But do you have any sockets they could use? And more to the point, are you happy about this? They'll be running or on stand-by all the time they're here.'

Marnie shrugged. 'We did agree to have them, can't back out now.'

Anne offered to talk to the riggers so that Marnie could get back to work. It was half an hour later before she returned to the office barn.

'Right. I think they're sorted out now.'

'You're a treasure, Anne.'

'You had no idea they were coming?'

'None at all. Did they say any more about what the cameras are for?'

'They don't say a lot, but they've put them up so they can see over the whole dig area. Dick says it's part of their style; they can switch from dig to dig around the country and compare what's going on. And they're controlled from a thing called an *OB* when it's on site.'

Marnie nodded. 'Outside Broadcast van. A lorry with a control centre inside. So what now?'

'That's it. We can just forget about them. The cameras are black and quite small, mounted at roof level or in trees. If you didn't know they were there, you'd probably never spot them.'

Marnie was grateful that for the rest of the day the smooth running of Walker & Co was able to proceed uninterrupted. She and Anne concentrated on their tasks, which in Anne's case included regular visits to the archaeologists with chilled water and to mop the occasional fevered brow on the crash pad.

When Anne made her daily trip to the post-box at four-thirty, her bundle of mail included copies of Fellheimer's article for DS Binns at the police station and Adam Lewisham, the programme researcher at *Timeline*. She felt confident there would be no more talk of Sarah Anne Day being involved in witchcraft.

Back at Glebe Farm, she saw Angela's Ford Escort parked beside the garage barn. In the office, Angela was standing beside Marnie's desk, talking in animated fashion.

'… so he's only doing it as a face-saver for the archdeacon, I think. Hallo, Anne.'

'Hi. Bad news?'

'No. Thanks to that article you brought me, the bishop's not going to stop us reburying Sarah.'

'So full steam ahead?'

'Not quite. He wants us to hold off while he conducts an investigation of the research.'

'What does that mean, in real terms?' Marnie asked.

'Not a lot. I think he just wants to have a word with Professor Fellheimer.'

'Who'll no doubt confirm the validity of his findings.'

'Yes, but it will mean the archdeacon's objections have been properly followed up, and a slight delay will allow time for things to cool off a little.'

'Good. Have you got time to stay for a cuppa? I want to tell you about a new development.'

Angela glanced at the clock. 'Quick one.'

'Okay. I want to tell you about a man.'

'I'm intrigued. Which man?'

'The man who never was.'

Angela grinned. 'I wish that was the archdeacon.'

Later that evening Anne was sitting on the giant bean-bag in her attic, reading. Music was playing quietly in the background – a tape borrowed from Marnie: Mozart's *Clarinet Concerto* – and she had lit a joss stick. After all the running around of the day, she was pleased to have some relaxing time to herself.

She was reading about the architecture of Le Corbusier and was becoming outraged at the sale by the state of the apartments and shops in his housing unit in Marseille, when the phone began ringing in the office below. Anne had turned the rapid descent of the wall-ladder into an art form and she was out of the bean-bag and at her desk before the answerphone cut in.

'Guess what, I'm bored again.'

'Danny! You *can't* be bored. This is the subject you've chosen to study for the next three *years*.'

'Oh gawd. It's all right for you, Anne. You *like* your subject. I bet you even read your course books for relaxation.' No reply. 'Anne? You do, don't you? I get it. That's what you're doing right now, isn't it?'

'I'm ... listening to music.'

'Anne Price, look me straight in the eye and tell me you're not reading a serious study book.'

'We're talking on the phone, Danny, I can hardly –'

'Huh!'

'Danny, I'd invite you to come up for the weekend, but we just freak you out. You think we're all *spooky*!' She made an exaggerated *woo-woo* sound that turned into a snort of laughter.

'No I don't.'

'Look me straight in the bloodshot eye and tell me –'

Danny screamed and laughed simultaneously. It was quite an achievement, though she nearly choked. When her coughing spasm faded she gradually regained the power of speech.

'I don't think you're spooky, Anne, or Marnie and Ralph, or your friends. I really don't.'

'You're welcome to come for the weekend if you'd like to.'

'Anything happening up there?' Danny tried not to sound wary. 'Anybody else around?'

'Nope. Just the three of us. We're hoping to have a quiet weekend before the onslaught.'

'The *what?*'

'*Timeline*. They're coming next week to begin filming. They've already installed some special cameras.'

'That sounds interesting. Just the three of you, you said?'

'Want to make it a foursome?'

'Usual time, usual place.'

22
Offence

Saturday fulfilled its promise. Anne collected Danny from the bus station, and mid-morning it was already hot and sunny. The newspapers had exhausted all the permutations of *Phew! What a scorcher!* headlines, and the media were talking about record temperatures and sunshine.

Within less than an hour of donning her bikini, Anne was forced to retreat to the shelter of the spinney to prevent herself from turning into a lobster. Dolly came to recline beside her sunlounger, while Anne read the latest issue of *Domus* magazine. Danny the sun-worshipper managed another half hour before she too moved into the shade.

After a short stint in her bikini, Marnie pulled on a T-shirt and disappeared on board *Sally Ann* to emerge minutes later with iced lemonade that she had made the evening before. Ice cubes were chinking in the tall glasses as she handed them round and joined Ralph under the parasol.

In a half-whisper Danny murmured. 'Amazing. Even Ralph's taking it easy, but I bet that's a textbook he's reading.'

Anne surprised Danny by calling out. 'Ralph, what's that you're reading?'

'It's a book on the overheating of economies in the Far East.'

Danny sighed.

Anne grinned and announced proudly, 'Most of the books he reads have got sub-titles two lines long.'

Danny tried not to snigger.

Anne added, 'And most of them are by people he knows.' She raised her voice. 'Who wrote that book, Ralph?'

'I did.'

Danny was incredulous. 'But if you wrote it, why d'you need to read it?'

'Partly for pleasure, partly to reassess my conclusions.'

Danny sipped her drink and slumped back on the recliner. 'You know, Anne, I wonder if I'm really cut out for university.'

Anne turned towards her friend. 'Look on the bright side. It's not all about lepers' graves, burnings and hangings, is it?'

Danny sighed. 'No. There is that to be said for sociology, I suppose.'

On Sunday afternoon, after a supine morning and a lunch of melon, Greek salad and yogurt with honey, they took *Sally Ann* for a tootle. The countryside looked parched and, for all the fine weather, few boats had ventured out in the heat of the day. They travelled for an hour before tying up under a tree for iced coffee.

Danny took the tiller for the homeward run and made a major effort to improve her steering. Anne stood watch beside her, giving moral support and the occasional nudge. Danny rarely strayed from mid-channel and felt pleased with herself as she handed the helm back to Marnie for docking, while Anne walked the gunwale to secure the fore end alongside *Thyrsis*.

As they cleared the footbridge, Anne turned and waved back to attract attention. She pointed ahead. Marnie, Ralph and Danny craned their necks to see what had aroused her interest. Standing on the bank between *Thyrsis* and *X O 2*, they saw Dick Blackwood and Celia Devere in animated conversation.

Dick broke away to take a rope from Ralph and help make *Sally Ann* fast. With their heads close together, Ralph spoke quietly.

'Is there a problem?'

Dick glanced round and saw Celia talking to Marnie. 'It's absurd. Celia's got her undies in a tangle over absolutely nothing. One minute she was just asking about progress, the next she's saying we've ditched her. *Crazy*.'

'Let's see if we can build bridges.' Ralph walked across *Thyrsis* and stepped ashore. 'Celia, hallo. Nice to see you. We weren't expecting you this afternoon, were we?'

'No. Er, Dick rang and said he was coming down to check things over before the dig tomorrow.'

'I wanted everything to be ship-shape,' Dick explained, 'with *Timeline* coming.'

'You're always punctilious about everything,' Marnie said.

Celia made a small sound that might have signified dissent.

'Is everything ship-shape?' Ralph asked Dick.

'Yeah, seems to be. One or two edges could be straighter, but I'll get the students onto that first thing, before the TV bods get going.'

Marnie turned to Celia. 'Did you come for something in particular? You're always welcome, of course –'

'I just wanted to know what was going on.' Celia sounded miffed.

Marnie was taken aback. 'Going on?'

'No one tells me anything these days. It was originally *our* dig, after all, before it got taken over and we got sidelined.'

'But I thought you said Dick rang you up.'

'What? Well, yes, in a way.'

'I rang Celia to let her know we'd be filling in Sarah's grave temporarily –'

'I wasn't happy to be *informed*. I would expect to be *consulted*.'

Dick spread his hands. 'We got a message from the bishop's office that the reburial was being delayed pending further investigations. We couldn't just leave the grave open like that.'

Celia looked exasperated. 'I would've thought the diocesan authorities would contact *us*, as owners of the land.'

'They are,' Dick said.

'They haven't.'

'No, but they're sending you a letter, a *formal* letter, if you like.'

'Then why did they tell you first?'

'It was urgent. They want the grave filled in before filming starts. We've got to get it done first thing Monday morning.'

'We could have told Henry Tutt to throw the soil back in. I don't see what –'

'Celia, it's a possible crime scene and an archaeological site as well as being a disturbed grave. It has to be treated differently from a normal grave. The bishop and the police want it handled by archaeologists. We'll record its condition then put down a membrane to protect the inside before backfilling.'

Celia scowled. 'And what's this about cameras being set up?'

'I'll show you them, Celia. *Timeline* only installed them on Friday.'

'But why wasn't I informed about them officially?'

Dick looked from Marnie to Ralph, at a loss to understand the situation.

Marnie came to his rescue. 'They just turned up, Celia. No one had told us, either. But it's what they always do, apparently.'

'These television people think they can do what they like.'

Dick made a gesture towards the spinney. 'Would you like me to show you them?'

A curt shake of the head from Celia. 'No thank you.'

'All right then, I'd better be getting along. I've still got things to check on the dig. See you tomorrow.'

For a few seconds there was an awkward silence as they watched Dick walk away. Marnie was the first to speak.

'Celia, I don't think any slight was intended by anyone. People are just getting on with their jobs. I'm sure they aren't being discourteous to you personally.'

'It's not just me, Marnie.'

'Your husband is unhappy about how things are being handled?'

'Well, no, not Hugh so much. But Marcus is getting very agitated about the whole thing.'

'Marcus?' Ralph said.

'My father-in-law. It's really getting under his skin.'

'There is a lot of upheaval, of course,' Marnie said. 'Older people can find things like that unsettling.'

'He was muttering about it only yesterday. I wouldn't be surprised if he went into a decline over it all. He's not well, you know. He's got some condition, with a long name.'

Marnie looked thoughtful. 'Perhaps it might be wise in the circumstances to hold off with your redecoration for a while. That's going to be much more disruptive than the dig going on down here.'

'It's not *this* dig that's bothering him, Marnie. He's hardly aware of anything happening down here.'

'What then?'

'The *grave site*, of course. It is on our land, after all. Imagine how unsettling that is for him, digging up that old witch –'

'She was only twenty-three, Celia, and she wasn't a –'

'All right, but you know what I mean. It's still a disturbed grave. Marcus is very agitated about it.'

'On religious grounds?' Ralph suggested. 'I believe you're church-goers.'

'Only me. Hugh doesn't do religion, but Marcus is RC.'

'The Deveres are catholics?'

'Of course. Hugh's lapsed, but the old boy has a visit from a priest once a month. Not that he's got anything to confess, I'd imagine, at his age.'

Celia declined the offer of tea and took her leave. Marnie walked with her through the spinney.

'All this will be over in a few weeks, Celia, then life will settle back to normal.'

'*Normal*? We've got a disturbed grave to be sorted out, a hideous burial ceremony to go through, an investigation into an unsolved murder and witchcraft going on in the woods.'

Marnie laughed gently. 'Since you put it like that …'

Celia glared at her and then, slowly, relaxed. 'There is also the other thing.'

'I'd really like you to look forward to having the house redecorated, Celia. It'll be beautiful when it's finished, and it won't take very long. You'll love it.'

'I didn't mean that. I suppose I'm feeling distraught because Hugh told me he'd be away on business for a couple of days again this coming week.'

'Norwich?'

'You guessed.'

'It's a major centre for business.'

'And – more to the point – we have a cottage not far from there. Very convenient.'

'Sorry about that Celia business, Danny.' Anne waited until she had reached the dual carriageway that evening before starting the conversation. 'I didn't know *she* was going to turn up. Celia Devere always spoils the atmosphere.'

'Oh no. I enjoyed that bit. She's amazing, looks just like Princess Di. Having her around must be like living in a soap opera.'

'A soap opera? Well, she's never dull, that's for sure.' Anne laughed and glanced sideways at her friend. 'Does she qualify as another weirdo?'

'Yeah, but I can manage that sort. Is she rich?'

'Probably.'

'She acts like she owns everything. Does she live in a big manor house?'

'Yes, Knightly Court. It's gorgeous: beautiful house, beautiful grounds.'

'Anne, I've had a great weekend.'

'But we didn't do anything.'

'So what? I can't wait for the next episode.'

23
Timeline

Monday began like any other working day, but changed dramatically at nine when the archaeologists arrived. Anne went out to check they had everything they needed, as usual. It was another bright sunny morning. At the farmhouse, Bob and a carpenter were carrying timber through the doorway, chatting about the works. Anne was calling *hallo* when she saw something that stopped her dead.

Beyond the buildings and reaching up above the treetops stood a monster, a huge dinosaur rearing up over the land. Anne blinked and took one step backwards, mouth open. Seeing her, the builders put down their load and rushed over.

'What's up, Anne?'

She pointed. The three of them watched in amazement as the thing turned its head in their direction. It was a giant crane, taller and somehow more sinister than anything Anne had ever seen before. In the platform on top they could now make out two men, tiny figures operating a camera.

'What the hell,' Bob began.

'It's them. It must be. *Timeline*.'

As they stared up at the sky, a helicopter buzzed past the dinosaur and circled over the site. Through a gap in its side they saw a camera protruding.

Bob was still muttering. 'It's like the *War of the bloody Worlds*.'

'*Day of the bloody Triffids*,' Anne agreed.

At the HQ barn, Anne found the students grouped round the Land Rovers and minibus, looking upwards, hands shading their eyes, a colony of meerkats at full stretch. In the middle of the group, Dick was clapping his hands for attention.

'Come on! Come on! Gotta get going. Let's show these TV types how real archaeologists work.'

While the students went for their equipment, Dick turned to Anne. 'Morning! I'll swear some of this lot are wearing eye make-up and blusher.' He chuckled. 'And I wouldn't put it past some of the girls, either.'

Anne grinned. 'What about the grave site?'

'Got a team up there already, dropped 'em off on the way in.'

Returning to the office barn, Anne found her way converging with a man. He looked like one of the archaeologists, but she had not seen him before.

'Hi! Are you looking for Dick Blackwood and the others? Their barn's round the corner.'

'Marnie Walker,' he replied. 'I was told her office was opposite the cottages. Are you from the dig?'

'No. I'm with Marnie. You're pointing in the right direction.'

In the office the stranger extended a hand to Marnie and introduced himself as Rufus Maitland, consultant on the *Timeline* project.

'I just wanted to come and say hallo. You probably know of me.'

Marnie held his gaze. 'I don't think we've met.'

'No, but I know your brother-in-law, Paul Sutton. We're both at UCL.'

'Right.'

'And Steve Ellington, of course. He's a colleague. I believe you and he were … seeing each other for a time?'

'Yes.'

'I thought you might've heard of me.'

'Possibly. So you're here with *Timeline*?'

'Just for today, initially. I may be back later in the dig, depending on what they find.'

'Are you an expert on witchcraft?'

'Not exactly. Medieval monasticism is my current area of research.'

'What do you hope – or should I say, *expect* – to find round here?'

Maitland smiled and shrugged. 'You can never be quite sure.'

'But you must have some idea, presumably. I mean, you don't just go around the country digging holes in the ground, hoping for evidence of witches, do you? Or are you specifically interested in Sarah Anne Day?'

'That's a good question.'

Marnie waited, still looking Maitland in the eye. He seemed to find the experience uncomfortable.

'Well, we have some background evidence, research findings and so on. The rest, we'll have to wait and see. That's what makes it so interesting.'

'I hope you find what you're looking for.'

Anne watched this exchange without speaking, sitting at her desk going through the morning's post. Marnie escorted Maitland to the door and watched him walk past the windows. She stood thinking in the doorway for a while before turning back to her desk.

'You do know about him, don't you, Marnie? He's the one who said the poem about the man on the stairs, isn't he?'

'Yes.'

'But you didn't want him to know that Paul had been talking about their conversation?'

'Partly that.'

'What else, if you don't mind me asking?'

'A lot of people seem to know more about what's going on in Knightly St John than they say. I think the less I tell them, the better.'

'Why do you think he's here? Isn't it just to see how the dig goes, like he said?'

'You know, Anne, I'm not sure even he knows what's going on. The question is, who does?'

By the end of the morning Anne could contain her curiosity no longer. She announced that she was going to do the post run earlier than usual and take the opportunity to look in on the grave site. Two Land Rovers in the green and yellow livery of *Timeline* passed her coming down the field track. In the first, she caught a glimpse of one of the programme's presenters, a strikingly attractive young woman who had become a national icon.

The high street reminded her of war films. *Timeline* vehicles were spread along the road like an invading army. A cluster of people stood outside the churchyard gate, surrounded by boxes of equipment. Passing them, she caught a snatch of conversation.

'... inconclusive, so Terry wants to open up four or five more test pits.'

'Why not open up a trench and have done with it?'

'That'll come later.'

Anne posted the letters and turned to enter the shop as two men walked out. One of them was Rufus Maitland, the other a tall, rangy figure with white hair, dressed all in black. She recognised him as the programme's lead presenter, a professor from somewhere, but she could not recall his name. Neither man noticed her, so intent were they on their discussion.

Anne went direct to the post office cubicle and asked Richard Appleton for a pack of one hundred first class stamps. His wife, Molly, came over, eyes sparkling.

'Did you see them, Anne? That was Barny Guthrie.'

'Who?'

'The professor on *Timeline*. He's very famous, lovely voice, very polite.'

'Oh, yes. Professor Guthrie.'

'He was being pestered by that other one. Don't know who he was, haven't seen him on the programmes.'

'How was he pestering him?'

'Well, he kept his voice down, so it was hard to tell, but I did hear him say something like, *Sooner or later it's got to come out.*'

'What's got to come out? What did Professor Guthrie say?'

'I couldn't hear very much. People in the shop, talking. It sounded like, *that's not for us to decide*.'

Anne wondered about what Molly had said as she walked through the churchyard and pushed open the gate in the wall leading into Martyrs Close. Yellow tape still marked off Sarah's grave, but there was no longer a policeman on guard. Instead, Dick Blackwood was talking with Celia Devere, pointing at the grave. He broke off as Anne approached.

Celia turned and gave her the briefest of smiles. She was dressed in fawn slacks and safari shirt with a matching silk neckerchief that once again made her look like the star of a Hollywood blockbuster.

'Hallo. Sorry. Didn't mean to interrupt, just came to see how things were going up here.'

'Nothing is going up here.' Celia's voice had an edge to it.

Clang! Anne thought. Dick looked as if he was less than pleased that Anne had encouraged Celia to express her opinion.

'Right. I'll, er, leave you to it, then.'

Anne glanced at Sarah's grave. It was now covered with a dark grey tarpaulin, secured with tent pegs. She was turning to go when Celia spoke.

'Tell Marnie I'll be down to see her later on, will you?'

'Okay.'

Anne walked off. The maid had been sent on her way.

Back at Glebe Farm, Anne entered the office to find Marnie on the phone.

'Sure, Beth, it is very interesting, but *totally* disruptive.'

She listened some more.

'No, it's not their fault. They get on with their work. It's just so fascinating, I have to go out every now and then to see what's happening. Now, it's like a film set out there, all these famous faces in our little village. It's hard to concentrate on the job in hand.'

When Marnie ended the conversation she looked across at Anne. 'All okay?'

'Yes. Had a look at Sarah's grave. It's all wrapped up like a parcel. The good news is, I got the stamps we needed.'

'And?' Marnie looked suspicious.

'*Madam* gave me a message to pass on.'

'Celia? No doubt she was standing guard over *her* grave site?'

Anne nodded. 'Not so good news: she's coming down to see you later on.'

Marnie reflected. 'Thank you, my girl. No reply. You may return to polishing the silver in the pantry with the under-valet.'

'Yes'm. Forgive me if I don't manage a curtsy. My apron seems to have got tangled up in my computer.'

Marnie and Anne escaped to the sanctuary of *Sally Ann* for a sandwich lunch. Ralph joined them from *Thyrsis*. While they ate, Anne outlined what she had heard that morning.

'What could it all mean?' she asked.

Marnie shook her head. 'It could mean anything.'

Ralph swallowed. 'I think there are some indications. First, we can see there's more going on than just the *Timeline* dig and the university excavations.'

'It doesn't tell us much, though, does it? Or are you going to give us one of your impenetrable insights?'

Ralph pretended to ignore the question. 'Second, we can deduce that some of the people here know what is going on in the background.'

'Who?'

'That's the question. Obviously, Rufus Maitland *isn't* one of them.'

'So who does know?'

'The *Timeline* people,' Anne cut in. 'They must.'

Ralph nodded. 'I think you're right, but in my view, it can only be a few of them.'

'Professor Guthrie? He's the top man on the programmes.'

Ralph raised a finger. 'Guthrie's the top man *in front of* the cameras. The producer's the top person overall. He'll know what's going on.'

'What about Rob Cardew?' Marnie asked.

'No. Neither Rob nor his wife has a clue, I'm sure of that, even though her work is at the heart of the investigation.'

'Which means that someone else in the background is setting the agenda. Who could that be?'

Ralph folded his arms. 'Someone at a higher level than Guthrie or anyone else at *Timeline*.'

'Do you think Celia knows the whole story?'

'I very much doubt it. If she had the slightest idea, she'd be regaling us with tantalising snippets to show that she was in the know.'

'We're up against a brick wall with no way of getting any further.'

Ralph looked thoughtful. 'Not quite. We do have a secret weapon.'

'Oh?'

'Professor Fellheimer,' Anne chipped in. 'He might come up with something.'

Ralph smiled. 'Perhaps. We shall see.'

That evening Anne lay on her bed reading about Le Corbusier and his grand designs while Vivaldi and a sandalwood joss stick kept her company. Marnie and Ralph had gone for a drink in the village pub.

When Danny rang on the mobile, Anne settled in for a chat.

'Celia didn't show up in the end, probably retired to her tower in the north wing of the castle with an attack of the vapours.'

Danny laughed. 'Probably waiting for her Sir Galahad.'

'No, he's apparently away on *so-called business* with his floozy, or should that be trollop?'

Danny hooted. 'Anne! Are you kidding?'

'That's what Celia says.'

'She tells *you* that kind of thing?' Incredulous.

'No. She entrusted it to Marnie, valuing her discretion and on pain of death –'

'Naturally.'

'I heard about it when Marnie told Ralph. He then wrote it down and sent it to the editor of the *News of the World*. I made that bit up.'

'Soap opera – I *told* you!'

'So presumably you'll be booking your usual penthouse suite for the weekend?'

'How about Wednesday?'

The conversation had been over for barely five minutes when the mobile chirped again. Donovan.

'You've got a better social life than I have. Every time I try to phone you, your line's busy.'

'It was Danny wanting the latest news on the hotline to the stars. Anyway, how are you? *Mutti* gone home yet?'

'Uschi went Saturday. She was a great help, but, ah, the freedom!'

'Are you hobbling?'

'I can manage without a stick most of the time. Do I take it you've got the TV people there?'

'They're all over the village. Danny's coming up on Wednesday for a few days to gawp.'

'Wednesday?'

'Why?'

'I was wondering ...'

'Are you fit enough to travel?'

'Thought I might come up, see you for a day or two, then bring the boat back at the weekend. Would I be in the way?'

They agreed to meet at the station at ten o'clock.

24
Fame

On Tuesday morning at nine o'clock sharp, Marnie found her thoughts straying to Celia Devere and her eyes straying to the phone. She looked across the office at Anne.

'Didn't you give me a message that Celia would be coming to see me yesterday afternoon?'

Anne looked puzzled. 'That's right. It was delivered by the under-chambermaid, I seem to recall.'

Marnie smiled. 'I'm sure she doesn't really think of you like that.'

'Of course not. She just treats me that way.'

By mid-morning there was still no word from Celia. Anne went out on her rounds with the chilled water and spotted Dick Blackwood in the HQ barn talking to – or rather being talked *at* by – Suzi Fraser-Jones, the *Timeline* assistant producer. Poor bloke, she thought, constantly being hectored by forceful women. She passed by with a friendly wave.

'Anne!' Suzi called out. She abandoned Dick and strode towards Anne.

'All going well?' Anne asked.

'Great, great. Is Marnie about?'

'In the office, trying to meet a deadline.'

'Good. I'll need a minute or two if she could spare it.'

'Lunchtime, perhaps?'

Suzi checked her watch and clipboard.

'Earlier if possible. It won't take long. *God*, I'm running behind.' She spoke rapidly. 'Anne, could you please just say we'd like some shots of local people – herself, you, anyone else from Glebe Farm – a little later in the week. Also, I may ask her to do a short interview on camera with Barny, depending on what we find. Could you do that?'

'Sure.'

'Great. See you later.'

Suzi turned and sped off, pulling the mobile from her pocket. Dick came over, breathing out audibly between his teeth.

'Everything all right?' Anne asked. She could guess the reply.

'Wonderful.' Dick's tone was not overly enthusiastic.

'You've got problems? Sorry. Silly question. Every time I see you, you're being harangued by some woman or other.'

'You should've seen me yesterday.'

'I did, up at the grave site.'

'No, down here, later in the afternoon. We nearly had a mutiny, or a *riot*.'

'Whatever happened?'

Dick looked pained at the memory. 'You know how hot it's been …'

Anne waggled the water container. He continued.

'When it got to afternoon break time, some of the students began packing up to come down.'

'Clear up your loose?' Anne suggested.

'Yeah, only we aren't shouting that at present. It interferes with the soundtrack of the filming. So they kept an eye on the time and cleared up for their break. They were gasping. Next thing, they're told to get back in their pits by the TV people. They needed them to stay for *continuity*. With a few groans they got back to work, some of them putting on sunhats – it was nearly forty degrees up there. *Take off the hats*, they were told.'

'Continuity again?'

'Yep. So we had one girl pass out in her pit and another one threw up in hers.'

'I bet the TV people got the message then.'

'Oh yeah, they were very concerned, concerned that their filming was ruined.'

'What?'

'You heard me right. The students just abandoned their test pits and came down here to protest to me. To *me*! I thought they were going to walk off, go up to the pub or something.'

'Did they?'

'No. I managed to pacify them, said it wouldn't happen again.'

'You did well.'

'Not according to Suzi Fraser-Jones. She then came down and gave me a right earful for letting them desert their posts. Honestly!'

'What did you do?'

'When they got their break I told them they had to wear sunhats and carry water bottles with them at all times, sunblock too.'

'Good idea. I'd better keep out of the way so as not to spoil their shooting. I'll leave supplies of water in the HQ barn instead.'

'Oh no, they want you in view.'

'Me?'

'Sure. *Timeline* want shots of you taking water round. You're extra atmosphere on the dig, local colour.'

'Fame at last.'

'Fame is a fickle mistress, Anne.'

Anne smiled ruefully. 'Not your day.'

'Oh no, the Celia episode ended all right. I had to tell her *she'd* be wanted for an interview, too.'

'I bet she liked that.'

'Absolutely. She set off immediately to buy clothes, muttered something about staying overnight in London.'

After she had completed the water run, Anne explained Celia's absence the previous day to Marnie. They were pondering the hardship of having to decide what the well-dressed *châtelaine* wore for an interview on television, when one of the students appeared in the office. They had run out of milk and the tea-drinkers were gasping.

Anne offered her a litre of semi-skimmed, and she departed, pledging that it would be replaced later that day. When the student left, Marnie looked thoughtful.

'You know, Anne, I'm wondering if it would make sense to take a break sooner rather than later and catch up after they've gone. It's hard to settle down to work here with all this going on.'

'Should I put Danny off?'

'No. Let her come, but we may have to be flexible. D'you think she'd understand?'

'No probs. We're just one big soap opera to her.'

25
Pendant

'Keep an eye out for traffic wardens, Danny.' Anne scanned the car park in front of the station. 'They travel about on mopeds and strike like paratroops.'

It was Wednesday morning, and Anne met Danny from the coach before crossing to the railway station to meet Donovan. She double-parked immediately opposite the main entrance where they had a strategic view of every coming and going. Danny nudged Anne as a crowd of people issued out from the concourse.

'What does he look like, your boy- … er, Donovan?'

'Blonde hair, slight build. He'll be dressed in black, maybe dark grey.'

'How d'you know that?'

'Just guessing.'

Another nudge. 'Looks like you're right. Could that be him?'

Donovan emerged from the station and looked around. Anne waved. He nodded before setting off across the road. Predictably he was wearing grey jeans and a black shirt, the edge of a white T-shirt visible at the open neck. He was carrying a black hold-all and walked more slowly than usual.

'He's not as tall as I expected, not bad looking, though. His colouring's like yours.' Danny laughed. 'Pale and interesting.'

Donovan insisted he would be fine in the back of the Mini, but Anne noticed that he winced when climbing in and sat with his legs stretched out across the footwell as they travelled back to Glebe Farm.

Anne had deliberately left the lorry tarpaulin in place so that Donovan could see how well *X O 2* had been concealed. The three of them unrolled it together and stacked it on the bank. Once Donovan had dumped his hold-all on board and opened all the windows and doors, Anne suggested a tour of the dig sites. First, they headed for the office barn to leave Danny's pink hold-all in the loft. They turned the corner to find an Audi convertible in the courtyard.

'Uh-oh.' Anne pulled a face.

'What is it?' Danny asked.

'Soap opera time.'

'That belongs to your Princess Di look-alike?'

'You guessed.' Anne turned to Donovan. 'The *Lady of the Manor* is paying us a call.'

'Not your favourite person?' Donovan said.

'She acts like she owns the place, keeps insisting that Sarah was a witch, has to be the centre of attention at all times and treats *me* like a scullery maid.'

'Apart from that?'

'She's charming.'

'And she really does look like Princess Di,' Danny added.

They dropped the hold-all in the office and walked round to the HQ barn. Celia was holding court at the edge of the field, surrounded by *Timeline* people, listening attentively to Crispin Wade, the producer, who was pointing towards the slopes. It was obvious from the expressions on the faces of the TV crew that they regarded Celia as a gift from the gods. They were already working out which were her best angles and they were spoilt for choice. Standing there in a royal blue silk knee-length dress, Celia could feel the camera lenses aching to zoom in on her. She looked happy and relaxed.

Marnie, standing a little outside the charmed circle, wearing her everyday office clothes of shirt and jeans, spotted Anne and her friends and came over.

'Hi. Nice to have you back, Danny. Donovan, glad you could make it. Feeling better?'

'One day at a time.'

'Good.'

Anne canted her head slightly and spoke in a whisper. 'We're about to be honoured.'

Marnie waited until Celia spoke before turning round. 'I'm sorry I didn't get down to see you yesterday, Marnie, as I hoped. Something urgent came up.'

'That's all right. I had plenty to keep me occupied. You know Danny, of course, but I don't believe you've met our friend Donovan.'

'Hallo.' Celia smiled. 'Are you an archaeologist, too?'

'No.'

In the absence of further elaboration, Marnie explained.

'Donovan had an accident, injured his foot, so we offered to take care of the boat until he was fit enough to come for it.'

'I'm so sorry.' Celia oozed sympathy. 'Are you better now?'

'Much.'

'So you fancied a trip to see the filming?'

'No. I just came for my boat.'

'Ah, yes, of course, only I've noticed that whenever TV cameras appear they always attract their share of onlookers and hangers-on.'

Donovan continued looking straight at Celia. He said nothing. Marnie broke the silence again.

'Oh, that's all right, Celia. You're welcome to come down at any time, you know that.'

Celia struggled visibly to maintain her composure. Danny had a sudden coughing spasm, giving Anne the opportunity to dash to the HQ barn to fetch a cup of water. Donovan remained impassive, though he flicked an admiring glance at Marnie, who took Celia's arm and led her off to visit the dig.

Danny spluttered trying to drink the water, while Anne bent beside her, doubled-up in silent laughter.

'Nice one, Marnie,' Donovan muttered under his breath, watching the two women rounding the corner of the HQ barn.

Danny straightened up, gasping, a grin splitting her face in two. 'Whoo! That was good.' Seeing Anne's expression, Danny lowered her voice. 'You're not afraid of her, are you?'

'She's a client, a pain in the butt, but still a client.'

'Sorry.'

'No harm done. So what shall we do?'

Donovan shrugged. 'I'm easy.'

'Danny?'

'Let's go and see the dig.'

Archaeology is usually about patiently digging, shovelling and trowelling for hours or even days on end, picking up tiny apparently insignificant objects, each one a clue to something in the big picture. That day was an exception. Celia and Marnie barely had time to reach the first test pit when one of the older archaeologists set his trowel aside and knelt on the ground. He carefully parted the soil with his fingers, lifted something from the earth and laid it in the palm of his hand. It glinted as the sun reflected off a shiny surface.

'What's that you've got, Michael?' A girl student walked over to inspect his find.

Between thumb and forefinger he held it against the skin below her throat to admire it, before letting her hold it.

The girl tilted it to catch the light. 'Is it gold?'

'Possibly gold gilt, a pendant, I think. It suits you.' He smiled as she gave it back to him.

'Who does it belong to?' Celia held out a hand. 'May I see?' She examined it, turning the object over with exquisitely manicured fingers. 'It's a fleur-de-lys, isn't it?'

The archaeologist agreed. 'It has a loop at the top, you see, where a fine necklace passed through.'

'How old would it be?'

'Could be thirteenth or fourteenth century. That design was popular around then.'

Celia turned it over in her hand. 'Do you think it belonged to the lady of the manor?'

'That isn't the right question,' Donovan said.

'Oh?' Celia frowned. 'What is?'

'What was she doing down here?'

'Ah, yes. What would a lady of quality be doing in a place like this, a muddy farm?'

'Perhaps she had an assignation with someone from the farm,' Danny suggested.

'Archaeology isn't about guessing games.' No one had noticed Dick Blackwood arriving on the scene. 'It's about facts and evidence.'

'We don't even know if there was a farm here at that time,' Donovan said.

'Exactly, though it is quite possible. We need more evidence and to get that, we need to get back to digging. Come on, everybody!' Dick clapped twice. 'Come on!' Lowering his voice, he said to Celia. 'Can I have that, please.'

'What will happen to it?' She handed it over, as the archaeologists went back to work.

'It's got to be bagged, logged and put with the other finds.' Dick looked at Donovan. 'I don't think we've met. Are you with *Timeline*?'

'No. I'm just a friend.'

'It's hard to know who's who these days, with so many people around. I'm Dick Blackwood, site director.'

'Donovan Smith.'

They shook hands.

In the OB van a technician adjusted the view from one of the surveillance cameras. It was mounted on the end of the barn, giving a clear shot of the group gathered round the fleur-de-lys. Although there was no sound feed available, the pictures told their own story: the precise moment when a find was made; colleagues, including the beautiful lady, clustered together in discussion; a flash of sunlight on gold; the site director ordering the archaeologists back to work; a congratulatory handshake for one of the team. It was a perfect episode.

Marnie had managed to extricate herself from the visiting party and had retreated to the office, where she was able to work uninterrupted for over half an hour before Anne put her head round the door and suggested a tea break by the water.

When Marnie came through the spinney, she found Celia seated at the table under the parasol with Dick Blackwood. Anne had made lemon tea. Danny was arranging biscuits on plates. Marnie did not recognise the type, but they looked appetising.

'Donovan brought these,' Anne said, pouring tea. 'They're German.'

'Thanks, Donovan. They look nice.'

'You're welcome. They're good at biscuits in Germany. My aunt brought these over, thought I'd share them.'

'It's like a teddy bear's picnic,' Celia said, smiling. She turned to Dick. 'And we'll have no talk about witches or anything unsavoury to spoil the occasion.'

Dick smiled innocently. 'I wasn't going to talk about anything of the sort.'

'Good. Tea-time would be spoilt if we started on about witches being burnt at the stake and so on.'

'They weren't burnt at the stake,' Anne corrected her.

'I'm glad to hear it.' Celia accepted a biscuit.

'Anne's right,' Dick confirmed.

'Splendid.' Celia nibbled.

'They were hanged in England, weren't they?' Danny looked pleased with her knowledge.

'Or drowned,' Dick added.

Celia's smile was fading rapidly. 'Really?'

'Really.' Dick drank his tea.

Danny looked doubtful. 'I've never heard that before.'

'Would that have anything to do with ducking stools?' Anne asked.

'Stop!' Celia held up her hands. 'I thought we'd agreed we weren't going to talk about such things. They're *horrible*.'

'Your biscuits are really good.' Marnie attempted to change the subject. 'These have a kind of vanilla flavour.'

'*Kipferl*.'

Everyone looked at Donovan as if he had landed from Mars.

'They're called *Kipferl*,' he explained. 'That's their name, sometimes *Vanilla Kipferl*.'

They sampled the *Kipferl* in a silence that was appreciative but awkward. The conversation had been fractured by Celia's intervention.

'Er …' Dick hesitated.

Celia shot him a warning glance.

'I was only going to say –'

'Nothing about witches, I hope.' Her tone was ice cold.

'Well, what if I told you an *amusing* story about them?'

'Is such a thing possible?'

'Trust me.'

'I don't know.'

Marnie was not happy that Celia appeared to think she could dictate what was discussed at the table, *her* table, where Celia was a guest.

'Perhaps,' she began. 'Perhaps it might prick the bubble, make the subject less of a taboo, less intimidating?'

Celia frowned. 'I think –'

'What harm could it do?' Marnie smiled. 'Hm?'

'Go on, Dick,' Danny flashed him an encouraging smile. 'Tell us your funny witch story.'

Celia drank her tea without looking up.

'Okay. It happened in this very county, actually. That's what made me think of it. A woman was accused of being a witch, denounced by other people in her village. The lord of the manor agreed she should be put to the trial.'

'I don't think I'm going to like this story,' Celia murmured.

Dick continued. 'It was decided that she'd undergo ordeal by water.'

'A ducking stool?' Danny suggested.

'No, in the river.'

'How does that work?'

'The idea is, you throw the accused witch into the river. Remember, most people couldn't swim in those days. If she drowned, that proved she wasn't a witch but a normal human being.'

'Too bad that she's dead,' Danny observed.

'This is meant to be amusing?' Celia had regained her voice.

Dick resumed his narrative. 'That was the theory. If the woman floated, it proved she was a witch after all, protected from drowning by the Devil.'

'A lose-lose situation,' Anne said.

'Well, yes. If she floated and was therefore identified as a witch she was –'

'You did say this was an *amusing* story,' Marnie reminded him.

'Oh, yes. Well, on the occasion in question, everyone was lined up on the bank and the guards threw the denounced woman into the river. She bobbed up to the surface, so the vicar declared she was obviously a witch. Before she could be dragged out, a young woman, daughter of the so-called witch, rushed forward to beg mercy of the lord of the manor. She threw herself at his feet with such force that he stumbled, slipped and fell into the river. As he knew how to swim, he too floated and managed to climb out of the water.' Dick paused for dramatic effect.

'Go on,' Celia said.

'The crowd all cheered, and the lord had no choice but to declare that such an ordeal by water was invalid. He ordered that the woman be pulled out and set free, then he stormed off to change into dry clothes.'

'Lucky for the woman that her daughter caused an accident,' Danny observed.

Dick turned to face her. 'You think it was an accident, really?'

'You mean –'

'Exactly. She did it on purpose, knowing the lord could swim.' He looked across at Celia. 'There you are, how's that for a happy ending?'

'Is it true?'

'Yes. We have it on record.'

'The lord wasn't a Devere was he?' Celia asked.

Dick hesitated. 'I'm sure it was some other part of the county.'

Celia seemed mollified, and there was no further talk of witches, trials or ordeals. When Marnie announced that she had to get back to the drawing board – *I'm working on your project at the moment, Celia* – the party broke up and Celia went home.

Donovan went to sort things out on his boat, while Danny wandered off to watch the archaeologists at work. Marnie and Anne were heading towards the office barn when Dick touched Marnie's elbow.

'I was going to say –'

'It's okay. I guessed.' She smiled at him. 'Did it happen here, or were you going to tell me it was all made up?'

'No. It really was documented and, well, yes, it happened, let's say not far from here.'

'I'm glad you didn't tell Celia that.'

'There was quite a lot I didn't tell Celia.'

'Such as?'

'The ending wasn't entirely a happy one.'

'Don't tell me, the lord chopped off the girl's head with his sword?'

'Nope.'

'They hanged the woman anyway, just to be on the safe side?'

'No. No, she was let off. Public opinion was on her side, you see. The twist in the tale was that from that day forth, they bound accused witches hand and foot and soaked their clothes to make sure they sank.'

Marnie and Anne exchanged bleak looks.

'Those were the people who preached *God is love*, is that right?' Marnie said.

Dick nodded. 'Yes, and knew how to control the peasants.'

Back in the office Marnie returned to her designs while Anne studied the scheme for refurbishing a hotel. Unusually, Marnie found her attention wandering, her concentration faltering. She looked across the office to where Anne was sitting, head bent over her papers, writing notes. Without warning, Anne suddenly looked up and caught Marnie staring at her.

'What's up, Marnie?'

'I was just … thinking about Dick's story.'

'Were you wondering if he'd made it up after all? I wonder what sort of account was kept of that sort of thing.'

'No, I believed him when he said it really happened. I expect something was written down, maybe a report for the church authorities.'

'So what were you thinking?'

'It's odd but when Dick told that story, I imagined *you* as the girl who'd pushed the lord into the water, accidentally on purpose.'

Anne laughed. '*Me*?'

'That's just the kind of thing you'd have done.'

26
Image

Early on Thursday morning the curtains were closed on *X O 2*, so nobody called to invite Donovan for breakfast. When they started work, Danny helped Anne for half an hour with the filing. Soon the first sounds from the dig reached them. A convoy of vehicles was heard. *Timeline* was on the move.

Anne and Danny went to watch the crew setting up. While they stood looking on, a young man from the TV company approached them and asked if they were connected with the farm.

'D'you know what time the university archaeologists arrive?'

'About nine.'

'Do you know Dr Cardew?'

'He's the one in charge,' Anne said.

'Are you likely to see him? Could you give him a message?'

'Sure.'

'Could you ask him to see Crispin Wade or Suzi Fraser-Jones? They want to arrange an interview with him this morning.'

'I'll let him know.'

'That's great.' He looked from Anne to Danny. 'You two were filmed yesterday, weren't you?'

Anne shook her head. 'No, not us.'

'You were. I saw it. Someone found a little pendant, a fleur-de-lys? You were talking to that posh woman about it, blonde, blue dress.'

Danny grinned. 'The lady of the manor.'

Anne looked thoughtful. 'Who filmed us? There wasn't a camera crew anywhere near.'

'You were caught on one of the location cameras.' He turned and pointed at a surveillance camera fixed to the end of the barn. 'One of those.'

'True fame.' Anne struck a pose, grinning.

'It could be,' the young man said. 'They're running a trailer tonight after the six o'clock news. You might be on.'

Half an hour of watching archaeologists scrape dirt with their trowels was more than enough for Danny. The temperature was rising, with not a cloud in the sky. The TV crew seemed to be locked in a discussion in the shade at the side of the field while the helicopter droned over the site in circles. With more than an hour to wait before her first run as water-girl, Danny set off through the spinney to the docking area.

On *X O 2* the curtains were open at the portholes, so she stepped onto the tiny stern deck and banged on the door. Donovan was barefoot, wearing black jeans and black T-shirt. After a moment's hesitation, he invited her in.

'Oh.' Danny stopped when she passed the bathroom and stepped into the sleeping cabin, where the bed was made up with white sheets and a pale grey duvet.

Donovan turned to look back at her. 'What is it?'

'Your boat's, I don't know, *different*. Not like *Sally Ann* or *Thyrsis*.'

'More functional-looking?'

'I suppose so.'

They went on through a narrow doorway. The interior was dim with only the portholes and a pigeon loft admitting daylight, an effect enhanced by the grey walls and ceiling and grey carpet tiles on the floor. The galley had grey-painted units, with black-lacquered shelving in a style that was continued further forward in the open-plan layout. Even the dinette had grey tweed upholstery.

'Functional,' Danny muttered.

Donovan indicated the seating unit, and Danny sat down. He took his place opposite her. She looked at the shelves where old Leica cameras were displayed, saw photographs of silver racing cars from days gone by, attached to the side of the shelving. Further on she saw bookshelves, many of the titles in German. She smiled to herself.

'A *U-boat*,' she murmured.

'Say again.'

'Anne says your boat reminds her of a U-boat, a submarine. I see what she means.'

'I tend to think of *X O 2* as a travelling machine.' He pronounced the name as *Exodos*.

Danny grinned. 'Anne also said it was a *stealth narrowboat*.'

Donovan nodded.

Danny cast her mind back. 'The first time I saw it, it was at night. I'd come out to fetch something from *Sally Ann* and I heard a boat but couldn't see it.'

'I like travelling at night.'

'Why? You miss all the scenery.'

'The scenery's still there. It just looks different in the darkness. Did you come for a particular reason?'

Danny was wrong-footed by the sudden change of direction. 'No, I just, well, I wondered whether you were up and had had breakfast.'

'I am and I have.'

'Whether you were all right.'

'That, too.'

'Whether you wanted to see the excavations.'

'Yes.'

'Good. Shall we go together, or have you things to do first?'

Donovan stood up. Danny noticed that he placed his left foot carefully, as if testing it.

'You okay?'

'Fine.' He shifted his weight from one foot to the other. 'It's fine.'

'Great. Then let's go and see the dig.' As an afterthought she added, 'We might be on TV tonight.'

'They film the dig at night?'

Danny turned to go. 'No. Apparently, they're using some stuff they filmed yesterday with us in it.'

Donovan reached forward and caught Danny's wrist. '*Us*? What do you mean, *us*?'

'It's for some sort of trailer.'

'You must be mistaken. No one was filming where we were.'

'You don't understand, Donovan. They've got these little black cameras dotted about. They're virtually invisible. They film everything that goes on.'

'And you're sure we're in it?'

'It's a possibility. Why? It's no big deal, is it?'

Donovan let go of Danny's wrist, his thoughts elsewhere.

Movement in the courtyard caught Marnie's eye and she looked up to see Rob Cardew walking quickly towards the door to the office barn. At the last moment he stopped, reached into his back pocket and took out a mobile. For some time he paced up and down outside, listening and talking, and Marnie returned to her work.

'He's always on that phone,' Anne observed from across the room. 'He's quite dynamic really, in a laid-back kind of way.'

'Mm ...'

'He seems to be worried now, though.'

Marnie looked up again. 'You're right. I wonder if having *Timeline* here creates problems with the university's dig.'

'Yeah, I wondered about that, although –'

Rob ended his conversation and knocked on the door before entering. He gave them the usual owlish smile.

'Sorry, don't want to interrupt your work, just want to say hallo and see if everything's all right.'

'All is well, thanks, Rob.'

'Good. Not being too disturbed by all the comings and goings?'

'No, we're used to having helicopters and TV stars about the place. It's normal for us here at the centre of the universe.'

'Just as I thought.' He grinned.

'How are things going with you, Rob?'

'Oh, modified rapture, really.'

'*Timeline* getting in your way?'

'Yes and no. They have a tendency to poach our students at inconvenient moments, but they do share their findings, which can be useful.'

'In what way? Have they found anything?'

'They're surveying all the excavation areas and analysing the results. They've hinted they've already found material, so I'm waiting to hear from them.'

'What about your wife's analysis of the remains in Sarah's grave?'

His cheerful expression faded. 'Not so good. Rosemary was just on the phone. The remains have been removed from her lab.'

Marnie sat up. 'Who by?'

Rob shrugged. 'Apparently, some sort of officials.'

'*Apparently*? What does that mean?'

'The director called her in this morning and told her the remains had been taken away last night for *further examination*. He couldn't be more specific, but these people had arrived with all the appropriate paperwork and that was that.'

'How did Rosemary feel about it?'

'Upset, annoyed, let down. She's taken it as a personal vote of no confidence.'

'Was she making any progress?'

'To be honest, not much. It's very galling having nothing to show for all her efforts.'

'Visitor,' Marnie murmured and looked meaningfully towards the courtyard.

Suzi Fraser-Jones strode briskly past the windows and came in through the half-open door.

'Hi. I just came to see if all was okay. I hope we're not getting in the way too much.' She looked at Rob and smiled.

'Great minds,' he said, the friendly smile back in place.

'We all realise how much of a nuisance it can be, Marnie, having us on the doorstep.' Suzi looked at her watch.

'I have to admit we do have quite a bit of work on our hands just now. In fact, I was thinking that we might take a spot of leave.'

'Go away?' Suzi looked concerned. 'When?'

'Over the next few days. Does that matter, from your point of view, I mean?'

'We want to include you in the filming. People don't usually go away when we're around.'

'I was thinking that we'd take a short break as it's not easy to keep focused on what we're doing. We'll probably not get another chance to take time off this summer. Then, when you're not here, we'll be able to get on.'

'Without being interrupted all the time.' Suzi completed the sentence for her. 'Yes, I can understand that. How long would you be away?'

'Just a few days … a short trip on the boat.'

Suzi's mobile began chirping. With an apologetic smile, she gave a fleeting wave and went out, hurrying off on her next mission.

Marnie looked at Rob. 'Where were we? Oh, yes, Rosemary's missing remains.'

The office phone began ringing. Anne grabbed it.

'Walker and Co, good morning … One moment, please. I'll see if she's free.'

Anne pressed the Hold button. 'Celia wants to talk about progress.'

Rob grinned and left.

Donovan stopped when he reached the HQ barn. Inside, two students were keying data into a laptop, while one of the older archaeologists was examining finds with another student. Danny looked on as Donovan scanned the area.

'Tell me about these cameras, Danny.' He spoke quietly. 'Where are they? How many? Are they static?'

'No idea.'

Donovan indicated the group in the barn. 'Will they know?'

Danny shrugged. 'Dunno. They're *Timeline*'s cameras.'

Donovan advanced slowly, looking up at the eaves of the barn. He saw the camera at the same time as Danny and stared at it.

'Flexible mounting,' he murmured. 'Aerial, remote control.'

He turned and walked into the HQ barn. 'Hi, good morning.'

Everyone looked at him.

'D'you know where the producer is, or whoever operates the surveillance cameras?'

The older man answered. 'It depends. I believe they run all the time. There's a van – the OB they call it – and when it's here they can guide the cameras, focus them, turn them and so on.'

'Is it here now?'

'Haven't seen it. It was here all day yesterday, parked by the bottom of the field track.'

'Thanks.'

Danny trailed Donovan round the garage barn, puzzled by his interest in the cameras. She figured it was a man thing. Technical stuff. He stopped when they were clear of the buildings. There were no vans in sight. Across the field slope small groups of archaeologists were attending to their pits and trenches in the gathering heat. At the furthest point a different group was clustered round a pit.

'What are they doing?' Danny asked.

'That's a film crew.' Donovan turned. 'I want to see if I can find those other cameras.'

'Okay. I'll go round to the office, see if I can do anything useful.'

They went their separate ways. Danny rounded the corner of the office barn as Anne came out.

'Hiya. I was coming to look for you. You okay for the drink run, Danny?'

'Yeah.

'Seen Donovan yet?'

'He's up and about, gone looking for the surveillance cameras.'

'Why?'

'Not sure. He seems bothered about them. I told him what that bloke said about us being on TV and it seemed to worry him.'

Anne reflected for a few seconds. 'How's his foot today?'

'Slight limp, says it's all right. He's not bad-looking, is he? So are you two an item, then?'

'An item?'

'That's why he's here, isn't it? It's not just on account of his boat.'

'Who knows? With Donovan you're never quite sure what's going on.'

That afternoon Marnie stopped on her way to the HQ barn to check the vehicles parked beside the end of the field track. She was looking for Rob Cardew, wanting to finish off their earlier conversation.

Her wish was granted. He crossed her path, heading towards a car that had just arrived. From a small hatchback Rosemary Goodchild climbed out and immediately began a heated conversation with her husband, prodding the air with a cigarette to emphasise a point. Marnie was on the point of turning away when Rosemary spotted her and waved.

Marnie sensed an atmosphere and looked for an opportunity to leave them to talk. Rosemary, on the other hand, was in no hurry for Marnie to go and suggested they look at the excavations together. She stubbed her cigarette out in the car's ashtray and they began walking. Marnie had a deal of sympathy for the team working in the heat on the exposed slope. A cry made her turn, and Danny came up with Donovan following on behind.

Introductions were made. Rosemary looked at Donovan.

'I haven't seen you before, have I? Are you with *Timeline?*'

'I'm just a friend passing through.'

'We're thinking of going for a trip,' Marnie added. 'A few days' break. It's our only chance of a holiday this summer and while all this is going on ...'

'I can imagine. You can't get any work done. I wish I was coming with you.' Rosemary's tone was weary and dejected.

'Don't you find it all exciting?' Danny asked. 'The TV people, the helicopter, the bustle of it all?'

Rob explained to Danny. 'Rosemary's had some problems in the lab.'

'What kind of problems?'

'My work has been interrupted.'

'In what way?'

Marnie spoke before Rosemary could reply. 'I'm not sure Rosemary's able to talk about it.'

'You mean it's confidential?'

Rosemary looked at Rob before speaking. 'I've been working on the remains found in the grave. They've been removed for analysis at another lab.'

Danny looked puzzled. 'That's confidential?'

'It's annoying. They came last night after I'd left and took them without any reference to me.'

Donovan, who had been standing in the background until then, stepped forward to face Rosemary.

'Who came and took the remains?' he said.

'They didn't say, but they acted as if they owned the place.'

'Someone must have authorised the removal, surely?' Donovan said.

'My director saw them. He stayed on after me, for once. Usually I'm the last to leave.'

'What about your notes, reports, findings, all that sort of stuff?'

'I was just asking Rosemary about that,' Rob said.

Rosemary frowned. 'They insisted on taking all the files.'

Donovan was incredulous. 'They took *everything*?'

'Yes. They just turned up without warning and took the remains, all the dossiers, computer disks, the lot.'

There were a few moments of silence.

'No they didn't.'

All eyes turned towards Donovan.

'What do you mean?' Rosemary said.

'They didn't turn up without warning. They must have arranged to see your director beforehand, made an appointment for a time when you wouldn't be around to object.'

Rosemary put a hand to her mouth. 'Of course. It was odd, the director being there at that time. I'd not thought of it before, but since you mention it …'

'Presumably,' Marnie began, 'there's nothing you could've done about it, is there? You couldn't have stopped them.'

'I could've made a formal protest.'

'On what grounds?' Rob said quietly. 'It was a government-funded contract. The remains were theirs, technically speaking.'

'That isn't the point,' Donovan said.

Rob looked at him. 'What is?'

'If a formal complaint was made and an enquiry subsequently took place, the complaint would be made known. With no protest there'd be less likelihood of an enquiry and no record of any conflict that might arouse suspicion or comment.'

'They just wanted everything brushed quietly under the carpet,' Rosemary added.

'Exactly,' said Donovan.

'And I suppose I'll never find out why.'

'That's easy, and you'll know the answer better than anyone else.'

Everyone looked baffled.

'What do you mean?' Rob asked.

'It's obvious. The remains pointed to someone who wanted the truth about them to be kept hidden.' Donovan looked at Rosemary. 'You knew more about them than anyone, so you must know who could be compromised by the facts about them being made public.'

'But I don't know who might want the details kept private.'

'Are you sure about that?'

'I think I'd know if …' She looked thoughtful.

'What is it?' Rob said.

'Well, if they had official authority to have the remains taken away, presumably it's the government – or some part of it – that wants them kept secret.'

'What part of the government could it be?' Rob asked.

'That isn't the right question.' Donovan interjected.

'No? I'd have thought it –'

'No. The question is, what did the remains reveal?'

All eyes turned towards Rosemary.

'They were those of a man; not old but not in his first youth; remains largely skeletal with some skin tissue; medium height and build; seemed to have been fit and healthy; showed signs of a violent death; possibly by strangulation; buried about fifty or sixty years ago; distinguishing marks difficult because of decomposition, but part of what appeared to be a tattoo; no clothing but perhaps a shroud of some sort. That's about it.'

'No. There's more, much more.' Donovan's tone was firm.

'I don't know what you –'

'You were in intimate contact with him for days.'

'Intimate contact with a set of bones,' Rosemary protested.

Donovan shook his head. 'You *must* have formed an impression of who he was, at least what kind of person, how he lived and died. Was his general fitness due to hard manual labour? Did his bones reveal he was heavily muscled? What did his skull tell you about him?'

Marnie laughed. 'You sound like Sherlock Holmes, Donovan.'

'Sorry. I get carried away.'

'What do you do?' Rob asked. 'We don't know anything about you.'

'I'm taking a gap year before university.'

'And you're a friend of Marnie's.'

'He's Anne's –' Danny began. A sharp look from Anne stopped her in mid flight.

Marnie continued. 'Donovan was involved with us in the trouble we had with the far right last summer. His photographs were used in the papers. They made a tremendous impact at the time.'

'Photographs?' Rosemary murmured.

'Yes. He –'

'Photographs,' Rosemary repeated. 'My god.'

'You've kept some photographs?' Rob took her arm. 'You said they'd taken all the files, everything.'

'They did, but –'

'They're in your camera,' Donovan interjected.

'How did you know that?'

'It's obvious.'

'Yes. I shot a whole roll of film yesterday to update my records. I'll take them in to get them processed tomorrow.'

'Where?'

'We have a lab at work – the Imaging Unit – they do all our processing, high quality prints –'

'No,' said Donovan. 'You can't do that. They'll have been told to hand over anything relating to your work.'

'What else can I do?'

'Where's your camera?'

'In my bag in the car.'

'What kind of film is it? Colour?'

'No. We use black and white for this kind of job.'

'I can develop it.'

'You?' Rosemary looked at her husband and back at Donovan. 'I'm not sure.'

'It's not the kind of thing you can drop in to Boots like holiday snaps. Trust me.'

The dig was winding up for the day when the early evening news programme began at six. Marnie turned on the television in Ralph's study on *Thyrsis* and sat in the chair at his desk. Anne and Danny took the armchairs while Donovan sat on the floor between them. Ralph was on his way back from meetings in Oxford, held up in traffic on the by-pass.

With growing impatience they sat through the usual run of depressing items: a minister accused of sleaze, problems with the economy, famine and genocide in Africa. Towards the end of the programme the presenter took on a more cheerful air and announced that the hot weather would be persisting over the weekend. This boded well for the special summer edition of *Timeline* where at sites all over the country digs were in progress, their topic: witchcraft through the ages. As he spoke, the scene changed to a panorama, a panning shot of a sloping field in a rural setting.

'That's here!' Danny exclaimed. 'Those are our diggers.'

The view cut to a group shot of enthusiastic archaeologists clustered together, one of them holding up a tiny object, a pendant fleur-de-lys. The sun glinted off gold as he held the object against the throat of a girl in the team and the others admired it. The cameo scene concluded with another man, obviously in authority, shaking hands with a young fair-haired man dressed in black. The image froze and became a background picture covering the entire rear wall of the studio as the newscaster wound up. Conspicuous in the centre of the picture stood Donovan, staring out at millions of viewers.

Danny patted his shoulder. 'Hey! You're famous.'

Donovan said nothing. Everyone was smiling, everyone but him.

The talk at the dinner table that evening was of the trailer for *Timeline* and Rosemary's photographs. It was warm and muggy and they ate at the table on the bank beside the docking area. Ralph had returned too late to see any of the news programme, and Marnie brought him up to speed on the day's events in Knightly St John. His reaction to the photographs story surprised them.

'I wonder if Rosemary's contracts are covered by the Official Secrets Act.'

Ralph suggested they check with Rosemary before going any further. He pointed out that she could find herself in trouble for misappropriating material, as could anyone connected with the last roll of film. The latter was now sitting in a cupboard on X O 2, ready for Donovan to transport it back to his dark room in London.

Donovan was even more quiet than usual during the meal and took himself off for an early night as soon as they had finished eating. Danny remarked on this when she and Anne retired to the attic that night. She could not understand why Donovan was so concerned about having his face plastered on the TV news.

Anne thought back to Donovan's sudden disappearance the previous summer after the shooting of the far-right political leader, Garth Brandon. It was suspected that the gunman had been one of Brandon's inner circle, a blackshirt like all his followers. These memories Anne kept to herself.

27
Getaway

The door to the office barn swung open on Friday morning and Celia Devere made an entrance. Marnie was bent over her drawing board deep in concentration and did not look up. Anne was adding up a column of figures on the computer and could not take her eyes away for fear of making a mistake.

'What *fun*!' Celia exclaimed, radiant in the doorway. 'Isn't it *wonderful*?'

Marnie turned slowly, her mind still focused on her hotel project. Anne pressed the *Enter* key and raised her eyes. Celia was resplendent in a pale blue trouser suit, head tilted at a coquettish angle, arms spread wide, beaming.

'Wonderful?' Marnie repeated. 'Oh yes, nice suit.'

'Not the suit, *silly*.' A girlish laugh. 'All the *action*, the *life*. Haven't you been outside this morning?'

Words flashed through Marnie's mind: *No. Believe it or not, some of us have to earn a living, which means doing some actual work, you idle moron!* She said, 'Er, no, not really. We've been rather committed on the work front.'

'Of course you have. I expect you've been getting everything ready for the start on my redecoration. Am I right?'

'More or less.' Marnie hoped she sounded convincing.

'Excellent. Well, while you've been beavering away, the world and his dog have been beating a path to your door, or rather, to your field. If Anne was out there serving teas, you'd make a fortune.'

Anne dropped a mental curtsy, loaded a mental Kalashnikov, hurled a mental grenade. At that moment, the door was pushed wider and a man walked in, followed by a woman and a teenage boy. They began looking around the office.

'Good morning.' Marnie tried to conceal her irritation. 'Can I help you?'

'This the *Timeline*'s office, then?' The man began walking towards the display board where project plans and photographs were pinned up.

Marnie stood up and placed herself in front of him.

'No, this is the office of Walker and Co, interior designers. The archaeologists are based round the corner.'

Anne leapt to her feet. 'I'll show you. It's this way.' She led the man to the door and gave directions.

Celia smiled as the visitors trooped out. 'I think you have the patience of a saint, Marnie. You're always so polite to everyone.'

'It's part of being professional. It can be a strain at times.'

Celia missed the irony. 'You do it so well.'

'Thank you.' Marnie tried not to look at Anne, who was grinning in the doorway. 'I take it we have sightseers out there?'

Celia took Marnie's arm. 'Come and see for yourself.'

The phone began ringing. It was Molly Appleton from the village shop. She had been inundated with strangers asking directions to the *Timeline* dig. They were arriving by the minute. Marnie pondered the news for several seconds. She could not work out why Celia found it all so exciting. They walked round to the field with Anne and it immediately became clear.

No sooner had they reached the HQ barn than a small crowd gathered round Celia, identifying her as the glamorous lady seen in the TV trailer. Close up, dressed like the star in a Hollywood epic, she did not disappoint her public. Marnie watched Celia preening herself, basking in the glow of recognition. She suspected it was only a matter of time before autograph books came out.

Anne remarked to one of the students in the HQ barn that Dick Blackwood was nowhere in sight. She pulled a face in the direction of the crowd and explained that he had left in a hurry. A neighbour in Martyrs Close had warned him that a throng of visitors was milling around Sarah's grave site, apparently looking for souvenirs among the brambles. Dick had just phoned back to base camp asking for four students to join him at once to mount a guard to keep it safe from desecration.

While Anne was relaying this to Marnie, Danny and Donovan arrived. Danny had been sunbathing by the canal and had called on Donovan for a chat. She came wearing an open shirt over her bikini. Donovan was in black and grey.

A small group of visitors detached themselves from Celia's charmed circle to inspect the latest arrivals. Some of them recognised Donovan from the television trailer. He was unsettled to receive so much attention and flashed a concerned look at Anne. So many strangers bothered him.

One of the students in the HQ barn complained about the heat. Anne realised it would soon be break-time. As the crowd round Donovan grew, she walked to the edge of the field, cupped her hands round her mouth and called out.

'Clear up your loose!'

The diggers in the field needed no second urging. They broke all records tidying their trenches and set off for the HQ barn, leaving the visitors stranded where they stood.

Donovan raised a hand to shield his eyes and stared out across the slope. He turned and strode away, momentarily pausing to glance back at Anne with a barely perceptible nod.

Half an hour later, Anne slipped out of the office barn and walked through the spinney. Emerging on the other side, she found that X O 2 had gone. She was considering what to do next when her mobile sounded.

'It's me. Are you alone?'

'I'm by the boats looking at your empty space. Where are you, Donovan?'

'Just round the corner to the south. Off-side of the canal. Can you meet me?'

'Give me ten minutes.'

Anne was back in the office in less than two. Marnie was at her desk, sorting papers.

'Marnie –'

'I know. It's impossible to work here with all this going on.'

'Marnie, Donovan's gone.'

'Already?'

'I think he's spooked by all the attention. He's moored out of sight, wants me to go and see him.'

Marnie nodded. 'Of course. He thinks the far right might be on to him?'

'My guess is, he thinks he might've been recognised on TV last night.'

Marnie stood up. 'Maybe we should all go. We can leave one day early.'

'You don't think it might look odd?'

'No. We've already made it clear we can't work properly with so much disturbance.'

'Should I tell Rob or Suzi?'

'No need. They'll not notice us going. And if Donovan's right, the fewer people who know we've taken off, the better.'

Ralph was warming the engine on *Thyrsis* when they reached the docking area. Anne and Danny attended to casting off while Marnie left a message on the Burton's answerphone in cottage number one, asking them to feed Dolly for the next few days.

They rounded the corner and were lost from view to anyone on Glebe Farm land in less than a minute.

In the late morning heat the diggers were preoccupied with slaking their thirst, the camera crew with setting up their next shots, the trippers with gazing at the spectacle. If one or two visitors were mingling with the crowd and examining everyone connected with the dig at close quarters, no one noticed them.

Thyrsis drew level with *X O 2* and deposited Anne and Danny on the counter. After a hasty conference, Donovan disappeared inside, leaving Anne at the tiller while Danny pushed off from the bank. They cleared the lock at Cosgrove, and the small convoy headed south, observed only by a solitary heron.

28
Leighton Buzzard

Much of Saturday morning was spent travelling round Milton Keynes. The previous night the convoy had tied up in the most remote spot they could find. Donovan had offered to give up his sleeping cabin, but Anne and Danny insisted on sharing the convertible dinette. Breakfast was hasty and basic but adequate, and both boats were ready to move off by seven.

The landscape around the self-styled 'new city' is as varied as any to be found on the canal system, with no locks to interrupt progress from one end to the other. They passed through housing developments of varying styles, here a picturesque village, there old-established industry, in one sector wooded scenery, in another open moorland; a mixture that often surprised the visitor.

Donovan saw little of it on that journey, but stayed inside, leaving Anne at the tiller. For Danny the trip represented yet another opportunity for sun-worship, and she stretched out in her bikini on folded towels on the roof near the stern where she could chat to Anne as they cruised along.

They had decided to proceed with some distance between the boats so as not to draw attention to themselves. When *X O 2* approached the first lock of the day at Fenny Stratford, another boat was pulling away from the bank ahead of them, its crew already opening a gate. Seeing the two young women, a man at the lockside waved them to come forward and heaved open the second gate. *X O 2* had found a new companion for the journey, a hire boat returning to Leighton Buzzard at the end of a holiday afloat.

On *Thyrsis*, Marnie pulled over to drop Ralph ashore to work the lock and spotted *X O 2* in the distance following closely behind another boat. As the lead boat turned to take a bend, she recognised the light blue paintwork of a local hire-boat company.

That afternoon, twelve lock-miles later, the blue boat slowed and veered off towards the hire base. The companions went their separate ways and Anne settled down to cruise through her home town.

Rounding the next bend, she became aware of activity on the bank. Three policemen were standing in a group by the wall set back from the towpath. Seeing the boat, they stepped forward, one of them speaking into his lapel radio.

X O 2 proceeded unhindered past the policemen. They passed under a bridge and rounded a bend. As soon as they were out of sight, Anne grabbed her mobile.

'Danny, take the tiller. I have to make a call.'

Danny slipped down from the roof while Anne pressed buttons.

'Marnie? Listen, it's me. Are you in Leighton Buzzard yet?'

'Just approaching. Why?'

'There are police on the towpath looking at the boats going by.'

Marnie sounded puzzled. 'So? Can't have anything to do with us.'

'I know. It's just ... I had a funny feeling.'

'Anne, relax. There's absolutely no reason why ...' She paused. 'That's odd.'

'What is?'

'There's a policeman waving at us. I think he wants us to stop.'

'What shall I do?'

'You go on. We'll come when we can, or I'll be in touch.'

Anne disconnected.

Danny handed back the tiller. 'Everything all right?'

'The police have stopped *Thyrsis*.'

Danny looked alarmed. 'Why?'

'No idea.'

'So what now?'

'We carry on. Marnie will keep us posted.'

Danny resumed her place on the roof, sitting cross-legged facing Anne, her expression registering total bewilderment.

'Anne, I don't get it. We're handling the boat so Donovan can rest his injured foot, aren't we?'

'Ye-e-s.'

'And we came on the trip to get away from all the interruptions to your work. This is just a mini-cruise, right?'

'Yeah.'

'Then why are the police stopping Ralph's boat?'

Donovan peered out from the doorway.

'Good question.'

The policeman pointed at Marnie and waved her down. Throwing *Thyrsis* into reverse gear, she came to a halt beside him.

'Hi. What can I do for you?'

'Can you pull over?'

'There's no space just here.'

He stepped onto the gunwale. Ralph had been inside, changing the film in his camera, and he emerged onto the counter to find the policeman staring at him.

'Good afternoon.' Ralph smiled pleasantly. 'Are you a hitch-hiker?'

The constable seemed unsure how to take this.

'We need to moor the boat so we can talk properly,' he said.

Marnie raised a hand. 'Where do you suggest?' she asked in an even tone, wondering what *talk properly* meant.

The young officer looked in all directions. All the moorings were occupied as far as he could see. Ralph made a suggestion.

'Why don't we make *Thyrsis* secure alongside one of these moored boats and go inside to *talk properly*, as you put it?'

The constable signalled to another officer to join them while Marnie and Ralph tied the boat at bow and stern. Inside, they sat in the study.

'So,' Ralph began. 'What can we do for you?'

'You are Mrs Marnie Walker and Professor Ralph Lombard?'

'We are,' said Ralph.

'You live at Glebe Farm, Knightly St John, Northamptonshire?'

'Correct.'

'I must ask you to accompany us back to Glebe Farm.'

'Now?'

'Yes, miss.'

'Why?'

'The bodies have been discovered and you're wanted for questioning, both of you.'

'Bodies?' Ralph said. 'You mean *archaeological remains*, up on the dig site?'

'No, sir.' The policeman looked steadily at Ralph. 'Two bodies have been found at Glebe Farm … in shallow graves.'

Anne steered *X O 2* round the bends south of Leighton Buzzard and pulled over to the bank once they were clear of the town. All three of them stood on the steerer's counter, staring back the way they had come. Donovan checked his watch.

'How long do we wait here?' Danny asked.

Anne wondered if she was getting spooked again. 'Hard to tell. We'll stay a while. Marnie said she'd phone when she could.'

'What do the police want them for?'

Anne reached forward and turned off the engine.

'Your guess is as good as mine.'

Within half an hour of leaving Leighton Buzzard, Marnie and Ralph were back at Glebe Farm. They had taken the next available mooring by the supermarket, much to the annoyance of a boat-owner who thought he had seen it first. The police waved him on and Marnie guided *Thyrsis* back into the slot. The officers allowed them to retrieve their belongings and heave overnight bags into the boot of an unmarked police car before whisking them off.

A crowd was waiting by the entrance to the field track, held back by two constables as the car turned in. Marnie wondered if the archaeologists had been prevented from continuing their dig. As they bumped down the slope she saw they were still at work and the film crew was in action.

Marnie guided the driver towards the courtyard, and they parked behind a familiar grey Cavalier. DS Binns and WDC Lamb met them as soon as they climbed out of the car. Binns suggested they talk in the office barn. Marnie announced that she was going to make coffee or tea and went straight to the kitchen area.

'It's just the two of you?' Binns asked. 'Where's your assistant?'

'It's the weekend, sergeant.. We do have a life outside the office.'

'We'll need to talk to her.'

'I think,' Ralph began, 'it would be a good idea if you talked to *us*.'

'You know why we've brought you back.'

'One of your colleagues told us that remains had been found on the site.'

'You don't seem surprised, sir.'

'Well, hardly. It would be rather a disappointment if they weren't, wouldn't it? We have three dozen or so archaeologists toiling away, a team of geophysicists, numerous other experts, a TV crew and a helicopter. Finding remains is what it's all about, sergeant.'

'These were in shallow graves.' Binns invested the words with sinister meaning.

'Tea or coffee?' Marnie called from the back of the office.

'I'd prefer tea, if that's all right, Mrs Walker.'

'Me too, please, Mar–' Cathy Lamb bit her lip. 'Tea for me, please.'

The atmosphere became more domestic as they pulled chairs round to form a circle. Cathy Lamb opened a notebook. It seemed a very English interrogation, reminding Marnie of a Miss Marple story. She put out a plate of biscuits and poured tea into china cups.

'Sergeant Binns,' Ralph's tone was relaxed and conciliatory. 'I'm sure you have your procedures, but may I suggest we start from the premise that we are here to help in any way we can and that we are not suspects. I assure you we haven't murdered anyone and buried them in ... *shallow graves*.'

'You're right, professor. We do have procedures. That means I'm required to ask a number of questions.'

'Fire away.'

'Were you aware that human remains were buried here?'

'Not as such, no.'

'What does that mean, sir?'

'We've been led to believe that all manner of things *could* be found on the site. That's why all this is going on.' He indicated the outside.

'I thought I'd made it clear we weren't talking of archaeology.'

'Sergeant Binns.' Marnie put down her tea-cup. 'From what you've told us, I think you've made it clear that's what you *are* talking about.'

'In what way?'

'First of all, you're referring to *human remains*, not bodies.'

'That's just a –'

'I know, I know. But you're not asking us to establish where we were at a particular time, such as when the people concerned died and were buried in these graves. That suggests two things to me: you don't know who they are, and they died a long time ago.'

'That doesn't necessary follow.'

'Are the remains in any way connected with those found up at the other grave site?' Ralph asked.

'I can't answer that, professor.'

'Can you tell us where these *shallow graves* are situated?' Marnie asked.

'They're just by your docking area.'

Marnie looked startled. 'By our moorings?'

Binns reflected. 'A little to the north.'

'That's all just scrub land, a tangle of undergrowth and old trees by the footpath.'

'And that explains why the graves weren't found before now,' Ralph added.

'How were they found?' Marnie asked. 'Can you tell us that?'

'Part of the survey carried out by archaeologists working for *Timeline*.'

'Down there?' Ralph looked doubtful.

'You didn't give them permission to go there?'

'We just let them get on with it,' Marnie said.

'Coming back to my questions,' Binns paused. 'Why did you leave so suddenly?'

Marnie smiled. 'Do you honestly think we were fleeing a crime scene on a narrowboat?'

'You must admit the timing was odd.'

'It was pure coincidence.'

'How old are these remains, these bodies?' Ralph asked. 'Do you in fact know how long they've been there?'

'Not yet.'

'What condition are they in?'

'I can't tell you anything about them, sir.'

'What do you know? What could possibly be suspicious about them?'

Binns looked Ralph in the eye. 'They were found on your land, close to your dock, shortly after you left abruptly without telling anyone you were going. Does that sound suspicious enough for you, sir?'

~~~~

Donovan looked at his watch for the umpteenth time. Danny was back on bikini duty on the roof of the boat with Anne sitting beside her, legs dangling over the side.

'How long have we been here now?' Anne asked. 'Half an hour?'

Donovan nodded. 'Just over.'

'No word from Marnie,' said Danny. 'D'you think we ought to carry on?'

'I don't like not knowing what's happened,' said Donovan.

'Difficult to go back. We could be recognised.'

Anne looked thoughtful. 'Not necessarily.'

~~~~

The detectives showed Marnie and Ralph where the graves had been located, an area cordoned off about ten yards from *Sally Ann*'s dock, a similar distance back from the canal. Neither of them could understand why the *Timeline* geophysicists had carried out a search in amongst all the undergrowth. Of the graves themselves there was nothing to be seen except a mound of stony soil. Beyond them lay a pile of branches and vegetation.

The group stood in silence, contemplating the burial site. Marnie was thinking of all the laughter they had shared on and around *Sally Ann*, while just a short distance away two people lay in their graves, unmourned and forgotten.

'You didn't tell us what sex they were,' she said quietly.

After a moment's hesitation, Binns said, 'They were both male.'

'And were they –'

'Mrs Walker, I can't discuss them with you.'

'Can you tell us their orientation?' Ralph asked. Realising the ambiguity of his question, he added, 'Were they aligned east-west?'

Binns thought about it. 'Yes.'

'So, Christian burials, then, not witches' graves.'

'They were men, sir, as I said.'

'There are male witches, sergeant. Presumably they would've been aligned north-south like female witches.'

'But, Ralph,' Marnie interjected, 'these were surely wearing modern clothes, if the police think we might know something about them.'

'There are witches around even today,' Ralph reminded her.

'I suppose so. We're not getting anywhere, are we? Would anyone mind if I just popped to the loo?'

Back in the office barn, Marnie went into the toilet and pulled out her mobile.

No one paid any attention to the girl who strolled along the towpath into town, wearing pink T-shirt, blue jeans and baseball cap. When she walked onto the bridge and took a camera from her denim duffle bag, passers-by gave her space to take photos. It was a popular view, with all the moored boats creating a colourful ambience along the bank. She swapped the camera for a small pair of binoculars, leaving the camera dangling from its strap round her neck. Just another tourist.

Anne spotted *Thyrsis* about a hundred yards down the line. She slipped the binoculars back into the bag, hoisted it onto her shoulder and put on sunglasses as she sauntered back to the towpath. Like so many visitors to that part of town, she turned into the entrance of the supermarket and walked through the car park. It ran parallel to the canal for some way. Anne walked straight ahead, glancing occasionally through the planting at the boats attached to bollards on the other side of the path.

Thyrsis was moored close to the building, level with the parking spaces reserved for parents with small children. The end space was empty. Anne bent down to tie a lace on one of her trainers. She carefully checked the other one before straightening up and heading for the supermarket entrance.

Inside, she went directly to the toilet block and shut herself into a cubicle. She changed into a yellow T-shirt, swapped the baseball cap for a white sunhat and folded the duffle bag to half its size. She waited a few minutes, enjoying the air-conditioned interior, before leaving to return to *X O 2*.

Anne was back on *X O 2* cleaning the portholes when the mobile began vibrating in her pocket.

'Hallo?'

'Anne, listen, I haven't got long.'

'Marnie! What's happened?'

'We've had to come back to Glebe Farm.'

'How?'

'The police gave us a lift.'

'Why would they do that?'

'Anne, there isn't an easy way to break this to you.'

'Has the place burned down?'

'No. They've found remains.'

'The archaeologists?'

'Yes.'

'Why would the police –'

'Two bodies.' A gasp from Anne. Marnie continued. 'In shallow graves.'

'Oh my god! Where?'

'You know that overgrown patch beside *Sally*'s dock, by our path to the bridge?'

'That's awful.'

'Anne, listen, I've gotta go. Here's what I think we should do …'

Anne relayed the phone conversation with Marnie to the others. Donovan announced that he agreed with Marnie's plan.

They cast off and headed south into open country at action stations: Donovan inside; Anne at the tiller; Danny on the roof in her bikini. She turned over on her towel and looked at Anne.

'Why did you change your clothes in town?'

'CCTV.'

'I don't get it.'

Donovan appeared in the doorway by the counter. 'Anyone studying CCTV footage would probably not recognise her as the same person at a glance.'

Danny looked down at him. 'You really take all this seriously, don't you?'

'Look, Danny, our friends have just been picked up by the police; loads of strangers are crawling around Glebe Farm, so anyone could go there on the pretext of watching the filming; the far right are probably looking for me. Which bit of that do you think we should *not* take seriously?'

Marnie left the loo and rejoined the others by the new grave site to find Ralph pointing out that he and Marnie were now stranded. The police car that had brought them back to Glebe farm had returned to duty without waiting. Their boat was moored at Leighton Buzzard, several miles away.

Binns offered them a lift back with Cathy Lamb. They suspected rightly that he hoped Lamb would elicit further information from them on the journey.

They were just exiting the field gate when Ralph leaned forward from the rear seat.

'Cathy, there's absolutely nothing we can tell you about those graves or the remains found in them. I'm sure you know that.'

Marnie was in the front passenger seat. 'I think Sergeant Binns knows it, too.'

Lamb's reply was nothing more than a quick sideways glance at Marnie.

Marnie continued. 'So why go to all this trouble, getting us dragged back here from our journey? For goodness sake, we're only taking a few days off to get away from all the disruption.'

'I know.' Lamb sounded exasperated. 'Those remains are … never mind. I can't talk about them. But, for what it's worth – and you mustn't quote me on this – I don't think you have anything to do with the remains.'

'Then why all the –'

'Listen, I can't say why because I don't know why. What I do know is that a lot of people have got the jitters about Knightly St John, and it's got nothing to do with witchcraft or archaeology.'

'Do you mean your senior officers?' Ralph asked.

'I think it goes higher than that, quite a lot higher.'

After opening all the doors and windows on *Thyrsis*, Marnie and Ralph stood on the counter and watched Cathy Lamb drive out of the supermarket car park. They waited for several seconds, looking up and down the towpath, wondering if anyone was observing them, wondering if they were becoming as paranoid as Donovan. Concluding that they probably were, but that no one seemed to be keeping them under surveillance, they untied the mooring ropes and pushed away from the bank.

To the casual onlooker, they were just another narrowboat setting off on a journey, a tall man at the tiller and a woman perched up on the roof, chatting casually like any couple on a boating holiday.

Thyrsis took the left-hand bend immediately after the bridge past the water point, then the longer right-hand bend and was soon out of sight.

'Is this it?' Danny sat up as *X O 2* slowed and pulled over to the side. 'Aren't we going any further?'

She scanned the area in all directions. They were in a secluded spot with trees and bushes on both banks. Donovan came out to take the tiller while Anne stepped ashore and tied up fore and aft.

Danny persisted. 'Anne, are you going to explain? What are we doing here?'

'Waiting for *Thyrsis*. They'll be coming to join us shortly.'

'When?'

'In half an hour or so, probably, maybe a bit longer.'

'Anne, I –'

'Look, Danny, I've chosen this place specially for you. You see? I've moored in a sunny space so you can sunbathe. Normally I would've chosen a shady bank in this heat. Just relax. We're on holiday.'

Ralph saw *X O 2* minutes after clearing the town and smiled to himself at the sight of Danny taking in the sun. It looked as if they had deliberately chosen the sunniest stretch with her in mind. Then he realised that that was exactly what they had planned. The otherwise unusual – some might say *sinister* – boat looked relatively normal with a girl in a bikini on the roof.

The five of them gathered in Ralph's study. Armed with tall glasses of sparkling water with ice and lemon, they sat and reviewed the situation. Anne began by asking for more details about Glebe Farm. Marnie explained, but made no mention of Cathy Lamb's intuition that people in high places were involved in the developments in Knightly St John.

'So what now?' Anne asked.

Donovan looked at Marnie and Ralph. 'You'll be going back to Glebe Farm.'

Marnie nodded. 'I think we have to, yes.'

Danny was puzzled. '*Back?* But we've only just come away.'

'They can't be absent when so much is going on,' Donovan said.

'What about you?'

A wry smile from Donovan. 'I have to be absent. I'm going back to London.'

Marnie said, 'I think that's the one tricky aspect of our planning.'

'No it isn't. You have to go north; I have to go south. It's as simple as that.'

'You have an injured foot,' Marnie pointed out. 'And London is the other side of the Chiltern Hills.'

'The foot's improving. I can travel solo, go at my own pace at night.' He glanced at Anne. 'The *stealth narrowboat* has its advantages.'

And so the plan was agreed. The only other piece in the puzzle was Danny, who opted to return with Anne to Glebe Farm. While she lugged her hold-all on to *Thyrsis*, Anne stayed behind to help Donovan cast off. When Marnie announced they needed to take on supplies at the supermarket, Anne declared that she would go with Donovan to the next lock, a short way down the cut, to give him a good start to his journey. She could walk back into town and meet them in half an hour.

Donovan changed into his camouflage gear of light-coloured clothing, plus baseball cap and sunglasses, while Anne steered *X O 2* for what she believed would be the last time. He sat on the step inside the doorway.

Anne looked down at him, flexing his injured foot. 'Are you going to manage?'

'Sure.'

'I think you're right to be cautious about security.'

'I know I am, and you must be, too, Anne.'

'I'm not likely to forget the time we were attacked by neo-Nazi thugs in Northampton last year.'

'But we fought back hard. It's the only way with that sort.'

Anne frowned. 'Even so …' She thought back to the headlines when Brandon was shot in broad daylight, in cold blood.

'There isn't any *even so*, Anne.'

'But Brandon –'

'I know, but you can't think of it like that.'

'How else can I think of it?'

'Suppose, just suppose, someone had assassinated Hitler in the 1930s. Perhaps there would've been no war, no holocaust.'

'I'll try to see it that way.'

'You think it was wrong?'

'I find it all very confusing. I just don't know how it can be justified. But I do know one thing, Donovan. Inspector Bartlett once told me that no murder investigation is ever closed. The police never give up.'

Donovan looked up at her. 'Nor do the Nazis.'

Anne brought the boat over to the bank and handed the tiller to Donovan while she worked the lock. When *X O 2* emerged, Anne closed the gate. Donovan held the boat steady on the engine.

'Do you want me to go with you down to Church lock? It's not far.'

'No. You've brought me far enough, Anne.'

'Goodbye, then. Perhaps I'll see you again some time?'

'I came back, didn't I?'

Marnie had turned *Thyrsis* round to point north by the time Anne rejoined them. Ralph pushed the boat away from the bank and walked back down the gunwale. Marnie smiled at him, though her thoughts were with Anne, who had gone inside with Danny.

'Well,' she said, 'that's our summer holiday – a weekend trip to Leighton Buzzard.'

Ralph kissed her. 'I know how to show a girl a good time.'

29
Warned off

Marnie was surprised how refreshed she felt in the office on Monday morning after just a weekend away on the boat. The unrelenting spell of hot weather was expected to continue, and Marnie sat at her desk in a sleeveless top and lightweight cotton slacks studying the Knightly Court file. Anne had put it on her desk after breakfast. On that particular morning they had a special reason for wanting to be ahead of the game.

Marnie picked up the phone for her first call at three minutes to nine precisely and talked timings with the Knightly Court decorator. They scheduled an initial planning meeting for later that morning, ready for a start on Wednesday. The call lasted ten minutes. After disconnecting, she hit the button immediately for dialling tone and keyed in the next number. The curtain maker would be coming over that morning for a final measure-up. It was going to be a busy day.

On *Thyrsis*, Ralph received a call from Professor Fellheimer in Oxford.

'Guy here. I've been trying to phone you for the past few days.'

'I've been away.'

'I wondered. Not suffering from jetlag, I hope.'

'Only mildly. What can I do for you?'

'Are you coming to Oxford today by any chance?'

Ralph looked at the pile of documents waiting for his attention and thought of his publisher's looming deadline. 'I wasn't planning to …' Then he thought of Guy Fellheimer, who never said or did anything without a reason. 'But of course if you really –'

'Would it be convenient for me to come over to Knightly, Ralph?'

'Of course. Can you come for lunch?'

Sounds of paper shuffling. 'Er, thanks but I've got rather a lot on this morning.' More shuffling.

'Guy, if you'd rather I came to see you –'

'No. It's all right. I'd like to have a word with Cardew if he's around. Also, I'm curious to see the dig. Latter part of the afternoon all right?'

At ten-thirty Ralph went to the office barn for the usual coffee break. Marnie was putting the phone down as he closed the door behind him. She looked frustrated.

'How ironic. I make a big effort to get everything and everyone in place to start Celia's contract bang on time, and she's not even at home.'

'Today's the big day?'

'It's supposed to be.' She looked at the clock. 'God, is it that time already? Where has the morning gone?'

Ralph looked around. 'And where's Anne gone?' He went to the kitchen area and filled the kettle.

'She's out checking that everything's ready for the archaeologists' break.'

'There.' Ralph switched on the kettle and looked pleased with himself. 'Marnie, Guy Fellheimer's coming this afternoon. I think he wants to talk to me about the remains in Sarah's grave.'

'You *think* he wants to talk about the remains? Didn't he say? Why not just tell you on the phone?'

'I know. He sounded curiously evasive. He wants to see Rob Cardew as well.'

Marnie sighed. 'I'll be glad when all this –'

The door swung open and Anne came in at high speed.

'Hi, Ralph. Oh, kettle's on.' She grinned at him. 'You must've been having lessons.' She began putting mugs on a tray.

'Guess what,' Marnie said. 'Celia's not answering the phone. We've got contractors coming this morning and she's forgotten about them.'

Anne shook her head. 'Don't worry. She's here. I've just seen her talking to Rob Cardew, talking *at* Rob, I should say. What you might call a *heated discussion*. I swear she thinks the archaeologists are her own personal serfs.'

Marnie looked relieved. 'Oh well, could be worse. You'd better put another cup out, for Celia.'

Anne pulled a face and spoke in an ever-so 'umble voice. 'Yes ma'am, I'll put out the Royal Worcester, ma'am, or perhaps the Spode.'

She was performing a curtsy when the door opened and Celia stood in the doorway, resplendent in a cream shirt-waister dress. Anne lost concentration, wobbled and sat down heavily on the ground. With as much dignity as she could muster, she gathered herself up and turned to kneel by the cupboard to search for a cup.

'Celia, come in.' Marnie stood and offered her a chair.

As she sat, Celia spoke quietly. 'Does she go in for amateur dramatics?'

'The whole time,' Ralph replied in a stage whisper. 'It's her consuming passion.'

'Celia,' Marnie said brightly. 'Coffee? I've been trying to reach you all morning.'

'Really?'

'Of course. We have contractors coming today. Actually, it's just to make final checks before work starts later in the week, but we're ready to roll.'

'Oh, yes.'

'The decorator and curtain maker are both coming at about eleven. I hope that's convenient. You recall I mentioned it to you last week, before we went off on the boat?'

'Yes. Marnie, I'll not have coffee, thanks. Can we go up to the Court? I'd like a chat before your people arrive.'

Following Celia's open-topped Audi through the village, Marnie tried to guess what pressing matter was up for discussion. The possibilities ranged from cancelling the refurbishment altogether, to complaints about the archaeologists neglecting *her* grave site and renewed fears about witchcraft. Whatever was on Celia's mind, Marnie was in no mood for playing games.

On arrival, Marnie headed for the front door, but Celia steered her round to the terrace. The garden looked glorious, with sprinklers spraying a pale rainbow over the emerald lawn, reflecting the colours in the herbaceous beds on the far side. Celia made no move to sit but continued walking slowly, eyes cast down, arms folded. Marnie fell into step beside her and waited.

'Marnie, there's something I have to talk to you about.'

Marnie suddenly guessed what that *something* was. Celia continued.

'You're probably the only person in the world I can –'

'Celia, if this concerns your private life I'd really rather not –'

'Oh, Marnie!' Celia turned and took hold of her by the arms. Tears brimmed in her eyes. 'Please don't say that. There's no one else I can turn to.'

'Celia, after that unfortunate misunderstanding concerning your husband, I thought we'd agreed to let it rest at that.'

'I know that was a big mistake, and I apologised, Marnie.'

'That's okay. It's all in the past. I thought we'd moved on from there.'

Celia resumed walking. 'I need some help, and you're the only person I know I can trust to be discreet.'

'Of course I'm discreet, Celia, you're a *client*.'

'Aren't I a *friend* as well?'

She turned appealing doe-eyes in Marnie's direction. Marnie knew she had to choose her next words with care.

'Whatever our relationship might be, Celia, we mustn't lose sight of the fact that it has to be professional. We have to work together and it isn't a good idea to let personal –'

'That's what I have in mind, Marnie.'

'Oh?' Suspicion. 'I don't follow.'

'I want you to help me in a kind of ... professional way.'

The two women stopped, each assessing the other, but from vastly differing perspectives.

'Go on. In what *professional* way can I help you?'

Celia gazed across the lawn, avoiding eye contact. 'Hugh and I went to our cottage in Norfolk at the weekend ...'

This doesn't concern a redecoration job, Marnie thought. She said nothing.

'... and I'm convinced he'd been there with another woman.'

'That doesn't sound like a –'

'Hear me out, Marnie, please, before you jump to any conclusions. I've got proof this time, actual evidence.'

'Then you have two options, Celia. Either you confront your husband with the *evidence* and have it out with him, or you take steps to make sure he doesn't have the leeway to keep on seeing this other woman. Both courses have their own risks, and only you can judge which way to go. There, that's my advice on the subject.'

'But you don't understand, Marnie. It isn't as simple as that.'

Surprise, surprise. Marnie looked pointedly at her watch. Where *were* the trades people?

'Celia, I really can't get involved in your affairs. Sorry, I mean your private life. It isn't practical. If you think about it you'll realise –'

'I said I wanted your help in a *professional* way, Marnie.'

'How?'

'My evidence, the *proof*. I need help with it.' She produced an envelope from a pocket and held it out. 'It's in there.'

Marnie eyed the envelope with suspicion. Celia gestured for her to take it, but she shook her head.

'What is it?'

'It's only hair.'

Marnie imagined Celia scrutinising the pillows at the cottage, shouting *Eureka!* as she detected a long strand of auburn or brown hair where her blonde head usually lay.

'Celia, hair can get onto a pillow in a variety of ways. You should be careful before accusing Hugh of infidelity. He might've brushed against someone in a restaurant and later thrown his jacket on the bed.'

'It wasn't on the pillow, Marnie. It's not that kind of hair.'

Marnie did not want to pursue the matter, but she was becoming intrigued. Celia opened the envelope and held it out for inspection. Marnie was on the brink of leaning forward.

'It's *pubic* hair, Marnie. I found it on the loo seat.'

Marnie gulped and took a step backwards. 'It's *what*?'

'Yes. You see, I went straight to the loo as soon as we arrived. And there it was. I knew at once it didn't belong to Hugh or me.'

Marnie was aware that Celia was prattling on about finding an envelope and using her eyebrow tweezers, but she shut out the rest of the details. A dozen thoughts rushed through her mind. Several of them involved dashing to her car and roaring off down the drive, never to return to Knightly Court again. Then one thought rose to the surface above the others.

'Celia, how do you envisage me helping you in a professional way with *this*?'

'Well, I wondered if you could put in a word … with Cathy Lamb.'

'You think Hugh's involved with Cathy Lamb, the detective?'

Celia gave a girlish sigh. 'No, *silly*! You get on well with her and she has access to a lab where they do tests on things. I thought she might be able to get someone to have a look at the hair and provide proof that it came from another woman.'

'But that's a forensic lab only available to the police and –'

'Then I could confront Hugh and have it out with him, like you suggested.'

'*Suggested?* No, no, Celia. I didn't *suggest* anything. I merely pointed out what options you might have.'

'Well anyway, I don't suppose these labs are busy all the time and –'

'Listen! That's a car. If I'm not mistaken, the contractors have arrived.'

The meeting went well and at lunchtime, under the parasol on the bank beside the boats, Marnie outlined her encounter with Celia over a meal of houmous, tsatsiki and taramasalata, with chopped raw vegetables and 'designer water'. Ralph, Anne and Danny could hardly believe their ears.

'She's certainly singled you out to be her confidante,' Ralph observed.

'But why *me*? Why not someone like, say, Angela Hemingway?'

'Angela? Come on, Marnie. Can you imagine it? "*Oh by the way, vicar, I've identified strange pubic hair on the toilet seat. Could you provide me with a sample of yours ... purely to eliminate you from our enquiries, of course*".'

Anne and Danny hooted, and even Marnie had to smile at the thought.

'What gets me is she tries to make me feel guilty and heartless when I don't agree to co-operate.'

'Moral blackmail. Does she get tearful?'

Marnie smiled wryly. 'She's elevated it to an art form, Ralph. She can turn on the tears, but not so much that they actually flow and spoil her make-up. It's a wonder to behold.'

'She probably uses that waterproof mascara,' Danny suggested.

They were interrupted by Marnie's mobile warbling.

'Marnie Walker, good afternoon.'

It was a short conversation of one-word replies. Marnie disconnected with a thoughtful expression.

'That was Cathy Lamb. She and Binns are coming down this afternoon. They wanted to make sure we were going to be around. I wonder what they want.'

On their way back to the office after lunch they heard raised voices as they walked through the spinney. Anne and Danny veered off to investigate and found Dick Blackwood and one of the older archaeologists remonstrating with a small crowd of people milling round the HQ barn.

He turned to Anne and asked her to confirm that they were on private land and that only *authorised persons* were allowed to be there. Anne did her best to look impressive and announced that Glebe Farm had given permission to the university and *Timeline* archaeologists to work on site. Other visitors were strictly by invitation only, at the insistence of the *police*. She glanced meaningfully back towards the shallow graves site.

The unwanted visitors were mostly middle-aged, and Anne hoped they would be basically law-abiding. One of the women was muttering that Anne looked like *little more than a schoolgirl* when, as if on cue, two people came round the corner of the barn.

Anne addressed the group. 'Let me introduce *Detective Sergeant* Binns and *Detective Constable* Lamb.' She paused to let the identities sink in. 'Now I'm sure that if you leave *immediately* and I promise that Glebe Farm management won't press charges, the detectives will not detain you for trespassing and compromising their crime scene.'

The *unauthorised persons* jostled each other in their rush to get away, and within seconds the area was cleared.

'What was all that about?' Binns asked. '*Press charges … crime scene?*'

'This is why we went away on Friday,' Anne declared. 'Too many interruptions to our work. It's hopeless. I don't know how these people can be here on a Monday afternoon. Don't they have jobs to go to?'

'Morbid interest,' Binns confirmed. 'We see it all the time.'

'Are you coming to see us?' Anne asked.

'Shortly. Is Mrs Walker there?'

'Of course. Cathy phoned to make an appointment. We won't be running away, tempting though that may seem.'

Sergeant Binns came straight to the point.

'We've had results back about the bodies. They appear to have been in the ground for around two hundred years.'

Marnie indicated the chairs and sat down. 'Does that mean you're giving active consideration to taking me off the suspects' list?'

'We're giving it serious thought.'

'So who were they? Has this anything to do with witchcraft? Are the archaeologists involved?'

'Too early to know for sure, but we've had the remains moved to Oxford for further examination.'

'The Archaeological Materials Laboratory?'

A pause. 'That's the place.'

'Dr Rosemary Goodchild?'

'As usual, you're ahead of us, Mrs Walker.'

Ralph was engrossed in proof-reading an article he had just completed for *The Economist* when he heard knocking on the side door. As Guy Fellheimer came backwards down the steps, Ralph warned him about the low ceiling height and led him to the study, where he folded himself onto a chair and examined his surroundings.

'So this is the famous floating college I've heard so much about. Not a bad environment for researching. What do you do for a library?'

'Believe it or not, Guy, I get a lot of material from the Internet.'

'Yes, I suppose you can do that in your line of enquiry.'

'Tell me about your line of enquiry, Guy. I'm agog to know what it was that brought you here that you didn't want to discuss on the phone.'

Fellheimer stretched out his long legs, a serious look on his face.

'Can I offer you something?' Ralph asked. 'Coffee, tea, something stronger?'

'I'm driving, so I need to be careful, but a small Scotch wouldn't go amiss.'

Ralph went to the galley and returned with a tray holding a bottle of Glenmorangie, two glasses, a small jug of water and a bowl of ice cubes. He set them down on the footstool and invited Fellheimer to help himself. When they were settled, they clinked glasses and sipped.

'I'm being blocked, Ralph. You know, there's a lot more to this matter than meets the eye. When I raised the issue with Henry Eustace – my contact at Pembroke College, you remember – I thought he'd get back in touch with the inside story. I guessed it would have something to do with the man-who-never-was and that it would probably be something still covered by the Official Secrets Act, hence all the mystery.'

'Even though that relates to the second world war?'

'There's quite a lot that can't be discussed even today, Ralph.'

'I didn't realise.'

'Oh yes. I have a cousin, charming old spinster, lives in a flat off Maida Vale. I expect her neighbours think she's just a harmless old biddy, devoted to her cat and her memories. In fact, she came to Britain before the war as a Jewish refugee, escaping from Hitler. Fluent in English, mother tongue German, she was recruited into military intelligence. She ran a covert operations unit – what the popular press would call a *spy ring* – from an office in Curzon Street. That's all I know, except that she linked up with a group in Geneva.'

'After all these years.'

'Yes. Once you sign the forms, that part of your life remains secret for the rest of your days.'

'And you think that's what's happened in this case.'

'I can't think of any other explanation, Ralph. When I asked Eustace what he'd found out, he confessed that he'd got absolutely nowhere. We're not talking about a first-year undergrad here. This man has connections, years in the intelligence service, knows people. He says he ran into a stone wall.'

'Could he be holding something back?'

'It's possible, but I think he was being truthful. When you've played chess with someone for five years, you know the way their mind works, how they react to situations. I'm sure he was genuinely surprised to discover that even he couldn't make progress.'

'Thanks for trying, Guy.'

Fellheimer shook his head. 'Now, of course, you're wondering what I'm holding back.'

Ralph shrugged and smiled. 'When you've been a friend and colleague of someone for twenty years, you know the way their mind works. I don't imagine you had to travel here from Oxford just to tell me your chess partner had drawn a blank.'

'You're quite right. It is more than that. He actually told me he'd been warned off.'

Ralph's smile faded. '*Warned off*,' he muttered. 'Curious choice of words.'

'Even more curious if you knew Henry Eustace. He's not your run-of-the-mill don with a lifetime spent in libraries and seminars.'

'You don't think he's been out of the game so long his contacts have just moved on?'

'No. He's not past his sell-by date. In any case, you're never really out of the game, as you put it, once you belong to that circle.'

'So, no progress, stone wall, warned off.'

'A fair summary, Ralph.' Fellheimer drained his whisky and put the glass on the tray. 'And it can mean only one thing.'

30
Graves

Angela Hemingway phoned early on Tuesday morning to ask when would be the least inconvenient time to come to Glebe Farm. Marnie took the hint and suggested coffee time.

The vicar arrived to find DC Cathy Lamb talking with Marnie in the courtyard. Anne was walking back from the farmhouse and asked Lamb if she was staying.

'Wish I could. Interviewing this morning. You know how it is.'

'Are you any further forward with the two latest bodies?' Marnie asked.

'Not yet. We'll let you know when we've got anything. You are going to be around, presumably?'

'Sure. I've had my holiday for this year.'

When Lamb left, they went into the office and were soon sitting comfortably with mugs of coffee.

'It must be hard for you and Anne to get on with your work,' Angela said.

'To be fair, Angela, the archaeologists are no trouble. But frankly, the sightseers and all this *shallow graves* business are getting me down.'

'I must say, Marnie, you do seem a bit stressed.'

'Understatement.'

'You could do with some light relief. In fact, that's why I'm here. We were wondering – that's Randall and me – if you'd like to come for dinner one evening this week at his place in Brackley.'

Marnie gave the idea two milliseconds of thought. 'I'm ready now!'

'You mean tonight?'

'Well, not literally, I don't suppose –'

'Marnie, you yourself have often said that things done on impulse are the best.'

'Ye-e-es.'

'So why not tonight? I'll ring Randall and tell him that's what you'd like. What d'you say?'

'Just one snag: there are four of us here at the moment.'

Angela grinned across the office at Anne. 'What is it you usually say, Anne? No probs?'

Anne heard Marnie groan that afternoon and looked up to see DS Binns passing the window on his way to the office door. She saw Marnie take a deep breath and could almost feel the effort she was making to present a calm exterior.

Binns accepted a chair.

'I have some news for you, Mrs Walker.' He saw Marnie's expression change. 'Don't despair. I think you'll be pleased. It concerns the bodies in the shallow graves.'

'I'm touched that you think news about dead bodies a few yards from my boat will bring me pleasure. May I assume you're not going to be hauling me off to the cells?'

'Correct, at least for the moment.' He smiled. 'We've learnt that the graves contained the bodies of two men killed at the time the canal was being built.'

'Navvies?'

'It appears so.'

'That was quick work. This stretch of canal was built in 1794. You've traced them in just a couple of days?'

'Not quite. We, er, had some help with that.'

Anne stood up and walked across the office. 'Why weren't they buried in the churchyard, Mr Binns?'

'They weren't killed in an accident, were they?' Marnie said.

'Why do you say that, Mrs Walker?'

'Well, the men were basically just digging a big ditch. It wasn't dangerous work. I don't know of any account of men being killed along here. And presumably, as Anne suggests, they'd have been buried in a proper graveyard and it would have been in the parish records.'

'You're quite right. It seems there was a brawl and these two men were casualties. Nothing was ever reported at the time and the whole matter was literally covered up.'

'Then how did you find out about them so quickly?'

'The archaeologists?' Anne said quietly.

Binns nodded. 'Yes. Dr Goodchild got in touch with the university's local history department as soon as she saw what we'd sent her. A specialist in social history had them nailed in just a few hours. I was impressed.'

'Why had no one found them before?' Marnie asked.

'They could've been buried anywhere, including under the canal or a bridge. But once we had the bodies, the experts had a pretty good idea who they were.'

'Do you know their names?'

'No. Men just turned up for work in those days. They were paid cash in hand every week and travelled from job to job. Generally they couldn't read or write and often they just gave a first name or even a nickname.'

'What happens now?'

'As far as you're concerned, Mrs Walker, you'll get your land back and we'll leave you in peace, more or less.'

'What does that mean?'

'I've just made a statement to the media about the bodies for the early evening news on TV. There may be some morbid interest in the grave site for another day or two, but it should soon die down and that will be an end to it.'

Marnie had been right. Things done on impulse were often the best. Sitting in Randall's candle-lit dining room in the Georgian rectory in Brackley, she felt relaxed and free of stress. Even when the conversation turned to the bodies in the shallow graves, she was able to discuss them dispassionately.

Randall was pouring wine, a claret brought by Ralph. 'Is it true the navvies mainly came from Ireland?'

'Why do you ask that?' Marnie said. 'Do you think Irish lads would be more likely to get into fights?'

'No, I was just wondering. You see, if they were catholic, that might explain why they didn't get a church burial. Few RC churches round here.'

'Surely it was more likely they'd be buried by the others so they didn't get into trouble with the authorities.'

'I suppose so.'

Angela was clearing away dishes from the first course. 'Isn't it surprising that no one missed them? You'd think someone would ask what had become of them.'

'Not in those days,' Ralph said. 'People often went far away to find work.'

'But they were some mothers' sons.'

'That's the way it was in the 1790s. Communications were poor. They probably couldn't write anyway. It was quite normal for young men to leave home and not see their families for years, or ever again.'

'So, coming back to my question,' Randall said. 'Were they from Ireland?'

'Not necessarily,' Marnie replied. 'I was reading an article in one of the boat magazines. It seems quite a few of them were recruited locally.'

'What a sad thought,' Angela said. 'They could have come from villages in the county and been lying there in their native soil, their families not far away, never knowing what had become of them.'

A sombre mood settled on the room.

'I suppose there's nothing we can do about it now,' Marnie reflected.

Suddenly, Angela brightened up. 'Yes, there is!'

'Absolutely,' Randall agreed. 'There are lots of things we can do.'

The dinner guests were bewildered, but Angela was beaming.

'On Sunday we'll remember them in our prayers. That's a start. Then, when the remains are released, I'll arrange for them to be buried in the churchyard. We can have a proper memorial service. And then …' Angela looked at Marnie. 'Of course, it's for you to say, but if you didn't think it an imposition, perhaps we could hold a short ceremony down by the canal.'

'What kind of ceremony?'

'A sort of thanksgiving for their lives and all the hard work done by the navigators. I know you're not a believer, Marnie, but –'

'No, it's a nice idea. You're welcome to do it on our land. I assume you'd want to hold your ceremony near the grave site?'

'If that's all right with you, Marnie.'

'A blessing of the waters,' Randall added. 'To give thanks for all the canal builders, the engineers, the boat people and their families, living and dead.'

It had been a good evening and on the journey home in Ralph's Volvo Anne dozed on the back seat beside Danny. Marnie turned to speak over her shoulder.

'Not too spooky for you tonight, I hope, Danny?'

'No. It was okay. I got a bit worried when they started talking about the shallow graves, but maybe I've got used to that kind of thing now.'

'Good.'

'There was one thing, though. All that talk about memorial services and ceremonies by the water for the dead people who'd built the canals, what was all that about?'

'The power of ritual,' Ralph observed.

'I thought it was a bit creepy, couldn't see what good it would do.'

'Ritual helps people come to terms with events. It helps to draw a line under them, bring closure. That's all they want to do.'

They drove on through the dark, Marnie resting a hand on Ralph's knee, the girls leaning back against the head restraints, eyes closed. When Ralph slowed to turn off the dual carriageway, Anne yawned, blinked and looked up at the stars. A thin sliver of moon hovered over Knightly Woods, stars flickering between the trees on the hill, the silver outline of the moon in the inky blackness.

Ralph waited momentarily in the filter lane while a few cars passed, before crossing the highway. The oncoming headlights lit up the interior of the Volvo, and for a few seconds Anne was dazzled by the lights reflected in the side window. It was almost as if the beams were shining through the woods on the high ground above them. Were lights shining through the woods? Anne blinked and tried to focus. Had she imagined it? Then they were rolling again, down the last mile or two towards the village.

They turned off the road at the entrance to the field track and Danny leaned forward in her seat as the car's headlights lit up the terrain before them. As usual the field was alive with bobbing tails as rabbits scampered off in all directions. Danny laughed.

'That's something you don't see in Leighton – oh! What was that?'

Marnie sat up. 'Where?'

Danny pointed forward between the front head restraints. 'Down there, like little lights.'

'Reflections of eyes?' Ralph suggested.

'Maybe.'

'Could be the badgers. 'There's a sett at the bottom of the field, to the left of the spinney.'

'I've never seen badgers before,' Danny said.

'Nor have we,' Anne said. 'They're nocturnal and very shy.'

Ralph slowed down. 'Perhaps this is our lucky night.'

He stopped the car outside the garage barn to let his passengers out before driving in. Danny grabbed Anne by the hand and tugged her round the corner.

She spoke in a low voice. 'Is the sett this way?'

'Not sure,' Anne whispered. 'Ralph seems to think so.'

'Let's go and see.'

Rounding the corner of the barn, they immediately found themselves in total darkness, relieved faintly by starlight. Danny hesitated, but Anne had an idea.

'Wait here. I'll fetch a torch from the garage.'

'But they'll see it and run away.'

'I'll be careful. Just hang on a sec.'

Anne seized a torch from a shelf in the garage, muttering to Marnie and Ralph that Danny was intent on a badger hunt. She was turning to leave when a scream pierced the night. The three of them rushed out, Anne switching on the torch. Danny was not where Anne had left her. She swept the powerful beam across the ground.

'Danny!' Ralph called out.

Some way ahead they heard a sound like a whimper. Running towards it, Anne's torchlight picked up a shape on the ground. As they drew nearer they realised that Danny was in a hole.

Ralph knelt down to help her. 'Are you all right, Danny? Are you hurt?'

'I … I think I've fallen … into one of the graves.'

'Let's get you out.'

Ralph and Marnie took one arm each and heaved Danny out of the hole. They guided her towards *Thyrsis*, where they satisfied themselves that she had suffered no injury. Her clothes were dirty but undamaged and she dusted herself down.

'Sorry to be such a nuisance. I didn't want to miss the badgers, thought Anne's torch would scare them off. I never dreamt I was that close to the shallow graves. Ugh!' She shuddered.

'Shallow graves?' Marnie said.

'Yes. Didn't you see? There was another one nearby.'

Marnie and Ralph traded glances.

'Are you sure?'

'Marnie, I know a grave when I see one. I'm getting to be quite an expert on the subject.'

Ralph picked up the torch from the table. 'I'll be back in a minute.'

Marnie followed him out. 'I'm coming with you.'

Alone in the saloon, the girls looked at each other. Danny spoke first.

'Am I missing something here?'

Anne nodded slowly. 'You certainly are.'

'I don't get it, but that's not unusual these days.'

'Whatever you fell into, Danny, it wasn't one of the shallow graves. They're over there.' She indicated with a flick of her chin. 'You must have fallen into some other grave.'

Without speaking, Danny lowered herself onto a chair as the colour drained from her face.

31
Lights in the woods

In her attic room Anne propped herself up on one elbow in bed and opened an eye. The glowing alarm clock told her it was just on seven. Taking a deep breath, she slid her feet out from under the duvet and dropped them deftly into her slippers. Daylight was seeping through the window slit. She stood up and began tiptoeing towards the opening for the wall-ladder.

'No need to creep about.' A voice from the floor beyond the bed. 'I'm awake, sort of.'

'Hi, Danny. Restless night?'

'No. Actually, I slept rather well.' She yawned. 'I think I must be becoming immune to all the things that go on here.'

'Must be a good sign. All right if I use the shower?'

'Sure. I'm not going to rush off and fall into any more holes. Once is enough.'

'I didn't mean –'

'I know. I'm only kidding.'

'At least you didn't injure yourself.'

'But you were right, Anne. I should've stayed put and waited for you to get the torch.'

'You could hardly have expected to come across open graves in the field, Danny.'

'Do you think it was the archaeologists?'

'I did wonder, only they wouldn't have left holes open like that without some kind of protection. And it wasn't the badgers, that's for sure.'

Danny chuckled. 'Pity. I would've liked to see them.'

An image flashed through Anne's mind: headlights piercing the night. She was aware of Danny's voice in the background.

'I mean, who'd be digging graves down there anyway? And what – or who – were they burying?'

Anne stood poised by the opening for the wall-ladder, staring down the hole into the darkened office. Danny was still speaking.

'Just shows how I've got used to the weird goings-on at Glebe Farm. We're surrounded by grave-robbers and I manage to get a good night's sleep.' She laughed.

Anne turned and looked across the room.

'What did you say?'

Marnie was normally awake earlier than Ralph, so it surprised her to see him lying on his back beside her in bed, gazing up at the ceiling.

The previous night, they had found the second hole mentioned by Danny. They had shone torches down, wondering how deep a grave had to be to qualify as *shallow*.

Marnie stretched an arm under the duvet and wrapped it round Ralph's chest.

'Been awake long?'

He took her hand and brought it to his lips, kissing the tips of her fingers.

'Not very. I've been wondering whether we should've reported the holes to the police last night.'

'But we agreed, Ralph. What if it had been a careless young archaeologist, who didn't think anyone would walk round there in the dark? DS Binns wouldn't have thanked us for disturbing his beauty sleep.'

Ralph chuckled.

'It's not that funny,' Marnie said.

'I just conjured up this thought: Binns arriving with curlers in his hair, wearing teddy bear pyjamas.'

They laughed silently together in the semi-darkness. Only the palest light penetrated into the sleeping cabin, but even at that hour they could feel it was going to be another warm day.

'Are you working here today, Ralph?'

'Yes. We'll face Binns together.'

'But first we'll have to check with Dick or Rob, just in case it was an oversight by one of their students.'

Marnie shifted onto her back under the duvet and stretched both arms up towards the ceiling.

'You don't really think it was one of them, do you, Ralph?'

'No more than you do.'

Marnie sat up.

'But if they're not theirs, who dug them?'

At breakfast on *Sally Ann* the talk was of holes in the ground. Marnie had suggested to Ralph that they refer to *holes* rather than *graves* until they knew for certain what had been dug. This did not prevent the conversation from veering towards technical matters related to grave digging.

'How deep do you think the hole was?' Danny asked.

'You should know,' Anne said. 'You're the one who fell in.'

'I know, but I think I was in a state of shock. That seems to be my default setting these days.'

'I think it was three or four feet deep,' Ralph offered.

'So would that qualify as a *shallow grave*?' Danny asked.

'It's a pretty deep hole to fall into,' Anne muttered, 'whether it's a grave or not.'

Marnie took warm rolls from the oven and laid them in a basket on the table. 'I reckon a shallow grave would be about two feet. I also think there are more cheerful things to talk about over breakfast.'

'So how deep's a *regular* grave?' Danny asked.

Ralph laughed.

'What's funny about that?'

'Sorry, Danny. I realised I was about to say, you seemed determined to get to the bottom of it.'

The three females present scowled at him. Ralph raised both hands in surrender.

'All right. The serious answer to your question, Danny, is about six feet.'

'So these were neither shallow nor ordinary graves.'

'Perhaps the diggers were interrupted while digging them,' Anne suggested. 'Maybe our headlights took them by surprise and they …' Her voice tailed off.

'What is it?' Marnie said.

'What on earth could they have been burying?' Danny said. 'It's horrible to think that while we were driving home, someone was out there –'

Anne interrupted her. 'They weren't *burying* anything.'

'Then why dig the holes?'

'You said it yourself this morning, Danny.' Anne got to her feet. 'Excuse me a minute.'

She eased herself round the table in the confined space and headed down the boat towards the stern doors. The others hesitated for a second before getting up to follow her out.

It was a fine morning, the sky almost clear, the air warm and still. Anne led the way through the spinney, round the barns and into the field. Reaching the holes, she stared at the ground. Marnie understood at once.

'What are we looking at?' Danny sounded bewildered. 'What was it I said, Anne? You're getting as bad as Donovan.'

'Grave-robbers.'

'That's right,' Marnie agreed.

Danny pulled a face. 'How do you –'

'Look, Danny.' Marnie pointed. 'It's obvious. What's the first consideration you have if you're digging a grave?'

Danny shrugged. 'You want to bury someone?'

'So?'

Ralph stepped closer to the nearest hole. 'You make a pile of earth so that you can easily shovel it back in. Here, the soil has been thrown all over the place. Whoever dug these holes wasn't concerned with *burying* anything. They just wanted to open up the ground as quickly as they could.'

Marnie walked between the holes and peered in. 'And they're both roughly the same depth.'

Anne looked back towards the canal as if making a calculation.

'What is it, Anne?'

'There's another thing. I think these holes are aligned north-south, so if they were burials …'

Even Danny caught the inference.

'How did you come to work all this out, Anne?' Marnie asked.

'I suppose you could say, I saw the light.'

Anne had announced she wanted to clarify her thoughts before saying any more about the graves. She offered to clear away the breakfast things and wash up on *Sally Ann* while Marnie and Ralph went to phone the police and Danny took her shower.

Alone in the galley, Anne pressed buttons on her mobile. She listened to ringing tone for a long time. Surely Donovan should have reached home by now, she thought. Strange that the answerphone was off. She pecked out the number of his mobile.

The person you are phoning is not available. Please try again later.

Perhaps the solo journey was more difficult than they had imagined. Anne started thinking of everything that could have delayed him. After running through all the permutations, she tried both numbers once again and gave up. Her life seemed to be a series of *what-ifs* and *maybes* these days.

Back in the office barn, Marnie and Ralph seemed more cheerful. Ralph had made the call to DS Binns and explained that Marnie would be out at meetings for the first part of the day. Binns said he would call by that morning.

Marnie asked Anne to be ready to leave for Knightly Court at ten to nine. In the Discovery on the way up the field track, Marnie touched her friend's arm.

'It's good to be getting on with our normal life, even if it does involve Celia Devere.'

'Especially if it involves Celia, I think.' Anne grinned.

'What do you mean?'

'You don't want to risk being alone with Celia.'

Marnie laughed. 'Correct. And there is one other thing.'

'You want me to explain what I said about seeing the light.'

'I guessed you didn't want to talk about that in front of Danny.'

'I'm not sure of myself in this, Marnie. I could be mistaken but, well, frankly if I'm right, it could be *seriously* creepy.'

Marnie shot a sideways glance at her friend. 'Now you're making *my* skin tingle. Does this have anything to do with Donovan?'

'No.'

'Only, when you stayed behind after breakfast, it did cross my mind –'

'I rang to see if Donovan had got home safely, that's all.'

'Is he all right?'

'No reply.'

'Mobile?'

'Recorded message, not available.'

'How many days is it since we parted company?'

'He should easily have got back by now, Marnie.'

'Maybe he's just travelling at night, and he does have an injured foot. Anne, if there's anyone capable of looking after himself, it's Donovan.'

'I know.'

'So what did you mean about seeing the light?'

Anne gave a quick outline: the headlights shining in her eyes on their way home the previous night; her impression that lights were flickering up in Knightly Woods. She now wondered if the lights might have been fires. By the time she completed her narrative they were passing through the gates onto the drive of Knightly Court.

Marnie brought the car to a halt near the front door and turned off the engine.

'So what are you saying, Anne, exactly?'

'The holes at Glebe Farm weren't intended for *burying* anything, or anyone, were they? Someone had been digging something up, from holes aligned north to south, in a hurry, at dead of night.'

'I get the picture. And you think …'

'I think we'd better continue this later.' Anne nodded meaningfully over Marnie's shoulder. 'Here comes *la belle châtelaine*.'

As Celia approached them, Marnie opened the car door and climbed out. It occurred to her that in all her contacts with Celia she had never seen her wear the same outfit twice. On that day her client was wearing a short-sleeved summer dress in pale green silk; very much the Lady of the Manor preparing to meet the workers. To Marnie's relief the decorator's van arrived at that moment and pulled up beside the Discovery.

Marnie shook hands with Celia, who seemed distant, preoccupied. Anne joined them but remained unobtrusively beside Marnie. In the background, two men in white overalls were opening the back doors of the van and unloading equipment.

'Unless you need to change the schedule for any reason, Celia, we'll start in the drawing room, as planned.'

'That's fine, Marnie. Do I need to do anything?'

'Nothing at all. The men are quite self-sufficient.'

'So I can just leave them to get on with their work?'

'Absolutely. We've just come in case there are any last-minute queries.'

'My father-in-law always says you plan everything very … what's the word he uses? … *meticulously*.'

Marnie smiled. 'Is he here this morning?'

Celia stared at Marnie for some seconds before replying. She lowered her voice.

'Marcus is … unwell.'

'I'm sorry to hear that.'

'For some time he's been ill, Marnie, very ill. I'm sure I mentioned it to you.'

Marnie searched her memory. 'You did tell me he had a *condition*. I hadn't realised it was so –'

'Oh, yes. He's never had very good health, but for the past several months he's …' Celia's eyes flickered towards Anne. 'Well, let's just say things have got worse, much worse.'

In the car on the way back to Glebe Farm, Anne was the first to speak.

'That went all right, didn't it?'

'It was fine. We know their work. They're reliable. They'll do a good job.'

'Pity about Mr Devere. You like him, don't you, Marnie?'

'He's a nice old chap.'

'Do you think he really is very ill, or was that just Celia acting a part, as usual?'

'Sadly, I think that was genuine.'

'Did you notice, Marnie, she didn't want to say any more with me there? *Not in front of the servants*. Huh!'

They lapsed into their private thoughts until they reached the high street.

'Anne, tell me about the lights in the woods. What were you going to say about them?'

Anne sighed. 'I know it'll seem daft, but I was wondering if whoever dug up whatever was in the holes on our site was, well, reburying it up in Knightly Woods, or even cremating remains.'

Marnie blew breath out through her lips. 'Bloody hell!'

'I know but, of course I could've been mistaken, though I'm pretty sure I saw something up there.'

'I think that would probably qualify as *fairly creepy*. So who d'you think was doing all this digging up and reburying or cremating?'

'I dunno.' Anne shuddered. 'Some sort of weirdoes, I suppose.'

'How certain are you that you really did see lights up there?'

'Fairly. It was dark, though, and I was a bit dazzled by oncoming cars.'

Marnie slowed and turned left into the field leading down to Glebe Farm.

'You see, Anne, the question is, what do we say to good old DS Binns when he puts the thumbscrews on us?'

'Binns?'

'Sure. He's going to be asking all sorts of questions about what he'll regard as more graves on our land. They may not be shallow, but he won't care about that. To him, they'll be graves. And as far as he's concerned, we'll have some explaining to do.'

'Do you think he'll be lying in wait for us when we get home?'

'That's a thought.' Marnie stopped the car halfway down the track and reached for her mobile. She hit a speed-dial button and waited. 'Ralph, it's me. Any sign of Binns of the Yard?'

'He's been here, but only for a fleeting visit. He looked in and asked what time we got home and what car we were in. Then he said he was going to the site of the new graves –'

'He called them *graves*?'

'Yes. He said he'd be back later. I haven't seen him since.'

When Marnie parked in the garage barn she was surprised to find a small posse waiting for her. First to approach her was Danny wearing a flimsy muslin shirt thrown over her bikini. Behind her came Rob Cardew and Dick Blackwood.

'The police are here, Marnie. They've cordoned off the place where I fell in last night.

The sergeant's been to see Ralph.'

'Did he say anything to you, Danny?'

'No. I was putting the li-lo out on the roof of *Sally Ann*. He just gave me a look.'

'Can't think why,' Dick said with a twinkle in his eye, glancing down at Danny's suntanned legs.

She turned and flashed him the heavy eyelids. Rob Cardew stepped forward.

'You've had another visitor, Marnie.'

'Really? I wasn't expecting anyone. Who was it this time, the Gestapo or the Witchfinder General?'

'An elderly lady.'

Marnie raised an eyebrow at Anne, who shook her head. They could only think of one person of their acquaintance who matched that description, Mrs Jolly, a friend from Little Venice.

'What was she like, pleasant, homely, motherly type?'

Rob reflected. 'Not really. She was petite, with quite striking features, a rather challenging manner, the type who has definite opinions.'

'You can say that again,' Danny chipped in. 'I saw her too. I was lying on the roof of the boat when I heard someone come up. She seemed to be examining *Sally* from front to back, nodding her head as if she knew her. When she noticed me, she gave me a look like she didn't approve of the bikini.'

'I do,' Dick said.

The others ignored him. Marnie was lost in thought.

'I wonder ...'

'D'you know her, Marnie?' Anne asked.

'Possibly.'

Danny laughed. 'Maybe it was Donovan in disguise!'

Marnie grinned. 'Very likely.' She turned to Rob Cardew. 'Did you want to talk to me about anything else, Rob?'

'I wanted to give you an update on where we are with the dig.'

'Is the visitor still about?'

'She left ...' Rob looked at his watch. '... about half an hour ago. She said she'd come back another time.'

'Rob, I'd love to hear about the dig, but I think I ought to see Sergeant Binns.'

Rob's expression became serious. 'You might like to have a word with me first, Marnie.'

They agreed to split up. Anne went off to open the office with Danny. Dick returned to supervising the dig. Marnie went with Rob to the HQ barn.

* * *

The red light was glowing on the office answerphone. One message. Anne pressed the button.

'Hi. Ring when you can. Mobile.'

That is one succinct message, Anne thought. She had no need to look up the number.

It answered on the third ring. Donovan had made the journey back to London in reasonable time, travelling mostly by night. He was sure no one had followed him, no one was watching the house.

Anne told him about the new graves, the return of the police and the arrival of the old lady. As usual he listened without interruption. His questions all concerned the visitor. Did they have any idea who she was? Had she come alone or with others? How had she travelled there? Was she coming back? When? Did she ask about anyone in particular? Did she ask about him?

When Anne could answer none of his questions, he became silent. Anne scoured her brain for anything she could tell him.

'Donovan, listen. I think I saw lights up in the woods when we were coming home last night. I was wondering if people were burying whatever they dug up from down here.'

'Do the cameras show anything?'

Anne was thrown off-balance by the sudden change. 'What cameras?'

'The *surveillance* cameras, the ones that got me on the TV news.'

'I'd forgotten about them.'

'Worth checking if they run all the time, even at night.'

'I will.'

'I'd better go.'

'Glad you got back all right.'

'Yeah. It seems like they don't know who I am.'

~~~

In the HQ barn Rob took a marker pen and drew four small circles on the cellophane sheet over the site map pinned to the wall. He explained to Marnie that they had discovered two further opened graves when they arrived on site that morning. The holes had certainly not been there when they left the previous day. All of them were aligned north-south. Current thinking was that they were pagan burials, and the hot money was on witch-graves.

Marnie asked if he had any idea how old they might be. He was not prepared to speculate.

'Why were they buried down here?'

'There could be all sorts of reasons, Marnie. There are indications of a spring, so they could be associated with some ancient holy place. This site is very secluded, little risk of being seen.'

'You think the graves predate the building of the canal? These aren't more navvies killed in brawls?'

'I'd be very surprised.'

'I wonder where they've taken the remains.'

'I have no idea. Have you, Marnie?'

'Without actual evidence, I couldn't possibly comment.'

Rob flashed her the owlish grin and walked with her out of the barn.
~~~

'There was one other thing I wanted to tell you, Marnie. Celia phoned Rosemary yesterday to ask if she'd analyse a hair sample she'd found in their cottage.'

'You're kidding!'

'I kid you not. She was quite offended, apparently, when Rosemary explained – diplomatically – that what she was asking was impossible.'

'That's why she's got the sulks.' Marnie sighed. 'Oh, that woman.'

Their stroll had now taken them round the HQ barn and into the field. The slope was dotted with small clusters of archaeologists at work. Marnie tried to imagine the field without the diggers and realised that for all the upheaval, she would probably miss them when they were gone.

On the lower ground, away to their right, she could see areas cordoned-off by the police. To one side she made out a group of plain clothes officers, including Binns and Lamb, locked in conversation.

She tried to imagine the scene the night before. Somehow someone had known about the graves and had decided to move their occupants to prevent disturbance. Could Anne have been right? Marnie suddenly felt an overwhelming desire to share her idea with Rob.

'Do those spy cameras work after dark?'

'How extraordinary, Marnie. That's exactly what Sergeant Binns asked when he arrived this morning.'

'What did you tell him?'

'I didn't know. He went off to talk to the technicians in the OB van.'

'Was that before or after going to see Ralph?'

'First thing when he drove down here. Is there a problem?'

Marnie was about to answer when Anne came running round the corner of the barn. She spoke breathlessly to Rob.

'Those cameras, the surveillance ones, do they run at night?'

Rob pulled the mobile from his pocket, pressed buttons and spoke rapidly. He disconnected.

'They watch the site round the clock.'

Ralph had the slightly unfocused look that Marnie recognised as deep concentration when she and Anne burst in on him in his study on *Thyrsis*, followed by Danny. He turned briefly back to the computer and pressed the Save button.

Marnie wasted no time. 'Binns isn't interested in us for this one. He knows our movements and the timing of whatever went on down here last night. The surveillance cameras saw everything.'

'Are you sure? It was very dark.'

'I'm sure he knows the exact time we came home.'

'And the people digging?'

'My guess is, he could see their lights well enough to know they were at it long before we got back.'

'Good. So that's that all cleared up.'

'Not quite, Ralph. Anne has a theory.'

Anne explained about the lights she had seen on the high ground in Knightly Woods. 'What I can't explain is exactly what was going on up there.'

Danny's expression combined distaste and confusion in equal measures. 'You think someone dug up the dead bodies of witches, dragged them all the way up to the top of that hill and then had a rave to celebrate?'

Anne frowned. 'I know I saw something and I don't believe in coincidences.'

Ralph pinched the bridge of his nose. 'It's a possibility.'

'More than that, I think,' Marnie said quietly. 'There's something I haven't mentioned before.'

Anne's eyes narrowed. 'About the lights?'

'About Knightly Woods.'

Marnie told them how Celia and her husband had walked in the woods and stumbled on a witches' circle on the top of the hill.

'Do we tell Sergeant Binns about this?' Anne asked.

Marnie turned to Ralph. 'What do you think?'

'On balance, we probably should.'

'And if it was just some sort of party up there?'

'We'll look foolish and we'll have wasted his time.'

'So shouldn't we check our facts first?'

'That might be wise.'

'I'd like to go,' Anne said.

'If we all went it would look odd,' Marnie pointed out.

Danny looked uncomfortable. 'Perhaps –'

'You should stay here, Danny.' Marnie grinned. 'You and your bikini are our best decoy.'

Ralph smiled. 'I suppose you want me to stay behind to add a tone of respectability to the camouflage?'

Marnie looked at Anne. 'Seems like it's you and me, babe.'

It was cooler in the woods, at least before Marnie and Anne began climbing to the top. From the car park they took the designated footpath and followed its gentle incline until they realised it had been designed to skirt round the hill rather than ascend it. They spotted a steeper route through the undergrowth and struck off towards higher ground.

Their heart rate and temperature rose in line with the steepness of the gradient as they clambered steadily upwards without talking. The light between the trees was deceptive, patterning the ground in mottled shade, making them take extra care not to trip over roots and stones on the way. The woods were dozing in the noonday heat. All around them was silence, with only an occasional note of birdsong reaching them from far off.

Just as they were beginning to think the hillside would go on forever, they arrived in a clearing and could see ahead of them a final wooded slope to the top. Exposed to the sun, neither wanted to pause for breath in the open space. Marnie led the way across to the trees and picked out a track. The summit was as devoid of growth as a monk's tonsure and they walked its perimeter, searching for indications of disturbed ground.

They found nothing. Marnie and Anne sat down on mossy ground out of the sun, leaning back against trees, disappointed. Anne spoke first.

'Was it just a late night ramble?'

Marnie shook her head, taking deep breaths. 'Who knows what it was?'

'Whatever it was, this has been a wild goose chase.'

'The lights you saw might've been on some other part of the hill.'

Anne's turn to shake her head. 'No. You can just about see the main road from over there. I looked.'

Marnie stood up. 'Come on, then. Let's check it out again.'

They walked side by side, systematically covering the whole of the open ground. After several minutes of searching, Marnie was starting to wonder if they were in the wrong place. If this was the clearing that Celia had described to her, where was the witches' circle?

Anne was about to repeat her concern that they were wasting their time, when she trod on something. Looking down, she realised that the dust on the ground was in two colours: the brownish soil and a finer grey powder, both mixed together. She stepped aside from where she had trodden and squatted down, running her fingertips through the fine dirt. Her nail brushed against something small and firm. She picked it up and shook the dust from it while Marnie looked on. Anne stood up and blew away the last ash. She was holding the stub of a candle, a black candle.

'We're there,' Marnie said.

32
Winterburn

It was not like Marnie to fret when the police failed to turn up on her doorstep. On Thursday morning she dropped a notebook into her shoulder bag with the Polaroid camera and got up from the desk. It was ten to nine and she was setting off for Knightly Court. She had left a message for Sergeant Binns the previous day, but so far there had been no response. Marnie looked at the wall clock and then checked her wristwatch.

Anne grinned. 'I don't think there's a difference in time zone from one side of the office to the other.'

'I don't want to be out if Binns suddenly appears.'

'Then let *me* go to the Court. You only want to make sure everything's going smoothly so that Her Ladyship ...' Anne mimed a curtsy while remaining seated. '... isn't getting her frillies in a twist.'

With most other projects Marnie could just let Anne pay a routine visit to the work. But on this job they both knew that Celia would think she was being fobbed off with the *under scullery-maid*. The problem was solved when DC Cathy Lamb breezed into the office with a perfunctory knock.

'What's this, Marnie? Fleeing the country?'

'It's tempting.'

'You wanted to speak to us.'

Marnie gestured to a chair. 'No Sergeant Binns?'

Lamb remained standing. 'We've split forces. Too much going on. You'll have to make do with me this morning.'

'I take it that means you don't think we're involved in the latest grave-digging episode.'

'Course not. We know what time you came back from Brackley. The intruders were long gone by then. Right now, we're more interested in where they went.'

Marnie flashed a look at Anne before replying. 'You could try Knightly Woods.'

'Really?'

'Anne has something to tell you.'

Lamb pulled out her notebook and flipped it open. 'Maybe we should sit down, after all.'

Anne craned her neck to stare back down the slope towards the new grave sites as Marnie drove the Discovery up the field track. As soon as they had described their visit to the woods the previous day, Lamb had left at high speed to report back to her sergeant. Marnie wasted no time in heading for Knightly Court.

'Can you see anything, Anne?'

'Not really, just a few of the uniforms by the taped-off area. Why the hurry to get away?'

'If Binns had caught up with us we'd have been there half the morning. He would've wanted our story at least three times and then told us to stick around in case we were needed again. The police forget we have a business to run.'

'Cathy seemed very interested in what we told her.'

Marnie smiled sideways at Anne. 'Just doing our duty as good citizens.'

By the time Marnie swung the car in through the gates of Knightly Court, the decorators' van was standing by the main entrance, its rear doors wide open. Nearby, Celia's Audi was lined up as if ready to leave, hood folded down, boot lid standing erect. Celia herself came out trailing behind her a small Louis Vuitton suitcase on wheels followed by a man in overalls. As Marnie pushed her car door open, she saw Celia retract the handle, stand back and point into the boot. The decorator lifted the case in and closed the lid.

Anne joined Marnie beside the Discovery. 'We all seem to be making quick getaways today,' she said softly.

'I wonder why,' said Marnie. 'Let's find out.'

Celia stood waiting beside her car, wearing a simple cream cotton dress and light tan slip-ons.

'Oh, Marnie, I'm so glad to have caught you.' A languid tone of voice.

'You're going away?'

Celia sighed. 'I have to. It's just too ... how can I put it?'

'Has something happened?'

Celia gestured towards the house. 'I can't ... it's ... the paint. The smell is giving me a *constant* headache. I know if I stay a moment longer I'll go down with the most *frightful* migraine.'

'I see. Normally, if you can leave the windows and doors open it clears quite quickly. In this weather –'

'It's no good, Marnie. I'm going away for a few days to our cottage in Norfolk. The decorators have a key, and you'll be here to keep an eye on everything.'

Marnie counted to three before replying. 'What about your husband?'

'Didn't I say? Hugh's off on business. He's staying at the cottage as well.' She beamed. 'I thought it would be a pleasant surprise for him when I turn up.'

Oh boy, Marnie thought.

On the drive back to Glebe Farm, Marnie stopped the car on an empty stretch of road outside the village and turned to Anne.

'What's bothering you? D'you want to talk about it?'

'What do you mean?'

'You're so quiet.'

'Only in comparison with Danny.'

Marnie chuckled. 'What is it about that girl?'

'You mean apart from the fact that she seems to be tanned all over and runs around half-naked most of the time?'

They grinned at each other.

'At least she doesn't seem to be so spooked by everything these days.' Marnie became serious. 'Are you seriously worried about Donovan? Is that what it is?'

Anne screwed her face up. 'Not in the way you mean, Marnie. But there is something. I can't quite put my finger on it.'

Marnie switched off the engine. 'Try.'

Anne drew in a long slow breath, staring ahead through the windscreen.

'Things don't match up somehow. It's odd, but I get the impression we're not all looking in the right direction, or even in the same direction.'

'You've lost me.'

Anne sighed. 'I've lost *myself*. I don't know how to put it.'

'Why not make one of your famous lists, then?' Marnie smiled encouragement.

Anne paused. 'First on the list I'd put the witch thing. We've got the weird goings-on up in the woods that scared Celia. Then *Timeline* and their excavations and now the witches' graves – if that's what they are – down by the canal. And the whatever-it-was in the woods on Tuesday night.'

'That's all clear enough.'

Anne nodded. 'As far as it goes, yes. But there's something else going on here, isn't there?'

'So what comes next on your list? And is there a connection?'

'A connection? Yes. It's ... it's Celia, I suppose.'

'Go on.'

'There's the body in Sarah's grave. We all know that's got nothing to do with the witches. The question is, why were those remains taken away from Rob's wife? Who removed them from her laboratory? And what has all that got to do with the poem about the man on the stairs, who wasn't there?'

'There's something else about that, Anne. You know Ralph's been talking to Guy Fellheimer?'

'Sure. He was going to follow it up with a friend at another college.'

'It seems Guy's friend tried to find out what was going on and was warned off.'

'*Warned off*? That sounds ominous.'

'Worse than that, really. The friend used to be in the secret service – probably MI something or other – and he has connections. On this occasion they were of no use.'

'Or he knows what's going on and can't – or won't – say,' Anne surmised.

Marnie nodded. 'So there's your list. Two headings: witches and the mysterious remains. And you think Celia's the link between the two columns?'

'Could be, but it's not Celia that bothers me. There may be another link.'

'Donovan?'

'Yes.'

'But, Anne, surely no-one's looking for Donovan on account of *witches*. How can he be a link?'

'He got caught on camera at the dig site, so if anyone is looking for him, they'll associate him with the archaeologists. And he was certainly recognised from the TV news by those people who came to look at the dig the next day.'

Marnie sat thinking. 'I'm not sure you're right about Donovan being connected with both strands or even with either of them. He just turned up and got filmed by accident.'

'And was seen by millions of people.'

'True.'

'And he *is* connected with the remains in Sarah's grave, Marnie.'

'In what way?'

'He has Rosemary's roll of film.'

Marnie leaned back against the headrest. 'I'd forgotten about the film. But only a few of us know about that.'

'I know it may be only a remote connection, Marnie, but it is a link.'

'Maybe, but I don't think you need have any worries there.'

'It worried Donovan enough.'

'He always worries. I'm sure if anyone did see him on the TV news, they don't know who he is.'

'It's funny. That's what Donovan said.'

'There you are, then. Nothing to worry about.'

Marnie started the engine and drove off.

'Your lists have their uses, Anne. It was helpful talking about the two headings like that.'

Anne looked out of the window thinking they were none the wiser, and that Donovan didn't scare easily for no reason. She kept her thoughts to herself.

Back at Glebe Farm, Marnie and Anne were intercepted by Bob the foreman on their way to the office barn. He looked sheepish.

'What's up, Bob? Something bothering you?'

'Well, someone was here, looking for you, Marnie.'

'What sort of someone?'

'Scary.'

Anne looked over her shoulder and quickly dug out the office keys.

Marnie frowned. 'Can you be more explicit?'

'You'll think I'm daft but it was a little old lady.'

Marnie had a flashback. It was three years earlier while travelling solo on her sabbatical first journey on *Sally Ann*. On a windswept afternoon in the middle of a heavy downpour she had come across an old lady with an injured ankle, miles from anywhere. Her name was Iris Winterburn. She had been one of the so-called 'idle women' who had served on narrowboats during the second world war.

With the help of a skinhead sheltering from the storm in a shed, she had managed to get the old lady onto the boat and had taken her to the skinhead's home village nearby, where he had a car. Ms Winterburn – her austere manner did not encourage the use of forenames, even in memory – had nicknamed him *Attila*. Marnie's last sight of the injured party had been her departure in Attila's battered orange Triumph Spitfire, resplendent in Iron Cross, Confederate flag and raccoon's tail swinging from the radio aerial, blasting off into the rainy gloom to a fanfare of *Colonel Bogey* on the horn. The memory made Marnie shudder. She was brought back to the present by a nudge from Anne.

'What?'

'I said presumably this person is not Mrs Jolly. Do you know who it might be, Marnie?'

'I have a rough idea.'

'Shall we go and find her? Poor old thing might be gasping for a cuppa.'

'Anne, if this is Iris Winterburn, she won't need looking after. She's as tough as old boots, spent two years in the war taking cargoes in and out of some of the most wanted waterway targets on the Luftwaffe hit list. If Hitler had known she was on the other side, he'd have thrown in the towel before the Normandy landings.'

Bob's expression suddenly contorted. Before Marnie could ask if he was all right, she heard a voice behind her.

'I think that's an exaggeration. He'd probably have waited till the allies crossed the Rhine.'

Marnie and Anne turned slowly. At the corner by the office barn stood a diminutive, neat figure in a light jacket of royal blue cotton over a fawn dress. On one shoulder she was carrying a small rucksack. Sharp features, silver hair and piercing blue eyes gave her a striking appearance, and her voice had a strength that belied her years.

'Iris Winterburn,' Marnie said quietly.

'So it *is* you.' The visitor eyed Marnie appraisingly. 'My rescuer from the storm.'

'Shall we ...' Marnie's voice had become a croak. She cleared her throat and gestured towards the office door. 'Would you like to come in and have a cup of tea, Ms Winterburn?'

'Why not? It's your usual reaction on meeting me. And it's *Miss*.'

As they crossed the courtyard, leaving Bob grateful to return to his work, Anne felt relieved that the newcomer had not heard her comment about the 'poor old thing'. Unlocking the office door, she stood aside to let Marnie and their guest enter. In the doorway, Iris Winterburn turned to Anne as if to thank her.

'You were right, young lady. I am gasping.'

Anne gulped, followed her in and headed straight for the kitchen area to put the kettle on. Marnie moved the spare chair over to her desk, noticing the red light glowing on the answerphone and the morning post still piled in the in-tray. After brief introductions, they settled down with tea and biscuits.

Marnie attempted friendly conversation. 'I wonder what became of Attila.'

'*Attila?*' Winterburn considered the name. 'I'm not that old.'

Marnie smiled. 'The *skinhead*. Almost your first words when we got you on board *Sally Ann*. You said he looked like Attila the Hun at a vicarage tea party or something like that.'

In the background Anne sniggered.

'Did I?' The old lady reflected. 'I must have been feeling charitable.'

'You were feeling a lot of pain, as I recall.'

'It took the best part of a year to get over that. A bad sprain, that's all it was, but at my age …' She shrugged.

'It could've been worse,' said Marnie. 'We were lucky Attila was there to help me transfer you to the boat. I've often wondered how you got on.'

'Did you think we'd eloped to Gretna Green?'

Looking at the old lady, with the slightly Roman curve to her nose and the firm pointed chin, a question was forming in Marnie's mind. She did not delude herself that this was a journey to express gratitude. Her visitor could not have known that Marnie now lived there. So why had Iris Winterburn come to Glebe Farm?

'I heard you'd discharged yourself from hospital, Miss Winterburn.'

'Who told you that?'

'The nurse in charge of your ward. She sounded Scottish, I think.' Marnie could have added that the poor woman also sounded as if in shock.

'Oh yes, prim woman with red hair. I never trust people with red hair. So you phoned the hospital.'

'I was worried about you, wanted to know you were all right.'

'The … er … *Attila* took me to where I was staying. I offered him ten pounds towards his petrol, but he declined. I slept badly and the next day I went home. Some holiday that was!'

Winterburn looked up at the ceiling where the spray of lavender was hanging, her expression thoughtful. Her eyes strayed to the wall-ladder leading to Anne's attic room. She drank her tea.

'Your injury doesn't seem to have done any lasting damage, Miss Winterburn. In fact, you don't look any different from when we met. That must be about three years ago.'

'Oh, I expect I creak in a few more places, but I manage to survive.' She put her cup down and looked at Marnie's desk. 'So this is where you work.'

'Yes.'

'You have a lot to do, judging by the amount of paper there. I mustn't get in the way. I'll leave you to it.'

The old lady stood up. Marnie and Anne got to their feet.

'It's been nice to see you again, Miss Winterburn. I'm glad you suffered no lasting effects from your ordeal on that awful day.'

The old lady paused before replying. 'I'm glad to have had the opportunity to thank you for helping me.'

Marnie did not point out that Miss Winterburn had not so far expressed any thanks.

'But that isn't why you came, is it?'

For the first time Winterburn smiled. 'You're very perceptive, Ms Walker.'

'Sometimes, perhaps, and it's *Marnie*. It used to be *Mrs*, but now Marnie will do. You're right about me having a lot of work to get through, but I wonder, would you like to come for dinner on Friday?'

A hesitation. 'That would be most agreeable. I have to return home on Saturday.'

'Shall we say seven o'clock?'

Winterburn nodded. 'Can I meet you here?'

'We'll eat *al fresco* beside the boat, but I can meet you here if you'd like that.'

'I have my reasons. Don't show me out. I know the way to my car and you have things to do. Until tomorrow, then.'

Anne collected the tea cups and plates on a tray when she and Marnie were alone again.

'You must tell me how you met her, Marnie. What was that about rescuing her from a storm?'

'It was during my summer sabbatical on *Sally*, not long after I first met you. I'll tell you all about it later.'

'Okay. One last thing before we get back to the grind, what do you think she meant when she said she *had her reasons*?'

'No idea. Perhaps we'll find out tomorrow evening.'

Danny surprised Marnie by preparing a ploughman's lunch for Walker & Co plus Ralph, and they ate it beside the docking area. Danny announced that while she was at Glebe Farm she would like to do what she could to help, adding that she didn't want to outstay her welcome. Marnie assured her that she could stay as long as she wished, and Anne suggested they might do the post run together that afternoon.

Danny duly appeared at four o'clock and changed out of her bikini into shorts and T-shirt ready for the trek up to the village. Anne gathered up that day's letters for posting, together with a shopping list and they set off, calling in to check that all was well in the HQ barn on their way.

Dick Blackwood was examining photographs outside the barn and he bounded over when the girls went by.

'Your tan's coming on well, Danny.' He managed to keep his smile just short of a leer.

'Sociology obviously agrees with me.'

Anne was trying to figure that out when Dick turned his attention to her. 'Is your friend Irish?'

'I think I'm missing something here. Danny comes from Leighton Buzzard, like me.'

'The other friend, the *boyfriend*, the one dressed in black.'

'Why d'you ask?'

'Someone was asking about him. They'd seen him on the TV news.'

'Who had?'

'Some young guy. I hadn't seen him before.'

'Not an archaeologist?'

'No, a sightseer. I heard him asking one of the girls. She said she thought perhaps he was Irish; he had an Irish name. She couldn't remember it, though, said it was something like Dooley or Donnelly. I couldn't quite remember it myself.'

'Not a bad guess,' Danny said. 'Actually it's –'

'Why was this man so interested?' Anne interrupted, shooting a sharp glance at Danny.

Dick shrugged. 'Dunno. He was just wandering around, looking at the dig, just seemed to be making conversation with one of the girls. Does it matter?'

'Not sure. Dick, if anyone else asks about him, just say he was with the TV people and leave it at that. Okay?'

'Fine by me.'

Anne checked her watch, said they had to catch the post and led Danny off up the field track. Danny chatted merrily as they walked along, while Anne only half listened. Her thoughts were on Donovan. She was becoming convinced that perhaps he wasn't paranoid after all. She heard his voice: *they don't know who I am*. Maybe not, she thought. But how long before they find out, whoever *they* are?

That night on *Thyrsis* when Marnie came out of the shower, she called through to Ralph in the sleeping cabin.

'Can I borrow one of your shirts as a dressing gown?'

'Of course. I always wanted to live with a transvestite.'

Marnie went through and sat on the bed, wearing a pale blue shirt with double cuffs that flapped about. She waggled them provocatively at Ralph.

'You'll find the cufflinks in the second drawer down if you wish to be formal,' he said.

Marnie laughed. 'Do you think it would add to my allure?'

'Unquestionably. Anyway, what's become of your dressing gown?'

'I lent it to Danny. She's running out of clothes.'

'I didn't realise she wore any.'

'Ah yes.' Marnie grinned. 'You must have a good view of her from your study, lying there in the sun on *Sally*'s roof all day. I hope she doesn't distract you too much.'

'I don't so much as spare her a glance.'

'Good. I wouldn't want her giving you any wicked ideas.'

'Although, actually, if I did just happen to ... *accidentally* cast half an eye in her general direction, absentmindedly, you understand, I might just observe that she now spends most of the time reading.'

'Magazines and chick-lit?'

'Textbooks, I'd say. If I was noticing anything at all.'

'Of course.' Marnie smiled sweetly. 'Talking of bodies –'

'Were we?'

'Oh yes, I think we were. What about the bodies in the not-so-shallow graves? Why did people come and take away the witches' remains, if that's what they were? Any ideas?'

'Possibly they just didn't want them dug up by anyone else.'

'So they removed them for cremation? Is that what they were doing up in Knightly Woods?'

'Seems reasonable.'

'Perhaps we'll find out tomorrow, if Binns comes by.'

'Talking of tomorrow, Guy Fellheimer rang this afternoon. He said he might come over. I was wondering if he might stay and have dinner with us. Would that be all right?'

'Fine. We'll see what he makes of Iris Winterburn.'

'I think he has some more news about the man who wasn't there.'

'Good. Is he kosher?'

'Guy? *Absolutely*. He's regarded as one of the foremost modern historians in Britain. He has an international reputation.'

Marnie laughed so much she rocked the bed. Ralph looked bewildered.

'What's funny about that?'

'I meant *foodwise* kosher. He is Jewish, isn't he? And Friday is a special evening, the start of the Jewish Sabbath. Gammon followed by cheesecake may not be appropriate.'

Ralph reached up to the shelf over the bed for his mobile.

'It's not too late to ring him to find out. He's a night owl.'

The call was answered at once. Fellheimer confirmed that he would be pleased to stay for dinner and that he was not strict about the food laws. Ralph was chuckling when he disconnected.

'Guy says to tell you he doesn't go the whole hog.'

Marnie grinned and sprawled across the bed, propping herself up on one elbow.

'It should be an interesting evening. Oh sorry, am I creasing your shirt?'

Ralph leaned forward and began undoing the buttons. 'Talking of bodies,' he murmured.

'Were we?'

'Oh yes, I think we were ...'

33
Unanswered questions

To Marnie, Friday felt almost like a normal day, at least by the standards of that chaotic summer. In the office by seven-thirty, she had completed a full hour's work before the post arrived, while Anne occupied herself with the finances and made a things-to-do list as she sorted out invoice records and budget statements, humming quietly to herself. Dolly took up station under a reading lamp on Marnie's desk, purring softly, eyes closed. From time to time Marnie absent-mindedly stroked the velvet ears while concentrating on a design or a brief. The office was in total harmony.

After a quick visit to Knightly Court to check progress, Anne surprised Marnie by asking if she could have some time to herself that morning.

By the end of the afternoon Marnie felt she had put in a solid day's work for the first time in weeks. Leaving Anne and Dolly in charge of the office, with Danny on the post run, she strolled to *Sally Ann* to prepare the meal. It was to be a light summer collation of smoked salmon, asparagus quiche with mixed salad, strawberries and cream. Three bottles of *sauvignon blanc* from Gascony were chilling in *Sally*'s fridge.

Sliding the quiche into the oven, she saw Guy Fellheimer come out of the spinney and head towards *Thyrsis*. The sight of him made her realise she had hardly given a moment's thought all day to the unresolved questions of the remains in the various graves dotted about the village. What would Fellheimer add to their knowledge, she wondered, before returning happily to more mundane matters.

Twenty minutes later, Ralph and Guy were setting the table under the parasol so that all would be in place for them to eat as soon as they came back from tootling on *Sally Ann*. Leaving the quiche to cool in the galley, Marnie crossed the docking area to change her clothes on *Thyrsis* while Ralph showed Guy round the dig sites.

Clouds were gathering in the west as Marnie set off from the boat to receive her visitor, and she worried that history would repeat itself. Her first meeting with Iris Winterburn had taken place in a ferocious storm, with howling winds and near-horizontal rain. Ralph and Guy ambled out from the trees and readily accepted the task of opening a bottle of wine.

On her way through the spinney, Marnie met Anne and Danny, both changed into tank-tops and fresh jeans. Anne handed Marnie the office keys and announced that so far their guest had not arrived. Anne warned Marnie that she had propped some 'things' up in the kitchen and asked her to be careful not to disturb them if she went there.

Within moments of Marnie reaching the office door, Iris Winterburn drew up in her car and parked it beside the farmhouse. She climbed out with no trace of stiffness. There was also little trace of a greeting, other than a brief nod.

'Shall we go through the spinney?' Marnie asked.

Winterburn looked up at the office barn. 'I'd like to see in there first. May I?'

'That's the office, where we sat yesterday.'

'I know. I'd like to see inside again, if it's not too much trouble.'

'Of course.' Marnie turned to unlock the door. 'Let me open the barn doors. You'll see better that way.' She pulled the heavy doors aside to reveal the glazed frontage.

Winterburn walked in and stood in the middle of the space, taking in her surroundings. Marnie watched her without comment.

The old lady walked over to the wall-ladder and pointed upwards. 'What do you keep up there?'

'That's Anne's attic room. We've turned it into a kind of bed-sitter.'

'May I see it?'

'The ladder's the only way up, Miss Winterburn.'

'I know. Perhaps I should ask her permission?'

'There's no need. She'd be happy for you to see her room. Shall I go up first to put the lights on? There isn't a window, other than a narrow slit.'

'Yes.'

Marnie climbed the ladder and reached up to the light switch. She was surprised to find Winterburn close behind her. Marnie stood aside and let her wander round.

Before descending the ladder Winterburn muttered, 'Creature comforts.'

Back down in the office, the old lady turned her attention to the spray of lavender suspended from the ceiling.

'Did you hang that up there to conceal the hook?'

'The hook? I didn't actually; Anne did. But if that had been its purpose, it's failed completely if you can see it so easily.'

Winterburn shook her head. 'That will do now. Thank you … Marnie.'

The stern deck on *Sally Ann* was more crowded than usual when Anne untied the mooring ropes and Marnie reversed out of the dock. With one foot on the bank, Anne pushed the bow clear and skipped down the gunwale.

Marnie pulled the lever into forward gear in mid-channel. She turned towards Iris Winterburn, who was standing at the rear of the deck, looking out at the countryside.

'Miss Winterburn, the tiller is yours.' For a few seconds their eyes locked. 'Please.'

Without a word the old lady stepped forward and grasped the steel bar firmly. *Sally Ann* motored on, her course straight and true. All eyes were on the steerer, who seemed totally focused on the task in hand; all eyes except for Anne, who turned away to look out across the passing meadows. Marnie touched her friend on the shoulder and heard a faint intake of breath. Anne simply nodded without turning round.

'I believe you have some experience as a boat captain, Miss Winterburn,' Fellheimer said.

'Some, but not since 1945.'

'You haven't lost your touch.'

'I was used to bigger boats, a motor with a butty, but this one, *Sally Ann*, runs well.'

Anne went below, followed by Danny. When they reappeared, Anne was carrying glasses of white wine on one tray, while Danny brought bowls of nuts and olives on another. They cruised for an hour, with Iris Winterburn at the helm all the while.

On the return run, approaching the final bridge, they noticed activity in the field where the police had cordoned off the grave sites. A uniformed officer was pointing at them, talking to a man in plain clothes, DS Binns.. By the time they reached home base, he was waiting for them, standing beside the table and the parasol.

Normally at this point when a guest was steering the boat, Marnie would take over, tactfully pointing out that the entrance to the docking area was narrow and tricky. On that evening, perhaps because it seemed inappropriate to ask an *idle woman* to relinquish control, they left Winterburn in command.

Setting the engine to idling speed, she drifted in mid-channel until the bows were almost level with the entrance, then threw the tiller hard to the left and pushed the heavy gear lever into reverse. *Sally Ann* pivoted slowly on her axis, the nose coming round to face the dock entrance, the tail sliding towards the opposite bank. In one fluid movement, Winterburn pulled back the gear lever in mid-swing and pushed down on the accelerator. The water boiled at the stern within a few feet of the edge and, while the nose continued its trajectory, she eased back on power and let the boat slip quietly into the dock. The old lady gave enough reverse thrust to stop *Sally Ann* without a bump.

Everyone gazed at Winterburn, who stood with a slightly confused expression on her face.

'How do you switch off the engine?'

Marnie leapt forward and reached under the step.

'Er, slightly primitive arrangement here, I'm afraid.'

She pressed down on the cut-out lever and the Lister clattered to a gradual stop. Marnie withdrew a greasy finger. It was as if a spell had been broken. Marnie turned off the key in the ignition. Anne and Ralph set about the mooring ropes. The party stepped ashore where the detective was waiting for them. Danny produced a tissue from her back pocket and gave it to Marnie who wiped her fingers.

'Good evening, sergeant. A late call.'

'I thought you'd maybe done a runner again, Mrs Walker.'

'I'm not obliged to stay on the premises, am I? I'm not under house arrest.'

'Of course not. I have some news for you.' Everyone gathered round the detective. 'Our search found no burials in the woods.'

'Nothing? But surely –'

'I said no *burials*, Mrs Walker. But we did find evidence of a large bonfire. *Unfortunately*,' He gave the word special emphasis, 'much of the site had been *trampled* before we got there. *You'd* been there first.'

Marnie shifted uneasily, glancing at Anne. 'Oh dear.'

'Quite. However, our scene-of-crime officers were able to identify different types of ash scattered over the hilltop and raked into the ground. We've sent samples off for analysis.'

'Can ash tell you much?'

'It should reveal whether the fire consumed more than just wood.'

'Will you be able to let us know the outcome?' Ralph asked. 'Assuming that we haven't sailed *Sally Ann* off to South America in the meantime, of course.'

A hint of a smile. 'I'll be in touch.' Binns looked at Marnie. 'You did after all point us in that direction.'

After Binns had left, Anne and Danny set out the first course while Marnie put the quiche in the oven to warm and Ralph opened more wine. As they began eating, Marnie explained to the guests the background to the detective's visit. Fellheimer and Winterburn listened attentively, though Marnie knew Ralph had probably already outlined the situation to Guy.

Winterburn dabbed the corners of her mouth with the napkin.

'So you're thinking that these were witches' graves on your land and that modern witches – or whatever they call themselves these days – removed the remains and cremated them on a bonfire. That was to prevent anyone from touching them?'

'That's what we're wondering,' Marnie said.

'And they did that on a hill somewhere round here?'

'Up in Knightly Woods beyond the village, the other side of the dual carriageway.'

The old lady looked thoughtful.

'What's on your mind, Miss Winterburn?'

'Presumably, they must have been buried by their own kind down here for some particular reason?'

'They would have chosen a site of special spiritual significance,' Fellheimer interjected. 'Pagan sites were often associated with a spring, for example, or some other feature like a rock or a glade or dell that they considered to have some kind of mystical quality.'

'They deliberately chose not to scatter the ashes on consecrated ground?' Winterburn said.

'They have their own views on what constitutes consecrated ground.'

'What's so special about the place in the woods where they had the bonfire?'

'Well,' Marnie began, 'we've been told that modern-day witches use it for festivities, ceremonies, special occasions, you know.'

'So presumably, when you went up there and *trampled* the site – as your detective put it – you were probably *trampling* on the dusty remains of various dead witches.'

Marnie made a face. 'Nicely put, Miss Winterburn.'

The old lady shrugged. 'That's how it was.' She took a sip of wine. 'And it's … *Iris*.'

Marnie smiled. 'It's still a sobering thought … Iris.'

'What's new?' said Danny.

When the dishes were cleared away and the next course was served, Ralph asked

Fellheimer to bring them up to speed on his enquiries.

'Do I take it you all know about the *Man Who Never Was*?' Heads nodded round the table. 'Good. Well for some reason not readily apparent, there seems to be quite a lot of renewed interest at the moment in that episode in the war. It's hardly a state secret. There have been books about him and a film, plus TV documentaries.'

'So why now?' Marnie asked.

'It appears someone has been carrying out research to establish who he really was.'

'Hasn't that been established?'

'Not hitherto. In the film he was a Scot who'd died of pneumonia. There was a touching scene in which his father gave permission for the body to be used to serve his country. That was pure fiction.'

'You're sure of that?'

'Reasonably. This new research cut across a project being run in London. It apparently suggests the real man was a Welsh vagrant, who may have been buried in a cemetery in Treorchy, an alcoholic who died in Cardiff after ingesting rat poison. It contains cyanide which leads to chemical pneumonia.'

Ralph leaned forward. 'Why wasn't it picked up through the research council, Guy? You wouldn't normally expect two people to be researching the same topic. Waste of resources.'

'It seems the work in question was being pursued as a kind of hobby. The person doing it was outside the university world. No one in academia knew it was going on until an *amateur* historian in Cardiff contacted a publisher who brought it into the open.'

'What happened to the London University project?' Marnie asked.

Fellheimer raised a long finger. 'That's where it starts to get interesting. This research fellow at Queen Mary College, Nigel Penrose, was feeling pretty disgruntled after nearly two years spent on his project. He'd been in touch with a lecturer at King's Cambridge who had similar interests, and she sympathised with his position.'

'Would this be someone in Rob Cardew's department?' Marnie asked.

'No. She's a historian, not an archaeologist. Dr Zoë Maltravers. She met Penrose at a seminar in Oxford at a time when he was desperately looking for other leads. Maltravers had come across some papers from the period in question while researching a topic on Germany's post-war economic recovery. Sorry, this must sound terribly boring.'

'Not at all,' Marnie said. 'But I think, Guy, we're probably wondering how this connects with Knightly St John.'

'It doesn't, except by implication. You see, Maltravers had come across references to a dossier relating to Hitler's plans for governing Britain after invasion. Penrose arranged to examine the dossier in Cambridge in the library of Cantwell College. He followed all the correct procedures and travelled up from London to discover ... that the dossier had been removed.'

'By who?' Marnie corrected herself. 'I mean, by whom?'

Fellheimer raised both hands. '*That* is the question.'

'To which you have no answer,' said Ralph.

Fellheimer nodded.

'Just like the remains at the Archaeological Materials Laboratory in Oxford,' Marnie said.

'I think that may be your link with Knightly St John,' Ralph suggested.

Marnie turned to Fellheimer. 'Guy, what sort of thing is this *dossier*? What's it like? Is it a folder of papers or a report or a book?'

'I've not actually seen it, of course, but I understand it's a collection of papers and a policy document.'

'An official German government document from wartime?'

'That's what I understand, according to Henry Eustace.'

'So it might be possible to find other copies of this document around?'

'Who knows?'

'Can I ask something?' Anne's voice caused everyone to look in her direction. 'Would this dossier be like secret plans, Hitler's plans for who'd take control of Britain if he won the war?'

'His plans in general are quite well-known, Anne,' Ralph said.

'So who would've been in command?'

'It's been understood for some time that King Edward VIII would have been installed as a kind of puppet king under the direction of Hitler and his cronies.'

'The one who abdicated? He'd come back?'

'Apparently.'

'And run Britain for the Nazis?' She looked incredulous. 'He was on their side?'

'That's no secret, Anne. He was a sympathiser, and there's quite a lot of evidence that some parts of the British aristocracy admired Hitler. They saw him as a bastion against the threat of Soviet Russia and communism.'

'What has all this research stuff got to do with the body in Sarah's grave?'

To that question no one had an answer.

It was dark when Marnie walked with Iris Winterburn to her car. The others were still at the table, but the old lady wanted to go back to her hotel before it got late.

'I'm so glad to have seen you again, Miss … Iris.' Marnie smiled. 'I can't quite get used to calling you that.'

'At my age very few people – fewer as time goes on – ever call you by your first name. It makes a pleasant change, as has my coming here this evening. Thank you, Marnie.'

They reached the car and Winterburn opened the door.

'Don't hang around while I get ready to go. There's all that fumbling with the keys and the seat belt and so on. Go back to your guests.'

As they shook hands, Winterburn looked thoughtful.

'I have a request. May I call in tomorrow, just briefly, some time in the morning? Or would that be inconvenient?'

'We usually have coffee at ten-thirty.'

'I'll be there.'

On the way back through the spinney Marnie was surprised to find Anne running through the trees towards her.

'Oh *no*! Have I missed her, Marnie? She left when I was in the loo. *Damn*!'

'It's okay. She's coming for coffee in the morning. You'll be able to say goodbye then.'

34
Official secrets

Morning clouds were clearing by the time Danny was setting the table on the grass beside *Sally Ann*. Straightaway after breakfast, Marnie had baked biscuits and left them to cool in the galley. To both their surprise, Anne had been otherwise engaged up in her attic. Their surprise increased when she eventually appeared shortly before ten-thirty wearing her best sun-dress.

Danny was accustomed to being under-dressed, but on this occasion she decided to change out of her T-shirt and jeans. When she hurried off to the attic to put on her only dress, Marnie spoke casually to Anne.

'Nice dress.'

'Oh, yes. I thought I'd make a bit of an effort, as we had a guest coming.'

'A special guest.'

'How d'you mean?'

'I was just thinking about how you turned away when Iris took the tiller yesterday.'

'Oh, did I? I suppose …'

Anne blinked several times and her eyes became decidedly pink.

'What is it, Anne?'

Anne's voice was choked.

'Well, she *is* special, isn't she? I mean, she's one of the real *Idle Women*.' Two tears ran down Anne's cheeks. 'When I saw her at the tiller, it suddenly came over me. She was a living piece of history, and there she was, on our boat. It was …'

Marnie went over and hugged her friend.

'Yes, living history, but also a real person and I'm sure she'll be pleased that you've made an effort for her.'

'So have you, Marnie, and Danny is, too.'

'Everything all right?'

They turned to see Ralph coming across from *Thyrsis*. In blue shirt and cream chinos, he too looked as if he had dressed for the occasion. Marnie explained while Anne wiped her eyes with the back of a hand. Ralph kissed her on the forehead and she announced she would begin preparing coffee in the galley. She looked more cheerful as she walked away.

'Is she okay?' Ralph murmured when Anne was out of earshot.

'I think so. She was really moved by the idea that one of the famous *Idle Women* was actually standing beside her, steering our boat.'

'I'm glad it's nothing more than that.'

'Oh, there is more to it than that, Ralph. I'm sure of it. Anne's up to something and I haven't a clue what it is.'

The table was decorated by a posy of small pink and white roses that Iris Winterburn had brought as a gift for her hosts and Anne had arranged in a vase. As Marnie served coffee and offered biscuits, she had the feeling that Winterburn had something to say. They had hardly begun when she was proved right.

'I asked to come back this morning for two reasons, one of them personal the other … different.'

'What's on your mind, Iris?'

'I've been thinking about what's been going on round here and I don't think you quite understand what it was really like in the war. When you see films about that time, you know how it all turned out, so it may be frightening, but you know the Allies won in the end. We didn't have that insight and for much of the time we knew it could go either way.'

'Like *scary* or *what?*' Danny said, her eyes wide with alarm.

Winterburn ignored the interruption.

'What you may not realise is the importance of secrecy in those years. We were constantly being told not to talk about anything we were doing that was remotely connected with the war effort. One of my friends actually called the police and accused a man of being a fifth columnist because he was plying her with questions about what their boat was carrying, how long it took to travel from Birmingham to London by canal and so on. It took him some time to persuade the police that he was just … what's the expression?'

'Chatting her up?' Anne suggested.

'Exactly.'

'Why did you want to tell us that?' Marnie asked.

'Because you have to understand why no one knew about the *Man Who Never Was*. You see, if someone died, there were documents to be completed, procedures to follow. The real dead man had to have a funeral as part of the secrecy. They couldn't just whisk away a corpse without explanation, even in wartime. Suspicions could be aroused if there was no funeral. One careless word in a pub by a hospital porter or a nurse about a vanishing body could get back to enemy intelligence.'

'I'm sorry to seem stupid,' Anne said, 'but how does that tie up with the remains found in Sarah's grave in Martyrs Close?'

Winterburn stared at her.

'That's just the point, Anne. It doesn't. This person doing research in Wales who thinks the false remains – probably a load of sandbags the same weight as a man – are buried in somewhere like Treorchy cemetery may well be right. What is *absolutely* certain – unless I've got everything *completely* wrong – is that the remains found in the grave of the woman you mentioned are not at all connected with the man who ended up buried in Spain during the war. Anyone who thinks they are connected is looking in entirely the wrong direction.'

'You're quite right,' said Ralph. 'Those remains have nothing to do with that operation in the war and moreover, they have nothing whatever to do with witches.'

Marnie nodded. 'We're all back to square one.'

'Not all,' Anne muttered.

'What d'you mean?'

'Whoever removed the remains from Dr Goodchild's lab must have known something about them, something important.'

'Well, if the intelligence service have got hold of them, you'll never hear of them again,' Winterburn said. Her tone was emphatic.

Marnie got up and went to make another cafetière while the others sat mulling over what had been said. When she returned, the conversation was still revolving around security during the war. Anne was speaking.

'And didn't they put up posters saying *even walls have ears* and *careless talk costs lives*? I've seen them in books about graphic design.'

'Yes, but that was only part of it,' said Iris. 'Secrecy went far deeper than that and it continues to this day.'

Marnie bent over to fill her guest's cup.

'How does that work, Iris? I'm not sure I follow. It was all a long time ago.'

'Not in historical terms,' Ralph pointed out.

'I'm talking about *human* terms,' Iris persisted.

'Can you give us an example?'

'Let me just think.' The old lady stirred her coffee, an expression of deep concentration on her face. 'Yes, I'm sure that would be all right.'

Marnie took her seat again, and all eyes were on Iris Winterburn.

'I'm not going to mention any names for obvious reasons. I have a friend I've known all my life. She married shortly after the war. One morning last year she received an invitation to a kind of reunion. It was in her name only, not including her husband. They were both going through the post at the breakfast table. My friend told her husband about the invitation, saying she would like to go, as it would involve meeting wartime colleagues she had not seen for decades. When she told him the date, he said he was going to a reunion on the same day.'

'That's *amazing*!' Danny exclaimed.

'My friend asked her husband what kind of reunion it was. At first, he was evasive, so she asked him outright if it had anything to do with Bletchley Park. He was astonished and said it was indeed about Bletchley Park.'

'Presumably that's in Bletchley, the other side of Milton Keynes?' said Marnie.

'Exactly.'

'Does that have a special significance?'

'It was one of the most important top secret units in the whole of the war. Even though ten thousand people from several countries worked there for years, its existence was never revealed. It's where some of the most brilliant minds in Europe cracked the codes in the German communications system, called *Enigma*.'

'So the Allies could intercept enemy messages?'

'That's right, Marnie. The French and Poles did a lot of groundwork, but it's at Bletchley Park that the computer was developed and the interceptions took place.'

'Even so, your friend's husband seems to have heard of it.'

'Heard of it? He was *there*. They had both worked there at the same time but in different sections, different buildings.'

'And they'd never met each other?'

'What's much more astonishing is that they never talked about their war work throughout fifty years of marriage, and until now she never spoke of it to me, a lifelong friend.'

'That's incredible!'

'But true nonetheless. You see, people learned not to ask too many questions and they got into a habit of secrecy. And of course, people were different in those days.'

'Because the war was on?' Anne said.

'Not just that. People behaved differently, had different values. I doubt if your generation would understand.'

'I'd like to.'

Winterburn hesitated. 'I suppose we had certain standards. They'd seem old-fashioned now. People used to say, *an Englishman's word is his bond* or, *I give you my word*. You've heard things like that? They meant something to us. Also, a lot of people had to sign the Official Secrets Act. When my friend signed it, they told her she was bound by it for the rest of her life.'

'And she never talked about it, not ever?'

'That's the way it was. When you're up against the most powerful military machine in the world and just about clinging on, you know where your interests and your loyalties lie.'

The old lady looked at her watch and folded her napkin.

'It's time I was going. Sorry to have prattled on like that, but I thought you should understand the way things were. The man in the grave up behind the churchyard has nothing to do with the war. I'm convinced of that.'

Marnie walked with her guest through the spinney and Anne asked if she could go with them. Danny tagged along on the path behind.

Anne said, 'Miss Winterburn, may I ask you something? You said you had two reasons for coming back this morning.'

They emerged from the spinney beside the office barn. Winterburn stopped and looked up at it.

'I wanted to see the place again.'

'You knew Glebe Farm?' said Marnie.

'I stayed here once in the war. We had a series of breakdowns along this section of the canal.'

'I believe you told me you'd stayed in a village at one time, waiting for engine parts.'

'That was where our skinhead friend lived. A makeshift repair didn't work. We broke down again and ended up billeted here. Two of us slept up there in the attic for three or four nights, on camp beds.'

'My attic!' Anne exclaimed.

'So it appears.'

Anne suddenly dashed past the others and disappeared into the office barn. Marnie was wondering if her friend had been overcome with emotion again, when Anne came out carrying two bundles.

'I hope you don't mind, but I painted these for you, to remind you of your visit.' She turned the objects round to face Iris Winterburn. They were two watercolours, one of the office barn, the other of *Sally Ann*, both painted on board. 'I didn't have time to frame them.'

The old lady stared at the pictures for some time. When she eventually spoke, her voice seemed to come from far away.

'It was all so long ago, a lifetime, when I was young and strong, and the world was at my feet. Thank you, Anne. I am very … touched.' She reached into her handbag and rummaged around for some seconds before extracting a small round object. She held it up. 'Have you seen one of these before?'

It was a badge made of dark grey plastic. In the centre were the initials *IW* above two wavy lines, surmounted by the title, *National Service*. Anne held it in her hand.

'It's where the nickname came from, isn't it? *Idle Women*.'

'Yes. I want you to have it.'

Anne held it out. 'Oh no, I couldn't …'

'Why not?'

'It's part of your history, your life.'

'I don't need it. Keep it. I want you to.' She turned to Marnie. 'I don't suppose I shall see you again. Thank you for having me, and for the other things. Good luck for the future.'

Her voice was firm and without a trace of sentimentality.

'I'd have been very glad to have you on my boats in the war.' She looked at Anne. 'Both of you. You two would have made a good pair of *Idle Women* yourselves.'

She glanced at Danny without comment before turning back to Marnie.

'I don't know if you'll get to the bottom of whatever's going on round here, the grave business and so on, but let me give you a word of advice. Don't drop your guard, not for a moment, not ever.'

35
Oxford

At breakfast on Sunday Danny said casually that she thought it was time to go home. She had been uncharacteristically quiet the previous evening and after dinner she had listened to music on her Walkman in the attic room while Anne lay on the bed reading. Over coffee and croissants, Marnie assured her she was welcome to stay at Glebe Farm, but Danny's mind was made up.

When Anne went off to shower, Danny stayed on *Sally Ann*, clearing away the dishes with Marnie.

'Danny, I think you felt excluded by Iris Winterburn yesterday. I hope you're not feeling that you don't have a place here with us.'

Danny looked dejected. 'I'm not sure how I feel, Marnie. You make me very welcome and it's amazing, I actually want to get on with my studying here, but … I don't know, yesterday it was as if I was intruding.'

'Not because of anything I said, I hope.'

'No. It was when Miss Winterburn said she would've liked you and Anne as crew on her boat in the war. She, like, gave me a sort of look.'

'Danny, she was just being polite to her hosts. And in any case there were only three people in a crew on those boats. Didn't you realise that?'

Danny looked unconvinced. Marnie put an arm round her shoulders.

'I've got just two things to say to you. The three of us, we two plus Anne, are the *Idle Women* of *Sally Ann*. You're part of the crew. You know that.'

Danny smiled in a half-hearted way, and Marnie thought for a moment that she was going to become tearful.

'Thanks, Marnie. But I do think I ought to make tracks. My parents are wondering if they'll ever see me again.'

'I understand.'

'Perhaps I could come back in a little while? I really can study here, despite all the comings and goings. It somehow makes it easier.'

'Come back as soon as you like.'

'You said there were *two* things you wanted to say. Was that the other one?'

'No. The other thing was that if you left, I'd be faced with complaints from the archaeologists – the male ones at least – about your absence. That bikini of yours …'

Danny grinned. 'I wouldn't like to disappoint them.'

Marnie and Danny were on their way through the spinney when Anne came running towards them, waving at them to stop. She held one finger up to her lips for silence and drew them into a huddle.

'We've got a visitor,' she whispered. 'There's a car round the back of the archaeologists' barn. I heard it arrive. I think the driver coasted down the last part of the track.'

'You don't recognise it?'

Anne shook her head. 'Never seen it before, a Golf.'

Marnie looked at Danny. 'Any ideas?'

'Nope.'

They skirted round the spinney to approach the barn from the side. Almost immediately they saw the car, parked close to the rear wall. Marnie's first response was surprise tinged with relief. Anne and Danny picked up on her reaction.

'What is it?' Anne said softly. 'You know the car?'

'No, but somehow I can't get excited about a geriatric beige Golf diesel.'

The two girls studied the intruder's car in the light of Marnie's assessment. They agreed she had a point. It was about ten years old and gave the impression it had not been washed since the novelty of ownership had worn off about nine years earlier. As they looked on, they became aware of a muffled voice emanating from the barn.

'More than one of them?' Danny murmured.

They strained to hear what was being said, but it was impossible. Anne reached into a back pocket and pulled out her mobile. She pointed at it and then at the barn. The gaps in the speech made it clear; the visitor was speaking on the phone.

Marnie gestured that they should advance. She moved rapidly out from the trees and covered the open ground to the barn in a matter of seconds. When Anne and Danny caught up with her she was standing in the entrance. Inside, sitting at a table, Rob Cardew looked up, smiled and raised his free hand. He brought his conversation to an end.

'So I'll see you when I see you … okay … then why don't we get a takeaway? Fine … ring when you're leaving. See you!' He switched off and put the phone on the table. 'Hi folks. Hope I didn't disturb you.'

'We spotted the unfamiliar car, not your usual Land Rover.'

'No. That's the university's. This one is mine.'

'So what are you doing here today? Are the others coming?'

'Just me. Rosemary's gone in to the lab – she'll be there most of the day – so I thought I'd catch up on paperwork.'

'Her lab's open on a Sunday?'

'She has authorisation, her own keys, knows the alarm settings.'

They left Rob to get on with his work. While Danny was packing, Anne received a phonecall. She went out to sit on the bench in the courtyard. Donovan reported that his foot was improving by the day.

'Sounds like you're being sensible.'

'Yeah, just pottering about, taking it easy, tidying up the motorbike, reading.'

'Did you get anywhere with Rosemary's photos?'

'I've developed them, but …'

'No good?'

'Not really. I've tried enlarging them, but my equipment isn't hi-resolution when they're blown up. I'm going to phone Rosemary after this call.'

'Try her mobile. She's not at home this morning.'

'You keep her social diary now? I knew you liked to organise everyone, but –'

'Rob's here. He said she's gone in to work today.'

Anne was listening to silence.

'Donovan?'

A pause. 'I'm here, thinking. Why's she gone in to the lab?'

'Rob said she had work to do. Why?'

'I had been wondering about taking her images to a studio I know in London.'

Anne heard a voice in her head: *don't drop your guard, not for a moment, not ever.*

'I don't think that would be a good idea, Donovan. The fewer people who know about –'

'That's what I was thinking. Anne, there's an imaging facility at Rosemary's lab, isn't there?'

Anne tried to act casually on the drive down to Leighton Buzzard. It was not difficult; Danny was back to her normal chirpy self. By the time they drew up outside Danny's front door, Danny was planning to return to Glebe Farm very soon on the grounds that the atmosphere was conducive to her studies.

Citing the need to tidy up some things in the office, Anne declined the invitation to come in for coffee and excused herself on the doorstep. Danny and her mother waved Anne off, neither of them staying out long enough to notice that she turned left instead of right at the end of the street.

The University of Oxford Archaeological Materials Laboratory – known simply as the AML – was situated not far from the city centre in a tree-lined residential street. It had been converted from two late-Victorian houses, and its domestic bourgeois exterior disguised the hi-tech activity conducted within its solid dark brick walls. When Dr Rosemary Goodchild, research fellow in the Institute of Archaeology, left the building, she closed the door carefully behind her after resetting the alarm system.

They had chosen a bistro as their meeting place. Anne arrived two minutes before Rosemary came through the door. The place had just opened and Anne had had no difficulty finding a corner table. Rosemary joined her and they placed their orders.

'It's very good of you to let us do this, Rosemary,' Anne said quietly.

'I'm the one who should be thanking you, and Donovan, of course. Is he really fit enough to drive?'

Anne shrugged. 'His choice, his decision. He wouldn't have suggested this if he wasn't up to it.'

Neither of them paid any attention to the motorcycle that stopped outside the bistro, or to the rider who pushed open the door while removing his helmet. It was Donovan, a fact that surprised both the people waiting for him. Anne glanced out at the bike. It looked old-fashioned compared with modern machinery, mostly black and steel-grey, with a modicum of chromework. The fuel tank was adorned with a blue and white roundel, displaying three letters: BMW.

Donovan went to the counter, pointed at their table and gave his order. He crossed the floor with hardly a trace of limp, wearing leathers and boots. Anne was not surprised that the whole ensemble was in black, including the helmet and its tinted visor. When he sat, he placed the helmet carefully on the floor and came straight to the point.

'Everything set up?'

'Yes. I'm the only person in the lab today.'

'Good.'

'Do you have access to all areas?' Anne asked.

Rosemary nodded. 'There's one security code on the door to my part of the building. The imaging unit is on my corridor.'

Over coffee they agreed that only Donovan would accompany Rosemary back to the lab. Anne would keep watch on the building from her car parked along the street. When they were ready to go, Rosemary gave Anne directions. She set off at once and was already in position when Rosemary and Donovan rounded the corner and approached the building.

Anne felt uneasy, as if she was the one being watched, rather than acting as look-out. As Rosemary and Donovan climbed the steps to the front door, Anne wished she had thought to pop into the loo before leaving the bistro.

~~~

'This is my room. Perhaps you should leave your helmet in here.'

With its high ceiling and tall windows looking out over a paved courtyard, Rosemary's office had evidently once been a ground floor reception room in the days of long gowns and frock coats. Now, it was a mixture of study and laboratory, with walls painted in white emulsion and light grey carpet tiles.

The blonde wood desk and chairs at one end of the room were typical of modern design, as were the grey filing cabinets. A workbench extended the full length of one wall, with a single stool parked beside it. On its surface stood a number of instruments, including two microscopes and something that resembled a microwave oven. The walls displayed a collection of black and white photographs in plain glass frames showing excavations in progress.

Donovan set the helmet down out of sight behind the desk. From a small black rucksack he produced a folder, left the rucksack with the helmet and followed Rosemary to the door.

They passed three doors before Rosemary stopped. She knocked twice, waited a few seconds, took a deep breath, went in and turned on the lights. The unit was roughly twice the size of her office and was filled with media equipment and computers, some items looking as if they had been taken from a science fiction film set.

'Oh my god,' Rosemary breathed.
~~~

'What?'

'Well, I mean, look at it. I'd forgotten it was so *daunting*. Do you know how to operate this stuff?'

'I only want to scan in some pictures, convert them to digital and enlarge them. I don't have to run the whole show.'

'I'll leave you to it. You know where I am.'

Donovan walked slowly round the room inspecting the equipment. It was state-of-the-art in all departments: scanning, recording, editing, processing, printing, copying. He felt almost intoxicated at the thought that he had been let loose in this treasure trove. It took him two minutes to locate the macro photography system.

Back in her office, Rosemary was finding it hard to focus on her project. Half an hour after leaving Donovan in the imaging unit, she realised she had spent barely ten minutes on productive work. Her subject was the need for a balanced approach when dealing with human remains in excavations. She had written a sentence on the importance of reconciling issues of religious faith with respect for the dead and the concerns of science, and she found herself staring at it. These days, she seemed to spend much of her time thinking about remains found in an unconsecrated grave in Knightly St John.

Donovan meanwhile had no such impediments to progress. He had taken a decision to rephotograph the pictures he had developed in his own darkroom and use the macro digital photography equipment to blow up the images. It took him a short time to come to terms with the technology, and it surprised him that, for such a well-equipped unit, there was so little attention to security.

None of the machinery required him to enter a password. The unit itself was not locked, though the whole corridor was protected by a coded lock on the access door. He had noticed that there were no surveillance cameras either inside the building or on the external walls. He was pondering the significance of that, when he heard the faint warbling of a mobile phone somewhere nearby.

Rosemary jumped when her mobile began ringing. As soon as she heard Anne's voice, she knew something was wrong.

Donovan heard hurried footsteps in the corridor a few seconds before Rosemary burst into the room.

'Security guards!' she blurted out.

'Where?' Donovan was gathering his things as he spoke, switching off equipment, replacing a cover on the machine he was using. 'How many?'

Rosemary pointed over her shoulder. 'Approaching the building, two of them. Anne just phoned.'

'Is this normal?' Donovan was on his feet, leading Rosemary to the door.

'Yes. They make routine visits out of hours.'

'Good.'

'*Good?*' Rosemary stopped and stared at Donovan. She was more accustomed to dealing with people who had died centuries earlier and rarely had to take snap decisions.

'Sure. It's just routine. Come on. We've got to get back to your office. We mustn't be found in here.'

'What shall we say to them?'

'I'm a new assistant or something.'

Rosemary looked at Donovan's black leathers and shook her head. 'You're not, I mean, you don't look like –'

'Don't worry about it.'

'But you haven't got a security pass.'

Donovan pulled her out through the door and closed it behind them. They could hear voices in the entrance hall. He looked at the empty corridor; there was nowhere to hide. Overhead, signs indicated the emergency exits, the fire extinguisher, toilets. *Toilets!*

'Come on!'

He seized Rosemary by the wrist and dragged her away. The toilets were round the corner to the left. He looked back. The guards were not in sight.

'Rosemary, where will they be? Think!'

'Er, probably checking the directorate offices first.'

'Are the toilets locked?'

'The toilets? No.'

Donovan stood thinking. Rosemary was frowning.

'What can we –'

'Listen. Go back to your office. Get a handbag or something and wait until you hear the guards opening the door to this corridor. Then come out and walk down here. Act relaxed but walk quite quickly and say hallo or something to them. Okay?'

Rosemary nodded. 'What about you?'

'I'll meet you in the Ladies.'

Rosemary looked puzzled. 'You'll meet me –'

'Go in and take the nearest cubicle to the door. I'll be there.'

'But they're bound to inspect the toilets.'

'Good. I'm counting on it.'

Rosemary's frown deepened. Donovan touched her arm.

'Trust me. Just do it. Go quickly.'

Rosemary had barely entered her office when she heard the door open along the corridor. Shouldering her bag, she stepped out and began walking at a brisk pace. She glanced back and raised a hand in the direction of the two security men, calling out a cheery greeting. By the time she reached the corner, they were pushing open the doors of the offices. She hurried along and dived into the Ladies.

The place looked deserted, and she wondered if Donovan had climbed out of a window, but there was only one, protected on the outside by bars. She pushed against the first cubicle door and gasped as she went in. Donovan was standing on the lavatory bowl.

'Are they coming?' he whispered.

'Any minute.'

'Shut the door.'

Rosemary pushed home the bolt. 'What now?'

'Sit on the loo.'

Donovan shuffled back to leave space for her to sit down. As she turned, he patted her on the shoulder and pointed to the bottom of the partition. There was a gap of about eight inches to the floor. Rosemary shook her head; she didn't understand. He leaned forward to whisper.

'I'm sorry, but you're going to have to take down your jeans.'

Rosemary's mouth opened, her expression stunned. He continued.

'It's important to look authentic if they come in.'

Rosemary now understood why Donovan had specified the first cubicle. Slowly, she turned her back on him, unzipped her jeans and rolled them down around her ankles before sitting on the loo seat. A sudden sound outside told them the security guards were coming. After three loud knocks on the door they heard it swing open.

'Sorry about this, miss. We have to check.'

Rosemary kept her voice matter-of-fact as she called out through the partition.

'That's all right.'

'Thank you, miss.'

Anne checked her watch. Five minutes had elapsed since the security guards had entered the building. She wondered if Rosemary's office had a cupboard where Donovan could hide. Would it matter that he was there? Perhaps he might be a visitor or a courier delivering material to the lab. On a Sunday?

That voice again: *don't drop your guard, not for a moment, not ever.*

So what could she do to help? It was agonising having to sit and wait, powerless to do anything useful. Or was that the case? Anne gripped the mobile in her lap and pondered. Gradually, an idea began to take shape in her mind. She lifted the phone and scrolled through its memory.

Rosemary stood, quickly pulling up her jeans and zipping them. She left the top button unfastened. Inclining her head round to Donovan, she spoke in a whisper.

'How long do we need to stay here?'

'You should go now.'

'What about you?'

'I have to wait till they're clear before I can come out.'

Rosemary hesitated. Donovan pointed at the handle on the cistern.

'Don't forget to flush and wash your hands. The guards will expect to hear the sound of the water and the roller-towel.'

'That's just it, Donovan. I'd, er, actually like to use the loo.'

'Sure.' He climbed carefully down, wincing as his left foot touched the floor. 'I'll go to another cubicle. Sorry.'

Musing that nothing in her lengthy studies right up to doctorate level had ever prepared her to handle experiences such as this, Rosemary used the loo, rather self-consciously, and exited the toilets after making all the appropriate sounds. Feeling relieved in several senses of the word, she turned the corner and found the two guards waiting for her. Their demeanour was stern.

'We need to have a word, miss, on a serious matter of security. Strictly speaking, we ought to make a report about this.'

'What is it?' Rosemary hoped they didn't notice she was shaking.

'Your office. When you came out to use the, er, facilities, you left a cigarette burning in the ashtray.'

'Oh!' Rosemary knew she was blushing.

'First of all, that posed a fire risk, and secondly, smoking is only permitted in restricted areas. As a member of staff, you should know that.'

'You're quite right. I'm really sorry. I must have been so absorbed in my –'

All three heads turned. Not far away a phone was ringing.

'I think that's mine.' Rosemary tried not to reveal how elated she felt at this intervention.

'Like I said, miss, we should normally make a report to our office, but …'

The ringing continued, its persistent sound intruding into their conversation, demanding attention.

'That's very sweet of you. I'll not let it happen again. In fact, I'm planning to give it up altogether.'

'Fair enough, miss. There's no more to be said, then.'

'Thank you.' Rosemary looked down the corridor. There was no end to the phone ringing. 'That must be urgent. I'd better get it. Are you coming this way?'

The three of them made their way back along the corridor, Rosemary hurrying ahead of the men. She turned and gave them a grateful smile as she entered her office. Racing across the room, she seized the mobile from the desktop.

'Hallo.'

Donovan waited a full five minutes. When he stepped down from the loo seat in the end cubicle, he examined the window. It was of frosted glass, a typical Victorian sash window like all the others he had seen in the building, and he guessed that it could only be opened a small amount for ventilation. He turned the fastener and took hold of the two brass lifting handles. He was right. The opening was limited to about four inches. Kneeling, he peered out through the gap, twisting his head to gain a view on all sides.

The AML was larger than just two houses, with a full-height extension at the rear, covering three floors in total. The security guards would have to patrol the rear part of the building.

It was almost noon. He walked rapidly to the door, opened it smoothly and stuck his head out. Silence. In the corridor, he eased the door shut without a sound and walked briskly back to Rosemary's office, the thick soles of his boots noiseless on the tiled floor. Without hesitating, he opened her door and slipped inside.

Rosemary raised a hand to her forehead. She looked drawn.

'What now?'

Donovan nodded towards the door.

'Where are they?'

'I don't –'

'Presumably they inspect all parts of the building.'

'Yes.'

'So they must be upstairs by now.'

'Must be.'

'Come on, Rosemary. Time you had an early lunch.'

'Food is the last thing I –'

'It's not about food. It's about getting out of here.' He handed her a large envelope. 'Take these. It's the blown-up photos.'

'But shouldn't you –'

'If I get stopped, they'll search me. No one will touch you. We gotta go.'

Rosemary stuffed the envelope into her bag while Donovan grabbed his helmet and rucksack from the floor. Pausing at the door, Donovan opened it a crack and listened. Nothing.

'We're going to sneak out while they're upstairs?' Rosemary whispered.

'No. You're going to call them.'

'But they might be in the rooms at the back.'

'Precisely. They might just as easily be in the rooms at the front.'

He told Rosemary what she had to do, then took her by the arm and ushered her out. He pulled open the access door between the corridor and the entrance hall, and they listened again for sounds of movement. Donovan flattened himself against the wall, invisible from the stairwell, and nodded at Rosemary. She took a deep breath and called up the stairs.

'Hallo!'

No response. Donovan nodded at her again.

'Louder.'

'HALLO! HALLO!'

Footsteps. A voice from high up.

'Yes, miss?'

'I'm just popping out for lunch. I'll leave you to set the alarm. Okay?'

'Will you be coming back?'

Donovan nodded.

'Probably,' she called.

'You'll remember what we talked about.'

'Yes I will. Don't worry. Bye!'

'Bye, miss.'

They strained to hear the guards' footsteps. Donovan immediately crossed to the front door, and they were outside in an instant. Rosemary turned to shut the door firmly. When the lock clicked, she looked round. Donovan was nowhere to be seen.

She walked down the steps onto the street. Pausing, she checked her shoulder bag and located her wallet. She hitched the bag back into place and, on impulse, looked up at the façade. As she did so, a face moved into view at a window on the second floor. She smiled and gave a brief wave before walking off towards the city centre, alone.

Somewhere down the street she heard a car door shutting.

Later that afternoon Marnie received a phone call from Anne. She outlined what had happened in Oxford and gave her ETA for returning to Glebe Farm. She declared that she would not want much to eat, despite having had only a small lunch, but she would be desperate for a Pimm's and a 'flopping out' by the water. Marnie promised both.

She was disconnecting when there came two knocks at the office door. Rob walked in looking puzzled.

'Marnie, I've just had a call from Rosemary.'

Marnie nodded. 'I've heard about their activities at the lab.'

'Okay. Tell me about Donovan?'

'What about him? You've met him yourself.'

'Sure, but, who exactly is he?'

Marnie considered this before replying.

'That's a good question.'

36
Henry Eustace

The first call of the week took Marnie unawares. It came in at exactly nine o'clock on Monday morning, and she should have known who would be on the line. There was no preamble.

'I must say, Marnie, I find it *all* rather disappointing.'

'Celia? Good morning. What do you mean?'

A sigh. 'I really thought *you* would be different, but it's the same old story. People just don't do what they say they'll do.'

Across the room Anne was stuffing a notebook into her bag and picking up her car keys. She saw Marnie take a deep breath before replying.

'Celia, the works are on target. In fact, if anything, they're running slightly ahead of schedule.'

'I can't see how they possibly –'

'Please listen. All the woodwork has been prepared and undercoated, and they're well advanced with glossing.'

'Well, it doesn't look to me as if much work has been done at all since I left. I hoped they'd have finished at least one room by now. How much longer will it take?'

'A couple of weeks. Trust me, Celia. The work is going well, you'll see.'

Another sigh from Celia. From the other side of the office a concerned look from Anne, who was hovering by her desk. Marnie listened to a silence she was determined not to break.

'Have you had any news about the body in the grave?' Celia's tone suggested that that too was Marnie's responsibility. 'Only, no one tells me anything, of course. I thought *you'd* probably be in the know.'

'I haven't heard anything further from the police. They certainly don't confide in me.'

'So what's happening this morning? Will the decorators be turning up at all?'

'Of course, any minute. Anne's on her way up to see them.'

'Well, there's no sign of any. Oh, wait a minute. Someone's arriving. It's them. I hope they know what they have to do.'

At about the time Anne was arriving at Knightly Court, Ralph had his first phonecall of the week. Guy Fellheimer sounded bemused. Was Ralph going to be in his study that morning? Could Henry Eustace, the chess friend from Pembroke College, ring him? Ralph agreed to be called and tried to draw Fellheimer on what Eustace wanted to discuss.

'He'll have to tell you that himself, Ralph.'

Ralph knew better than to press him further. Afterwards, sitting at his desk thinking about the conversation, Ralph reached an unexpected conclusion: Guy didn't know what

Eustace wanted to talk about. It was for his ears only.

An hour later the phone rang.

'We haven't met, Professor Lombard, but I believe you know about me from Guy Fellheimer.'

'Of course, Dr Eustace. What can I do for you?'

'Well, professor, it's actually quite difficult to know where to begin.'

'You could start by calling me Ralph.'

'Thank you. Look, I don't suppose there's any chance we might get together?'

'Certainly. I'm probably coming over to Oxford later in the week.'

There was no immediate response. Ralph sensed that Eustace was in need of more than a quiet chat over a glass of wine. He was looking at his diary when Eustace spoke again.

'Would it be at all possible for us to meet today? I could come to your office if that wasn't inconvenient.'

'My office is out of Oxford. In fact, it's a boat on the canal.'

'Yes, I know. Guy told me.'

They agreed to meet at three.

Anne swept into the office, crossed the room without speaking and flopped into her chair with a sigh worthy of an Oscar nomination. Marnie looked up, an inscrutable expression on her face.

'Need I ask whether you ran into Celia on your site visit?'

'I couldn't take any more. I've finally done it.'

'Really.'

'Yep. I cut off her head with a meat axe and chopped her into tiny pieces. Then I fed them to the fishes in the canal. You'd better make the call, Marnie.'

'The police?'

'The RSPCA. I'm going to turn myself in. They'll want to put me on a rap on the grounds of cruelty to fishes.'

'They'll probably give you a good grilling.'

Anne winced. Marnie got up and went to the kitchen area to switch on the kettle.

'Cup of cyanide?'

'Please, with strychnine, two lumps.'

'I'm not sure they make strychnine in lumps, Anne.'

'Granulated, then. I don't want to be a nuisance.'

Henry Eustace was quite different from Fellheimer: of medium height and stocky build, with a round slightly florid face, bald on top with red hair at back and sides. Something about the way he moved gave Ralph the impression that he knew how to take care of himself.

They shook hands and walked through the spinney. Emerging from the trees, Ralph veered towards *Thyrsis*. For a few moments Eustace brightened up; the idea of a leading academic working on a narrowboat caused him some amusement.

'Thank you for agreeing to see me so soon, Ralph.'

'It's good of you to come all this way.'

'I wanted to be sure we could be alone with no risk of being overheard.'

'So what brings you here at a few hours' notice for a discussion in what some might describe as secrecy?'

'Guy Fellheimer has told you that I was, shall we say, discouraged from pursuing any enquiries relating to the remains found in the grave near the churchyard.'

'*Warned off* was the expression he used.'

'Quite.'

'And my guess is that you didn't allow yourself to be *discouraged*.'

'These days there are so many avenues of enquiry that it isn't really possible to block every one, if only because no individual can know every angle that might be examined.'

'You pursued the matter from another direction.'

'Yes.'

'I would've thought whoever was warning you off would have been aware of all your research activities.'

Eustace permitted himself a trace of smile.

'You know that my own field has recently been the fifth column in the second world war.'

Ralph nodded. Eustace continued.

'For the past year I've been acting as a kind of external tutor to a research student in Bonn. His name is Günter Kroll and he's writing a doctoral thesis on military intelligence in preparation for the invasion of Britain.'

'That doesn't sound much of a threat to our security. The deployment of the Home Guard is hardly controversial any more.'

'That's right. But they were assembling a huge amount of data.'

'*They* being your fifth column, presumably.'

'Yes, plus the usual airborne photo-reconnaissance and naval observation. The Germans compiled a vast amount of material in enormous detail: coastline features and coastal defences, potential landing areas, centres of population, just about everything imaginable.'

'And now out-of-date by half a century,' Ralph observed. 'So no one here is going to get very excited about it.'

'Which is possibly why no one here tries to interfere in my contact with Kroll. I've been over to see him a couple of times and we've examined the material in the Federal Archives. You wouldn't believe how much they've got, Ralph, tonnes of dossiers, literally, maps showing key services, harbours, power stations, electricity supply cables, road and rail networks, even phrasebooks of questions that would be useful for interrogation.'

'So you see how they planned the invasion from the German side, using information partly gathered from agents based in Britain. British intelligence surely knows all about this.'

'Of course. It was the British army that captured it all during the invasion of Germany.'

'Henry, I think the time has come for you to explain what it is that's brought you here today. What you've told me is very interesting, but none of it is confidential. It's been open to public scrutiny for years.'

Eustace sat in silence for some time. Ralph was beginning to wonder if he was having second thoughts about divulging what he knew when Eustace began speaking quietly.

'Kroll has stumbled on something by chance. It concerns Nazi sympathisers in Britain.'

'At the time of the war?'

'At that time, yes, but it has far-reaching consequences today, consequences that go to the top echelons of the British establishment.'

'You mean the *monarchy*?'

'Possibly.'

'And you believe that is why you've been warned off.'

'Yes.'

'Let's get this straight, Henry. Your colleague in Germany, your student, has found something in his researches that implicates the British monarchy in Nazism. Is that what you're saying?'

'It's along those lines.'

'Presumably this isn't about Edward VIII and his association with Hitler. All that's common knowledge.'

'Of course.'

'It's also known that King George and the royal family would have nothing to do with him and that he was more or less banished, first to Bermuda during the war and then to a life in exile in France.'

Eustace shrugged. 'Common knowledge, as you say.'

'Henry, I think even the most committed republican would find it hard to believe that the present queen and her family are Nazi sympathisers.'

Eustace shrugged. 'No. But I keep coming back to my question: who is powerful enough to get me warned off when I start asking about that extra body in the grave?'

Ralph sat back in his chair and stared into the distance. The options were very limited. The monarchy? He dismissed the idea. The government? The conservatives had been in power a long time, but Major was a moderate and even Thatcher and her most dyed-in-the-wool cronies were no fascists, except to certain factions of their banner-waving far-left opponents. Who, then, could it be? Rogue elements in the security service? What could they want to cover up? What could be so important so many years after the war had ended? Ralph turned back to Eustace.

'Can you explain precisely what Herr Kroll discovered?'

'Before I do, Ralph, let me say that I've been through the same thought process as you. I don't know what you've concluded, but frankly, so far I've drawn a blank.'

'Tell me about Kroll's research. You said he'd stumbled on something.'

'It was entirely by chance while he was looking for something else.'

Ralph's turn to shrug. 'That's the nature of scholarship. Look at Alexander Fleming and penicillin.'

'Exactly. The Federal Archives in Bonn contain files on hundreds of agents based in Britain, possibly thousands. Kroll was carrying out a survey on how many were picked up by British intelligence services and in what areas. He was looking for potential case studies on how the agents were detected and what happened to them subsequently.'

'Are you sure the army intelligence officers didn't go through all that after the war?'

'There's stacks of the stuff, Ralph. Most of it was very mundane: codenames, weekly returns – much of it inconclusive – password changes, notes on bomb damage, shipping movements in and out of ports, details gathered from newspapers. Most of it was out-of-date as soon as the war ended.'

'But not all of it.'

Eustace shook his head. 'Kroll came across a file in the Abwehr – military intelligence, you know – relating to the capture of an agent based in Oxford. That's what first attracted his interest. Under interrogation the agent offered information about high-up Nazi sympathisers as a deal to save his life. Convicted spies were of course hanged at that time.'

'Were such deals common?'

'Rare, but not impossible. The file dried up at about that point and –'

'Sorry, Henry. I don't quite follow. How did the Abwehr officer – presumably the agent's handler – know about the interrogation and the deal?'

'That's the interesting point. The agent's last official message back to Berlin told of his suspicion that he'd been rumbled. When he failed to report in at the next appointed time, the Abwehr officer – a Major Manfred Hallgarten – suspected he'd either been arrested or killed. A week or so later Hallgarten received a letter that was only to be sent to him from a member of that agent's family in Germany if he was caught.'

'How would they know that?'

'Possibly from a contact in Britain who knew what had happened.'

'I see. And this letter?'

'It explained that the agent had a kind of insurance policy. It seems he'd deposited with a colleague a document detailing everything he knew about Nazi sympathisers in the British establishment. It was to be passed to the authorities in the event of his death or disappearance.'

'So the agent would certainly have used this in his interrogation.'

'Undoubtedly.'

'What became of the agent?'

'There's no mention of him again in any of the Abwehr files that Kroll has so far examined. Technically his file was closed.'

'And the document, Henry? Do we know what became of that?'

'No, but there was an oblique reference to something that might have been it in wartime cabinet papers that were made public last year.'

'Fifty years after the end of the war, and it's still reverberating after all this time. Is that the end of the line?'

'Kroll has managed to track down the agent's handler in the Abwehr.'

Ralph sat up. 'Has he spoken to him?'

Eustace pursed his lips. 'No. He died in 1988.'

'All very frustrating. So the trail has gone cold.'

'There is one other thing, Ralph. Major Hallgarten had a daughter, Ingrid.'

'Had?'

'She's alive and well and a professor of social anthropology at one of the universities in Frankfurt.'

'Interesting.'

'The bad news is, she refuses absolutely to discuss her father's career as an army officer and a Nazi.'

'Is she on the far right herself?'

'Quite the opposite. She's regarded in political circles as a hard-line left-winger.'

'There's no chance that she might be willing to talk to Günter Kroll?'

'She's adamant. A brick wall would be more co-operative.'

Anne had spent the afternoon in Milton Keynes, first in the library, then on a visit to the food centre with a long list. She returned in time for tea.

'No Ralph?'

'He has a visitor from Oxford, a friend of Guy's.'

'Why did this friend come here? Ralph goes to Oxford every week. Couldn't it wait?'

Marnie put her pen down and sat back in the chair.

'Everything seems so surreal these days. I wonder where it's all going to end.'

Anne walked over and perched on the edge of the desk.

'That business in Oxford yesterday was weird. I mean, what could possibly be so important about a body that's been in the ground for fifty years that it gets everyone jumping about? It's not as if Knightly St John's the centre of the universe, is it?'

Marnie reached into a desk drawer and pulled out an OS Explorer map. She spread it open, and Anne swivelled off the corner of the desk.

'You're checking to see if Knightly actually *is* the centre of the universe? I think you might need a bigger map.'

'I just wondered how Sarah Anne's grave site related to the Court and its grounds. It must be about here.'

They pored over it together, Marnie tracing a line with her finger from the back of the churchyard, past the executive houses to the grounds of Knightly Court.

'This doesn't help much, just shows how it looks now. I remember we talked about this with Randall. It didn't quite sink in at the time.'

Anne straightened up. 'Hang on a minute.' She crossed to her desk and grabbed a folder from the pending tray. 'I've got some bits and pieces in here, in the archaeology file.'

Marnie was amazed at how much material Anne had collected. The folder was thick with notes, photographs, maps, diagrams and plans. Anne extracted one document and unfolded it as she carried it back to Marnie.

'Look, this is one of Dick's sketch maps of the area. It's a copy from something in the county archives, shows most of the village from the church to down here soon after the civil war.'

Marnie retraced the line from church to manor house. She found it interesting that so much had changed in over three hundred years. Knightly Court looked smaller then, and the church stood in a more isolated position, the village seeming little more than a cluster of houses, quaintly drawn on the plan, with a few lanes leading off one main street. In the area where the development of Martyrs Close now stood there was nothing indicated but trees.

'I'm not sure I'm much further forward,' Marnie muttered.

'We did this in geography at school, interpreting maps,' Anne said, looking over Marnie's shoulder. 'It's surprising how much you can tell.'

Marnie sat back to give Anne a clearer view. 'There you are, then, surprise me.'

Anne leaned over and studied the map in silence for a full minute.

'It's interesting, isn't it?'

'I'll take your word for it, Anne. D'you want to give me a clue?'

Anne tapped a finger-nail on the spot where they knew Sarah Anne Day was buried.

'It's interesting to see what isn't there.'

'I'm willing to be persuaded.' Marnie sounded dubious.

'Well, I think maps in those days were partly drawings and partly diagrams. You can see how the cartographer has drawn little cottages in the high street.'

'Okay.'

'And so these trees drawn where Sarah's buried probably mean that the whole site was fairly dense woodland. See? He's drawn them close together. They still do that on modern maps.'

'They buried her in a spot where the grave was well concealed, you mean.'

'Yes.'

'Is that what you meant when you said you were interested to see what wasn't there?'

'No. What isn't there is the gate in the churchyard wall.'

Marnie craned forward, her nose almost touching the surface.

'Would you expect a map to show that kind of detail?'

Anne pointed again. 'Look. The other gate's marked, with the footpath from the Court.' She ran her finger along the wall towards the trees. 'But no path or gateway at this end.'

'I see what you mean. If this is accurate, there was no doorway back then.'

'Of course not,' Anne said.

'Why *of course not?*'

'Because that was the way the Knightly Court estate workers went to church in Victorian times.' Anne indicated a place between the Court and the church. 'They built cottages about here for some of their staff.'

'You're right, Anne. That must have been about two hundred years after Sarah's death.'

'She was buried well away from where people would walk.'

Marnie nodded. 'Until they wanted to create a path through the woods to gain access to the church so that the workers wouldn't share the same route as their employers. Do you have a plan from that time in your folder?'

'Probably. I've got just about everything in here.'

True to her word, Anne soon dug out an estate plan from the end of the nineteenth century. Marnie spotted the new footpath at once.

'There it is! What do you make of that, map-reader *extraordinaire*?'

Anne returned to sitting side-saddle on the desk.

'Actually, I'm not sure what this proves, Marnie. The Victorian footpath doesn't really go very near to Sarah's grave. It skirts the churchyard wall along there, and the area was still heavily wooded.'

'Until when?'

'Dunno. Perhaps until they built Martyrs Close? I haven't any modern plans at that kind of scale. What are you trying to find out, exactly?'

'I was wondering at what point Sarah's grave was revealed, that's all.'

Anne began gathering up the papers. As she picked up the oldest plan to fold it together, she paused to look at it, smiling.

'I love the detail they included in those days, Marnie. Look at this bit here.'

On that part of the map showing the fields that now extended down to the canal and Glebe Farm, the cartographer had drawn in sheep dotting the slope all the way down the hill. Anne laughed gently.

'Perhaps if he came back now he'd draw archaeologists on the hillside.'

Marnie smiled at the sheep. Every one had its own individual face, as if they had sat for portraits. She tried not to let her smile fade too quickly at the thought that that same land later contained the graves of dead labourers and witches.

37
War grave

On Tuesday morning Marnie braced herself for the call at nine on the dot. It never came. Anne had already left for Knightly Court, and Marnie was pleased that her strategy of heading off Celia's bleating seemed to have worked.

Anne arrived back some twenty minutes later to report that Celia was nowhere to be seen. Marnie's cunning plan was working. With luck, by the end of the day the master bedroom would be repapered before Celia had time to think about it. Marnie was convinced that that part of the programme would deliver a major psychological advantage. Once Celia saw the tangible result of the redecoration in her own bedroom, it would become a haven and she would become less critical. At least, that was the idea.

Anne was reporting on progress at the Court when the sound of a car arriving made them both freeze. It had come to a halt beside the farmhouse. But it was not the svelte, designer-label Celia who wafted past the window on the way to the office door. In familiar cheesecutter and tweeds, George Stubbs hove into view, tapping twice on the plate glass as he plodded by. The cheesecutter was doffed as he poked his head round the door.

'Good morning, fair ladies.' His voice was rich, like thick gravy on a Sunday joint. 'Not disturbing you, am I?'

'Come in, George. You're rather early for coffee.'

He waved a dismissive hand. 'Just popped in as a courtesy. Come to see the excavations, if it's no trouble. Haven't been down for a while.'

'Do you know Dick Blackwood, the site director?' Anne asked. 'I could take you round and introduce you, if you like.'

He beamed. 'Best offer I've had all day.'

As Anne turned to go, Marnie said, 'Just a sec. George, can I ask you something?'

'Are you back on your missing persons trail, my dear?'

'Only indirectly. Come in for a moment.'

As George advanced into the office, Anne pulled up the visitors' chair, and he lowered himself onto it.

'How can I help? I spoke to my cousin Albert about people going missing in the war, but he's no wiser than I am.'

'Did you ever play in the woods as a child?'

'They were private property in those days, Marnie.'

'You haven't answered my question, George.'

He grinned. 'Yes, of course. *Sherwood Forest*, we called it, played Robin Hood there.' He winked and tapped the side of his nose. 'Don't ask what we got up to with Maid Marian!'

He guffawed at his joke, but rapidly subsided in the face of Marnie's non-reaction.

'Would that include the woods where Martyrs Close now stands?'

'Ah, that was much more difficult. The Court's back yard, so to say.'

'Can you remember how long ago they felled the trees in those woods, the ones by the churchyard?'

'Quite some time ago now.'

'Was it when they came to build Martyrs Close in the seventies?'

'Oh no, much earlier, during the war, nineteen-forty, forty-one perhaps?'

'As early as that?'

'Of course. The country needed the timber. It had to come from British sources. Supplies from overseas weren't reliable. The Jerries were all over Scandinavia, U-boats in the Atlantic.'

'So they chopped down mature woodland trees. Such a loss. Presumably they replanted with saplings?'

'Absolutely, although …' George took on a faraway look. 'Funny, now that you mention it, never occurred to me at the time. I was just a small boy.' He grinned again. 'If you can imagine that.'

Marnie and Anne tried not to.

'What was funny, George?'

'After the old trees had gone, they replanted with new ones, but in parts they planted *brambles*.' He said the word as if he couldn't quite believe it.

'Like the ones round Sarah's grave,' Marnie prompted.

'Exactly, all round there. Some people said it was to keep us kids out. I don't know. But the estate workers thought they'd be in for blackberries galore.'

'No doubt.'

'Not a bit of it, Marnie. They were forbidden to take them.'

'Why? Did they want them up at the *Big House*? It all sounds terribly feudal.'

'That's what was funny. It was not like the Deveres to begrudge their staff a bit of fruit, but the curious thing was, even the Deveres didn't touch them. It was awful to see the blackberries withering on the bushes. Food was in short supply, but no one picked them, officially, I mean.'

'Which means that you and the *Merry Men* did? And Maid Marian, no doubt?'

George shrugged. 'We did the odd bit of scrumping, of course we did. My mother made the odd blackberry pie, bramble jelly, but access wasn't easy. High walls up there. And you'd soon get chased out if you were seen.'

'I wonder why.'

'Oh, we all thought we knew why, Marnie.'

'Go on.'

'The family turned in on itself when Roland Devere was reported missing behind enemy lines. He was the blue-eyed boy. Old Mr Devere, that was Quentin, never really got over losing his number one son.'

'But that was much later, surely.'

'He was believed to be killed in action in about nineteen forty-two, I think it was. Then suddenly he came home on leave. It happened again the following year.' George paused, calculating. 'Yes, that would be about right, nineteen forty-three. Par for the course, they said, dangerous missions , incommunicado for long periods.'

'Did he come home again?'

'That I couldn't tell you, Marnie. The family did eventually find out that he'd definitely been killed the following year in France, on active service with the resistance, preparing for the invasion of Normandy.'

'Is it known where he's buried?'

'Oh yes. They have a photograph of the place up at the Court.'

'You've seen it, George?'

'Many times. It's in the library. I used to go there regularly for meetings of the local Conservative Association. Old Marcus Devere was chairman for some years.'

'Is it one of those huge war cemeteries?'

'No. It's a smaller one, just for the resistance, beautifully tended, by the look of it. I believe it's near Avranches, though I'm not sure where that is, exactly.'

A long way from Sarah Anne Day's lonely forgotten grave covered with brambles, Marnie thought.

Rob Cardew arrived on site early in the afternoon. He looked in on the HQ barn for a quick word with Dick Blackwood before going round to see Marnie. The door to the office was ajar and, looking in, he paused on the threshold for some seconds, observing Marnie at her desk. She was lost in her thoughts, a troubled expression clouding her face. In that moment he knew she was not pondering a question of design or colour and he realised how concerned she was at the events unfolding around her. He also realised for the first time – with a sense of surprise that this had not struck him before – that her face, especially now in solemn contemplation, possessed the serenity and beauty of a Canova statue.

Rob was on the point of drawing back to leave Marnie to her reflections when her eyes wandered in his direction and her anxiety changed first to surprise, then to a smile.

'Sorry, Rob, miles away.'

'I'm disturbing you, Marnie. I'll come back later.'

'No. It's fine. What can I do for you?'

'I have a message, from Rosemary.'

Marnie stood up.

'I could use some air. Have you eaten?'

'Eaten?' He gave the question some thought. 'Er, I don't think I have, not lately. I've just come from a meeting at the university.'

'Come on, then. We'll go to *Sally Ann* and get you a sandwich.'

They took the path through the spinney and found Anne sitting out on the stern deck, reading. Glad of a break from studying, she offered to make refreshments, and the three of them stepped down into the cabin. Marnie and Rob took seats in the saloon while Anne pottered in the galley. Rob came straight to the point.

'Rosemary doesn't know how to get in touch with Donovan. He didn't give her a number or any contact details, just said she should go through you two.'

'And what's her message?'

'What should she do with the photos? She thought Donovan was going to examine them and talk them over with her, but he wouldn't take them, said there was a risk he might be followed. Is he paranoid or something?'

'Don't you think he should be, after all that's happened at the lab?'

Rob shrugged. 'I know it's all very cloak-and-dagger, but when you think about it, nothing actually happened at the lab, nothing unusual. The security guards turned up on a thoroughly routine patrol.'

Marnie shook her head. 'You're starting from the wrong place, Rob. Donovan was only there because someone had intervened to remove evidence. He only needed the equipment because Rosemary had extra photos still in her camera by chance. And what if the guards had found Donovan at the lab?'

It was Rob's turn to look concerned. 'I don't know what's going on here, Marnie.'

'I think you do. At least, I think you have a better idea than we do.'

'No,' he protested. 'Why do you say that?'

'Two reasons. One: Rosemary must have been told something by the people who removed the evidence – or by her director. Whatever they said will have given her some kind of idea about what was happening. Two: you've been able to look at Donovan's blow-ups of the original photographs. That means you must know more about them than we do.'

Anne put a sandwich in front of Rob and he took a bite.

'This is great. Thanks, Anne. I'd forgotten I was hungry after all.'

'Well?' Marnie said.

'The director told Rosemary she should let the matter drop, forget she'd ever seen the remains. Future contracts depended on that. I don't know what you –'

'So it's definitely the government,' Marnie interrupted.

'Didn't we always know that?'

Marnie ignored the question. 'What about the photos? Do they reveal anything?'

'To be honest, Marnie, not a lot.'

While Rob continued eating, Marnie rested her chin on her hands, both elbows on the table. Anne came and sat beside her.

'Marnie?'

'Yes?'

'Don't you think we ought to get Donovan to see the photos? He might have more of an idea – oh, sorry, Rob. I didn't mean –'

'You're right.' Marnie looked determined. 'It was his idea, after all. Did you bring them with you, Rob?'

'No. They're at home.'

'Could you possibly bring them in?'

'When?'

Marnie pulled the mobile from her back pocket and pressed Donovan's number on the speed-dial. They spoke briefly. Marnie looked up.

'Tomorrow?' Rob nodded. Marnie confirmed and disconnected. 'Good. In the meantime, you've got them somewhere safe, no doubt?'

Rob looked sheepish. 'I think so.'

Marnie's expression became sceptical. 'Don't tell me you've hidden them in your sock drawer.'

'Not actually. I've, er, put them in a tupperware box, in the fridge, under the bacon.'

A smile tweaked the corner of Marnie's mouth. When she spoke, her accent was pure Russian spy from the movies.

'You are nobody's fool, meester Bond … licensed to chill.'

38
Tattoo

The elderly black VW Beetle burbled along the high street of Knightly St John. At the wheel, Donovan was pleased that the road was deserted. He was less pleased at having Danny beside him in the passenger seat. When he had spoken to Anne on the phone the previous night, she had just been talking to Danny who had hinted broadly that she would love to return to Glebe Farm, in the interests of pursuing her studies. It had seemed a good idea for Donovan to pick her up from home on his way north.

He had agreed but now, after listening to her incessant chattering for half an hour, he was wondering if his judgment had been impaired. It was a relief to drive down the field track, their short journey over.

He spotted a parking space among the archaeologists' vehicles between a Land Rover and a minibus, where his car would be out of sight to the casual observer. The Land Rover had University of Cambridge markings on the side and a pennant on the radio aerial. Danny mentioned that it was normally used by Rob Cardew. As he tugged her overnight bag from the back seat, Donovan paused to examine the pennant.

'That's Holbeach Man, that skull,' Danny said. 'He was a famous relic, apparently. Don't think they ever found the rest of him. I wonder how he got his head chewed off.'

Donovan opened his mouth to speak, thought better of it and closed it again. Danny failed to notice.

'Where d'you want your bag, Danny?'

They gathered in Ralph's study on *Thyrsis*, where there was little danger either of being interrupted or observed. It was cramped but manageable, with the photos spread out on the floor illuminated by Ralph's halogen desk lamp. Ralph looked down from his office chair; Marnie and Rosemary knelt on one side, Anne and Donovan on the other. Behind them, Rob and Danny perched on chairs to peer over the shoulders of the inner group.

From his bag Donovan produced a large magnifying glass mounted on a frame, which he positioned over the blow-ups of the tattoo. He invited the others to examine it and give their opinion on what it depicted.

Anne pointed at the first part.

'That looks a bit like an O. Could it be a name?'

Rosemary inclined her head from side to side. 'If it is a name, what might it be: Olivia, Odette, something of that length?'

Donovan stared at her and leaned over to re-examine the smudged mark closely, while the others looked on. He sat back and quietly muttered a single word.

'*Totenkopf*.'

The group reflected, each trying to interpret what he meant. Marnie was the first to speak.

'I'm not sure I quite see the –'

Bang! Bang! Two loud knocks on the door at the stern. Every head twisted round.

Ralph got to his feet. 'I'll go.'

He was about to step over the photos when he realised they were no longer on the floor. Donovan had scooped them into his bag and thrust it into the gap between the desk and a bookcase. Ralph closed the study door behind him and made his way through the boat.

Danny looked nervous. 'What do we do?'

'We wait to see who it is,' Donovan said. 'We're just sitting here talking about the dig with the project director. We wanted to be undisturbed. Okay?'

Everyone nodded. They could hear voices outside on the bank, Ralph and another man. Ralph's face appeared at the porthole.

'Darling, we have a visitor. It's Mr Devere.'

Marnie scrambled up and pushed open the doors into the cratch.

'I'll come out,' she called.

Hugh Devere, wearing a dark suit, was looking agitated. He made a perfunctory greeting.

'Oh, hallo, er, Marnie. Have you seen Celia?'

'No. She wasn't at the house when Anne met the decorators on site this morning. And she's not been here as far as I know.'

'That's most odd. She went out this morning and hasn't left any word about where she's gone. I called in at home on my way to a meeting and … no sign of her.'

'When did you last see her?'

'She was still in bed when I left at seven-thirty.'

'Is there a reason why you're worried about her?' Ralph asked. 'Has she done this before?'

'Not really.'

'There's probably a simple explanation,' Marnie said.

'And what might that be?'

Marnie ignored the sharpness of his tone.

'You must know she has a problem with the smell of the paint.'

'But they're not *painting* any more,' he protested. 'They're *papering*.'

Marnie wanted to say, *since when did a small detail like that interfere with Celia's mood swings?* 'Even so, perhaps she just wanted to be away from it all. Did you check to see if she had packed an overnight bag?'

Hugh looked aghast. 'What are you suggesting?'

'You're sure she hasn't done this before?'

He wavered. 'Well, perhaps once or twice, when we've … had words.'

'Have you *had words* now?'

'No.' Emphatic.

'Then my advice to you is to satisfy yourself she hasn't packed a bag. If she hasn't, my guess is she'll have gone to London for retail therapy. I'd suggest you check out the station car park.'

'The car park?'

'You won't even have to drive into the multi-storey. The person in the kiosk will remember Celia.'

'But I don't know what she's wearing, to give a description.'

'Just say *Princess Di*. That'll do the trick.'

Standing in the shower room on *Thyrsis*, Anne monitored the conversation through the narrow opening of the porthole. She was back in the study reporting to the others while Marnie and Ralph were taking leave of Hugh Devere.

'What d'you think's happened to her?' Danny sounded worried.

Taking a seat, Marnie made a dismissive gesture. 'Nothing. She's on her way to Bond Street is my guess.'

'But her husband –'

'Danny, Celia's a big girl, and a wilful one. She can take care of herself. We've got our own concerns.'

While the others were talking, Donovan had slipped his bag out from its hiding place and was studying the photographs again. Sitting on the floor in the corner, he seemed remote from everyone else. Marnie looked over at him.

'So, where were we?'

The others resumed their places and turned their attention back to Donovan.

'Donovan?' Marnie prompted.

Without looking up he said, 'I don't think Anne was right. The first mark might be a letter, but I think the rest looks more like a number.'

'If we can make that assumption,' Rosemary sounded doubtful, 'what does it signify? We've no way on this evidence of deciphering it.'

Donovan stared at Rosemary. 'You've seen the whole tattoo, you must've done. You must've photographed it.'

'Of course, but all those photos were taken away.'

'Even so, you must have some idea about what it showed.'

Rosemary shook her head. 'I took loads of shots of all the remains. You're forgetting that the skin was very discoloured. This tattoo only showed up when we started enhancing the images.'

Donovan held up the clearest picture. 'What were you actually photographing here?' It revealed only the faintest edge of the marking. 'What was the point of it?'

'I thought there were marks around the lower arm above the wrist.'

Donovan inspected the photo and quickly scanned the others.

'What sort of marks?'

'Like dark indentations in the skin. I did wonder if the person had had something tied round his arm.'

'Or had his arms bound?' Donovan suggested.

He passed the photos round the group for their opinions. As they studied the images, all their faces registered the same bewilderment.

Ralph borrowed the magnifier. 'I don't think we're going to be able to decipher this. It's hopeless.'

'You haven't any other photos, have you?' Anne asked Rosemary. 'I mean, the people in the imaging unit, would they have copies on a hard drive on their computer, perhaps?'

Rosemary shrugged. 'As far as I know, everything was removed. I've never even touched their equipment. Donovan might know if that's possible.'

All eyes turned towards him. Donovan was sitting with his back against a bookcase, looking blankly ahead, as if he had lost interest.

'Donovan?' Rosemary said. 'Would you know about that?'

'It doesn't matter.' He seemed far away.

'What do you mean? Isn't it what we're trying to find out?'

Donovan said nothing for some seconds. Anne wondered if he was in pain.

'Are you all right?' she asked.

'Even if we work out what the marks are, it won't help us. We'll have no way of finding out who they refer to. There's just not enough to go on.'

A cloud settled over the group. They realised that Donovan was right. If the tattoo was a number, even if they could decipher it, how could they find out what it meant? If it was the edge of a design, what could it tell them? If it was a name, what significance could it have?

'So we've drawn a complete blank,' Rosemary sounded disconsolate. 'Back to square one, if we were ever there.'

For a while they retreated into their thoughts, each of them searching for some way of making sense of what they had found.

'No.' Donovan broke the silence.

'No what?' Anne said.

Donovan seemed not to have heard her. 'Now that we have some idea about *what* it is, we might eventually be able to work out *who* it is.'

'You think you know what the marks mean?' Rosemary asked. 'You can decipher them?'

'That isn't the question any more.'

'But I thought –'

'No. The question is, why it was so important to stop us finding out. Why the cover-up? That's what this is about, always has been. So, yes, we are back to square one, but at least now we know why we're there.'

Marnie decided to visit Knightly Court that afternoon to check on progress. She also admitted to herself that she was curious to know if Celia had returned. The visit was a partial success. The decorators were pressing on at a great pace.

On the other hand, there had been no word from Celia. Her departure and absence hung like a question mark over the manor. It was only as she was turning to leave that Marnie realised that something was missing from the job. The decorators were working without their usual musical accompaniment. The radio was switched off.

When she remarked on this, the foreman explained that they had been asked not to use it because the 'old gentleman' was unwell. The butler had asked them to 'refrain'.

Marnie persuaded Donovan to stay for dinner that evening. The meeting with Rosemary and Rob had ended unsatisfactorily, with Donovan disappearing into a private world of his own. She wanted to tie up a number of loose ends before he returned to London. At six o'clock, when the archaeologists began pulling out, the black Beetle found itself alone and conspicuous in the field. Anne offered Donovan her space in the garage barn, which he accepted. Once the car was out of sight, he seemed to relax and accepted Marnie's further suggestion that he should stay overnight.

On impulse, Marnie had an idea: they would eat in the small walled garden at the back of the empty cottage number three. It was enclosed and private, and they could use the cottage kitchen and patio furniture. Anne announced that she would make the preparations with Danny and Donovan, and Ralph suggested a takeaway.

When Marnie finally tidied her desk for the day at seven, she walked across the courtyard and through the cottage to find everything in place. Tablecloth and napkins in yellow and white gingham added a cheerful air to the meal, and a festive touch was provided by a dozen nightlight candles in small glass holders glowing on the table. For half an hour or so they managed to forget their troubles, but inevitably the conversation returned to the matter that had brought Donovan up from London.

Curiously, it was Danny who brought this about.

'Donovan, what was that *Dummkopf* business about?'

There were smiles around the table.

'*Dummkopf?*' Marnie repeated. 'What d'you mean?'

Donovan was not smiling. He knew what she meant.

'I didn't say *Dummkopf*.'

'What did you say, then?'

Donovan shrugged. Danny persisted.

'I was sitting near you and I clearly –'

'All right. I actually said *Totenkopf*.'

'A death's head,' Ralph murmured. 'A skull, like on a pirate flag, with crossbones.'

'Or on a pennant,' Anne added, 'a university department's emblem?'

Danny understood. 'Holbeach Man! What's he got to do with the tattoo?'

Donovan mopped up sauce on his plate and seemed to ignore the question.

'Are you thinking,' Ralph began, 'it might be part of an identity number, the kind they used in concentration camps?'

Marnie turned to Ralph, incredulous. 'How could that be … in Knightly St John?'

'I suppose Donovan put the idea in my head, made me think about the Nazis, and that made me wonder about the tattoo.'

'I still don't see –'

'I think it could be the reverse,' Donovan cut in. 'They used tattoos for various purposes. The Waffen-SS had them, for example, giving the soldier's blood group. You could lose your dog-tag or paybook in battle and be unconscious, but with the tattoo in place the unit would always be able to give you an emergency transfusion in the field.'

'But Donovan,' Marnie protested, 'you're surely not suggesting that the body in Sarah's grave was a soldier from the SS?'

'No, of course I'm not.'

'Who was it, then?'

'Before we know that, we have some way to go.'

'But why here in Knightly?'

'Oh, I think we know that now.'

'Do we?' Marnie looked totally confused. 'I must've missed that part.'

Anne broke in. 'I thought you said this morning that it didn't matter.'

'No. I said it wasn't the main question.'

Danny made a strange growling sound and shook her head. 'These are just *riddles*, Donovan. Why don't you just say outright what you mean? Who do you think was buried in the grave? What's the tattoo about? Why here in this village?'

'I'd rather wait until I'm sure.'

'But you must have some idea, a *hunch*. It's obvious you do.'

Donovan looked pained. Before he could give an answer, Ralph spoke quietly.

'Danny, there's nothing wrong in clarifying your thoughts before revealing them. I've spent much of my life teaching students to do just that.'

Danny sighed. 'But he doesn't have to be so *mysterious* about it, does he?'

Ralph smiled. 'That's how you see it from the outside. From inside, things might seem very different.'

Anne climbed up to the attic that night to find Danny lying on her side in the camp bed, elbow on the pillow, head propped up on one hand.

'You're sure it's okay, Anne?'

'What?'

'Me sleeping up here and Donovan on *Sally Ann*?'

'He'll be comfortable enough on the boat with the Li-lo and sleeping bag.'

'That isn't what I meant. I meant –'

'I *know* what you meant. This is fine.' Anne's tone was emphatic.

'I only asked.' Danny looked pleased with herself. 'I think I've worked it out.'

'Well it may not be quite what you think, Danny.'

'No, listen. I meant about the body in the grave. What if in the war an enemy agent parachuted in, like a spy?'

Anne was doubtful. 'Parachuted in to Knightly St John?'

'Why not? It's fairly central, secluded, lots of places to hide.'

'And the risk of being seen,' Anne added.

'Yes! Suppose he was captured and killed by the locals. They'd have a grim secret – a sort of war crime. They'd probably decide to bury him somewhere he'd never be discovered, in an old grave. They'd think it would be safe. No one would disturb it, not even the risk of coming across it by chance while levelling the churchyard. What d'you think?'

'Well, it leaves a lot of other questions unanswered. I mean, why would the government want it hushed up now? Why would they want to take away all the evidence?'

'I don't have all the answers, Anne, but I think I could be on to something.'

Anne slipped under her duvet and yawned. She hoped Danny's theory wouldn't give her friend bad dreams.

Not far away, in the sleeping cabin on *Thyrsis*, Marnie was sitting on the end of the bed, brushing her hair. Ralph was sitting, propped up against his pillow, reading. Marnie turned to look at him.

'I must say, I thought Danny had a point this evening. Donovan can be rather maddening with his *mysteries*. Though, I suppose, to be fair, you were right to speak up for him. It must have been just as frustrating for you.

'On the contrary, my dear Watson. I think I've worked it out, too.'

'And you're going to be as maddening as Donovan, no doubt?'

'No.'

'You mean you're going to tell me what you've deduced, Holmes?'

'Not yet.'

'Meaning?'

'I thought I'd let you wheedle it out of me.'

'Oh? How will I do that?'

Ralph closed his book and slipped it onto the shelf above his head.

'I'm sure you'll find imaginative ways …'

39
Donovan's friend

Unusually, Marnie went for a walk alone that next morning before breakfast while Ralph was in the shower and the girls had not yet appeared. It was Thursday, and she realised with surprise that the university dig was almost at an end. She strolled from the spinney past the HQ barn and stood beside the witch-graves, recently filled in, staring out at the trench-pitted slope.

The previous night in bed, she had listened while Ralph outlined his understanding of the circumstances surrounding the body in Sarah Anne's grave. Or rather while he explained his interpretation of Donovan's line of thought.

'Come on, then, brainbox, tell all. What did *Donovano Mysterioso* mean when he said he knew what had happened here?'

Marnie had rolled Ralph onto his front and was running her fingertips up and down the length of his naked back.

'If you carry on like that I'll drop off before you've gained my full attention,' he muttered into the pillow.

'Wait till I turn you onto your back and start on the other side,' she whispered into his ear. 'I guarantee that will get me your full attention..'

He groaned. Marnie continued.

'Well? What did he mean? Start telling me while I search for the thumbscrews.'

'Working backwards, which is what you're doing rather effectively,' He arched his back as Marnie's fingernails drifted between his shoulder-blades. 'first of all, Donovan doesn't know whose remains were in the grave.'

'So we're no further –'

'However, there are one or two things we do know. The man must have died in suspicious circumstances. I know that's very obvious, but bear with me a moment. Whoever buried him probably killed him. Reasonable? So the first question is: why?'

'Why did he kill him?'

'It's two questions, really. Why did he kill him and why did he bury him secretly in a place where he was unlikely to be found?'

'Because it was murder?'

'All right, let's assume that for now. Marnie, don't stop doing that.'

Marnie shifted her position. She pulled Ralph's right arm out straight and lay face down across it, leaving her left hand free to continue its roaming.

'Not too uncomfortable?'

'Well within the bounds of the Geneva Convention on the interrogation of prisoners, I'd say.'

'Good. Carry on, then.'

'We're assuming of course that all this happened in the nineteen-forties, and I'm sure Donovan believes it took place during the war. He thinks the tattoo has something to do with the Nazis, hence his *Totenkopf* allusion.'

'All this we know. When are you going to tell me something new? The thumbscrews are just a shot away.'

'I'm taking things step by step, setting out the salient points in a – *ouch!* All right. This is where it gets interesting. Let's assume whoever was killed, it had something to do with the war. If it had been someone military, say, a soldier or an agent killed while trying to parachute in, there'd have been no reason to conceal the body.'

'The wicked Hun invader repulsed,' Marnie intoned. 'Good propaganda, medals all round.' She made a flourish on Ralph's back like a regiment of spiders scurrying about.

Ralph moaned with pleasure.

'Exactly. You know, Marnie, if we introduced this method into our examination procedures, I'm sure we'd get much better results in our *vivas*.'

'Your *whats*?'

'Oral exams.'

'*Orals*. Now you're giving *me* ideas …'

Ralph quickly moved on, before he lost concentration.

'You realise I'm trying to follow Donovan's reasoning in all this.'

'Not your own? I thought you agreed with him.'

'I'm using his ideas – as far as I can tell – as a starting point, a kind of working hypothesis.'

'Okay, but don't get too technical on me. I'm not used to the ways and methods of academia.'

'Your methods are *much* better, believe me. So, a man was killed, presumably because he was an enemy who had to be silenced.'

'But why conceal the –'

'It was obviously important that his identity should be kept secret. That's the question on Donovan's mind. He doesn't think we can work out *who* it was – even if we could decipher the tattoo – assuming it's relevant – but he does have a theory about *why* the burial had to be secret.'

'Which is?'

'I believe he thinks it was probably in case it gave away the identity of the person who had discovered the dead man's activities. The killer was worried about possible revenge.'

'By whom?'

'Thinking about what Donovan has let out and what Fellheimer's chess friend, Henry Eustace, has told me, I think it could be because there was an active fifth column group in the area.'

'You mean like spies?'

'Could be. And not just any common-or-garden spies. Whoever they were, they were somehow connected with the upper ranks of British society.'

'Let me get this straight. You think – that is, *Donovan* thinks – the man was a fifth columnist, killed for being a spy, and the killer hid the body for fear of reprisals. That right?'

'More or less.'

'That's your answer to Donovan's question: *why the cover-up?*'

'Seems logical.'

'What about the other question? Who killed our *spy* and how did he rumble him?'

'We have no way of knowing that, any more than we can identify who the dead man was, on the evidence we have.'

Marnie's hand was now describing languorous circles up and down Ralph's spine. Suddenly, he rolled onto his side, facing Marnie, easing his right arm gently out from under her.

'Actually, I do have a theory about who killed him, or at least an idea.'

Marnie rolled him onto his back and began slowly criss-crossing his chest with her fingernails.

'Is this your theory or Donovan's? It's getting difficult to keep up with you.'

'I think you're way ahead of me, Marnie.'

'Concentrate!'

'The Deveres.'

'You think one of them killed the man in the grave?'

'Why not? Don't you think that's why Donovan is being so cautious about naming the person he suspects? We know they have a history as patriots and war heroes. I'm sure the Deveres would react in a *very* hostile manner if they uncovered an enemy agent.'

The tips of Marnie's fingers were now flickering across Ralph's abdomen, heading south in a significant direction.

'They'd be able to conceal the body easily on their own land,' she murmured, 'and ensure the grave site stayed hidden under brambles to keep everybody away. D'you think I'm getting there?'

'Any time soon, I hope.'

Marnie grinned and laid her head on the pillow.

'It all seems possible,' she muttered, 'but somehow it doesn't ring true.'

'Mm?'

'Sure, they would have bumped off an enemy, with their track record in wars, but why wouldn't they be able to report it to the authorities and let them take care of things? Surely, that's what they would've done if they'd been involved.'

'Maybe.' Ralph's voice was drowsy.

'But it didn't have to be the Deveres themselves,' Marnie continued. 'It could have been someone who knew their estate, perhaps worked on the estate, though everyone in Knightly *knew* the estate, and many probably knew about Sarah's grave. Donovan's right. The question is: why the cover-up? Who were they trying to protect? Or perhaps, who scared them so much they had to conceal the murder to keep suspicion from falling on them?'

Marnie sighed and rolled onto her back. Her head was spinning. She had the sensation of going round in perpetual circles. No wonder Donovan didn't want to reveal his hand until he had things worked out. Ralph had been right. Donovan may have appeared mysterious on the surface, but deep down inside, he might have been undergoing the same inner turmoil that Marnie was feeling.

Of one thing she was certain: they had no way of finding the answers to the unresolved questions. Too much time had elapsed since the dead man had been lowered into Sarah's grave. Marnie closed her eyes, hoping for enlightenment, breathing deeply to calm her mind.

They had eventually fallen asleep without making love, entwined in each others' arms, and had awoken next morning to find the sleeping cabin lights still on. Both of them had a slight crick in the neck.

Marnie resumed her morning walk across the sloping field, squeezing the back of her neck, amazed at how many test pits and trenches had been cut into the land. Her head was still filled with the images conjured up the previous night.

Graves. All around her were graves. Away to her right down near the moorings were the shallow graves of the two navvies. Not far from them were the witch-graves whose occupants had probably been cremated on the heights of Knightly Woods. Up near the church was Sarah's grave with its shadowy interloper. Two outcasts, who had lain together undetected for half a century, unlamented and unmissed. A far cry from the local hero with his own personal war memorial in St John's churchyard, whose actual grave may have been in foreign soil in Normandy, but whose remains were revered in a plot carefully tended by his comrades and their respectful descendants.

Marnie turned back, anxious to return to the land of the living.

Anne's site visit to see the decorators at Knightly Court had become a daily routine, preferable to the possibility of an unpleasant surprise catching them unawares. On arrival, she spotted Celia's Audi parked in its usual place on the drive to the right of the front door. On the other side, the decorators' van occupied its usual place. After a few words with the men, Anne climbed back into the Mini to return to base.

She reached the high street in time to follow the convoy of archaeologists heading for Glebe Farm. When she walked into the office she was accompanied by Rob Cardew.

'Did you realise, Marnie, these are our last days trampling over your land? After Saturday you'll be rid of us.'

'We'll miss you.' Marnie hoped that sounded convincing.

'I'm sure.' He flashed the owlish grin.

'I'll be redundant as tea-girl,' Anne said.

'We'll miss you.' Rob spoke with absolute conviction. 'But before we leave, we'll be having an end-of-dig party on Saturday evening. If you're free we'd like you to join us, all of you from Glebe Farm.'

'We'd love to come.' Marnie reached for the desk diary. 'Where will it be held?'

'Er, we were wondering …'

Anne turned to Marnie.

'D'you think I'm about to move up from tea-girl to hostess-with-the-mostest?'

'You want to have the party here, Rob?' Marnie asked.

'If it's not too much –'

'Party?' Danny was descending the wall-ladder in pyjamas.

'She picks up key words by radar,' Marnie explained. 'What do you need from us, Rob?'

'Just the use of the HQ barn for putting out refreshments and somewhere to plug in the music machine.'

'No problem. Glasses?'

'No. We've got all that organised from the wine shop, better that way.'

'Will the *Timeline* people be vacating the site as well?'

'Yes, and they'll be at the party too. You'll finally be free of us all.'

Ralph walked the short distance from *Thyrsis* to *Sally Ann* and knocked on the stern door.

'Can we talk, Donovan?'

'Come in.'

Ralph passed through the sleeping cabin, where Donovan's bedding lay neatly folded on the duvet, into the galley-saloon. On *Sally Ann* all was rich colours, the red, blue and cream of the Liberty print curtains, the varnished pine tongue-and-groove cladding, the deep blue carpet tiles, the Oriental rug on the saloon floor.

'Not like your colour scheme, I understand. Anne said your boat was like a submarine inside.'

'You mean a *U-boat*,' Donovan corrected him.

They sat at the table in safari chairs. There was a faint, inviting smell of coffee in the air. Donovan offered to make a fresh pot and Ralph accepted. When they were settled, Donovan pushed the cream jug and sugar bowl across the table.

'So what can I do for you, Ralph?'

'I want to talk over your ideas about the remains in Sarah's grave.'

'I'm not sure I –'

'Yes, I understand that. But suppose I give you my interpretation of what I think you're thinking, If you see what I mean?'

Donovan picked up his spoon and began stirring.

'That would be helpful.'

Ralph outlined the points he had made to Marnie the night before. Donovan listened in silence, his face expressionless. When Ralph reached the end of his exposition, Donovan nodded.

'Yes. That's roughly how I see it.'

'There's just one thing I couldn't make out,' Ralph said. 'You mentioned a *Totenkopf*. What did you mean by that?'

'I once saw a photograph in a magazine of a Death's Head tattoo on the arm of a dead SS soldier on the Russian front.'

'Presumably he was in the SS Division named *Totenkopf*?'

'Possibly. They normally just had their blood group tattooed, but this could have been a personal thing added later.'

'And you think this man in Sarah's grave might have been such a soldier?'

'Not really. It's just an association of ideas. As I said, we don't have enough evidence to go on.'

'I agree with you on that, Donovan. But you think the man was possibly a Nazi?'

'I don't believe he'd been in a concentration camp, so I can't think what else it might be, if it's relevant at all.'

'Hallo, Marnie? It's Celia.'

Marnie cursed her bad luck in taking the call. Anne was out of the office.

'Morning, Celia.' Bright and breezy. 'All well?'

'I wanted to apologise for Hugh disturbing you yesterday. He shouldn't have gone to see you and make you worry about me.'

Marnie gritted her teeth. 'I was sure you'd be fine.'

'Yes. I went shopping in the West End.'

'Are you still finding the smell of –'

'Oh no. It's not so bad now. With our bedroom completed and the drawing room finished, I'm not so distressed by the contractors any more.'

'Great. They seem to be doing a good job. Anne gave me a report this morning.'

'Anne? You mean she was here, today?'

'Yes. She went up first thing to check that all was well.'

'How *sweet* of you, Marnie, to send her to find out about me. You really shouldn't be anxious on my behalf, you know.'

'I, er, well, I don't know what to –'

'Now I've embarrassed you. I'm so sorry. Anyway, I'm pleased with the results so far. I won't give my final verdict until all the work is done, of course.'

'Of course.' More gritting of teeth.

'Tell me, Marnie, when will you be wanting your next pay?'

Marnie imagined herself hovering deferentially outside the tradesmen's entrance.

'On a short contract of this sort there are no phased payments, Celia. I'll let you have a final account when everything is finished to your complete satisfaction.'

Celia giggled. 'Oh, I know it will be. I've already been telling my friends.'

'That you're pleased with the work?'

'More than that, Marnie. I've been putting the word around that I'm having a *Marnie Walker makeover*. You'll definitely be the *latest* fashion.' She laughed. 'I wouldn't be surprised if you were *begging* me to become your marketing manager as soon as our contract's completed.'

'An intriguing prospect, Celia.'

Marnie omitted to add, *over my dead body.*

Donovan was checking the oil level in the Beetle when he became aware that someone was standing behind him. He looked round slowly. Dick Blackwood stepped nearer.

'Hi. Did your friend catch up with you in the end?'

'Which one?'

'He didn't give his name. Sorry, didn't think to ask. Thing is … well, it's a bit embarrassing, actually. I know we were introduced, but I didn't quite catch your name.'

'What's that got to do with my *friend*?'

'He turned up again yesterday, at the end of the dig, just as we were packing up.' Dick looked thoughtful. 'That was odd.'

'My so-called friend didn't mention my name?'

'That's right. He just described you, black clothes, blonde hair, asked if you were on the site.'

'What did he look like?'

'Taller than you or me, thin rangy sort of bloke, very short hair, check shirt, jeans. D'you know who it was?'

'Had you seen him before?'

'I think so, when *Timeline* first came.' Dick looked thoughtful again. 'That's right! He thought you were with *Timeline*. I'm sure he did.'

'What did you tell him?'

Dick shrugged. 'I hadn't seen you.'

'Is he back here today?'

'Not so far.'

Donovan closed the engine cover, took out his keys and opened the driver's door.

'Do something for me?'

'Sure.'

'Tell Anne I had to go.'

He got in the car, started the engine and reversed out. Dick watched as the Beetle rounded the corner of the garage barn and headed up the field track. As the black shape disappeared from view, he realised that he still didn't know the driver's name.

40
Fleischer

From the moment Marnie walked through the spinney to the office barn after breakfast on Friday, she knew it was going to be one of those days. The *Timeline* helicopter was doing circuits over the village, and the camera tower-crane had taken up station dominating the field. It was barely eight o'clock.

She walked round to the HQ barn, where several vehicles in the company's dark green and yellow livery were already lined up, including the producer's Range Rover. Beyond, at the bottom of the field track, the black OB truck was in position, its satellite dish mounted on the roof. Once the university archaeologists arrived, the invasion would be complete. Marnie was grateful they had just two more days of shooting.

As she headed past the garage barn, she met Ralph hurrying to his car. She envied him his day of meetings in Oxford in the tranquillity of All Saints College. Although he was now a 'visiting professor', the college authorities had allowed him to keep his rooms overlooking Old Quad. No disruptive elements would penetrate the calm of those ancient buildings. *Bliss*, Marnie thought. They kissed and she waved him off.

Anne had the office up and running, as usual, and was filing papers when Marnie entered. The printer was rolling. In the background a steady hissing told her that Danny was in the shower; an early start by her standards. Marnie wondered if it had anything to do with the knowledge that *Timeline* would be in action that day.

Anne said, 'I'm running off this month's invoice for Willards, Marnie, plus the one for the office development in Towcester. What are we doing about the Knightly Court job?'

'I told Celia we'd not send an invoice until everything was finished … to her complete satisfaction.'

'Oh well, that'll be Doomsday.'

'Don't worry, she'll be delighted.'

Anne put down her filing papers and quickly crossed the office. The hissing from the shower stopped. Standing close to Marnie, Anne spoke hurriedly in a whisper.

'I'm worried about Donovan.'

'Did he phone last night?'

'I phoned him. Look, I know we say he's paranoid, Marnie, but he really is convinced someone is after him. He blames that TV shot of him on the national news, thinks someone recognised him from last year.'

'He is very distinctive.'

'So you think he's right.'

'I think he's no fool. Does he have any plans?'

Anne's expression clouded over. 'He says all he can do is lie low.'

Marnie took her arm. 'What is it?'

'He said they'd never give up until they'd caught him. He won't be coming back, Marnie, not ever. He said goodbye. It was for my own good not to see him again, too dangerous for all of us here.'

'Hi!' Danny emerged from the shower room, wrapped in a dressing gown, towelling her hair.

Marnie and Anne turned to face her, their expressions cheerful, determined to look relaxed and carefree. Danny frowned.

'What's the matter?'

Marnie smiled. 'Nothing.'

'You seem all tensed up.'

'Just a normal working day at Walker and Co.' Marnie hoped she sounded convincing. 'What are your plans, Danny?'

'Oh, you know, just be around. I was wondering what I should wear today.'

Marnie and Anne answered in unison.

'*Not* the bikini.'

~~~~

Marnie's worries about disruption proved to be unfounded. She made uninterrupted progress during the first half of the morning. Anne reported that the *Timeline* camera crew was conducting interviews, followed around by a small crowd of onlookers. She had been unusually quiet all morning.

She put the kettle on and wandered over to stand by Marnie's desk. Her manner brought a lump to Marnie's throat. Anne seemed as forlorn and vulnerable as a lost child. Marnie stood up and hugged her friend.

'I'm so sorry about Donovan, Anne.'

'Yeah.'

'Perhaps, some time in the future –'

'He was definite, Marnie. You know what he's like.'

'A strong character.'

'Yes. He says we've got to be on our guard.'

They walked together to the kitchen area where Anne began preparing coffee.

'It's hard to be on our guard, Anne, when we don't know who we're guarding against.'

'He told me last night that Dick said someone was asking about him. A tall thin man, with short hair. He said he was *rangy*, wearing a check shirt and jeans.'

'That could be almost any of the male students out there.'

'I know. Donovan said we must be careful not to let anyone know his name.'

'Have you mentioned this to Danny?'

Anne looked startled. 'No.'

'Go and fetch her. Tell her coffee's ready. Make sure she knows the situation.'

The phone began to ring.

'You go, Anne. I'll deal with things here.'

~~~~

Anne found Danny almost at once, standing on the edge of the group of onlookers a short distance behind the camera crew. She took her by the arm and led her off towards the HQ barn.

'Danny, have you spoken to anybody?'

'Like who?'

'Any of the visitors?'

'Said hallo to a few. One boy asked me if I'd been here before.'

'What did he look like?'

Danny shrugged. 'Dunno. He was about twelve. I asked him why he wasn't in school and –'

'Anyone else? Any men?'

'*Men*? What is this, Anne, the third degree?'

'Just tell me.'

A pause. 'Dick. I've spoken to Dick. He said he almost didn't recognise me with clothes on. You know what he's like.'

'Anyone else?'

'Don't think so.'

'Okay. Go to the office barn for coffee. Tell Marnie I'll be back in a minute.'

With that, Anne sped off to the HQ barn where she found Dick Blackwood examining a tray of stones. He looked up.

'Dick, I need to ask you about visitors. There are quite a few out there. Donovan said a man had been asking after him.'

'*Donovan*,' Dick repeated. 'Of course. That's right, yesterday.'

'Have you seen that man today?'

'No. I've been stuck in here most of the time.'

'Will you come and look now and tell me if he's on the site?'

Dick got up and followed Anne out. Shielding his eyes from the sun, he scanned the slope. Eventually he pointed to the far side.

'That might be him, green T-shirt, faded jeans.'

Anne screwed up her face and stared into the distance.

'By Rebecca's trench?'

'That's the one.'

'How certain are you?'

Without a word, Dick turned and jogged back to the barn, reappearing a moment later with a pair of lightweight binoculars. He adjusted focus.

'That's him. Have a look.'

Anne studied the man for several seconds.

'D'you know him?' Dick asked.

'No.'

'Just a friend of Donovan's?'

'I don't think so.' She lowered the binoculars, deep in thought. 'When's break time?'

'About ten minutes.'

'Great.' She thrust the binoculars at Dick and sped away. 'I'll be back.'

Anne nearly ran into Danny in the doorway of the office barn as she emerged backwards carrying a tray of mugs for the builders. She rushed in and scaled the wall-ladder while Marnie looked on. After a minute of scurrying about in the attic, Anne slithered down the ladder.

'Marnie, can I borrow the Polaroid?'

'Help yourself.' Marnie observed that Anne had changed into the old jeans and sweatshirt she used for working on the boat. 'What are you up to?'

'Tell you later.' Anne grabbed the camera and bolted. 'In a hurry.'

Her curiosity piqued, Marnie went to the door and was surprised to see Anne run round the side of the farmhouse into the untamed garden. Anne placed the camera on the paving slabs and knelt down on bare soil. She shuffled forwards on her knees, got up, dusted herself off and dashed back, clutching the camera. Without a glance in Marnie's direction, Anne ran up the field track and disappeared from view.

'What was that about?' Danny was walking back across the courtyard with the empty tray. 'I was just giving Bob his tea when I looked round and saw Anne doing a Toulouse-Lautrec impression in the shrubbery. Weird or what?'

'Definitely weird,' Marnie agreed. 'I wonder why.'

Danny shook her head. 'She looks as dirty as the students on the dig.'

Marnie nodded. 'That must be it.'

Up in the field, Anne went quickly to the farthest side and took a photograph in one of the trenches. The students looked up, recognised her, smiled and got back to their scraping. A young man in a green T-shirt was standing beside the next trench watching the students at work. Anne raised the camera and snapped again. While the Polaroid photo slid out from the base, she walked round to the other side of the hole.

'I'll get a shot from this angle, better with the light behind me. Rebecca, can you just move over a bit.'

'Sure. There's not much to see, Anne, just a few stones.'

'It's just for the records.' Anne raised the camera and they all heard it click. 'Bother!' she exclaimed. 'I touched the button too soon. I'll do it again.'

She peeled the photo out and held it in her fingertips while she took more care with the next one. Tucking the first two photos in her jeans pocket, she showed the students what she had taken. As they looked on, a cry went up from the bottom of the field.

Rebecca screwed up her face. 'What did he say?'

Anne said, 'Sounded to me like, *spruce up your goose!* Dick's getting demob happy.'

They all laughed. Anne turned and set off quickly while the students tidied the trench and their tools.

When Anne reached the HQ barn she thrust a photo at Dick Blackwood.

'Pin this on the board.'

Dick looked doubtful. 'It looks like a load of –'

'Dick, please, just do it. If anyone asks who I am, say I'm one of the team.'

He grinned at her. 'You sure look scruffy enough. What *have* you been doing?'

'Tell you later. I'll fetch the water.'

She jogged off round the garage barn while the students gathered for their break.

Danny climbed down the wall-ladder, placing each foot with caution on the rungs to avoid the risk of treading on the beach towel slung over her shoulder. She was wearing her bikini.

'I know what you're going to say, Marnie, but I've had all I can take of looking at stones in trenches, even if the place is being filmed.'

'I see you've changed into your studying attire.'

Danny picked up the beach bag. 'That's right. I've got my books. I'm going to sit and read by *Sally Ann*. Dolly's promised to test me on behavioural psychology.'

'That's good. Not many cats would do that.'

'I did have to offer an inducement, a tin of –'

The door flew open and Anne rushed in. She slipped two photographs out of the back pocket of her jeans, placed them on Marnie's desk and studied them.

'Danny, dig out the iced water, will you? I'm running late. Just take the bottle round to the HQ barn. They can help themselves.'

Danny dropped her things and set off for the fridge in the farmhouse. Marnie leaned forward for a better view of the photos.

'So what have we here?'

'It's the bloke who's been asking after Donovan.' Anne pointed. 'That's him in profile. I took it before he realised I was there. And that's a frontal shot. I pretended the camera went off by accident.'

'Asking after Donovan?'

'He asked Dick, but he didn't mention Donovan by name, just described him. He's been here before, after Donovan got plastered all over the TV news that time.'

'He looks a bit agitated in the second shot, seems to be raising his arm to … wait a minute. What's this?'

They both craned forward. Marnie held the photo up to the light.

'Oh gawd, not again,' she muttered. 'Look, Anne. There's a tattoo on his arm.'

Anne groaned, skipped across to her desk and returned carrying a magnifying glass.

'It'll probably just say, *I love Judy*, or something like that.'

'I don't think so.' Marnie turned the photo so that Anne could see it better. 'What do you make of that?'

Anne took the photo and steadied the glass over it.

'I wish it did say, *I love Judy*. Look.'

The tattoo was slightly blurred by movement but clear enough to leave them in no doubt. It was a simple design: a capital N and F joined together. The far right group they had encountered the year before. New Force. Donovan was right. They never gave up.

Danny had strained to put up the parasol on the bank of the docking area. She placed the beach bag of books in its shade and draped the towel over a steamer chair. True to her word, Dolly lay down beside her.

When Anne came out of the spinney, Danny hardly recognised her. Anne had changed out of her grubby clothes into a skinny top in primrose yellow, pale blue shorts, a sun hat, sandals and dark glasses.

'Don't get comfortable there. We're going for a tootle on *Sally Ann*.'

'What, now?'

'I'll explain once we've got going. Come on!'

While Danny cast off the bow rope, Anne dug out her mobile.

'Dick, it's Anne. Listen, if anyone asks after me, tell them I'm around somewhere. Don't say you haven't seen me, okay?'

Anne started the engine and reversed the boat out of the dock. She swung round and pointed the bows north towards some of the most secluded stretches of the Grand Union Canal in the county. They were observed only by Dolly, now relieved of her testing duties, sitting on the bank.

Marnie was blessed with strong powers of concentration and she used them to the full that afternoon. Alone in the office, she worked almost without interruption on the designs for a Willard hotel, a further scheme for the company's head-quarters and two private houses.

She could hardly believe it when, at six o'clock, Dick Blackwood stuck his head round the door to let her know the archaeologists were leaving. He had had no further contact with the visitor in the green T-shirt, no more enquires about Donovan or Anne. Marnie followed him out to watch the vehicles departing. She satisfied herself that no one was hanging around the site, returned to the office and phoned Anne to give her the all-clear.

As Marnie put the phone down it began to ring. It was Ralph.

'Sorry for the short notice, but there's a dinner in college tonight. I hadn't thought about going, but Guy Fellheimer has a colleague visiting from Germany, an expert on modern history from Tübingen. It might be worth meeting her.'

Marnie looked at the clock.

'What time is this dinner?'

'You'd need to be here for about seven-thirty.'

'Heavens!'

'I know. I've still got my rooms here, so you'll have somewhere to shower and change.'

'I'm on my way!'

Marnie kept clothes in the wardrobe at the back of the office, away from the smell of the boat. She was choosing a dress when Anne and Danny walked in. She quickly explained the new plan and grabbed a sponge bag from the shower room.

'There's plenty of food in the fridge. You don't mind fending for yourselves, do you?'

'No probs.'

The road into Oxford was relatively free-flowing, though the traffic on the other side of the carriageway was heavy and sluggish. On the journey, Marnie went through a mental checklist of things she had to take, convinced she must have forgotten something. A thought was niggling at the back of her mind. Was it something she had to tell Ralph, something she'd seen, something she had to do, somewhere she had to go? It was no good, she couldn't remember.

She glanced over her shoulder and saw the dress lying on the back seat.

Posh frock, shoes, make-up, sponge bag, hair brush. If she had missed anything, that was too bad.

In the city she had to concentrate to find the narrow side street that led to All Saints College, one of the smallest and least known institutions of the university. She managed to swing the Discovery off the main street and ease it down the cobbled lane, through the main gate. Ralph was waiting for her and indicated a reserved parking space.

'You've made very good time. Do you have an overnight bag?'

'You're kidding! I just grabbed some clothes and a toothbrush. It was all a terrific rush. Lead me to the shower.'

'Sorry about that, darling. The thing is, this person I want you to meet is leaving tomorrow. It was our only chance to see her.'

With the dress over one arm, they walked briskly across Old Quad. Marnie paused in the doorway at the foot of Ralph's staircase and looked back at the quadrangle.

'This is an amazing place. You'd never guess it was here unless you knew it, an absolute gem. I'm really looking forward to spending a night here.'

Ralph smiled at her. 'So am I.'

Unlike the larger Oxford colleges, All Saints did not possess a banqueting hall. Although its dining room could accommodate up to a hundred people, the atmosphere was inviting and intimate, with walls panelled in dark wood and low-level lighting supplemented by candelabra. It was situated in a building known as the 'New Extension', which had been constructed in 1629. Here, the ceiling was higher than in the older parts, with clerestory windows set in cream plasterwork above the panelling. Looking up, Marnie saw pale grey clouds drifting past in a blue sky.

The Master had arranged for Ralph and Marnie to sit at his table, and during the first course – a salad of artichoke hearts and mushrooms – he enquired about progress with the renovation of Glebe Farm. Over the main course of roast guinea fowl with new potatoes and broccoli, he asked whether they were finding time to use the boats. As they launched into summer pudding, he mentioned that he had seen snippets about the 'archaeological activities' on television and asked if Marnie would be relieved when the 'activities' finally came to an end on Saturday.

It was only when the cheese platter arrived that he referred to their other guest that evening, Professor Dr Karin Fleischer, who was sitting at an adjacent table being entertained by the Dean of Studies and a Senior Fellow.

Marnie had been observing her, discreetly she hoped, throughout the meal. Dr Fleischer seemed to be about forty and was obviously creating a more than favourable impression on her hosts. The occasional peal of laughter from their table gave Marnie the opportunity to look their way without appearing inquisitive. The visitor was wearing a trouser suit in a very dark green material that looked like velvet. It combined with a closely-cut hairstyle, dark brown with highlights, chunky amber jewellery and artful eye make-up to create an impression of intellectual intensity and sophistication.

When the Master became drawn into conversation with a professor of Roman law about aspects of constitutional government, Marnie spoke to Ralph in a low voice.

'Will I get a chance to talk to Dr Fleischer?'

'Over coffee. It's all arranged. The Master will introduce us.'

'What do you know about her, Ralph?'

'A very interesting character, apparently, with quite a colourful past.'

'She seems rather young to have a past.'

'She's known to be politically active on the left of the spectrum, at least she used to be. She may be less directly involved these days. It's rumoured that she had a liaison with a high-up figure in the SPD, the Social Democrats, the Prime Minister of one of the *Länder* – you know, the German states – a man tipped to take a cabinet position when his party regains power at national level.'

'So she's not a sympathiser with the ...'

'Definitely not, though I've heard it said she's flirted with quite a few other groups, including the Greens. In her youth there were rumours of a relationship with radical elements. I think that's all behind her now.'

'You *think*?'

'I'm pretty certain.'

'Ralph, what do you mean by *radical elements*?'

'She wrote a series of articles in the press about the Red Army Faction.'

'The who?'

'Otherwise known as the Baader-Meinhof Group. They were anarchists, responsible for bombings, riots, street battles with the police, shootings. She must have had inside knowledge to write those articles. I read that she visited Andreas Baader in the high-security prison in Ziegenhain for one such piece.'

Marnie shook her head. 'This is all outside my range. I've not really heard of them.'

'They were like the Red Brigades in Italy or *Action Directe* in France. Basically they wanted to overturn capitalism and, because they were young, some sectors of the press tried to make them look like romantic idealists. The truth was, they killed a lot of innocent people.'

'My god,' Marnie muttered under her breath. 'Do I really want to meet this woman?'

'Marnie, Fleischer wasn't one of them. She was studying them, saw them as a modern phenomenon, tried to understand the dynamics of extreme political action. It's a legitimate field of study. Jean-Paul Sartre interviewed Baader on one occasion.'

'All right. I'll take your word for it.'

'Fleischer applied to interview Ulrike Meinhof as well, but she committed suicide before the interview took place. Fleischer was only about twenty-two at the time, and a student.'

'And you think she might know something about the people responsible for the remains in Sarah's grave? It seems a long shot to me.'

'She has connections, Marnie. She knows – or at least *knew* – Ingrid Hallgarten. They were students together in Frankfurt.'

'I can't wait.'

When the meal ended, the Master led the diners across New Quad for coffee in the library, one of the oldest parts of the college. Ralph steered Marnie to a window near the corner. Through small panes of glass which must have dated from the fifteenth century, they watched the distorted shapes of the assembly processing towards the entrance lobby. On impulse, Marnie turned to Ralph and spoke in a whisper.

'I think you should do most of the talking for us.'

'But you're really the one who –'

'No, listen, Ralph. I have the feeling this woman will respond better to a man. Gut instinct. Trust me.'

As the distinctive form of Karin Fleischer reached the building, the Master detached himself from the gathering and drew her aside.

'Professor Fleischer, I'd like you to meet my colleague Professor Lombard and Ms Marnie Walker.'

After shaking hands, the Master completed the introductions and withdrew to attend to his other guests.

'I have long wanted to meet you, Professor Lombard. I'm sure you know your books have had a great influence on political thinking in Germany.'

Fleischer had a deep voice and spoke English clearly and slowly, with little trace of accent. All the while, she looked directly into Ralph's eyes with an expression that bordered on ironic amusement.

'I hope they were a positive influence. I've had a fair amount of correspondence with German colleagues over the years.'

Fleischer laughed quietly.

'I wonder if you knew that Andreas Baader had copies of both *We're Going Wrong* and *Public Need versus Corporate Greed* on the shelf in his prison cell?'

'As a matter of interest, Professor Fleischer, how would you know what he had in his cell?'

'One of the questions in my interview with him was to ask for the titles of all the books he had.'

'I read your whole series of articles at the time, though my German is modest, but I didn't recall that aspect.'

'No. Much of the material was for including in other publications and research papers.'

'Of course.'

'The Master tells me there were some questions that you wanted to ask me. How can

I help you? I must warn you, my knowledge of economic theory is probably more limited than your German.'

Throughout this exchange Fleischer did not so much as glance at Marnie. Her eyes never left Ralph's face.

'I wanted – or rather, *we* wanted – to ask you about your contact with Professor Ingrid Hallgarten.'

The mention of the name brought an immediate, if fleeting, reaction from Fleischer. Her smile vanished and her eyes narrowed momentarily before she relaxed again.

'Ingrid, ah yes. Well, I haven't seen her for some time.'

'But you were students together.'

'We were contemporaries, yes, but not close friends. What did you want to ask about her?'

'This will only make sense if I explain to you a situation that has arisen not far from here during an excavation.'

Fleischer nodded and Ralph outlined the events following the discovery of the second body in Sarah Anne Day's grave. He included the graves of the exhumed witches and mentioned the interest apparently being shown by the far right. He also referred to the incidents the previous summer surrounding the death of Garth Brandon.

During the narrative, Fleischer concentrated intensely. When Ralph ended, she blew air out between her lips as if smoking a cigarette.

'All of this happened on your property? Extraordinary.'

'On Marnie's property, to be precise.' Ralph inclined his head.

For the first time, Fleischer looked in Marnie's direction.

'I take it, you are not an academic, Ms … Walker?'

'That's correct. I'm an interior designer.'

'Of course. You have a much too developed sense of style to be a professor.' There was little warmth in the smile. 'So, what is the connection with Ingrid Hallgarten?'

Marnie replied. 'We believe Professor Hallgarten's father was in the intelligence service in the war. He had an agent in this area. His daughter may know something about her father's work. It's a very tenuous –'

'I don't see what this has to do with me,' Fleischer interrupted.

Ralph intervened. 'We would like to meet Professor Hallgarten, but we know she doesn't normally grant interviews about her father. She insists on keeping a distance from elements – shall we say – from the right of the spectrum, who might want to exploit the family name for political reasons.'

'You think I can help you with an introduction?'

'Yes. If you could assure her that we were not –'

'Professor Lombard, I have to tell you that Ingrid Hallgarten and I … how do you say this … *fell out?* … several years ago.'

'I see.'

'No, I think you do not see, Professor. This was not a question of academic rivalry.

It was a personal matter.'

'So you're unable to help us,' Marnie said.

Fleischer turned to look out of the window. She stared for so long that Marnie thought she was dismissing them. Ralph stood and waited. Eventually she spoke.

'If you obtained information from Ingrid, what would you do with it?'

Marnie was taken aback by the question. She had been compelled by the aim of resolving the mystery for so long that the actual outcome had become an end in itself.

Fleischer persisted. 'You must have a reason for wanting to question Ingrid. What is the purpose of your enquiry?'

'A body has been discovered in a grave in our village. We just want to know whose remains they are.'

'And then?'

'If we find out who it is, perhaps we could at least give them a proper burial.' Even as Marnie said the words, she realised how feeble they sounded.

'No, you don't understand me.' Fleischer turned back to Ralph. 'Are you wanting to publish the results of your enquiry? Or is it a matter of the police trying to find a killer? Ingrid would want to know how you planned to refer to her father and in what context.'

'Professor Fleischer,' Ralph glanced at Marnie. 'It isn't that kind of enquiry. There will be no publication. No one is going to mention Major Hallgarten by name. As Marnie says, we have a body; we need to know what to do about it. Curiosity can be a legitimate motive in itself.'

Fleischer fell silent again, deep in thought. She looked at Marnie.

'No. There is more. You do not come to a college dinner in Oxford and ask the Master to arrange an introduction so that you can find the name of an unknown person buried in a small country village. If you want me to help, you must tell me what you are doing, and why.'

'Professor Fleischer, you're right,' Marnie said. 'Someone is trying to prevent identification of the man whose remains were in the grave.'

'Someone?'

'Possibly the government.'

Fleischer stared. 'Why?'

'We don't know that.'

'You think this is a … what is the word … a *cover-up*?'

'Yes.'

'And Ingrid could help because she is outside the country.'

'That's what we thought.'

Fleischer shook her head. 'It is strange, after so many years, there are still secrets.'

'Will you help us?' Marnie asked. 'Would you be willing to approach Professor Hallgarten?'

'I must consider this. But even if I decide to contact Ingrid, I can make no promises.'

It was still light when Marnie and Ralph took their leave of the Master and Fellows and strolled round Old Quad. While they had been taking coffee a summer shower had fallen on Oxford and it had passed, leaving the college glowing and refreshed in late sunlight. Tucked away in its hidden corner of the city, unknown to most of the outside world, All Saints smelled of damp grass and cool air. They paused briefly beside a climbing rose. Drops of water fell from the petals of one flower onto the back of her hand as Marnie raised a bloom to her nose and breathed in deeply.

'Wonderful,' she murmured. 'You know, Ralph, there are times when I find it hard to believe you gave up all this to live on a canal boat.'

'No contest,' he said. 'Anyway, I didn't give anything up for a boat. I gave it up for sound career reasons and to be with you.'

Marnie gave a slight bow. 'Thank you, kind sir.'

'I mean it.'

'I know.'

'Actually, Marnie, you bring a balance into my life, among other things. In the academic world it's easy to get drawn into a mindset comprising only concepts and theories.'

Marnie looked back towards the library. 'I know what you mean. Meeting someone like Professor Fleischer makes me realise how intense everything is in that world. All the time walking on eggshells, wondering if someone is going to catch you out, prove you deficient in some way.'

Ralph smiled. 'Not everyone is like Karin Fleischer. We can still enjoy the beauty of our surroundings. It is a privilege to be here.'

Marnie grinned. 'It's so refined, perhaps I should've brought a nightdress?'

Ralph took her arm and led her to the corner staircase. When they reached his door, Ralph turned to Marnie.

'Don't worry, we're not formal in everything. You won't need a nightdress.'

'Thank you for that assurance.'

'Anyway,' He turned the key in the lock and opened the door. 'I seem to recall we have unfinished business from last night …'

41
Tenure

Marnie swung the Discovery into the high street on Saturday morning. She and Ralph had had an easy drive back from Oxford, and she was astonished to find herself in a traffic jam in the village. The way ahead was blocked by the transporter moving the giant TV crane, picking its way ponderously between parked cars and vans while the *Timeline* helicopter circled beyond it. Marnie lifted her foot from the accelerator and they drifted slowly forward. They were rolling gently when a car nipped out from a side street into a tiny gap in front of them and braked heavily.

'Isn't that Celia?' Ralph said.

'Yep. Typical. Thinks she owns the street.' Marnie reflected for a moment. 'Probably does, I expect.'

The crane lorry, the Audi convertible and the Discovery processed in convoy down the high street, past the church, pub and school and through the field gate. As soon as they entered the field, Celia yanked the wheel hard over and bounced past the truck, her tyres throwing up clouds of dust. The crane turned off the track and lumbered away down the slope.

Driving cautiously on the hard rutted ground, Marnie glanced over and saw that the field was alive with activity. Everywhere, small groups of archaeologists were clustered about their pits and trenches. The camera crew were filming an interview in the middle of the action, with Rob Cardew in front of the camera, pointing across to a far corner of the site, a microphone on a pole dangling over his head. Ralph yawned.

'Surely you're not tired, Ralph.' Marnie smiled. 'We did have an early night, after all.'

'Precisely.' He sat up in his seat. 'That's Anne down there, isn't it?'

Marnie twisted her head to see. 'Looks like she's taking photographs, a final record, last day of the dig.'

They turned to drive into the garage barn and found their way blocked. For the second time that morning Marnie was looking at the rear of Celia's Audi; it was parked directly in front of the barn. Sighing, she climbed out and headed for the office.

To Marnie's surprise, the door was ajar.

'Not like Anne to leave it like this,' she said to Ralph.

'Let me go first.' Ralph pushed the door wide.

Perched on Marnie's desk with her back to the door, wearing a cheesecloth shirt over a bikini, Danny was picking up the phone.

'Walker and Co, good morning ... I'm afraid she's not in the office at the moment. Can I take a message?' Danny turned to reach for the notepad and spotted Marnie and Ralph in the doorway. 'Oh, she's just come in. May I know who's calling? ... Hold on please.' Danny held up the phone. 'Mrs Vane-Henderson of Hanford Hall.'

Marnie took the phone while Danny picked up her bag of books and went out, smiling at Ralph. When Marnie finished the call she made a note on the pad.

'Another recommendation. One of Dorothy's friends wants me to visit.'

'Celia was right. You are becoming flavour of the month, Marnie.'

'Come on. Let's go and see what's happening on the dig.'

Not surprisingly, they found a small crowd outside the HQ barn. This was normal whenever the *Timeline* team was around. And on that morning the visitors thought they had found a star. In their midst, radiant in a white dress comprising layers of light cotton stood Celia Devere. Marnie was convinced her shoes were Prada. Even at ten o'clock on a Saturday morning she looked as if she had stepped out of the pages of *Vogue* magazine, fresh from the hairdresser's.

Spotting Marnie and Ralph, Celia turned and glided through the throng towards them, beaming.

'Lovely to see you both.' She air-kissed them on the cheeks, then lowered her voice. 'Dick Blackwood was just telling me they're going to have a party this evening to mark the end of the dig. I think they want me to be …' She made a self-deprecating gesture and spoke even more quietly, 'guest of honour. I expect all the TV people will be there.'

Celia glanced round to bestow a smile on her crowd of admirers, but found them turning to look in another direction. At that moment Danny skipped by in her shirt and bikini, and all eyes followed her. Celia frowned momentarily before regaining her composure.

'Oh, I forgot to ask where the party's being held.'

'It's here,' Marnie said.

'*Here?*'

'Yes.'

'You knew about it? You were invited?' Celia seemed to find the idea strange.

'Yes.'

'When were you invited?'

Marnie looked at Ralph. 'Thursday, wasn't it?'

Ralph nodded. Celia's frown returned, this time deeper.

'And it's going to be *here*?'

Marnie pointed. 'Refreshments in the barn, socialising and no doubt dancing out in the open. It should be a nice evening for it.'

'I see.' Celia looked at the ground. 'I don't think I'll be coming. Not really my sort of thing.'

'Really?'

Celia shook her head. 'All those students, swigging beer from bottles, no doubt, heavy petting behind the barn. Ugh!' She shuddered. 'No. I think not. Excuse me.'

Celia turned on her heel and walked off, almost colliding with Angela Hemingway, who was surprised when her friendly greeting went unreturned.

'What's up with Celia? She's looking like a wet Wednesday.'

'She doesn't want to play with us any more,' Marnie said. 'She's taking her toys and going home.'

Angela giggled. 'You're terrible, Marnie. I came to see what was going on and to give you the latest news.'

'And it's coffee time,' Marnie observed. 'What a coincidence.'

'Isn't it?' Angela grinned.

'So what's new?'

'The bishop says Sarah can be reburied in the churchyard as soon as the police enquiry is closed. He asked them for more information, but that's all they'd tell him.'

Marnie was about to comment when Rob Cardew came round the corner of the barn and went straight over to join them.

'Well, that's it, my moment of glory on the screen, famous for fifteen minutes, as they say.'

Angela began telling Rob about the news from the bishop, but noticed that his attention strayed to something over her shoulder. Turning, she saw Celia advancing on them, her expression less than cheerful.

'Is that your Land Rover, Marnie? Would you mind moving it. You're blocking me in.'

Ralph extended a hand to Marnie.

'I'll do it. Can I have the keys?'

Marnie handed them to him without speaking. He smiled at Celia and they set off. Marnie was still counting to ten under her breath when Celia stopped and looked back at her.

'You will remember that I'm expecting the redecoration to be completed by the end of the coming week, won't you, Marnie? There still seems a lot to be done.'

Marnie nodded and began counting to herself from scratch. After Celia had gone, she took a deep breath.

'Well, that puts me in my place, doesn't it?'

The others made sympathetic noises.

'You'll be glad when that job's finished,' Angela observed. 'Will it be completed on time?'

'Yes.' Marnie's tone was emphatic.

Rob reached forward and patted her arm.

'This one too, eh? You'll be glad to have us out of the way and things back to normal.'

'Normal.' Marnie looked quizzical. 'Now there's a thought ...'

True to her word, Celia did not put in an appearance at the party. Had she known how it would turn out, she would have been more than a tad disappointed. Nobody was going to tell her.

The TV people stayed on and even filmed part of the celebrations to provide atmospheric footage for broadcasting. The setting looked magical, with fairy lights – Anne's idea – draped over the HQ barn, extending into the trees. Garden flares burned at the perimeter of the gathering and funky music provided a festive background. The students had gone back to their campsite to shower and change for the evening and had returned transformed, barely recognisable as the dust bunnies who had spent the afternoon filling in holes, restoring the site to its previous condition.

The finds tables in the HQ barn were filled with quiches, dips, salads and nibbles, supplemented by burgers and sausages from two barbecues, and the wine, albeit from the more modest end of the supermarket shelves, flowed in abundance.

In an ambience of gaiety that had sometimes been lacking during the dig, Marnie and Rob stood eating together watching Danny's efforts to teach Ralph the latest dance, egged on by Anne who was spasmodically engulfed in laughter.

'I'm sorry it hasn't always been enjoyable for you, Marnie.' Rob's owlish smile was tinged with melancholy. 'We know we can't tell in advance what we'll dig up, but it's usually less dramatic than this excavation has been.'

'It's been an experience, Rob, and a pleasure to get to know you all. Which reminds me, I haven't spoken to Rosemary this evening.'

Rob nodded towards the dancers. 'There she is over there, gyrating with Dick.'

'Ah yes. She looks happy and relaxed.'

'Yes.'

Something in Rob's voice made Marnie study him.

'She is happy, I take it, Rob.'

'Very.'

'For any particular reason?' Marnie recalled Rosemary saying something once, at a time that now seemed long ago, about hoping to start a family. 'Do you have some exciting news? Or shouldn't I ask?'

To Marnie's surprise, Rob looked uncomfortable.

'Rob, I didn't mean to pry. I hope I haven't spoken out of turn.'

'No, no, Marnie. It was an innocent question. It's just, well, actually we do have some news, perhaps not what you seemed to be thinking.'

'Then forget I asked and get me some more wine.'

Rob turned to face Marnie.

'Rosemary has just learnt that she's getting a new project, funded by the government with quite a generous budget.'

'That's great news.' Marnie wondered why Rob seemed embarrassed. 'I must congratulate her.'

'That's not all, Marnie. They've told her she's likely to be given tenure, you know, her post made permanent.'

'Better still!'

'Yes. It's all just suddenly happened, out of the blue.' He drained his glass. 'I'll get you that wine. It's the Spanish red, isn't it?'

Marnie watched him go, then turned her attention to the dancers, where Rosemary was whirling round Dick Blackwood in gay abandon.

'I don't see why I should be the only victim.' Ralph had appeared unnoticed at Marnie's elbow, breathing heavily, his cheeks glowing. 'Isn't it time you tripped the light fantastic?'

Marnie smiled and Ralph's expression changed.

'What is it, Marnie? Something wrong? Was my dancing that bad?'

'Highly original.'

'Oh god.'

'No, Ralph, it wasn't your dancing.'

'Tell me what's happened.'

'Rob's just given me the news, Rosemary's getting tenure plus a big new project, government funded.'

Ralph pondered this for some seconds.

'In exchange for ...?'

Marnie shrugged.

'I wouldn't like to speculate, but something tells me she won't be pressing for information about a certain set of remains. In fact, I doubt if she'll be asking any awkward questions at all.'

42
Abandoned

Marnie slipped out from under the duvet without disturbing Ralph, pulled on a sweatshirt and jeans and went ashore. Sunday morning. Not just any Sunday morning. It was six-thirty and she had the place to herself, or so she thought. There was a stillness about the sloping field and a coolness in the air, as if the archaeologists had taken some of the heatwave with them, wrapped up in their groundsheets.

The first surprise came when she walked past the HQ barn. The lights were still hanging in place from the night before, but of the dig, the diggers and their final celebration there was no evidence in sight. Just as on all the days of their excavations, they had removed every trace of their presence.

Rounding the corner, Marnie stared up the field. Here too she could discern no indication that they had ever disturbed the land. Only when she walked up for a closer inspection could she see where the turves had been re-laid. The diggers had stamped them back in place and given them a light watering. In a few weeks, Marnie thought, you would scarcely be able to tell that the dig had ever taken place.

They had even taken the trouble to fill in the witches' graves so that they too were receding into the soil. Only the *shallow graves* showed signs of disturbance, if you knew where to look among the bushes.

There was a strange emptiness about the silent slope, a sense of abandonment. Suddenly it occurred to Marnie that although she had spoken with Rob, Dick and the others many times, she had gained little impression of what they had actually discovered. She knew they had found traces of buildings up the field, plus one or two artefacts like the pretty pendant so coveted by Celia Devere, but what it all showed or proved she had no idea. No doubt she would have to watch the programmes to find out what they had learnt.

The more she thought about it, the more curious it seemed that Rob had not offered to debrief the residents of Glebe Farm on the outcome of their weeks on site. In fact, in those last days she now had the distinct impression that he had been avoiding all but the most fleeting contact with her, ostensibly on the grounds that he did not want to disturb her work any more than necessary.

But was that the reason? Marnie thought back to the previous evening and her chat with Rob. If she had not referred to Rosemary, would he have told her about the new project, the government funding and the granting of tenure?

Back near the HQ barn, Marnie stood looking up the field, imagining the ghosts of the diggers who would now be in her memory every time she saw the place. She thought of those other ghosts whose remains had lain in the ground unknown to her for years, some of them for centuries before she ever came to live there.

Marnie turned to retrace her steps back to *Thyrsis* and almost fell over Dolly who had followed her out. She bent down and picked up the cat, who warbled a greeting in her arms.

'You teddy bear, Dolly.' Marnie buried her face in thick-pile fur. 'You great teddy bear.'

The cat's front paws clenched and unclenched rhythmically against Marnie's arm and she snuggled her head under Marnie's chin, amber eyes blinking slowly in contentment. Marnie felt the warmth of the sturdy black cat against her body. It was a comfortable uncomplicated relationship, stability in an uncertain world.

For some time Marnie stood there with Dolly, unwilling to break off. The cat began a deep slow purring and seemed to be drifting into sleep. Marnie smiled. The amber eyes opened wide. Infallible radar; breakfast time was approaching. With one last glance up Glebe field, Marnie turned away.

One thing was certain: the place would never be quite the same again. How often had she had that thought since moving to Glebe Farm?

43
Negatives

In the week that followed the departure of the diggers, life at Glebe Farm returned to normal.

For Marnie, that meant steady progress on her projects, site meetings with Willard managers and her new contact from Dorothy Vane-Henderson. For Ralph, it meant uninterrupted concentration on the beginning of a new book on warning signs for the world economy that would probably bring him renewed notoriety.

For Anne, it brought a welcome return to routine. Each morning after dealing with the post, she drove up to Knightly Court to meet the decorators and satisfy herself that the programme was running on target. For Danny, it meant the peace and calm that most people needed for studying. Instead, she complained that it was too quiet. She had found it easier to focus on her reading when the archaeologists were busy in the field.

For Dolly, it meant ceaseless vigilance in the quest to protect her friends from mouse attack. To achieve this, she curled up on the hatch of *Sally Ann*, pretending to be asleep for several hours each day. The subterfuge fooled everyone.

The outside world seemed to have deserted the residents of Glebe Farm. Both sets of tenants were on holiday. Angela was attending to her committees and her flock. Celia made no attempt to contact Marnie, and the decorators told Anne they only caught glimpses of her as she came and went.

There was no contact from Donovan.

~~~

On Monday while tidying her desk at the end of the working day, Anne suggested a tootle on *Sally Ann*. Marnie thought it was a good idea and proposed that they eat on the boat. That pattern repeated itself every evening in the days that followed. After closing the office they cast off and pointed the bows in whichever direction they pleased. Simple meals were prepared while they cruised along: quiches, salads, garlic bread, artichokes, asparagus, avocadoes, salmon, pizza.

On that first trip Marnie stood at the tiller, wine glass in hand, watching the sunlight on the crops ripening in the fields and the cattle and sheep grazing in the meadows. She felt the soothing influence of *Sally Ann*, easing away the tribulations of the past weeks. Those pastoral outings reminded Marnie of why she had come to Northamptonshire, why she had moved away from the metropolis, why she had sought out the peace of the countryside and the solace of a narrowboat.

When the storm broke and the tranquillity of their lives was shattered, they would look back on those evenings as the best of the summer.

~~~

On Friday while they were preparing breakfast, Danny announced that she thought it was time to return home. Marnie and Anne said they would miss her. It was agreed that Anne would take Danny home on Saturday morning and combine the trip with a visit to her own family for the weekend.

Ralph commented that Danny seemed to be making useful inroads into her university reading list. While he was speaking, his eyes drifted towards the window.

Marnie poured his orange juice.

'Everything okay, Ralph?'

'Oh, yes.'

'You don't sound terribly certain.'

'No, it's just that … It's nothing.'

'Ralph, if something's bothering you, chances are it isn't nothing.'

Danny stared at him. Anne got up and went to look out of the window.

'I know it'll sound odd,' Ralph began, 'but I had a feeling – just for a split second – that I sensed something in the spinney.'

'*Sensed* something?' Marnie prompted. 'Like what?'

'Perhaps it was Dolly,' Danny suggested.

He shook his head. 'She's on the bed back there. No, it was movement, but not on the ground, a sort of change in the light patterns.'

Marnie got to her feet. 'Come on. We can sit here surmising all morning. Let's go and see for ourselves.'

There was a scramble to follow her out. Once on the bank, Marnie told the others to spread out and walk quickly through the spinney in line abreast. It took only a minute to sweep the area. Next, they turned to the HQ barn. Empty. The garage barn showed no sign of disturbance. They regrouped in the field behind the barns.

'What did you expect to find, Marnie?' Ralph asked.

'Dunno. I thought anything was better than sitting on the boat, wondering if there was someone poking around outside.'

They walked back to the docking area which looked as it had when they left. Anne led the way on board and stopped at the foot of the steps down into the sleeping cabin.

'Where's Dolly?'

Marnie peered over her shoulder. 'What d'you mean?'

'She was on the bed when we came out.'

'Probably joined in with the manhunt,' Marnie suggested, looking round.

'Dolly!' Anne called. 'Dolly!'

With a quiet miaow, Dolly emerged from under the bed and rubbed her flank against Anne's legs.

'What were you doing under there?' Anne said, reaching down to stroke her. 'Did something spook you?'

The cat didn't reply.

Just before four o'clock Marnie and Anne drove up to Knightly Court for the final handover. It was Anne's second visit of the day. At her morning meeting she had checked that everything was on target for completion. The decorators had assured her they would have everything ready that afternoon. Celia had agreed to see them at four. She had made no contact with Marnie during the whole of the week and sounded subdued on the phone when Marnie had called her.

'That's a good sign,' Marnie said as they rolled onto the drive.

The decorators were loading equipment into their van. Celia's car was in its usual parking place by the front door.

'Can't talk,' Anne murmured. 'Speech is impossible. I've got everything crossed, including my vocal chords.'

'You're not nervous, are you, Anne? It's just a routine end-of-contract meeting.'

'Please refer to my previous statement.'

Marnie was smiling as she climbed out of the car.

'Hallo, John. All well?'

The chief decorator wiped his hand on his overalls before shaking hands.

'Fine. Nice to see a smiling face.'

'Oh? Problem?'

John glanced over his shoulder at the house and leaned towards Marnie.

'Misery guts in there – the *Fairy Queen* – seems to be worried about cracking her make-up.'

'John, have you finished the work?'

'Yes.'

'Are you satisfied with the outcome?'

He grinned. 'It's a cracker.'

'Then show me round. Do you know where Mrs Devere is?'

'On the terrace, when last seen.'

Marnie nodded at Anne who went to find her.

When they were all assembled, they began in the hall and worked through to the drawing room. Marnie and Anne were delighted with the results of their designs. The first negative moment came when Marnie asked if they might take some photos for the file.

Celia frowned and said quietly, 'I don't think that would be appropriate, for reasons of security.'

Marnie looked at her clipboard. 'I think we've covered everything.'

Anne knew that at this point the property owners normally pronounced themselves as *pleased*, *overjoyed* or *ecstatic*, often all three plus a few more superlatives. Marnie paused for a moment.

'Are there any points you'd like to raise, Celia?'

'I don't think so.'

'Then it only remains for me to thank you, John, and your team for an excellent job. Once again you've done us proud. I'm delighted with the results.'

'It's been a pleasure working for you, Marnie.'

For the second time that afternoon they shook hands. Celia's arms remained resolutely olded across her chest.

John looked at her, inclined his head briefly and muttered, 'Thank you.'

He was leaving via the French windows onto the terrace when Celia spoke up.

'Oh, there is one other thing, I suppose.'

John paused and waited. Celia turned to Marnie.

'When will these people want payment? Will they want cash?'

John went out. Anne lowered her eyes. Marnie's cheeks reddened.

'We'll be sending you an invoice in the post.'

Marnie held out a hand. After a moment's hesitation, Celia shook it.

Walking out through the front door, Marnie and Anne saw the white van leaving the lrive. Like John, Marnie could not get away fast enough. They were in the high street efore Marnie spoke.

'That *bloody woman*! *These people*, she said, *these people!* John was standing there, robably thinking she was going to thank him for a job well done. *Will they want cash?* I've ever known such *rudeness*, Anne. Not a cup of tea, not a smile, not a word of thanks.'

'It'll be good to close the file,' Anne said. 'I'll send the invoice off on Monday. Then we can forget all about Celia Devere.'

Marnie turned through the gate onto the field track.

'Let's hope so.'

∾∾∾∾ ∾∾∾∾

Marnie could not settle. She knew Ralph would be arriving in the office at around five-hirty, but she needed to walk to release tension and she wanted to tell him about the handover. Stepping down into the galley on *Thyrsis* she could hear him speaking on the phone. She waited until he disconnected before walking along to his study.

Ralph looked up as Marnie entered. 'That was Karin Fleischer.'

'Back in Germany, presumably?'

'Yes. I got a message from All Saints saying she wanted me to contact her. She spoke with Ingrid Hallgarten this morning.'

'Don't tell me.'

'You guessed. She refused to discuss her father's work in the war. Fleischer assured her that you had no hidden agenda, but even so ...'

'I wonder how hard Karin Fleischer pressed our case.'

'Oh, I think she tried. At one point she actually thought Hallgarten was going to agree, but in the end she reverted to her usual position.'

Marnie flopped into a chair. 'That's another door closed. First Rosemary, now this.'

Ralph steepled his fingers. 'I suppose we'll never know whose remains were in Sarah's grave.'

'Frankly, Ralph, I don't think I care any more. Some time soon Angela will arrange Sarah's reburial and that will be an end to it. We'll be able to close that file, too.'

44
Straight talking

Danny was assembling her bags at the foot of the attic wall-ladder on Saturday morning when Marnie's phone began ringing. It was exactly nine o'clock.

A shampoo sachet had burst in Danny's sponge bag and while Danny finished packing Marnie was wiping it out with tissues. Her fingers were covered in sticky gel, so Anne picked up the receiver.

'Walker and Co, good morning.' Her face relaxed into a smile. 'Hi, Angela. Yes, she's here. Hang on a sec.'

Marnie pressed the handsfree button with the dry tip of her little finger.

'Angela, good morning. How are things?'

'Good question, Marnie.' Angela's voice echoed in the room from the speaker on the phone. 'I've just had Celia bending my ear.'

Marnie sat down. 'Really. Lucky you.'

'She was terribly distraught.'

'What's new?'

'Seriously, Marnie. She was talking about taking legal action … against you.'

'*What?*'

'That's what she said.'

'But the decorators did an *excellent* job. The Court looks like a *palace*. If she wasn't happy, she could've said so.'

'Sorry? I don't follow, Marnie.'

'We completed her redec project yesterday. Isn't that what she's distraught about?'

Angela sounded baffled. 'No. She didn't mention that to me.'

'What then?'

'She, er, well, it was about Hugh, and you.'

Marnie's turn to sound baffled. 'Run that past me again.'

'She said she'd seen you, Marnie.'

'Doing what? When? I haven't seen her husband for days, not since he came round here looking for her last week.'

'She didn't mention that, either.'

'What did she say, Angela?'

'That Hugh had phoned to say he was going to be so late finishing his meeting in London that he'd decided to stay on in a hotel. He was rather vague about which one.'

'When was this?'

'Friday, a week ago. She's been brooding over it ever since, apparently.'

'That's the day I had to rush off to Oxford for a dinner.'

'Ah …'

'*Ah* what?'

'She said she'd just spoken to Hugh on the phone before going round to the village shop. On her way, she saw you dashing past in your car, and put two and two together.'

'She thought I'd raced off to London to make passionate love to her husband in a hotel?'

'Well, yes.'

'Angela you can tell her from me she got part of the story right. I did dash off. I did go to meet a man and we did spend the night making passionate love. But my assignation wasn't with her husband. It was with *my* lover. Got it?'

No reply.

'You can tell her that from me.'

Silence.

'Angela? Are you there?'

'I'm here, Marnie.'

'You heard what I said?'

'Yes. It's just ...'

'What?'

'I'm not sure that's the kind of message lady vicars normally pass on to their parishioners.'

Marnie faltered. 'No. I suppose not. But perhaps you could give her an abridged version. I don't want to speak to her myself.'

'Okay. Will do.'

'Was that everything?'

'Yes. Marnie? Is your phone all right? Your voice sounds rather echoey, as if you're standing in a tunnel.'

'It's on handsfree mode. My fingers are sticky.'

'That explains it.'

After they disconnected, Marnie sat thinking for some seconds, shaking her head. Suddenly she became aware of movement, a faint shuffling behind her. She turned to find Danny staring down at her shoes and Anne trying without much success to suppress a smile.

On the drive south to Leighton Buzzard Danny sat quietly beside Anne, who was happy to concentrate on her driving. It was only as they saw the first signs to their home town that Danny spoke.

'I've had a great time. It's been nice to stay with you and Marnie and Ralph.'

'It's been good, despite the odd ...' Anne glanced quickly sideways at her friend. '... happening.'

'You seem to have quite a few *happenings* in your life, Anne.'

Anne grinned. 'Yeah.'

Danny hooted. 'And Marnie doesn't exactly mince her words, does she?'

They motored on, both smiling, in silence for a couple of miles before Danny spoke again.

'Anne?'

'I don't expect so.'

Danny blinked. 'Don't expect what?'

'What you were about to ask me.'

'You don't expect to see Donovan again?'

'No.'

'You sound awfully definite about that. Is that what you want?'

'What I want doesn't come into it. Donovan believes any contact could be risky.'

'Who for?'

'All of us. If his enemies come looking for him at Glebe Farm, we could be in danger. At the same time, we could lead his enemies to him.'

'They don't know where he lives?'

'He's pretty sure they don't. In fact, he doesn't believe they actually know who he is, yet.'

'And you're worried they might use you to track him down.'

'Maybe. I think there are pretty good reasons for me not being able to see Donovan again.'

'Not ever?'

'Not ever.'

45
Journeys

With the departure of the diggers followed by Danny's return home, a calm descended on Glebe Farm in the last weeks of summer. To Marnie it almost seemed as if the events that had so disrupted their lives had never happened.

A week of showers helped the turves removed by the diggers to blend in with the grass in Glebe Field, and every trace of the excavations faded away. The police tape round the shallow grave site had been removed, and it was virtually impossible to identify the spot where the two navvies had been buried. Marnie kept away from Sarah's grave, but she knew from Angela that preparations had begun for the reburial.

Celia disappeared from their lives. On the Monday after her redecoration had been completed, Anne sent off the final invoice. She had had misgivings about it, convinced there would be all manner of hassle and disputes. She was proved wrong. The first item she opened in the post on Wednesday was a cheque for the full amount, signed by Hugh Devere. There was no accompanying letter, just the cheque by itself. Anne noticed that the handwriting on the envelope looked different from Hugh's signature and was in a different colour ink. With a feeling of relief, Anne looped an elastic band round the project file and placed it in the archive for storage.

Ralph spent most days in his study, working on his new book, preparing lectures for a tour of the Far East and honing an article for a journal.

Danny phoned Anne two or three times a week and chatted about her pre-university reading, some clothes she had bought for the coming term and a boy she had met at the local reference library. On one occasion she began asking a question that had been constantly on her mind.

'I don't suppose you've heard anything from –'

'No,' Anne had replied abruptly. 'And I'm not going to, so you don't have to ask me again.'

***

A period of unsettled weather blew in from the south-west in September, and the only trip on *Sally Ann* was to a boatyard south of Milton Keynes for hull blacking. They made the journey in six hours on a bright blustery Sunday. The school holidays had ended and traffic on the canal was reduced. Even so, they had to concentrate all the way in the breezy conditions, especially rounding tight corners and approaching narrow bridge holes.

Marnie, Ralph and Anne found the journey exhilarating, but opinions were divided at the thought that the boat would not be craned out of the water until the Monday morning. Anne had wanted to watch the spectacle and take photos of *Sally Ann* 'flying through the air'. Ralph was neutral on this, but Marnie announced that she would be glad not to spectate for the sake of her nerves.

It was to be their last boat trip for a while. Ralph was due to fly to Singapore early the following week, leaving Marnie and Anne to ferry *Sally Ann* back without him. The boat would be put back in the water on the Monday, exactly one week later, and Anne consoled herself with the knowledge that she could arrange her college timetable to be away that day.

Marnie drove Ralph to catch the airport bus for Heathrow the next day, Tuesday. She had offered to take him all the way, but he had insisted that the shuttle bus would be fine; she had work to do.

When they kissed goodbye at the coach station, Marnie said she couldn't wait for Ralph to be home again. He assured her the two weeks would pass quickly, and they would be able to resume their normal life together.

For once Ralph's forecast was to be proved wrong.

46
Timeline broadcast

t was what Anne usually called a 'college day', and not just because that was where she was going on the day in question. Wednesday 18 September was overcast and damp, hreatening rain. She had spent the first part of the morning sorting the mail, dealing with routine office tasks and checking an essay she was due to hand in that afternoon.

Shortly before eleven she took mugs out to Bob and his mate who were rebuilding an upstairs wall and chimney breast in the farm house. On her return to the office, she found Marnie leafing through the desk diary, muttering to herself.

'Oxford. Now when was that?'

'Did you say Oxford, Marnie?'

'I was wondering when it was that I went over to meet Professor Fleischer.'

'Has she been in touch?'

'No.'

'Is everything all right?'

'Probably.'

Anne reflected. 'Must've been just before the end of the dig. You and Ralph came back on the day of the final party.'

'That's right, August. That would be about six weeks ago. Yes, the end of the dig.'

'That reminds me, Marnie.' Anne set a mug down on Marnie's desk. 'Bob's just said we're on TV tonight.'

Marnie looked up. '*Timeline*?'

Anne nodded. 'Fame at last.'

'Did he say what time?'

'Eight o'clock.' Anne pointed. 'Better put it in the diary.'

Marnie came off the phone after speaking to Ralph in Hong Kong ten minutes before the programme began. For the next few days he would be travelling between venues, delivering lectures in universities and business schools, ending in Shanghai. It was a punishing schedule, but it kept him in touch with leading economists in the Far East. It also earned him as much in fees in one month as a university professor would normally earn in a year.

They settled down to watch and record *Timeline* on the small television in Anne's attic room.

There were six sites in different parts of the country, with continuity provided by Professor Barny Guthrie. They were both surprised how much he dominated the programme. In Knightly St John he had seemed to merge quietly into the background, but he had no doubt been at the centre of the filming up and down the field. There he was on the screen, popping up everywhere, taking a leading role at every excavation.

Watching the programme, it became clear that witches of various forms were active in every region. It gave the impression that Britain was just one big coven. The first digs shown were in the north of England, in Lancashire and Yorkshire, but just before the commercial break the scene shifted south to a view that was highly familiar.

In hot sunshine a find was made in a trench at Glebe Farm. A map appeared locating them beside the Grand Union Canal in south Northamptonshire. Back in the trench an archaeologist was wiping dirt from a tiny pendant, gleaming in gold, which he held up against the neck of one of the girls. In the next shot he was shaking hands with a young man dressed in black. Donovan was shown in close up. His image froze and filled the screen as Barny Guthrie explained what they would be discovering after the break. Donovan looked out at the nation for some seconds before he faded and the adverts began.

'Oh dear, he won't like that,' Anne said, pressing the pause button on the recorder control to eliminate the commercials.

'D'you think he'll be watching the programme?' Marnie asked.

'Dunno. Perhaps I should warn him.'

'Maybe you should.'

Marnie looked pensive. On the television a talking frog was explaining to an enraptured housewife that her sink could be unblocked with one squirt of the latest bleach. All her troubles would be over.

Anne frowned. 'D'you think people might come here looking for him?'

'It's possible, I suppose. And we might get over-run by sight-seers again. It'd be better if we weren't here.'

'*Thyrsis*?' Anne suggested.

'Yes. We could go down to Willowbridge and bring *Sally* back in convoy on Monday.'

'Trouble is,' Anne began, 'I've got classes till lunchtime on Friday.'

'That's okay. We'll set off early on Friday evening; a nice leisurely cruise. We can spread it out over the weekend.'

'Great.'

Anne pressed the VCR button to resume recording as the adverts ended and the second half of the programme began. They were feeling better already.

Anne had an early start on Thursday, but before breakfast she sent Donovan a quick e-mail.

Hi
The Timeline programme was on television last night.
The images of you shaking hands with Dick were prominent.
Thought you'd like to know.
Take care,
A

Just before she set off to brave the morning rush hour into Northampton, Anne checked her computer. No reply.

It was a long day. By the time Anne got back to the office it was after six and she flopped into her chair with a histrionic sigh. Marnie grinned at her across the room.

'So, what's new at the chalk face?'

Anne shook her head. 'I don't know what the younger generation's coming to. Half the class don't seem to have read the chapter Mr Boyd set for homework.' Anne pressed buttons to boot her computer into action. 'One of the girls told me she's thinking of dropping out, says she's finding the work too hard. I didn't like to say, but I had the impression she wasn't actually doing ...'

'What's up?'

'Nothing from Donovan. He hasn't replied to my e-mail from this morning.'

'Perhaps he's away.'

'Yeah.'

'Fancy a cup of tea?'

Anne made to get up. 'I'll make it.'

'No. You stay there. My turn. You've been gallivanting.'

Anne glanced across to the kitchen area.

'Where are the builders' mugs? Don't say you've washed them up and put them away.'

Marnie looked at the empty draining board. 'Must still be outside.'

Anne smiled. 'Standards decline when I'm not here.' She got up and headed for the door. 'I'll fetch them while you make us a delicious brew. How's that for division of labour?'

Anne entered the farm house by the front door and went upstairs. The wall and chimney breast in one of the bedrooms were finished and ready for plastering. Progress was slower than Anne would have wished, but the standard of workmanship was first class. She wandered from room to room, mentally working out how much more was to be done. The mugs were nowhere to be seen. She looked through a window down to the garden. The foundations had been laid for the conservatory, and slabs were lined up waiting to become the terrace. The tray containing the two mugs was resting on top of the slabs. Anne skipped downstairs and walked round to the rear of the house.

It had been a bright day, and the men must have had their tea break in the open air away from the dust of the brickwork. Anne looked up at the house and tried to imagine it with curtains at the windows, rattan furniture in the conservatory and tubs of flowers on the terrace. By this time next year, she thought, it will be completed.

She turned to look at the wilderness that would one day be a garden again. Weeds stood chest high, but over to one side a climbing rose was valiantly fighting for light and air. As she looked at it, she spotted a path through the jungle. It was barely visible, but Anne followed it. She decided to cut a few roses to put in a vase. Turning to fetch the secateurs, she realised that from where she was standing she could see directly into the courtyard, with a clear view of the door into the office barn. Something on the ground caught her eye.

Anne knelt down to examine a small mound of earth that seemed to have been scuffed aside. She sniffed. A faint smell rose from the earth: tobacco. She parted the soil with a finger to reveal a cluster of cigarette butts. Separating them, she counted seven filter tips. She had never seen either Bob or his mate with a cigarette, even while taking a break.

Anne pushed the earth back into a heap so that it looked undisturbed. If not the builders, who might have been standing there, smoking? Anne's mind was racing. Could the butts have been lying there for a long time? She was sure they smelled too fresh to have been in the ground for more than a few hours. How long would it take to smoke seven cigarettes?

Anne began walking slowly back to the office, all thoughts of roses and secateurs banished from her mind. The builders would have left the site at about four o'clock. It was now almost half past six. Someone had been watching the office. Suddenly, it occurred to her that that person might still be lurking in the 'jungle'. She quickened her pace.

47
Blood on the carpet

For once, Anne was the first person out of college when her classes ended at lunchtime on Friday. She raced to the carpark, threw her bag into the Mini and set off for the supermarket.

Before grabbing a shopping trolley, she dashed inside to the payphone, unwilling to trust the security of her mobile. She pressed buttons for the office number, desperate to ask Marnie if there had been an e-mail from Donovan. By the eighth ring, she was convinced she had dialled the wrong number. She tried again. Same result.

Where was Marnie? Answer: probably on *Thyrsis* making lunch. Anne dialled her mobile.

The person you are phoning can't take your call. Please try again later.

Damn! Anne rang the office number again. Ten rings later she disconnected. Think. Marnie must be around; the answerphone was off. Don't panic, Anne told herself. It's obvious. Marnie has gone over to speak to the builders; they sometimes leave early on a Friday. There was no point in wasting time here. She rang Donovan.

No reply. *Of course*. No answerphone. Anne sighed and got on with shopping. She was reluctant to waste more time phoning. The sooner they got underway, the better.

Anne ignored her self-imposed speed limit of sixty miles an hour on the way home. In light traffic she made good time, only throttling back through the village and down the field track. She pulled up in the courtyard, noticing the absence of the builder's van. The office door was half open. Good, she thought. Marnie's around.

Anne walked across to the kitchen area and began emptying the shopping onto the counter. A small round cheese enveloped in a bright red wax casing made a bid for freedom and launched itself over the edge, rolling across the floor to halt in the middle of the office.

It was as she bent down to retrieve it that Anne saw the bloodstains. A pattern of drops, each the size of a penny, dotted the deep blue carpet tiles like a small red constellation. Anne touched one of them with the tip of her little finger. The blood was dark red. She stood up and scanned the room. A few feet away, in the direction of the shower room, she saw a brownish smudge.

'Marnie!'

Anne raced to the shower room and knocked on the door. No reply. She pushed it open. It was empty, and there were no stains to be seen. She rapidly checked the floor of the shower, the toilet bowl and the loo-roll holder. Nothing.

She was racing across the office to search outside when the phone began ringing. Anne forced herself to calm down before picking up the receiver.

'Walker and Co, good afternoon.'

'Everything all right, Anne?'

'Who's calling please?'

'It's Molly Appleton from the shop. Are you and Marnie okay?'

'Why are you ringing, Mrs Appleton?'

'Well, I saw the ambulance coming from your end of the village about half an hour ago. I tried ringing to see if you were all right, but there was no reply. Richard just said he thought he'd seen your car go by so I –'

'What ambulance was it?'

'Well it was just an –'

'Northampton or Milton Keynes hospital?'

A pause. 'I'll ask Richard. He might know. Hold on.'

Anne heard muffled sounds, a hand placed over the mouthpiece, before Molly came back on the line.

'Richard thinks it was a Two Shires, so probably MK General.'

'Thanks, Mrs Appleton. Gotta go.'

Anne flipped open the filofax, found the hospital's number and pressed buttons. The nurses' station confirmed that a woman had recently been admitted from Knightly St John. The nurse asked for a description and then took down details: name, age, address, religion. She would give no information, but advised Anne that it would be an hour or two before she would be able to see Marnie, if at all.

When Anne disconnected she slumped at the desk, head in hands, breathing in short gasps. She could feel her heart pounding, her head spinning with a thousand questions. Why couldn't Marnie tell them her own name? Why did they want to know her religion? Why wouldn't they say what had happened to her? Why couldn't Anne see her? Why had she said, *if at all*? What had happened to Marnie?

Anne placed both hands palm-down on the desk, closed her eyes and forced herself to take six deep breaths. *Think what you have to do, Anne. Calm down. Get organised. Think. Think.*

She opened her eyes and struggled to rationalise her thoughts.

Something serious had happened here. An ambulance had been called. Marnie had been – *stop!* Wait a minute. Who had called the ambulance? Anne picked up the phone and checked previously dialled numbers. No emergency call was showing. She checked the speed dial and scrolled down to Marnie's mobile. Anne hit the button. Immediately a faint warbling emanated from across the room.

Taking care not to tread on the bloodstains, Anne rushed to the source of the sound. The mobile was lying on the floor under her desk. She pressed buttons and checked numbers. The last call was three nines. *What did that mean?* Had Marnie called for an ambulance? The builders had left. The tenants in the cottages were at work. Glebe Farm was deserted.

Anne suddenly felt isolated and vulnerable. She thought of the pile of cigarette butts in the garden. At once she propelled herself across the room and locked the door onto the courtyard. Her mind was steady now. Anxious she may have been, but she had things to do and was making a mental list.

Seizing the pad, she began scribbling notes.

PHONE:
Beth
Mrs Appleton
Police?
Ralph
Check Thyrsis

She couldn't get the image of the cigarette butts out of her mind. After all the activity of the summer, when Glebe Farm was crawling with TV crews and archaeologists, plus all the visitors from outside and within the village, the place was now deserted. Or was it? Anne was alone and needed back-up. The more people who were aware of the situation, the safer she would feel. She grabbed the phone.

'Beth? It's Anne. Listen. Something's happened.'

It was a brief conversation ending with Beth telling Anne she was on her way.

'Mrs Appleton? It's Anne. You were right about the ambulance. Something has happened to Marnie. She's in MK hospital. Do you know anything else about what's been going on?'

The Appletons knew nothing except that a customer had seen the ambulance going down the field track, and they had seen it on its return leg.

After hanging up, Anne sat back in the chair and reflected on what she knew. Marnie had met with a mishap of some kind, perhaps an accident. She had called for help and been taken to hospital. That was the simplest explanation. Then why had she left no note for Anne? Why hadn't she phoned Anne to let her know? Why was the mobile lying on the floor under Anne's desk?

Perhaps there had not been an accident. Perhaps Marnie had been attacked. Then how had she been able to phone for an ambulance? All questions; no answers.

Anne looked at her list. There was little point in phoning the police. If it was necessary, that could come later. Locating Ralph would be complicated, and it would be better to present him with facts rather than just worry him when he was in Hong Kong or Shanghai or somewhere, unable to do anything but fret. She had no desire to walk through the spinney to check *Thyrsis*.

Her course was clear. Her place was at the hospital. She picked up the phone and rang A & E. The duty nurse was no more forthcoming, but she was glad to learn that Marnie's sister was on her way.

Anne grabbed her car keys and opened the office door. Outside there was no movement. She silently locked the door behind her and sprinted across the courtyard to the Mini. Jumping in, she pressed down the door button, simultaneously twisting the key in the ignition. Performing the fastest three-point turn on record, she gunned the little car up the field track, keeping one eye on the rear-view mirror. At any moment she expected to see a car or a whole squadron of Hell's Angels in pursuit.

That Friday was obviously National Illness Day. Everybody in the country seemed to be at Milton Keynes General Hospital. The visitors' car parks were full to overflowing. On her third lap Anne managed to find a narrow slot and she mentally gave thanks for the compactness of the Mini.

Strangely, the Accident and Emergency unit was not the bedlam that Anne anticipated. There were certainly people waiting for treatment, but the atmosphere was calm and purposeful. At the nurses' station two women and one man were checking papers. Anne walked over and waited till they looked up.

'I'm here about Marnie Walker.'

The male nurse glanced down at a list.

'Ah yes, you're expected.'

Anne was about to protest, but bit her tongue.

'Can you tell me how she is? Can I see her?'

'Your sister is in theatre. When she comes out she'll be transferred to Obs and Gynae.'

Anne was bewildered. 'But I thought she'd been involved in an accident.'

'I'm sorry. I don't know how you got that impression. She's suffered a miscarriage, and there are complications. I can't tell you more than that. Excuse me.'

He turned to reply to one of the other nurses and became drawn into a discussion. Anne moved away and took a seat. A miscarriage. The blood on the carpet. Marnie phoning for help and dropping the phone under the desk. She had had to cope with the pain and the shock all alone with no one to care for her. Anne's shoulders sagged. Had Marnie known she was pregnant? Anne thought back to when she had found Marnie checking her diary for the day she had rushed off to Oxford. Six weeks had elapsed since she had taken off to join Ralph and meet the German professor. It all added up.

Anne stood and walked out. She needed fresh air and would wait for Beth outside. *There are complications*, the male nurse had said.

48
Prognosis

For Anne the weekend passed in a blur. Beth and Paul had arrived while Marnie was still in the operating theatre, and afterwards she was too drowsy to receive visitors. Cottage number three was vacant, so Beth and Paul installed themselves while Anne busied herself on the phone trying to track down Ralph. This was no easy task. In between engagements he was staying for a day or two with friends before moving on. Anne left messages at a number of hotels asking him to phone home.

On Saturday morning Anne phoned Molly Appleton and told her Marnie was recovering from an accident and would be back in the office in a day or two. That provided an official version to circulate in the village.

Before visiting hours, Anne devoted herself to tidying the office. Every paper was filed, every invoice printed and posted, every scheme checked and annotated. The to-do list grew but gradually every item save one was ticked off. *Sally Ann* was due to be craned back into the water on Monday.

Anne rang Danny, whose reaction surprised her.

'Have you told Donovan? He'll want to know.'

'I told you, Danny, I'll not be –'

'Don't be silly, Anne. You *must* tell him. He's a friend.'

'But –'

'Okay, he might not want to reply, but the least you can do is let him know. It's only right. Think about it.'

Anne did think about it, for half the morning and finally sent an e-mail.

Hi
Got some bad news. Marnie's had an accident.
She's in hospital – had an operation.
Haven't spoken to her yet.
Doctors say she'll be OK. Visiting later.
Ralph's away in Far East.
Beth and Paul here for the weekend.
Sally's in the marina for blacking. No idea when I'll be able to fetch her.
Hope all is well.
A

When they arrived at the hospital the duty nurse told them Marnie was in a single room, with only two visitors allowed at any one time. Anne sat in the corridor while Beth and Paul went in. They reappeared after a quarter of an hour, and Anne was shocked to see

Beth in tears. She jumped to her feet.

Paul had an arm round Beth's shoulders and, seeing Anne's startled expression, he mouthed, *It's all right*, and tried to look reassuring. The nurse told Anne she could have five minutes.

When Anne opened the door and slipped into the room, Marnie gave a weak smile.

'Don't be alarmed, Anne.' Her voice was faint and slightly hoarse. 'I look pale because I lost quite a lot of blood. Everything's all right. I'm going to be fine. Really.'

Anne put her bunch of grapes on a side table and sat by the bed, reaching to take Marnie's hand.

'I'm doing all I can to get in touch with Ralph.'

'Beth told me. Thanks.'

'I think I know what happened, Marnie.'

Another smile. 'Of course you do.'

'You checking your diary, that dash to Oxford …'

Marnie nodded. 'Forgetting to take my pills.'

'I figured.'

'Just one of those things. It went clean out of my mind.'

'So, are you all right?'

'The surgeon said I … probably won't be able to have children.'

'Oh Marnie.'

'Apparently one tube had to be removed. The other was badly damaged.'

'I'm so sorry.' Anne could feel warm tears on her cheeks. 'Really sorry, Marnie.'

'It could be worse. Anyway … I have my family.'

Anne could find no words. She buried her face beside Marnie's hand.

49
A surprise return

Anne had everything worked out. It was not the first time she had found herself in charge of the office, nor even the first time she had to run the company while Marnie languished in hospital, but on that Monday morning she felt utterly miserable and close to tears. Her therapy was to devote all her energies to keeping the firm running.

Beth and Paul had gone home the previous evening, satisfied that Marnie was on the mend. Anne had opened the office at seven, sorting through Marnie's in-tray over toast and coffee. She took a policy decision: she would tell none of the clients about Marnie's absence or its causes. She could initial any letters and handle any correspondence. If a cheque was needed, she would take it in for Marnie to sign during visiting hours.

College would just have to wait. Anne was ahead of schedule with her work and could keep up with reading outside office hours.

By eight she was in the farmhouse checking what building work was in prospect for the week when Bob and his mate arrived. She told them Marnie was unwell but would be back to work soon. In the meantime they knew what they had to do.

Half an hour later the post was delivered. By nine, everything had been processed and Anne was finishing the last of the reply letters when she heard a car pull up in the courtyard.

Angela Hemingway walked slowly past the plate glass window and came into the office. Anne thought that a vicar must regard the comforting of a parishioner as a normal part of her professional duties, but one look at Angela's face told her that this was personal. Anne had phoned Angela on Sunday evening to explain about Marnie. She stood up as Angela crossed the room, and they hugged each other in shared misery.

Angela looked at the desk, which was covered in envelopes, letters and notes.

'Come on, Anne. Let's get some fresh air. You look as if you've been working all night.'

They took the track through the spinney and made their way towards the towpath. Standing on the bridge over the canal, they gazed down at the water where *Thyrsis* lay at her mooring beside *Sally Ann*'s empty docking area.

'Molly Appleton has told people that Marnie had an accident. Did she get that from you?'

Anne nodded. 'I had to say something. They'd seen the ambulance.'

'You did the right thing. I'd like to visit Marnie. Would that be okay?'

'Sure. Visiting hours are three to five and seven to eight.'

Angela turned and leaned her back against the parapet.

'I was at Knightly Court the other day. From what I saw of the redecoration, it looks wonderful.'

'You went to see Celia?'

'No. I only saw the hall. I went to look in on Marcus Devere. He's now quite frail and doesn't leave the house. A pastoral visit.'

'I thought he was catholic.'

'He is, but he's a nice old chap and likes to have an occasional visitor. Actually, I bumped into Father Martin when I arrived.'

'Was that embarrassing?'

'Not at all. We get on very well with the Romans. Father Martin's really pleasant, very young. He's attached to the cathedral in Northampton. It's his first post.'

'How was Mr Devere?'

'Not bad. He has good days. That was one of them. He's gradually winding down. Anyway, let's not dwell on that. I just wanted to say what a beautiful job you and Marnie have done at the Court.'

'We were pleased with it. I hope Celia was.'

'I'm sure she was delighted. What about you, Anne? How are you bearing up?'

'I'm fine as long as I keep busy. My main concern is trying to get in touch with Ralph.'

'Where is he?'

'Somewhere between Kuala Lumpur and Shanghai. He might be spending a day or two with friends from Hong Kong Chinese University. Actually, Angela, I think I ought to get back to the office in case he's trying to contact me.'

'He doesn't know about the miscarriage?'

'No. And I'm not looking forward to telling him about it.'

Ralph's call came through in the early afternoon. He had just checked into a hotel in Shanghai. Anne made a huge effort to keep her voice steady as she gave him the news. It was a clear line and, almost six thousand miles away, she heard his intake of breath and felt his sense of shock. Reassuring him that Marnie was making a solid recovery, Anne offered to be at the hospital in the afternoon visiting time to make sure the portable phone was in Marnie's room so that he could speak with her.

After disconnecting, Anne rang the college to explain she would probably have to be absent for the rest of the week. Only two items remained on her to-do list. The first was *Sally Ann*. The boatyard had already told Anne she could collect the boat any day. She set that matter aside until she knew how the week was going to pan out.

The final item on the list was *Cottage 3*. Anne jogged through the spinney to collect bedding from *Thyrsis*. It took her half an hour to prepare the cottage as a temporary residence for Marnie and herself. They would have adjacent bedrooms, and Anne would be within easy reach if Marnie needed any help, day or night.

It was a long day, and by the time Anne went up to bed, she was bone-weary. She knew she had done everything possible to deal with the situation. Ralph and Marnie had had a conversation on the phone, and Anne was amazed at Marnie's composure afterwards. The office was running smoothly. The cottage was ready for Marnie's return. Anne tried not to think of her college work.

She lay back on the pillow and closed her eyes for a few moments to think about what jobs she had to do the next day.

Anne woke on Tuesday to find she had fallen asleep without turning off the light. It was strange to be in a normal house with perpendicular walls. She slid out of bed and opened the curtains. Opposite, the office barn seemed to nestle against the trees of the spinney. Anne yawned. It was six-thirty. She needed some light exercise to loosen up before taking a shower.

Dolly had slept downstairs in her basket, and the two of them stepped out together under an overcast sky with a cool breeze and the threat of rain in the air. Dolly trotted ahead of Anne, tail held high, along the track through the trees. Normally she had breakfast on the boat with the others, but for now –

At the edge of the spinney Anne stopped abruptly. Dolly pranced on and in her habitual fashion leapt up onto the stern deck of ... *Sally Ann*.

The boat lay in her docking area at rightangles to the canal a few yards from *Thyrsis*. Anne moved back into the shelter of the trees, twisting her head, scanning the spinney for any sign of movement. The curtains were all closed. It was impossible to know if anyone was on board.

Anne took a deep breath and covered the ground between the spinney and the boat in a few seconds. She reached into the gas bottle holder, dug out the spare door key and slipped it into the lock. The boat was empty, everything tidy and in its place. Outside, Anne lifted the central deck panel and reached down to touch the engine. It was faintly warm. *Sally Ann* had returned within the past hour or so.

Anne rapidly considered the possibilities. They were very limited. Had the boatyard staff brought the boat back? Unlikely. It was a six-hour trip from Willowbridge.

Anne lowered the deck panel back into place and perched on the lid of the gas bottle container to organise her thoughts. Someone had driven the boat back though the night and left her in the docking area. Whoever it was knew the boat, the boatyard people and *Sally Ann*'s docking arrangements. That person also had no problems with travelling in darkness. Only one name sprang to mind.

Donovan.

Anne had sent him a message that included the boat situation. He had not e-mailed her back. This was his reply. Then she saw it.

In one corner of the matt black decking a single impression could be seen: the faint imprint of a bicycle tyre. It was as good as a signature.

Soon after eight the phone rang.

'Walker and Co, good morning.'

'I would like to speak with Ms Marnie Walker.' A woman's voice, slightly accented, stern and businesslike.

'I'm afraid she's out of the office. Can I take a message?'

'Who is this speaking?'

'Anne Price. I'm Mrs Walker's assistant.'

A pause. 'When will she be returning?'

'May I know who's calling?'

'This is Professor Karin Fleischer, speaking from Germany.'

'Mrs Walker will be away from the office for a few days, professor.'

'I see. You are her secretary?'

'Not quite, but I have her diary and I am in contact with her each day.'

'I will leave a message. Tell her that I have spoken to Professor Hallgarten. Can you spell that?'

'Yes.' Anne stopped herself adding, *no probs*.

'I have persuaded her that Mrs Walker is not a neo-fascist. Dr Hallgarten would be willing to talk to her. You have understood?'

'Perfectly. I should perhaps explain that Mrs Walker is in hospital. She's had an operation, but will be back soon.'

'She is better?'

'Yes, thank you.'

'I will give you Professor Hallgarten's contact information.'

At nine Anne rang the boatyard and thanked the manager for releasing *Sally Ann* to their friend. He confirmed that 'Mr Smith', whose own boat had been blacked there the previous year, had come up from London especially to collect *Sally Ann*. They had tried phoning Marnie but only encountered the answerphone message. In the end they saw no reason to doubt Mr Smith's word; he knew where the spare key was kept and was obviously a friend.

It seemed he had travelled up by train with his bike and cycled to the boatyard from Bletchley station. Once the boat was delivered, he would be returning on the early morning train from Wolverton station.

'He's the only person we know who seems to prefer cruising at night. That's why we call his own boat the *Ghost Boat*.' The manager laughed. 'He said he wanted to give you a surprise.'

That's nothing new, Anne thought, as she disconnected.

50
Assignation

On Wednesday morning the temptation to phone Anne was enormous. The surgeon examined Marnie during his rounds and pronounced her fit to go home that day if she felt well enough. As soon as he left the room she was out of bed and on her way to the bathroom. Bathed and with fresh dressings in place, she changed into outdoor clothes.

Anne would be at college. Marnie wondered about a taxi, but the prospect of returning alone to an empty office did not appeal. She sat in the more comfortable of the visitors' chairs and tried to read a magazine. It was difficult. Never one to magnify a problem into a psychological melodrama, she sat in enforced idleness thinking calmly about her situation.

She realised that she had hoped one day to have children, but admitted to herself that it had not yet risen to the top of her agenda. Since the breakdown of her marriage to Simon she had focused on her career. Now she wondered if that was enough. Without being complacent, she concluded she had more than her share of good fortune. She knew that she lived her life surrounded by love. It was enough.

Marnie only knew she had nodded off when she heard the door click open.

'If you want to sleep, you should be in bed, Marnie.'

A brisk, crisp nurse with a ready smile and a Geordie accent looked at her in mock reproof.

Marnie blinked and sighed.

'It's boredom, Julie. Mr Hussein said I can go home and it's a long wait till Anne's due at visiting time.'

'You've got a visitor already.'

'How can I? It's much too early.'

'Some people think they can just do what they like and expect everyone to fit round them.'

'One of my friends?'

'So she says.'

'Who is it?'

Before the nurse could reply, the door swung open behind her and Celia Devere walked into the room.

'There you are, Marnie. The staff tried to tell me it wasn't the right time for visiting. You look fine to me.'

The nurse rolled her eyes at Marnie.

'Are you okay for a visit?'

Marnie realised how desperate she was when she agreed. The nurse left the room without a glance at Celia.

'You're up and dressed. Are you going home?'

'I shall be, later on.'

'But you're ready now, or so it seems. How are you, Marnie? When I heard you'd had an accident I –'

'I'm okay, fine. It's good of you to come.'

Celia sat on the edge of the bed.

'Oh, Marnie, I realise I've been *such* a fool, and an ungrateful one at that. After all the lovely scheme you did for the Court. It's *beautiful*. Things haven't been going well for me lately and, well, I rather took it out on you. Can you forgive me?'

One cliché after another, Marnie thought. 'Celia, there's nothing to forgive.' *Oh gawd, there goes another one.*

'Marnie, you're a star. So, tell me all about it.'

'It's rather personal and I'd sooner not –'

Celia raised a hand. 'Absolutely. I do understand. Painful memories, best put aside. Anyway, you're better now and are you in fact going home today?'

'When Anne gets back from college this afternoon.'

'Why don't I take you? I've got the car outside. Unless you'd rather stay here, of course.'

Marnie looked at the bare walls of the room, the bed where she had lain for five days and nights. She got up and grabbed the carrier bag in which she had stuffed her nightie and toiletries.

'Thanks, Celia. That would be nice.'

They stopped at the nurses' station and explained about the lift home.

'Thank you for everything, Julie. Is there any paperwork?'

'I'll deal with it, Marnie. You take care, now.'

'I'll bring the car round to the front.' Celia strode towards the exit, averting her gaze from the patients in the ward. 'See you downstairs in five minutes.'

Nurse Julie watched her walking away.

'D'you think she looks like Princess –'

'Everyone says so.'

'She's a friend of yours?'

'More of a client, really.'

'Marnie, when she arrived, she asked me something strange.'

'Oh?'

'She asked if a man had been to visit you. She started to describe him, tall, well-built, dark hair, city suit. I told her you hadn't had any male visitors apart from your brother-in-law. She seemed happy about that.'

'Amazing.'

'She wasn't talking about your guy, was she, the one in China?'

'No, her husband. She's got a thing about that.'

'And you?'

'And any woman.'

'The jealous kind, is she?'

'Yeah, drives me mad. I think I'll kill her.'

Julie looked at Marnie with a serious expression.

'I'll lend you a hypodermic.'

Marnie arrived at the front entrance to find Celia sitting in her open-topped Audi in a parking bay reserved for ambulances. A security guard appeared to be remonstrating with her, while Celia seemed to be assuring him that she was *virtually* an ambulance or performing that function.

When Marnie climbed carefully into the car, Celia reversed out, giving the guard a regal wave and a brilliant flash of smile. As soon as they were clear of the entrance she pulled over, pressed a button and the roof rose into place.

'I put it down so you'd find it easier to get in, Marnie,' she explained.

'That was thoughtful of you.'

They drove off.

'So, you were brought in by ambulance, I gather.'

'Yes.' Time to change the subject, Marnie thought. 'Angela came by a couple of days ago and said she'd been to the Court to visit your father-in-law. How is he?'

'Not very well, really, but then he's never had good health. Even as a child he was sickly, what they used to call *delicate*. It's amazing he's lived to such a great age.'

'I wonder if he'd welcome a visitor some time, or perhaps he'd find that too tiring.'

'A nice thought, Marnie. I'll ask him. Father Martin comes to see him every other Saturday. He's a priest from the cathedral in Northampton. He hears Marcus's confession – that can't take long – and they pray together. It's weird to hear Marcus call him *father*. He's only a slip of a boy.'

Marnie closed her eyes and leaned back against the headrest as the car swept down onto the dual carriageway. Celia set cruise control and glanced across at her passenger.

'Marnie, there's something I want to say to you. I know I've been rather self-centred, all this business about Hugh having an affair with another woman.'

'That's okay. Let's forget about it.'

'Thank you, Marnie. The thing is, I was feeling so hurt.'

'Understandable.'

'Yes. You see, I believe there is such a thing as loyalty. Don't you agree?'

'Of course.'

'I think marriage is sacred, Marnie. It has to be cherished and protected. No one has the right to damage it.'

'Absolutely.'

'I'm sorry. Here I am going on again. Everything always has to be about me. Me, me, me. I'm sorry not to have been more thoughtful about you, Marnie.'

'Don't worry about it.'

Celia turned off the dual carriageway and took the road for Knightly St John. Arriving at their next turn, Marnie looked up at Knightly Woods and thought back to the evening when Anne saw the lights in the trees. She tried to shut off her mind from thoughts of cremating witches. Suddenly, Celia pulled the car into a sharp u-turn, tyres squealing, turning right on the main road and accelerating hard. Marnie sat upright in her seat.

'What's up? Where are we going?'

'Didn't you see him?'

'Who?'

'*Hugh.*'

'You actually saw him?'

'Not quite, but that was his car. I'm sure it was.'

'You're following him?'

'Yes. And I know just where he's going.'

'Couldn't he be going to a meeting?'

'Marnie, he's in London today, or supposed to be.'

'So?'

'I hope you don't mind, just a little detour. It's not far.'

'Where are we going?'

Celia turned onto a small country road and continued at undiminished pace.

'Hugh always uses the main roads. I'm taking a short cut.'

'Where to?'

'It won't take long, Marnie. I'll soon have you home.'

After a mile they arrived at a village that Marnie had never seen before and pulled into a parking area behind the church. Celia tucked the car into a secluded corner, half shrouded by low-hanging branches from a tree.

'Celia, will you tell me what's going on.'

'It's what I said about loyalty, the sanctity of marriage and all that.'

'But why are we here?'

'I know Hugh's being unfaithful, Marnie.'

'What has this place got to do with it?'

'Don't you see? It's perfect for an assignation.'

'I don't understand. How did you know –'

'Marnie, this is where we used to come when we were having our affair.'

'You and Hugh?'

'Yes, of course. Who else?'

'Presumably he was married at the time?'

'To his first wife, yes. That's how it was an affair.' Celia spoke as if she was explaining something to a small child. 'This was our place, or one of them.'

Marnie leaned back and closed her eyes again. Words floated in her mind: *loyalty*, *sanctity*, *sacred*, *cherished*. She felt her jaw muscles tighten as a smile began spreading across her face. She couldn't help herself. The laugh began in the back of her throat.

'Sorry, Celia.' She reached into her bag for a tissue to wipe her eyes. 'Sorry about this.

It's just ...'

Celia reached across and put a hand on her arm.

'It's lovely to see you smiling, Marnie. I knew if anyone could cheer you up, I could.'

Back in the office, Marnie made herself a sandwich and a mug of tea. Seating herself at the desk, she was amused and touched to see a neat pile of papers marked for her attention. Significantly, there was no list of jobs to do. Anne had dealt with everything.

After five minutes waiting in the church car park, Celia had announced that Hugh must have another rendezvous place. Reluctantly, she had driven away and brought Marnie home, declining the offer of refreshment. Marnie wondered if she had other secret venues to investigate.

Marnie rang Anne and left a message on the mobile voicemail, telling her she was back at Glebe Farm. Two minutes later, the phone rang, but it was not Anne's voice on the line.

'Marnie, it's Molly Appleton. Celia Devere was in here just now and said she'd brought you home. Are you feeling better now?'

'Much better, thanks, Molly. Nice of you to ring.'

'That's good. Actually, I'm phoning because there's been a delivery for you. We took it here because there was no one at Glebe Farm to accept it. I'll get Richard to drop it down to you.'

'I could get Anne to collect it on her way home. She'll be back mid-afternoon.'

'It's no trouble, Marnie, and I'm sure you'd want this now.'

'That's very mysterious, Molly. What is it?'

'A surprise. You'll see.'

Anne breezed into the office with a huge smile and a hug for Marnie.

'It's *great* to have you back!'

'The pleasure is all mine, believe me.'

'I couldn't believe it when I got your message. I was going to get you some flowers, but I came straight back.'

'I'm glad you did.' Marnie looked pointedly across the room at Anne's desk. 'Someone saved you the trouble.'

Anne turned. A huge bouquet of flowers in a vase occupied most of her desk space.

'Wow! They're fabulous. From Ralph?'

'The gift card said simply, *Anonymous*.'

'*Anonymous?*' Anne repeated.

They looked at the bouquet. It comprised white roses, oriental lilies, gypsophila and chrysanthemums. Everything apart from the leaves was white. It was a monochrome collection. Marnie and Anne exchanged glances.

'Donovan,' they said in unison.

51
Invitation

Autumn set in, bringing with it a run of mellow days, a time for healing and adjustment. Marnie and Ralph spent many hours in each other's company, drawn even more closely together than before. They realised that they had spent little time talking about having children and now, in the knowledge that there would probably be none, they comforted each other, gradually coming to terms with their situation. Both were determined to ease each other's pain. Both drew strength from each other's love.

Anne, for her part, did all she could to show how much she understood their pain without adding to its intensity. Her warmth and positive approach to every part of their lives had never been so important as in those difficult weeks. Her cheerful nature helped banish the melancholy that might have been.

The mild weather was ideal for tootles on *Sally Ann*. Marnie, Ralph and Anne wrapped themselves in warm clothing to enjoy the late sunshine and cruise through an ever-changing landscape of gold and yellow and brown, punctuated by morning mists and hints of frost at the water's edge with the tang of woodsmoke in the air.

The golden days gave way to a period of gusting winds that sent clouds of dry leaves from the spinney flying round the courtyard at Glebe Farm. It brought new tenants to cottage number three and more contracts for Walker and Co.

Life assumed a steady pace of alternating work and rest. Marnie felt her strength gradually returning and was glad to spend those days quietly on designs at the drawing board. Ralph was free of overseas commitments until the spring and applied himself to caring for Marnie and researching for articles and a new book. Anne diligently made up for lost time at college and devoted herself to caring for Marnie and charging ahead with her studies.

On the surface, life had become humdrum and peaceful. On some evenings they watched the *Timeline* programmes and caught occasional glimpses of the dig at Glebe Farm. There was no repetition of the Donovan image, though they were all visible in the background in some of the shots.

Anne was mindful of Donovan's warning and occasionally had the feeling that someone was watching them. She hoped that Marnie had forgotten the cigarettes episode and was constantly on the watch for any indication of an intruder.

The builders were working on the construction of the conservatory, and Anne used her refreshment visits to examine the ground for traces of an outsider. On a day when building work was held up waiting for materials, she suggested they might usefully spend some time in cutting down the jungle in the garden. Marnie agreed that was a practical suggestion, not realising that Anne had an ulterior motive. With the weed growth chopped back, there would be less cover for surveillance.

Anne had sent an e-mail to Donovan to thank him for Marnie's flowers, and they embarked on an occasional electronic exchange of brief notes. Each weekend she had a phone conversation with Danny, and they spent time together in late October when Danny went home to see her parents and Anne returned to see her own. It was a joyous coming together filled with laughter as Danny recounted her involvement with a series of disastrous boyfriends and Anne chided her friend – the *party animal* – for spending so little time on her course work.

The countryside gradually fell asleep as the hours of daylight shortened. Life at Glebe Farm settled into a calm routine, a time of uninterrupted progress at work, quiet relaxation on country walks and the occasional boat trip on milder days. It might have remained that way if the incident with the staples had not intervened.

⁂

It was a Thursday morning in late November when Marnie found her stapler had run out. She hunted in vain for a box of staples before giving up. Knowing that Anne would certainly have some in her desk, she crossed the office and began opening drawers. In the second drawer she had to move a notepad in her search, and a name stared up at her from the top page. Hallgarten.

For a few seconds Marnie could not place it. The name seemed like an echo from a long time ago. Hallgarten, of course, the one-time friend of that German professor, the woman she had met in Oxford. Marnie blinked and banished thoughts of that day from her mind. But why had Anne written the name on her pad? Marnie picked it up and read the note.

M not neo-fascist. Hallgarten willing to talk. Fleischer.

The rest of the note was an address and a phone number. What did it mean? How long ago had this note been written? Why had Anne not shown it to her? It was not hard to guess the answers.

⁂

Anne arrived back from college as the light was fading. She dumped her backpack on the desk and went straight to the kitchen area to put the kettle on, tugging off her gloves, unwinding the long apricot scarf and shedding her blouson jacket.

'Hi, Marnie. There'll be a frost tonight. My nose is already going pink.'

Marnie rang through to Ralph on *Thyrsis*, and he joined them in the office. When they were sitting comfortably grasping their mugs, Marnie mentioned the Hallgarten note. It took Anne a while to remember. She raised a hand to her mouth with a gasp.

'The message. Professor Fleischer. I'd forgotten about it. It happened when you were …' Her voice faded.

'That's okay, Anne. You certainly had more than enough on your plate. I don't think I'd have been able to contact Professor Hallgarten back then, even if I'd known she was willing to talk to me.'

'Even so, I should've –'

'No. It's fine, really.'

'What do you want to do about it, Marnie?' Ralph asked.

'I don't know. Such a lot has happened since we were wondering about the body in

Sarah's grave, though in a way, nothing has changed. What do you think?'

'I must admit I'm curious, though I'm not sure if Hallgarten will be able to provide any firm answers to the question of who it was. I wouldn't want to cause you any more anxiety.'

Marnie sat in silence for several seconds, and neither Ralph nor Anne wanted to break in on her thoughts. Eventually she looked up.

'Angela phoned this afternoon. It seems the bishop has finally given approval to reburying Sarah in the churchyard. There are just one or two formalities and it can go ahead.'

'Closure,' Anne said quietly.

'That's what I was thinking.'

Ralph sipped his coffee. 'Would you like me to phone Professor Hallgarten?'

Marnie smiled. 'You don't think she'll take you for a neo-fascist?'

'Not too much risk of that, I think.'

'I'll phone her. As Fleischer contacted her on my behalf, it's the least I can do. I'll ring her in the morning.'

The phone rang twice before Marnie was connected.

'Ahrweiler, Institut für Sozialforschung, guten Morgen.'

'Oh, sorry. Do you speak English?'

The reply was heavily accented.

'Whom do you wish to speak?'

'Professor Hallgarten, please.'

'Your name?'

'Marnie Walker. I'm phoning from England.'

'Naturally. One moment.'

Marnie felt foolish. The complicated rush of German had almost stunned her into silence. She was musing that it would probably have been better if Ralph had phoned after all when a new voice came on the line.

'Hallgarten.'

'Good morning. This is Marnie Walker. You told Professor Fleischer that you would be willing to talk to me about the work of your father in the war.'

'But you did not take up my offer. Why was that?'

'I was in hospital. I only just received your message.'

'I see. What do you want to ask me about my father?'

'It's difficult on the phone.'

'I wouldn't talk to you on the phone. I just wanted to know what you wanted to ask me.'

'About the agents he ran in Britain, or rather in the part where I live.' The line went quiet. 'Hallo?'

'Yes. Why do you want this information – assuming I can give you anything – what do you want to do with it?'

'We have found a body in a grave. No one knows whose it is, but we believe it dates back to wartime.'

'And?'

'It was a man. He was somebody's son or husband or whatever. His family has a right to know what happened to him, to be able to bury him in his own grave.'

'You are concerned about this man, even though he may have been a traitor to his country?'

'We don't know that. We don't know anything about him. Perhaps he was German.'

'An enemy.'

'A person. The war is history. We have to move on. Whoever his family might be, they have a right to know what became of him.'

Another silence.

'Professor Hallgarten? Hallo? Would you be willing to see me?'

A pause. 'Yes, but only you, no one else. When will you come?'

'Soon. When would be convenient?'

They agreed on a date in the first week of December. When Marnie told Ralph, he was horrified. To make matters worse, Marnie told Beth when her sister phoned that afternoon.

'Are you out of your *tiny mind*?'

'Beth, I'll take a flight to Frankfurt. I'll stay overnight in a hotel, see Hallgarten the next day and fly home that evening. What's the big deal?'

'Are you *serious*?'

'I'm serious.'

'Marnie, nothing is ever that simple. Haven't you learnt that by now? And what about your health?'

'I'm feeling much better.'

'Only two days ago you told me you were still feeling tired.'

'I can –'

'And don't tell me you can sleep on the plane. And another thing –'

'Okay, okay.'

'Listen to me. You're forgetting all that Nazi business.'

'That's all over now,' Marnie protested.

'Then why are you going to see this, this … *spymaster's* daughter? I thought that was the whole point, that it *isn't* all over.'

'So what do you want me to do, just drop the whole thing?'

'Got it in one.'

When later that evening Marnie returned to the subject and had a similar – though less fraught – conversation with Ralph, they arrived at the same conclusion: Marnie was in no state to go to Germany to rake over old troubles and risk stirring up new problems.

That night in bed in her attic room, Anne lay thinking. It was all very unsatisfactory. Hallgarten would only see Marnie, but there was no realistic chance of Marnie being able to travel. They had reached the end of the line. She had no way of knowing that everything was about to change.

52
Donovan returns

Anne was glad the next morning was Saturday. She had slept fitfully, worrying about Marnie and the unwelcome invitation from Ingrid Hallgarten. In the early hours, before drifting off to sleep, she had reached a decision: she would break her vow of silence with Donovan. She wanted his advice. They all needed it.

Straight after breakfast she booted her computer and sent him an e-mail.

Hi

Must talk to you. Something has come up. Urgent.

A

She was surprised to receive a reply almost at once.

Not a good idea.

Anne hit the keys.

I wouldn't ask if it wasn't really important.

Another rapid reply.

Ring me at home.

Anne dialled Donovan's home number at once.

'I'm here. So what's the problem?'

Anne outlined Marnie's call to Hallgarten and explained that Marnie was not well enough to travel.

'Can Ralph go?'

'She says she'll only talk to Marnie.'

Anne counted the seconds ticking by before Donovan spoke again.

'*Sally Ann*. Tonight at six.'

The line went dead.

Anne made her way through the spinney with fifteen minutes to spare. It was already dark, and frosted leaves crunched under her shoes on the path. Through the trees she could see lights burning on *Thyrsis*. She had told Marnie and Ralph that Donovan was coming, and they had suggested she meet him alone at first. They would eat together later.

Not for the first time, Anne felt slightly absurd on Donovan's account. Was all this cloak-and-dagger stuff really necessary? Were there really neo-Nazis lurking behind every blade of grass? Glebe Farm was tucked away in a peaceful corner of Knightly St John, sheltered from many of the cares of modern life. Then she thought of the cigarette butts in the garden, the strange visitor to the dig site and, further back, her encounters with New Force the previous summer and the mayhem and tragedy of those confrontations.

She stepped aboard *Sally Ann* and immediately sensed that something was not right.

One look told her the doors were closed but not locked. She pulled on the handle and the doors swung open. Faced with the darkness of the interior, she hesitated, not knowing whether to run or call out to Ralph for help. Then the smell reached her. An aroma of coffee floated out from inside, and a smile spread across her face. She walked confidently down the steps into the arms of Donovan Smith.

Marnie went on board at seven, joined soon afterwards by Ralph. Pasta was cooking on the stove, and Anne was chopping up tomatoes, cucumber and peppers for a salad while Donovan was setting the table. A rich fragrance of garlic bread pervaded the air. Passing through the sleeping cabin, Marnie wondered if she imagined that the bed cover looked slightly less tidy than usual, but she refrained from comment. Ralph concentrated on opening a bottle of Australian Shiraz Cabernet. Marnie mixed a French dressing, then lit candles and oil lamps as they took their places at the table. In the subdued glow it was hard to imagine any threats from the outside world.

The first part of their conversation centred on catching up with news, with Marnie's gradual recovery from her hospital treatment and Donovan's reaction to his first term on the new course. They all seemed reluctant to broach the subject that had brought them together. Inevitably it was Donovan who raised it.

'So, Hallgarten. She wants to meet you, Marnie.'

'I think I'd say she was *willing* to meet me, probably against her instincts. There's nothing for her in this, after all.'

'I wouldn't be so sure. If she had nothing to gain, she wouldn't have agreed in the first place.'

'She didn't; Professor Fleischer persuaded her.'

'Or thinks she did.'

'How could Hallgarten possibly benefit from meeting me?'

'It could be nothing more than a matter of conscience or perhaps she needs to find out more about her father. It's not an easy burden to bear, knowing that your father was a leading figure in the Nazi war machine. Anything that shows he was just doing a respectable job would be worth knowing.'

'Running agents would be regarded as *respectable*?'

Donovan nodded. 'At least he wasn't working in the death camps or involved in war crimes. Intelligence work is nothing to be ashamed of.'

'Donovan,' Ralph began, 'however Professor Hallgarten might regard the situation, we've agreed that Marnie isn't up to taking on this assignment.'

'I can understand that.'

'I was wondering,' Marnie said, 'whether you might be able to talk to her – on the phone, of course – and find out what she knows.'

'She might feel more comfortable speaking German,' Anne added.

A rueful smile. 'I'm touched at your faith in me, but don't you think I may be a little out of my depth here?'

Marnie said, 'Your German is flawless, which is a good start. Also you think quickly and you keep a cool head.'

'Well,' he said, 'I'm willing to try.'

'Thanks, Donovan. When do you think you might be able to phone her?'

'What number do you have, private or work?'

'The university.'

'Then it has to wait till Monday,' Ralph said.

'Do you have an address for her?'

Marnie took a slip of paper out of her shirt pocket and handed it across the table.

Donovan read it. 'This is private.'

'Yes.'

'With this I can get her home number from directory enquiries. No need to wait.'

They sat in the office after dinner, with Donovan in Marnie's chair. He rang enquiries and spoke first in English before changing to German.

'That was the easy part. Are we ready? I phone her now?'

'What time is it in Frankfurt?' Marnie asked.

'Just after nine. That's quite acceptable in Germany.'

'Are you ready, Donovan?' Ralph said.

'I suppose so.'

Anne smiled at him. 'Go for it.'

Donovan collected himself before pressing the buttons. After a few seconds he began speaking. The others listened, catching the odd word, including Marnie's name. They noticed that he gave his own name simply as *Donovan*. It quickly became clear that the conversation was not going well. Donovan was frowning. Eventually he stopped and handed the phone to Marnie.

'She wants to speak to you.'

Marnie announced herself and assured Hallgarten that she was indeed the person who had spoken with her the previous morning. The professor reiterated that she was willing to meet Marnie in person but not conduct a long discussion on the phone. On that point she was adamant.

'Then I must thank you for your time, professor, but decline your invitation. My current state of health does not permit me to undertake the journey.'

'You had an accident?'

Marnie hesitated, not happy about explaining her medical condition to a stranger. But then, what the hell. 'I had a miscarriage with a number of complications. This required two operations to rectify. I'm self-employed and I need to take care of my health for obvious reasons. Fortunately I have an excellent colleague who keeps everything in order.'

'The young man I spoke to?'

'No, he's a friend.'

'And he is German.'

'Half German, on his mother's side.'

'Does he have connections with the … former regime?'

'I think he'd better answer that question himself.'

'Please. I would like to speak to him again.'

Marnie passed the phone back to Donovan. This time the dialogue seemed more relaxed. They recognised the name of Donovan's German grandfather, Professor Klaus Herrmann. This seemed to spark off a lengthy exchange. When he disconnected, his expression was thoughtful and troubled.

'What is it?' Marnie asked.

'She said she was a great admirer of my grandfather, asked me all sorts of questions, as if she wanted to be sure I was who I said I was.'

'I see.'

'No, Marnie, you don't see. She wasn't just chatting.'

'What then?'

'She said she would be willing to meet *me* to talk about her father's work, if you couldn't travel.'

53
The best-laid plan

It had been a strange weekend. Donovan had gone home on Saturday night, retrieving his bicycle from its hiding place in the spinney and riding off down the towpath to catch a train from Wolverton. They had all agreed to think about Professor Hallgarten's suggestion and confer again on Monday.

On Sunday morning the consensus at Glebe Farm was that Ralph should go with Donovan. As a renowned and respected academic, he would bring added weight to the discussions in Germany and reassure Hallgarten of their honest intentions. By lunchtime they were wavering.

Would Hallgarten worry that something she revealed might reach others in the university world and find its way into publications? Could Ralph visit the university without making his presence known to the authorities as a matter of courtesy?

By Sunday afternoon they were considering the possibility that Donovan might prefer to travel alone, reasoning that he was a loner by temperament. By Sunday evening they were totally confused.

Donovan had no lectures in the first half of Monday morning and they gathered round the office phone, which Marnie set to handsfree mode, and rang him at eight-thirty. She asked how he felt about travelling to Germany with Ralph, insisting that whatever was decided, she would pay all travel costs.

Donovan hesitated. 'I'm not sure why I think this, but maybe we'd be more conspicuous.'

'You think we'd appear an unlikely team?' Ralph said.

'Possibly. No offence, Ralph, but it might be easier for me to travel light.'

'But what if you needed back-up?' Marnie asked.

'Why would I need back-up?'

'I don't know. I just have an uneasy feeling. You're always saying how careful we have to be. You might need someone to watch your back, that's all.'

There was silence on the line. Donovan was thinking that Ralph had great qualities, but they were in the field of economic theory. He was not the first person you'd think of when it came to quick thinking in tricky situations. He was trying to compose a diplomatic way of phrasing that when Anne spoke.

'It's obvious, isn't it?'

Anne came down the wall-ladder, pulled on her apricot scarf and picked up the rucksack. Marnie was at her desk, chewing a thumbnail, her expression pensive.

'I'll be back by five, Marnie.' As usual Anne sounded chirpy. 'See you later.'

'Right. Anne, I'm not happy about this.'

'It'll be a doddle.'

'Frankly, I don't think I give a damn about whose body was in that grave. Who cares?'

'It seems to be bugging a lot of people who want to cover something up.'

'It was all a long time ago, and we've got no guarantee that Hallgarten will be any wiser than we are.'

'Look, we've come all this way, Marnie. This may be our only chance of finding out what's gone on here. Sure, we can give up, but let's have one last try.'

'Maybe you're right.'

'Why not? I'm looking forward to it. I've never been to Germany before. Donovan said they put up Christmas trees with white lights on everywhere. He says it's really pretty in Germany at Advent time.'

'And you really want to go in the Mini?'

'We'll see more that way. We can share the driving, which reminds me. I've got a list of things to do: insurance, AA cover, car ferry bookings.'

'You've got it all worked out.'

'Donovan's term ends on Wednesday. I can miss a couple of days of college at the end of the week. That's okay; I'm well ahead with my work.'

'As simple as that.'

'No probs. We'll just be two students going to Germany for a break. No one's going to pay any attention to us. We'll drive over on Thursday, visit the university on Friday and drive back on Monday. A nice weekend jaunt. What could go wrong?'

Marnie forced a big smile as Anne went out, though her stomach was churning. What could go wrong, indeed?

54
Sleigh ride

On Thursday morning Anne climbed into the red Mini, optimistic and excited about her first motoring tour on the Continent. Marnie and Ralph kept their misgivings to themselves and waved her off up the field track.

An arm protruded from the driver's window in a farewell flourish as Anne disappeared from view near the top of the field. Marnie leaned her head on Ralph's shoulder.

'I don't think I'll feel right until she's safely back.'

'Do you think I should've insisted on going with Donovan?'

'No, my darling, I don't. Donovan's plan of just blending in with the other students in Frankfurt is sound.'

'I suppose you're right.'

'The only snag is, they've got to get there first.'

Anne pulled out onto the dual carriageway and headed south. Beside her on the passenger seat lay a folder with all their papers and tickets for the journey. She was thrilled at the prospect of a trip to Germany. During the week she had taught herself some basic German phrases from a book and recited them as she drove along. Of course, they would be unnecessary, given Donovan's fluency in the language, but that was no excuse for not trying.

In the days leading up to departure, Anne had become sensitive to all the German things in her life. They had a Bosch electric drill in the tool kit. There was a Braun food mixer and a Liebherr fridge in the office kitchen. She thought of Celia's Audi convertible and all the other German cars on the road. At that precise moment she was taking particular notice of a dark blue VW Passat that was two cars behind her. It pulled out every now and then but moved back into its lane.

This struck Anne as unusual. All the other larger cars were rushing past at high speed. This one was following at a steady sixty. Anne heard Donovan's voice in her head: *be aware, be watchful.* Time for an experiment. The first exit from the bypass was coming up.

Anne signalled and slipped off the main carriageway. The Passat followed, keeping well back. At the elevated roundabout she took the third exit, the access road leading back down to the dual carriageway. She was relieved to see that the Passat did not follow; it proceeded past as if to take the next exit off the main road.

Anne chided herself for being neurotic. Returning to her usual cruising speed, she watched the rear-view mirror sporadically, having a clear view back down the road. She had travelled barely half a mile when she spotted a gaggle of cars approaching fast. Some of them were executive expresses, some of them German. They swished past in rapid succession, but one, a dark Passat on the tail of the queue hung back and joined the inside lane some distance behind her.

Was it the same car? Anne felt her hands grow damp on the steering wheel. She made herself take deep breaths. What would Donovan do?

She checked the mirror by moving her eyes only. It was still there, keeping station about fifty yards back. There could be several reasons for its doing so, but she could only think of one. Anne struggled to keep her mind on the road but at the same time try to work out a plan. She could speed up, but the Passat could go faster. She could slow right down, but that would only reveal that she was aware of its presence. To take action meant having a choice of options. That time had not yet come.

A signboard came up indicating the next turn-off. The plan formed itself instantly. At the two hundred yard board Anne indicated a left turn and slowed for the exit. On the climb uphill from the bypass she looked in the mirror without moving her head. Still there.

She followed the roads round to the central station and pulled into a parking slot two rows from the entrance. There was no time for precautions. She rang Donovan on her mobile and explained what was happening.

Silence for three seconds.

'How long can you stay in the car park?'

'Four hours, I think.'

'Right. Here's what you do. Get a parking ticket for four hours. Then get a train to Watford. On the train phone Marnie and tell her where it is. She'll have to collect it just before the four hours are up. Just say we've decided to change our plans.'

'Okay.'

'Ring me when you know your arrival time in Watford. I'll meet you there.'

'Where?'

'I'll be in the car park as close as I can get to the station. Look out for my black Beetle.'

'Why Watford?'

'No one will expect you to be going there.'

Anne heaved her hold-all out of the Mini's tiny boot and walked calmly into the station. With an enormous effort she restrained herself from looking back across the car park.

Anne spotted the Beetle across the road from the entrance. As she walked over to it, Donovan made no attempt to get out and help her with the hold-all. He pushed the passenger door open and indicated that she should put her bag on the back seat. When she climbed in beside him his face told her at once that something was wrong.

'What's up?'

Without replying, he started the engine and drove off.

'Donovan, what is it? Are you annoyed with me? I couldn't help being followed, if I was followed.'

'It's not you. Having to change our plan is difficult.'

'I'm sorry, but –'

'No. I'm sorry.' He took the main road up to the M25, the London Orbital motorway, and headed out of town. 'The thing is, this car isn't up to making such a long journey. It's not fully restored.'

'So what do we do, go by plane?'

'Have you any idea of the cost of booking a flight at the last minute, or a train for that matter?'

'Hire a car?' Anne was feeling desperate.

'Too complicated at our age, at short notice, for taking abroad.'

'So what are you saying? We haven't got a car, so we can't make the trip?'

'No. We do have a car.'

'Another one?'

Donovan nodded.

'And it can do the journey?'

'Oh yes.'

'So that's okay, then. Problem solved. Isn't it?'

'Not quite.'

Half an hour later they stood in Donovan's garage. He had pulled the cover off the car in the end stall, and Anne looked at it for the first time. Its black bodywork shone in the harsh fluorescent light; its chrome gleamed brightly.

'Does it have anywhere for luggage?' Anne asked.

Donovan pointed to the front. 'Under there. Enough for two hold-alls, not much more.'

'Does the hood go up?'

'Yes.'

'What is it?'

'A Porsche 356, built 1955.'

'It'll get us there and back?'

'Sure.'

'Not exactly inconspicuous, though,' Anne observed.

'That's the point.'

'Do we have any choice?'

'Can you ride a bicycle?'

Anne smiled ruefully. 'Let's do it.'

The journey to the coast was uneventful, but the atmosphere in the little sports car was tense. Anne was surprised at how smoothly the Porsche ran for such an old machine. It felt like sitting low down in a bathtub, with only a few instruments and an old-fashioned gear stick, but a very sporty-looking steering wheel with a polished wooden rim.

They hardly spoke until they had left London and joined the motorway to the south coast. Then Anne asked the question that had been bothering her all morning.

'Do you believe I was being followed?'

'Yes.'

'New Force?'

'I think so.'

'Why?'

'You yourself said someone had been watching you.'

'But why did they follow me today of all days?'

'You'd been getting the car ready for a journey. I think they're taking a lot of interest in you, as the one most likely to lead them to me.'

'D'you think they saw you meeting me from the train?'

'It's possible, but I'm hoping they might be confused by the change of car.'

For much of the way they travelled in silence. Every now and then Donovan would speak. He had produced a list of jobs to do, which she found comforting, together with a list of key phone numbers.

'Ring the harbour. Tell them we've had to change cars. Give them this registration number. Check the sailing's on time. Tell them we may be early, may want to take the first available crossing.'

Anne enjoyed having things to do. It took her mind off the thought that she may have been tailed that morning.

'Ring my insurance broker. Tell him we're taking the Porsche abroad. Get him to give you a reference number for a green card. Say I can't speak personally as I'm driving.'

Anne happily ticked off the items as she completed them. It felt almost like being in the office at home.

'Ring the AA. Tell them we're using a different car and give them the details. We'll need a new reference number.'

When they were heading south on the motorway Anne asked Donovan about the car.

'It was my father's pride and joy. He inherited some money as a young man and bought this almost from new. Got if for a good price from a lady owner who said she found it too much of a handful and hardly used it. He thought she didn't like the colour.'

'But you certainly do,' Anne observed.

'That's right.'

Anne looked at Donovan. He was wearing black jeans and trainers, a black leather blouson jacket and driving gloves of fine black leather with small holes punched in the backs of the fingers. The ensemble was completed with a pair of gold-rimmed Ray-Ban *aviators*. His blonde hair made a marked contrast with his clothes. It was not surprising that, seeing them together, some people took them for brother and sister.

They were running at a steady seventy, the engine growling softly behind them, eating up the miles with no risk of attracting the attention of the highways police. Suddenly, without warning, Donovan turned sharply off the motorway and took the exit for Folkestone.

'What are you doing?'

'Precautionary measure.' He was looking in the rear-view mirror as they passed over the carriageway. 'We need fuel. We're making good time.'

They pulled into a Shell station where Donovan slotted the car into the furthest bay.

He got out quickly and watched the road from behind the pillar before filling the tank.

'See anyone?' Anne asked.

'Don't think so.'

They left the station and threaded the coast road along to Dover. At the eastern docks they checked in and were allocated a place on the next ferry. Anne's enthusiasm began to replace her anxiety as they lined up in lane 95 surrounded by travellers who looked calm and relaxed. Several people walked over to look at them, but only to admire the classic sports car. They smiled and nodded at its two young occupants.

After embarking and making their way to the restaurant, Anne had shaken off her cares and was in holiday mood. Even Donovan seemed at ease as they perused the menu in the *Brasserie*.

'You don't think we were followed here, do you?' Anne asked.

He looked at her over the top of the card. 'No.'

'You sound pretty sure of that.'

'As sure as I can be.'

Anne sighed. 'That's a relief.'

Donovan tried not to think about pursuers, who by now were possibly waiting for them in Calais.

Anne tucked the receipt for the meal into her travel folder as they rolled down the ramp out of the bowels of the ferry and queued through passport control. It was early afternoon in France, and Europe lay before them. Anne had the road atlas open on her lap, and it was clear that the best way to Germany was to head towards Brussels and pick up the southern motorway – the *autoroute de Wallonie* – direction, Aachen.

She was surprised when Donovan suddenly said, 'Can you see the A26 on the map?'

'Hold on … yes. It goes more or less south-east towards Reims via Arras.'

'That's the one.'

'Isn't that the opposite direction to where we're going?'

'Yes.'

Anne felt perplexed. What did Donovan have in mind? She remembered what Marnie said about him: *he's not unreliable*. No. Anne trusted him. So what was the game?

'You're laying a false trail in case we're being watched.'

'Let's hope they're not as quick on the uptake as you are, Anne.'

'Who?'

'Whoever.'

Anne felt uneasy again. 'The motorway is that way.' She pointed at the signboard. 'Arras, here we come.'

Donovan followed the lane indicated, but two minutes later turned off the bypass and made for *Centre Ville*.

'Not Arras, then,' Anne muttered.

'Not yet. Look out for signs showing *Toutes Directions* as we go into town and then see f you can spot one marked *Autoroutes*.'

They wove through residential suburbs until Anne saw a blue motorway sign leading nto an industrial estate. Donovan murmured, *good, good*, and they slipped into a queue of juggernauts pointing east. He kept in line as they lumbered onto a motorway.

Anne was trying to read signboards but it was difficult from their place in the procession.

'Are we back on the A26?'

'We are indeed.'

'And are we being followed?'

'We'll have to wait and see.'

After a mile or two with the juggernauts, Donovan eased into the outside lane and accelerated to seventy, his eyes flickering constantly towards the mirror. Anne read a road sign and checked their position on the map.

'How far are we going on this road?'

'Quite a way.'

'What does *péage* mean?'

'Toll. We have to pay from the next section onwards. Take my credit card from the wallet. The machine will be on your side.'

The toll motorway was smooth with relatively light traffic, and they ate up the miles with ease. While waiting their turn at the second toll plaza, Anne noticed an argument going on between a motorist and a traffic cop – a *gendarme*.

After they had gone through the booths, Anne said, 'What was that all about?'

No reply. She looked across at Donovan. He was studying the rear-view mirror, frowning.

'What is it?'

'Not sure.'

'You think we're being followed?' She swivelled in her seat and looked out of the tiny rear window. 'Which car is it?'

'Possibly that grey BMW with the red and white number plates. Belgian.'

'Can we outrun him?'

'No chance.'

'So what can we do?'

Donovan accelerated and pulled in behind a large white Renault van that was bowling along at a fair speed.

'We take cover.'

'He'll still be able to see us.'

'Yes, but not run us off the road.'

Anne gasped. It had not occurred to her that they might be forced into an accident. They settled into a steady rhythm a few cars' lengths behind the van, and Anne remembered her earlier question. She asked Donovan about the row between the gendarme and the driver.

'The speed limit in France is eighty miles an hour. That man's average speed in that sector must've been substantially higher. The cop was booking him.'

'Speed cameras?'

'No. The toll ticket records entry and exit times from one plaza to the next. Written evidence, irrefutable. They can fine you on the spot and hold you up.'

Anne was silent for a minute.

'Donovan, how fast can your car go?'

'Not fast by modern standards, but she can do a hundred and five comfortably all day.'

Anne checked the map.

'Donovan, do it.'

'What?'

'Go at that speed till we get to the next toll booths.'

'What?'

'Trust me. We've got thirty miles to the next toll thingy. Go at a hundred.'

Donovan reflected, then smiled. He signalled and pulled out into the centre lane. Anne felt the seat press into her back as he hit the accelerator. The growl behind them intensified and the car surged forward. For mile after mile the Porsche flew along. Soon the first signs indicated the toll plaza ahead. As they slowed, Anne pointed to the hard shoulder on the right at the edge of the road.

Donovan swung across the highway and brought the car to a halt. Beside him, Anne was doing a calculation in her notepad, muttering to herself.

'A hundred miles an hour, thirty miles, that's roughly … eighteen minutes. Is that right?'

Donovan was watching the traffic.

'*Yes!*'

'You agree with my figures?'

'What? Oh, not sure. The BMW's just gone past.'

'Good. So thirty miles at, say, seventy. I make that … just over twenty-five minutes. Here, check my calculations.'

Donovan read her notes.

'Seems about right.'

'Can we sit here for another five minutes?' Anne asked.

'We'll have to, or we'll get booked by the gendarmes, as our friend in the BMW is being.' There was a note of triumph in his voice. 'Anne, you're a genius.' He leaned over and kissed her before getting out of the car.

'What are you doing?'

He raised the rear engine cover.

'Checking the oil. I expect we're being watched on CCTV. No one's going to query this with such an old car.'

Donovan made a show of pulling out the dipstick, wiping it and checking the oil level. Next, he opened the luggage compartment at the front of the car and took out a can of

Castrol GTX.

'Are we using oil?' Anne asked from the passenger seat.

'No, but a drop or two more won't do any harm.' He poured some oil then wiped the engine with a rag. 'How're we doing for time?'

'Another minute and we can go.'

Donovan put the oil bottle back in the boot and closed the covers front and rear. He walked once round the car as if checking the tyres and climbed back in.

'Okay now?'

'Spot on.'

They took their place in a queue of vehicles and found themselves behind the same Renault van that they had followed earlier. Anne handed the credit card and toll ticket to the operator in the booth, who passed them back with a *merci, bonne route*.

Pulling out from the booth lane, they accelerated quickly towards the next stretch of motorway. Both pairs of eyes scanned the plaza. Away to their right a gendarme was writing on a pad in front of a motorist who was gesticulating wildly with both hands. They were standing beside a grey BMW with red and white Belgian number plates.

Donovan pulled out to overtake the white van.

'How far to the next intersection?'

'That's a junction with the A2, about twenty miles or so.'

'Direction Brussels?'

'Yes.'

'Work out a route to Liège. We're looking for Mons, Charleroi, Namur. Can you see them?'

Anne ran her finger over the page. 'Got'em.' She noticed that they were travelling faster than their usual seventy. 'Any sign of the BMW?'

'Not yet. I want to be well away before he can catch up.'

At the approach of the intersection Donovan pulled into the right-hand lane and turned off, following signs to Mons. They had barely taken the A2 when he groaned, looking in the mirror.

'What now?' Anne was aghast. 'The BMW?'

'No. Could be worse. Police, coming up fast in the outside lane.'

Anne realised that theirs was the only car in that sector.

'We're not doing anything wrong, are we?'

'You never know what kind of trick they might pull.'

The car drew alongside and Anne looked across. The word *Gendarmerie* was emblazoned on the side in blue letters. The policeman in the front passenger seat smiled at her. She made a big effort and smiled back. The police car remained in position beside them. Donovan looked over.

'What are they playing at?' he muttered.

To their surprise, the policeman waved them on. While Donovan kept the Porsche at a steady eighty, the man waved more quickly.

'I think he wants us to go faster,' Anne said.

Donovan looked over again and saw the gendarme smiling and waving. Anne pointed forwards and raised her eyebrows in a question. The gendarme nodded and waved again. Donovan took it up to ninety. The police car caught up, the gendarme still waving.

'I never reckoned on a police escort,' Donovan murmured, 'but the quicker we get away, the better.'

He hit the throttle and the engine growled. They left the police car behind as they passed a hundred. In the mirror Donovan saw the police car flashing its lights in farewell, receding into the distance.

'What was all that about?' Anne asked.

'Enthusiasts, I suppose. This kind of car attracts that kind of attention sometimes.'

'But they were *gendarmes* and they encouraged you to break the speed limit.'

Donovan shrugged. 'This is France.'

'But not for much longer at this speed. Belgium up ahead.'

Donovan slowed back to eighty and a minute later they were passing through the frontier, where the border police hardly glanced at their passports.

For the next two hours Donovan held a steady eighty and they gobbled up the *autoroute de Wallonie*, the southern motorway which, as he had promised, was light on traffic. They made good progress but neither of them could relax, and Donovan constantly watched the mirror, wondering where the next problem was coming from.

Approaching Liège, Anne read the road signs carefully.

'I suppose we follow the E42 then the E40, direction Aachen. Is that right? Seems the logical way to go.'

Donovan looked at Anne.

'What did you say?'

'Our road is the –'

'No, I meant about it being logical.'

'Well, I assumed that was where we're going. Aachen is just over the border and it's the direct road into Germany.'

Donovan was shaking his head.

'No. This is wrong. That's what anyone would expect. Aachen … Köln … Koblenz … Frankfurt. We're too conspicuous in this car.'

'But we're going to Germany and it's up ahead on this road.'

Donovan shook his head again.

'No. That's asking for trouble.'

'Another change of plan?'

'There's a motorway south from Liège. Can't remember the number.'

Anne searched the map.

'There are two. The good ol' A26 goes roughly towards Luxembourg.'

'That's the one.'

'It cuts through the Ardennes. That's a very scenic area, isn't it?'

'Beautiful, but we'll not get to see it.'

Anne looked alarmed. 'Why not?'

Donovan pointed through the windscreen. 'Look outside.'

The light was fading rapidly as they bypassed Liège on the ring road.

'The darkness will help us.' Donovan switched on the headlights. 'You'll find a torch in the glovebox.'

'Are we still aiming to cross into Germany this evening?'

'It should take a couple of hours from our turn-off.'

Anne was reading a road sign and glancing at the map.

'I think this is it. Yes. A26 … E25: Bastogne, Arlon, Luxembourg.'

'That's great. You can relax now, Anne. We just take this road till we join the connection to Luxembourg.'

Anne closed the atlas and slipped it into the footwell. Donovan took the filter lane and swung round to pick up the new motorway. Outside night had fallen, an all-enveloping cloak of darkness that promised safety. They had barely reached cruising speed when the first snowflakes scurried towards them in the headlight beams.

'Whoa!'

Donovan twitched the steering wheel left and right to correct the skid. They were already down to forty and had been gaining altitude and losing speed for the previous half hour.

'What was that?' Anne peered forwards. 'The road seems to be straight.'

'Black ice. Every now and then the steering gets lighter and we lose grip.'

On the emergency hard shoulder they had passed numerous lorries that had pulled off the carriageway, all of them caked in snow. In the headlights they saw two parked petrol tankers that seemed as long as *Sally Ann*. The consequences of either of those crashing were horrendous.

Anne was studying the atlas again.

'What are our options, Donovan? We've still a long way to go through the Ardennes. I'm assuming that's where we are. I haven't seen a sign for ages.'

'We've passed Bastogne,' he said. 'The next landmark must be the junction with the road that cuts east to Luxembourg.'

'What's the plan?'

'Try to reach Arlon.'

They were crawling along at less than forty, Donovan muttering quietly to himself.

'What did you say?' Anne asked.

'I was just thinking about the Battle of the Bulge.'

'Where's that?'

'Right here where we are now. In 1944 the German army mounted a huge counter-attack when the allies were least expecting it. The Panzers came roaring through the Ardennes in the snow, took everyone by surprise.'

Anne looked out of the window at the snow swirling by in the darkness.

'I'm so glad you told me that.'

At ten-thirty Anne was too tired to eat and Donovan looked drawn. Twice the Porsche had skidded sideways on the motorway at low speed and each time Donovan had only just managed to keep the car pointing in the right direction. Complaining that they could travel faster by sleigh, they finally reached the exit for the town of Arlon and gratefully parked outside a small hotel in the centre. The whole place was blanketed in snow.

Anne was amused to see that the receptionist took Donovan's passport and booked them in as *Monsieur et Madame Smith*. They took the lift to the second floor, where their room overlooked the street, and stared down at the Porsche parked under a lamp. It was the only car not covered in snow, as if the gods had deliberately made it stand out for the benefit of their pursuers.

Anne leaned against Donovan.

'D'you think we could be the only people in the world still involved in a war that everybody else thought ended fifty years ago?'

'Have you forgotten about the grey BMW or the person who was watching the office at Glebe Farm?'

Supper was a bar of KitKat, followed by a banana. Anne insisted they toss a coin to decide who took the first shower. She lost.

When Donovan came out of the bathroom with a towel tied round his waist, Anne had a sense of *déjà vu*. The same idea occurred to Donovan.

'This is just like last year,' he said. 'Do you remember that night we spent together in the school?'

'I don't think that's an occasion anyone ever forgets. You said it was your first time too.'

'Didn't you believe me?'

'Yes. It's just that you were older than me and I thought you'd probably … you know …'

'There had been someone, once, but it didn't work out.'

'Who was she?'

'Her name was Annette, Annette von Droste-Hülshoff.'

'A German girl. What happened?'

'She'd been dead … for a hundred and fifty years.'

Anne laughed. 'That's a pretty good excuse for not requiting your feelings.'

'Being dead? Yeah, I suppose it is.'

'That put you off girls, did it?'

Donovan shrugged. 'When someone lets you down like that …'

When Anne came out of the shower, Donovan was lying across the bed, sleeping. She gently moved his legs, kissed the top of his head and draped the duvet over him. Before turning off the light, she looked out of the window.

It was snowing again.

55
Dead end

When Anne awoke the next morning she thought they had slept late. It was light in the room and Donovan was in the bathroom. She rolled out of bed and drew the curtains. The snow brightened up the morning under a cotton-wool sky. Down in the street the Porsche was safely tucked under a camouflage coating and blended in with the other parked cars.

After breakfast Donovan borrowed a broom from the hotel and swept the car clean. He had a small shovel in the boot and dug snow out from around the cars' tyres. They made slow progress back through the town and onto the motorway for Luxembourg. When Donovan yawned, his breath clouded in the chilly cockpit. It took several minutes before the heater raised the temperature.

Anne was studying the atlas.

'Which way are we going, round Luxembourg past Koblenz and pick up the A3 going south?'

Donovan pulled a face. 'I asked at reception about road conditions. There are big hold-ups on some of the motorways, jack-knifed lorries and the like. The Köln – Frankfurt *Autobahn* is the busiest road in Europe. That's the A3.'

'So we find another route?'

'I think we have to.'

Anne turned a page, shaking her head. 'There isn't any logical alternative motorway, just country roads that the motorways go round. Are there mountains in the way or something?'

'Not mountains, no.'

'What then?'

'You said you were looking forward to seeing how pretty Germany is. Now's your chance. Once we're past Luxembourg we'll stay on the motorway till beyond Trier. Then we'll turn off and go down the Mosel valley.'

'Will the roads be open?'

'Snowploughs will've been out all night keeping them clear. It won't be fast but it'll cut off a huge corner, and at least we won't risk getting stuck in a motorway tailback.'

Donovan's plan proved to be sound, at least until the snow began falling again mid-morning. Up till then, Anne had been enchanted, gazing out at the Mosel landscape. Tree-covered hills encircled them. Vineyards spread out in all directions from the gently winding river. The towns and villages looked as if they had slipped out of the pages of story books from her childhood. She caught glimpses of half-timbered houses, turrets, cobbled streets, arches, steep gables, squares with fountains. And everywhere she looked, Christmas trees had been set out, their white lights burning in the frosty air.

When the first barge cruised by, Anne had a flashback to home. The Grand Union

Canal was like a stream compared with the Mosel. The narrowboats – even the old working pairs of seventy-foot motorboats and butties – seemed like toys compared with the substantial craft plying this river. That first barge flew a Luxembourg flag of red, white and pale blue horizontal stripes, and carried a small car on the deck. She thought of Donovan's bicycle on the roof of *X O 2* and smiled at the memory.

At first the snow dropped languidly from the sky, big flakes drifting in still air. They looked perfect in the fairytale countryside. Gradually, they began to blot out the view and soon the wiper-blades were inadequate for the task of clearing the windscreen. Donovan muttered a quiet oath. Anne felt helpless beside him.

'I think the next place is Piesport. We seem to cross over the river before it and go through the town. Perhaps it'll be easier there.'

Before Donovan could reply, a gust of wind blew a solid wall of snow straight at them and he had to brake to a halt, unable to see the road in front of their faces. Not daring to stop for more than a few seconds, he shifted into second gear and eased the car along at a crawl. They inched forward, gradually gaining speed until they were rolling at little more than jogging pace in third gear.

Donovan shook his head. 'My gamble isn't working.'

'It was our best chance.'

'Anne, ring Hallgarten's number at the university.'

'Shouldn't you speak to her?'

'I don't want to stop. We could get stuck.'

Anne rang the number, bit her lip, took a deep breath and asked for Hallgarten in German.

'*Guten Morgen. Ist Professor Hallgarten zu sprechen?*'

Donovan stared at her in amazement.

'*Mein Name ist Anne Price.*' After a pause she spoke again, this time in English. 'I'm sorry about this, professor, but we're stuck in heavy snow.'

'Yes, I heard the *Autobahn* was blocked near Koblenz. So what are you planning to do?'

'We're on our way but we're going to be much later than planned. I'm really sorry.'

'You have my private number and address? You can find it?'

'Yes, in Offenbach, across the river Main from Frankfurt.'

'Good. Ring me when you know what time you will arrive.'

'Thank you.'

The snow eased off for a while, and they stopped in Piesport to buy rolls: ham sausage for Donovan, smoked cheese for Anne. The bakery where they bought them smelled wonderful, and Anne wanted to stay there forever. Back on the road, they ate as they drove along, finishing their meal with a banana and the promise of a stop at the next town for coffee.

They pulled over in Brauneberg, where sleeping vineyards climbed steeply up from the river. Donovan told Anne they produced some of the best wines in the region. Coffee and a slice of cheesecake fortified them for the next leg of their journey, and they set off in better spirits.

<center>~~~~ ~~~~</center>

By late afternoon they had left the Mosel valley and picked up a motorway not far from Bingen on the Rhine. As dusk descended, Anne was enchanted by the spectacle of so many Christmas lights. Had it not been for the thought that somewhere out there, someone was plotting against them, she would have fallen in love with Germany.

Grateful that the motorways from Mainz to Frankfurt were clear of snow, Anne gave Donovan directions to the south side of the river, and they took a road running alongside the Main through an industrial area. It was a very different world from the lush, pastoral Mosel. She remembered Hallgarten's request and pulled out the mobile.

'What are you doing?' Donovan asked.

'She said to ring when we knew what time we'd arrive. We should be there in ten minutes or so.'

'No. Wait. Ring when we're there.'

'Don't you trust her?' Anne knew the answer as soon as she had spoken. 'Of course. *Be aware. Be watchful.*'

'Exactly.'

'But do you trust her?'

'I don't know her.'

Anne's estimated time of arrival was accurate. They parked in a tree-lined street facing the river, opposite the small block of flats where the professor lived.

'Ring her now, Anne. Say we'll be there in ten minutes.'

They sat and watched the street as the minutes ticked by. On the other side of the river they had a panorama of downtown Frankfurt, with tower cranes in the docks silhouetted in darkness against a backdrop of skyscrapers. One or two cars ventured along the professor's quiet side street, but all of them cruised by without stopping. At the agreed time, Anne and Donovan climbed out and crossed the road.

Donovan checked the names beside each bell and pressed a button. A woman's voice told them to come up to the first floor. A buzzer sounded and Donovan pushed the front door open. As they approached the door to the flat, it swung inwards and they were greeted by the professor. She was not what they had expected.

'Come in, come in.' She stood aside in the doorway with a welcoming smile, gesturing them to enter. 'You must be frozen and hungry.'

Tall, with a mane of hair held back by an Alice band, Professor Ingrid Hallgarten was wearing a striped apron, her hands covered in flour.

'Please excuse me. As you see, you find me baking my Christmas biscuits. I'm late as usual, always too much to do.'

She ushered them into a spacious open-plan living area with subdued lighting and comfortable, inviting sofas. Her personality seemed to fill the room with warmth.

'Now, I've made some soup. I hope you'll have some. It's vegetable with mushrooms, an old recipe from my grandmother.'

Donovan thanked her in German. With a glance at Anne, she continued in English.

'Please take your jackets off and make yourselves comfortable. If you need a bathroom, it's through there.'

To their surprise, a young woman appeared from the kitchen, wiping her hands on a towel. In jeans and a smock top, she was slim and pretty with bobbed hair and glasses, smiling broadly. Hallgarten introduced her.

'This is Helga, one of my students. She likes baking biscuits. She's volunteered to help me.'

They shook hands. Whatever Anne had expected, it was not such a friendly informal reception. She relaxed, and even Donovan seemed at ease.

While Anne and Donovan ate their soup, Hallgarten sat with them at the table, leaving Helga in the kitchen.

'This is wonderful soup, professor, just what we needed.'

'Good. You've had a long and tiring journey. So, how do you like Germany, Miss Price?'

'It's beautiful, specially with all the Christmas trees up.'

'Have you seen many?'

Anne pictured the Mosel valley in her mind. She was about to mention it when she sensed Donovan stiffen beside her.

'Quite a few. You can see them from the *Autobahn*.'

'Of course.' Hallgarten became more serious. 'Before we speak about the reason for your visit, you must first promise me that if anything of what I tell you is to be published, you will ask for my approval beforehand.'

Anne shook her head. 'Nothing is to be published, professor. That's not why we're doing this.'

'But you *must* promise nonetheless.'

'I do promise, definitely.'

'Very well.'

Hallgarten stood up, went to an antique polished bureau in the corner of the room and picked up a folder.

'When I was asked by Professor Fleischer if I had any information about my father's activities during the war, my first reaction was that I had nothing that would be of direct use to anyone, apart from academic historians.'

'Something changed your mind?' Donovan said.

'It was the name. I thought about it. Somewhere I had seen a name that could be connected with your enquiry.'

'The name of an agent?' Anne asked.

'Yes.'

'You know the actual name of that person?' Anne felt her heart beating faster.

'Yes. The name in the papers was … Knightly.'

Anne was perplexed. '*Knightly*? That's the name of our village, more or less.'

'And the name given to my father's contact.'

Of course. Anne realised that any agent would have a codename. They might not even have come from the area; it was just the place where they operated. They had travelled to the centre of Germany to be given the name of their village.

'What else do you know about this agent Knightly?' Donovan asked.

'I don't know if it was a man or a woman. Let's call him *he*. Like all the agents, he had a general role.'

'Spying,' said Donovan.

'He gathered information about military and economic activity in the area: transports on the road, passage of aircraft, movement on the canals.'

'The *canals*?' Anne found it hard to imagine an enemy spy watching the boats plying the Grand Union Canal. 'That's beside where we live.'

'I see.'

'Did he have any other duties?' Donovan said.

'He was to infiltrate pacifist groups and encourage them to undermine the civilian population. For example, he gave them money to pay for printing posters. He planted rumours that German paratroops had already landed in England and were disguised as foreign allies: Czechs, Hungarians. He also had to help fascist sympathisers to escape to Germany.'

'A busy man, if it was a man,' Donovan observed.

'That's not all. One of Knightly's main tasks was to gather support for the Nazi cause among the British upper classes.'

Donovan stood up and crossed to the window, looking out through the venetian blinds.

'Does that mean he was connected with Knightly Court?'

'What is that, a manor house?'

'Yes.'

Hallgarten consulted the file. 'There is no mention of this manor.'

'But –' Donovan checked himself. He took his seat again. 'Is there any other information in your folder?'

'No. Like several of the files it ends abruptly. Knightly seems to have disappeared in September 1944.'

'You think he was captured or eliminated?'

Hallgarten shrugged. 'No explanation is given in these papers.'

'And that's everything you know?' Donovan sounded disappointed.

'My dear young man, there are scholars who write doctorates on less information than this.' She laughed. 'What did you expect?'

'Of course. May we have copies of the papers?'

'No. That's impossible. You must see that.'

'Yes, but I had to ask.'

He pulled a pad out of his back pocket and wrote rapid notes. When he had finished, he read them back in German to Hallgarten who confirmed the details were correct.

Helga emerged from the kitchen and took away the dishes. In the doorway she turned and asked if they would like tea or coffee. Donovan declined the offer and said they had to be on their way. The professor closed the folder and set it down on the bureau.

'Have you a long way to go?' Helga asked. She had a good accent.

'That may depend on the weather.'

Helga looked towards the window. 'It's snowing again, quite thick.'

Anne and Donovan thanked Hallgarten for the information and her hospitality. She took them to the door. Suddenly Helga appeared behind her, holding out a small packet.

'Some Christmas biscuits to take with you.'

Anne took them. They were wrapped in a gift box and tied with ribbon.

'Thank you so much. That's lovely.'

Helga smiled, nodded and retreated to the kitchen.

'I don't suppose this is how you imagined me,' Hallgarten said. '*Daughter of Nazi spymaster*.' She smiled. 'You must have been expecting someone like Mata Hari or Rosa Luxemburg.'

'Thanks for your help, professor,' Anne said.

'I hope what I told you is helpful.'

Donovan shook her hand. 'We'll know that when we get back.'

Outside, the night was growing colder and a deeper blanket of snow covered the ground. Donovan scraped the windscreen clear and climbed into the car beside Anne, who was consulting the atlas.

'Where to now?' she said. 'Should we stay somewhere in the town? It might be better than the country.'

Donovan agreed. He started up the engine and pulled on his driving gloves. Before pulling away, he glanced up at the flats. On the first floor he made out a shape behind open venetian blinds. Helga was looking down on them. She waved as they moved off from the kerb. Further down the street they made a three-point turn and headed back the way they had come.

'Can you see Sachsenhausen on the map?' Donovan asked. He spelt the name.

'This side of the river,' Anne confirmed. 'We're pointing in the right direction.'

'I think we'll find a hotel in that part of –'

Anne looked up. 'What is it?'

Donovan was staring in the mirror. 'We've got company.'

'Are you sure?'

He made no reply but accelerated hard. The Porsche's tail snaked on the slippery surface and Donovan twitched the wheel to control it. He took a turning and sped off past industrial buildings.

'I'm sure,' he muttered. 'A Merc.'

They came to a junction with a dual carriageway, where he turned left and raced off on a wet road that was clear of snow. Ahead was a roundabout with signboards indicating a motorway. They turned onto the roundabout, slipping in front of a lorry. She knew Donovan was using it as cover, but it could only give them a temporary breathing space. When the lorry turned onto the motorway access road, she was not surprised that Donovan continued round. They left the roundabout and regained the dual carriageway, now going in the opposite direction.

Anne recognised the road from which they had come. Donovan turned off the main road and made a number of left and right-hand turns in quick succession. They found themselves on a tree-lined road running parallel with the river which lay to their right. There were no buildings and the area was deserted.

'Are they still following?' Anne asked.

'Can't see anyone at the moment.'

Anne was beginning to feel safe when she spotted the road sign. They were in a dead end. She mentioned this to Donovan who was studying the mirrors. His expression was grim.

'Won't we be all right down here?' Anne asked.

Donovan shook his head. 'We've left a fresh trail in the snow.'

'Donovan, do you have a gun?'

'No.'

'Then what can we –'

With a jolt, Donovan pulled off onto the side of the road between the trees, where the surface felt firm but bumpy. He manoeuvred the car round to face back down the road and peered through the windscreen before turning off the headlights. They sat in the dark, watching another heavy fall of snowflakes swirling around them.

'Another fifteen minutes and our trail would be blotted out completely.'

'But we don't have that much time, do we?' Anne said.

'A minute or two at most, is my guess.' Suddenly he turned to face her. 'Anne, get out and take our bags from the boot. Quickly!'

Anne leapt out and grabbed the bags, slamming the car's front down firmly. Bewildered, she bent down to speak.

'What now?'

'No time to explain. Get the bags and take cover behind a tree over there. Whatever happens, stay hidden.'

'But –'

'Just do it! Please.'

Anne ran back and took shelter. It all seemed improbable, the empty street with only the twin tracks in the snow to show where they had come, the black Porsche hidden behind the trees in the dark with its lights switched off and the engine idling. For a minute that felt like an eternity she stood there, not noticing the cold, but aware that she was trembling.

Then she saw it. At the far end, lights appeared, and she heard a car coming quickly towards them. She ducked back behind the tree and glanced over at Donovan. Her heart froze in her chest as she saw him lean forward and touch the steering wheel briefly with his forehead.

The car was approaching fast and would soon be upon them. What was Donovan planning to do? If he was going to escape, why had he left her behind with the luggage? Would he try to evade their pursuers and come back for her? Seconds later, she had her answer, and it was more horrifying than she had imagined.

When the oncoming car was thirty yards away, the Porsche roared and leapt from cover, its wheels spinning. Donovan hit the accelerator at the same time as he turned on the headlights and raced out onto the road at full throttle. Anne winced, bracing herself for a head-on crash. Startled by the lights, the oncoming driver swerved. His car skidded across the snowy ground and smashed heavily into a tree. Anne heard metal crunching and glass shattering. As she gasped for breath, the air was filled with the smell of petrol. A second later, the car exploded in a fireball.

In its light she saw the Porsche skating across the road over snow and ice, Donovan fighting the wheel in a frantic effort to control it. The car slithered sideways, hurtling towards the river and vanished from view. Her stomach turned as she heard the grinding of metal followed by a deep splash.

Groaning, Anne broke cover and tried to run across the road. The snowy surface concealed impacted ice. She slipped, lost her footing and fell heavily on her back. She rolled over, trying not to look at the burning Mercedes or think of its occupants. Anne struggled onto her knees and stood up cautiously, aching all over. She turned and followed the new tyre tracks left behind by the Porsche. Already they were filling with snow. She spat flakes from her lips and wiped them from her eyes, aware of tears running down her cheeks.

The ground sloped steeply down towards the river and she quickened her pace. The next time she fell, she pitched forward landing heavily on her knees. Her head struck the ground. Throbbing in every part of her body, Anne paused to take a breath before standing and almost screamed when an arm took her by the waist and began pulling her up.

'Anne, come on. We've got to get away from here.'

When she looked into Donovan's face she almost fainted.

'But –'

'No time. Get the bags. We gotta go.'

It was almost an hour later when they walked into the entrance hall of a hotel in Sachsenhausen. They were both exhausted with fatigue and shock, and the warmth of the reception area made their faces tingle.

The young woman at the desk spoke rapidly in German, eyeing them with suspicion, but Donovan's reply and the ensuing exchanges seemed to satisfy her. They were allocated a room on the first floor, where they collapsed on the bed. During their walk through the snowstorm they had been unable to talk. Donovan had counted the minutes before they heard sirens in the distance as the emergency services converged on the blazing wreck.

The ensuite bathroom surprised them. Anne had expected the customary shower ubicle, but instead she found a large old-fashioned enamel bath. Gratefully, she filled it nd poured in a small bottle of lavender oil. Without a word, they stripped off their clothes nd lowered themselves into the steaming fragrant water.

'I thought you were dead,' Anne said quietly.

'So did I.'

'What happened?'

'You saw it. I made them take avoiding action rather than risk a head-on crash.'

'But suppose he hadn't been able to swerve like that.'

Donovan shrugged. 'What else could I do?'

'You went off the road. And your car …'

'Yeah.'

'You jumped out?'

'I rolled out into the snow as the car slid down the bank.'

'How deep is the river at that point, d'you think?'

'Probably quite deep. Big barges tie up along there.'

'So you've lost your father's lovely Porsche. I'm so sorry.'

'At least we're alive, Anne. You can't expect happy endings when you're up against eople like that.'

'I was thinking. How did they know where to find us? Was it Hallgarten?'

Donovan rested his head back against the taps and closed his eyes. 'That was my first hought. But then I wondered why she would do that after trying to help us.'

'Who then? Helga?'

'That's my guess. I wouldn't be surprised if she was a plant. Who'd be better placed to ccess Hallgarten's files?'

'But she looked so nice, so pretty and charming.'

'Perfect. You'd hardly infiltrate someone with a nervous twitch and an Iron Cross.'

Anne lay back in the fragrant water and stretched her legs.

'So what now?'

'Home. Germany's biggest airport is just down the road from here.'

'Home,' Anne murmured. 'It seems like a million miles away.'

56
More questions

Ralph was at the railway station early on Saturday afternoon to meet Anne and Donovan. They had caught a morning flight to Heathrow from Frankfurt, and Anne had been surprised when Donovan opted to go home with her. He seemed less worried about being watched or followed, though typically, he suggested that they be met at Wolverton, by boat.

They descended the steep stairway by the road bridge down to the towpath where Marnie was waiting for them on *Sally Ann*. Wrapped in winter clothing, they cruised home in still air under an opaque sky clutching mugs of steaming coffee laced with brandy. By the time they reached Cosgrove lock the light was fading, and dusk was coming down when they steered into the docking area at Glebe Farm. Anne felt like kissing the ground as she hopped onto the bank to tie up.

While trout and almonds baked in the oven, the four of them sat in the saloon with a glass of mulled wine and Anne and Donovan told their story. Anne tried to recount the events in as matter-of-fact a tone as possible. When she reached the final incident she handed over to Donovan.

'I was sure they were on to us and I didn't hold out much hope that we'd get away. They'd only stop looking for us if they were convinced we were dead.'

'And you think this student, Helga, tipped them off?' Marnie said.

'It's just an idea. Anyway, when we left Hallgarten's flat I saw we were being followed and all we could do was make a run for it. I thought we'd lost them when I realised I'd made a serious mistake, driven into a dead end. On one side was perimeter fencing around an industrial site, on the other was a steep slope down to the river.'

'You couldn't drive back out?' Ralph asked.

'That was my plan for if they came down that way. I turned the car round and parked off the road between trees, ready to rush out when they went past us. If they didn't come, we'd wait for an hour or two then take our chances on the road again.'

'But they did come.'

'Of course. It was Friday evening. Everyone had gone home from work. We were the only car leaving tracks in the snow round there. It was inevitable they'd find us. Sitting there, I suddenly had an idea. It was crazy, but I knew we couldn't out-run them.'

'How did you know it was them in the dark?'

'That wasn't difficult,' Anne interjected. 'They were racing like lunatics. Every other car we'd seen that evening had been crawling along.'

'Anne's right,' Donovan said. 'As soon as I saw their lights and heard their engine, I knew it had to be them. I waited till they were almost up to us. I just hoped the car would move fast enough in those conditions. The tyres bit into the rough ground under the snow and we lurched out onto the roadway. I turned on the full beams and hit the throttle. My car snaked but kept going. We were right in their path. The driver had no time to think. He just swerved, hit the brakes, lost control and skidded straight into a tree. He didn't stand a chance. I clipped the kerb and went off the road. The ground fell away steeply at that point. The brakes were useless; steering was impossible.'

'I heard the car hit the river,' Anne said. 'I thought Donovan had gone with it.'

Marnie held a hand to her mouth. 'My god!'

Ralph said, 'I think I could do with a spot more brandy.'

They spent the next half hour re-examining the events of the journey. Donovan was convinced the tyre tracks would have been covered by the time the emergency services discovered the burning car. Any traces not filled in by snow would have been obliterated by fire engines, ambulances and police cars. There were no witnesses to testify to the presence of the black Porsche that was now lying deep below the surface in the dark murky water of the river Main. It could be years before it was discovered, if at all.

Ralph brought them back to the original reason for the journey to see Hallgarten. Donovan took out his notepad and presented the facts given by the professor. It took less than two minutes.

'That's it?' Marnie said.

Donovan closed the pad. 'That's it.'

'So we're no further forward. After all you've been through.'

'I'm not sure we are no further forward,' said Ralph. 'One fact stands out, the date when *Knightly* lost contact.'

'September 1944,' said Donovan. 'I've been thinking about that. It must have been someone connected with Knightly Court.'

'The Deveres?' Marnie sounded incredulous.

'Not necessarily,' said Ralph. 'Let's look at possibilities. Marcus Devere was around at the time, so he has to be taken into account. He had a wife in those days. No one's mentioned her so far. He had a brother, though we know he was already missing in action in France and was later confirmed as dead. Any other family?'

'Was the dead brother married?' Marnie asked.

'Don't know.'

'Who would know?'

'George Stubbs,' said Anne. 'He was only a child back then, but I'm sure he'd know that sort of thing.'

'We could give him a ring,' Marnie said.

'Perhaps it would be better to sleep on it and contact him tomorrow,' Ralph said. 'Other questions might have occurred to us by then.'

Marnie nodded. 'Seems reasonable. A night's sleep would certainly be good for –'

They all heard the sound and turned their heads towards the stern. It was like a distant wailing. Anne got up and was walking back towards the sleeping cabin before anyone else reacted.

'It's Dolly!'

Anne was right. The cat warbled a greeting as she headed for her feeding bowl in the corner like a missile homing in on its target. Her fur was glistening.

'Look out of the windows,' Anne called from the stern.

Marnie pulled curtains aside and they stared out. During the meal snow had been falling. It covered the bank and was settling on the branches of trees in the spinney. Anne returned to the saloon holding a snowball she had scooped from the steps by the stern doors. She laid it ceremoniously on the draining board in the galley like a trophy.

'Talk about *Winter Wonderland*,' she said. 'If it lasts, it'll be my first ever white Christmas.'

The snow was falling steadily in large flakes unruffled by any breeze, like the ones that had covered their tracks in Germany. As they gazed out, Anne was thinking that snow would never seem quite the same again.

57
George

It was still dark and it had stopped snowing when Anne got out of bed on Sunday morning. She had a plan and knew exactly what she was going to do. In the shower, she thought about their discussion the evening before and knew that despite all their efforts they had reached a dead end. She also thought about Donovan and admitted to herself that she was slightly surprised that he had opted to stay on *Sally Ann* rather than join her in the attic room. It was the understanding of his motives that led to her plan.

Wrapped in her warmest clothes, she took the torch from its hook in the kitchen and went outside, edging her way along the front of the office barn. She swept the courtyard with the beam and was relieved to see the snow was undisturbed. Crossing to the farmhouse, she carried out the same manoeuvre in the garden, with the same result. There were no footprints around the outbuildings.

Anne turned towards the spinney. Keeping away from the path, she scanned as much as she could see, combing her way through the trees and undergrowth, watching the ground for footprints and any roots that might trip her up.

Anne reached the edge of the trees and suppressed a gasp. Beside the docking area, as close as possible to *Sally Ann*, was a distinct line of impressions in the snow. Someone had been checking the boat. She switched off the torch and pressed herself tight against a tree. Something was wrong. In the pre-dawn darkness, illuminated only by the snow, she sensed a presence nearby and knew she had given away her position with the torchlight.

Over to her right she could see lights burning on *Thyrsis*. Someone was in the galley and the shower room was occupied. She was wondering whether to run across and hammer on the door when it happened.

'There's no trace of an intruder.'

The voice spoke quietly, almost directly into her ear.

'Donovan!' Anne shrieked. 'You nearly gave me a heart attack.' She put a hand to her forehead. 'I feel faint.'

'Sorry about that. Seems we both had the same idea. You've checked round the house?'

'Yes.' She still sounded breathless. 'I should've guessed it would be you.'

'Can I use the shower?'

'Sure. Breakfast in twenty minutes?'

'Great.'

Marnie rang George Stubbs and arranged to see him at home after the morning church service. Donovan chose to stay behind on *Sally Ann*, while Ralph worked on *Thyrsis*.

In its snowy setting, The Old Farm House looked magnificent, and the effect was enhanced by the smell of woodsmoke in the air. Sheila Stubbs showed them into the living room where a log fire was burning in the inglenook and the French windows framed the view out to the frosty, snow-bound garden. When George came in, having changed out of his Sunday suit into a sweater and slacks, Sheila excused herself to return to her kitchen.

'If you have everything you need, I'll get back to my cooking.' She smiled brightly. 'The Aga calls.'

'Are you baking things for Christmas, Mrs Stubbs?' Anne asked, and for a second she had a flashback to another kitchen in Germany.

'Oh, no. I baked my cake and puddings back in October.' Her tone suggested that any later would be an affront to civilisation.

She went out and closed the door behind her. George smiled at Marnie.

'What can I do for you, my dear? Are you better now, after your accident?'

'I'm fine, George, thank you. I'd like to ask you some questions about things that might have happened here during the war.'

'Fire away. I'll do my best, but I was of course just a nipper.' He sat back, folding his thick hands across his heavy stomach.

'This concerns the body found in Sarah's grave. We'd like to identify it if at all possible.'

'Understandable. Can't have spare bodies floating about, can we?'

'Well, no. The thing is, we have reason to believe ... did I really say that? Anyway, we do. We think it might have some connection with ... there's no other way to put this, George ... with an enemy agent who was run by an officer in Military Intelligence in Berlin.'

George frowned. 'You think the body's some kind of German spy? Or d'you mean it's someone killed by a spy?'

'We suspect it might be a spy. I know it sounds improbable, and the more I talk about it, the stranger it seems.'

'Marnie, what on earth was a German spy supposed to be doing in Knightly St John?'

Anne said, 'I've just come back from Germany, Mr Stubbs. I met the daughter of the Intelligence officer. She showed us papers about an agent here in Knightly. In fact, Knightly was his codename.'

'Good lord!' George stood up and went to a side table holding a variety of bottles. 'I think I could do with a Scotch. Something for you, Marnie, Anne?'

They declined. George poured himself a measure of whisky, added a splash of soda and returned to his seat.

'Marnie, I don't see how I can help you with this. I was only nine when the war ended.'

'We believe the agent had connections here, may have been linked in some way with Knightly Court.'

George was shaking his head. 'In what way?'

'Can I ask you about the family?'

'The *Deveres*? Pillars of society.' He spoke with absolute conviction. 'Not of the church, of course, being catholics, but otherwise the backbone of the country.'

'What do you know about them?'

George sat upright, as if to make it clear that whatever he said would not alter his judgment of the Deveres.

'There was old Quentin Devere, father of Marcus. I never saw much of him. I believe he had a stroke or something in the war. He was then in his sixties, I think, died around 1958. Had two sons: Marcus, of course, the present owner, and Roland who was killed in the war, as you know.'

'What about their wives?'

'Good god! You're not suggesting –'

'That's right, George, I'm not suggesting anything. I'm trying to understand, that's all.'

'Well, Quentin's wife was called Beatrice. Don't know much about her, though I believe she came from a good family. Roland never married. I think I heard he'd been engaged but the woman broke it off. Not sure if I'm right about that.'

'And Marcus?'

'He's been widowed for some years. Gwen was a marvellous woman, type who organises the whole village, chairman of the parish council, stalwart of the WI. For years she was its county chairman. Very big in the Guides, too.'

'The local squirearchy,' Marnie observed.

'Absolutely, salt of the earth. Everyone looked up to them. You really can't be serious in suggesting they might have been involved with some enemy agent, Marnie. It's just too far-fetched for words.'

'George, there was someone here connected with Major Hallgarten. I don't believe his daughter was lying. She had the actual file on Knightly. Anne saw it in her flat on Friday evening.'

'All right, but if the name's the only thing you have to go on ...' He sipped his whisky, staring into the glass.

'We have a date, too,' Anne said quietly.

'What date?'

'Professor Hallgarten said the agent ceased communication in September 1944. Does that help at all?'

'Not as far as I'm concerned, Anne.' He smiled indulgently. 'I was eight years old at that time.'

Marnie realised she had made a mistake. George may have been around during the war, and he may know everything that went on in the village now, but as a child he could only have had the vaguest understanding of what was happening.

She began to get up. 'Well, thanks anyway, George. It was good of you to see us.'

George raised a stubby hand.

'I don't like to send you away empty-handed, fair lady. Let's just think round this for a moment.' He intertwined the sausage-fingers as if praying for divine inspiration.

Marnie said, 'I suppose the man most likely to know what was happening would be old Mr Devere, but he's –'

George looked horrified. 'Marcus Devere? *Unthinkable*. The man's a great patriot. Did you know he was chairman of the British Legion in this county for over thirty years? Awarded the CBE for his services.'

'George, I wasn't suggesting he was involved in anything, just that he would know what was what.'

'Of course, of course. But he's much too frail to be bothered now, Marnie.'

'I realise that.'

'September 1944, you say. I don't remember much about that time, but I know a man who might.'

George got up and went to the telephone on the bureau. He checked the speed dial and pressed a button. A few moments later he spoke into the receiver.

'Maureen, hallo. It's George. Is Albert about?' He placed a hand over the mouthpiece while waiting. 'My cousin might know.'

'Not too young?' Marnie said.

George shook his head. 'In his teens in the war.'

'Not called up?'

'Farming. Reserved occupation. Ah, Albert, I need to ask you some questions … Marnie's here … Marnie Walker … yes.'

Marnie and Anne listened while George explained about the *enemy agent* and asked about September 1944. The conversation was punctuated by *really? … you sure about that? … when would that've been? … good lord, I never knew that … telegrams the same day? … well I never … amazing …*

When George replaced the receiver he stood looking at the instrument for several seconds before resuming his seat. He looked across the room at Marnie, his expression puzzled.

'Well, that was strange and no mistake.'

'What was it, George?'

'That September was a sad month for the village. Albert's older brother, Arthur, came home on leave. It was the last time they saw him. He went back to his unit and a week or so later they heard he was missing in action.'

'Yes, I remember you telling me that, George. That wasn't what surprised you, was it?'

'No. I told you Arthur worked as a gardener at the Court.'

Marnie nodded. 'And old Quentin Devere went personally to tell his parents what had happened. You said.'

'Well, it seems the Deveres had a telegram themselves on the same day, telling them about Roland.'

'Missing in action?' Marnie said.

'Yes. What a horrible coincidence, on top of everything else.'

'Do you think the old man already knew his own son was dead and that was why he went to break the news to your cousin's family in person?'

'Wouldn't surprise me, Marnie. They're that sort of family.'

'You said *on top of everything else*. What else happened?'

'It was at that time apparently that old Quentin's butler got a letter telling him his father was dying. Quentin paid for him to go home to see him by train to Greenock. While he was up there, the butler was killed in a bombing raid on the docks.'

'How awful.'

'He'd been Quentin's batman in the army. Quentin had been a professional soldier. When the first world war broke out, he was too old for active service, but his batman wanted to join up. In 1915 he was badly wounded – shrapnel, I think – and was invalided out. The old man took him back as butler. He was devoted to Quentin and the whole family.'

'A horrible month all round,' Marnie said. 'I heard you tell Albert about the agent.'

'Oh, yes. He hadn't a clue about that, I'm afraid. If there'd been talk of foreign spies or fifth columnists, I'm sure he would have heard about it.'

'Not even a rumour?'

'Not a word, Marnie. Sorry.'

When Marnie turned the car round on the drive and George waved them off, Anne noticed that the snow had covered their tyre tracks while they had been inside. It fell in light flurries as Marnie turned cautiously onto the high street.

'At times like this I'm really glad to have the Discovery. Whatever the weather, it gets us home.'

Anne made no comment.

'Anne? You all right?'

'I was just thinking. War is so *awful*. I mean, look at Knightly. It's so pretty and peaceful, yet wars have brought it so much tragedy down the ages.'

'You're not just thinking about the last war, are you?'

'No. Think of all the heartbreak they had here in the Civil War. And we're still trying to sort out some of the aftermath now, Sarah's grave and all that.'

'You're right, Anne. But there were two bodies in that grave, and I can't help thinking the second one was Major Hallgarten's agent.'

'Perhaps nobody realised someone killed him because of all the tragedies going on that month.'

Marnie braked early for the turn-off through the field gate.

'I think virtually every month in the war brought its own tragedies, Anne. September 1944 was probably no worse than any other time.'

The car bumped down the field, its four wheel drive system making light of the snow packed on top of the rutted track. A faint glow in the sky revealed where the sun was trying to break through the cloud cover. It lit up the falling snow, illuminating the landscape before them like a Turner painting. For a second, Anne felt as if she could see all the way to Germany.

'We've drawn another blank, Marnie. I don't know what else we can do.' She remembered that summer morning when she had run down the field track to tell Marnie about the body found in Sarah's grave. 'We're back where we started.'

'But,' Marnie began, 'the body in the grave is still a mystery and, don't forget, someone is trying to cover up what happened.'

They arrived back on *Sally Ann* to find a scene of domesticity in the galley. Ralph was checking something in the oven while Donovan was cutting potatoes for a German-style *Kartoffelsalat*. Ralph apologised that the quiche was shop-bought, but he had found it in the freezer and thought it was just right for a snowy day. The bottle of Shiraz Cabernet standing on the table looked just right, too, Marnie thought.

Ralph served the quiche with the potato salad and roasted red peppers. Marnie outlined the main points from their meeting with George while pouring the wine. When she reached the end of the story, they began eating. Eventually Ralph spoke.

'So, Donovan, what are your plans?'

'I'd like to stay on for a day or two, if that's possible.'

'Of course.'

'Is it okay if I sleep on *Sally Ann*?'

They were all aware that he had not left the boat since their return from Germany.

'You want to keep out of sight,' Ralph said.

'Yes.'

'Do you still think …' Marnie paused. 'They're after you?'

'Not necessarily. For one thing, I'm still pretty sure they don't know who I am.'

'But they were following you,' Ralph said.

Anne shook her head. 'No. They were following me. I led them to Donovan, didn't I?'

Donovan said nothing. Anne continued.

'They watched me to see where I'd go. Someone must've followed me on the train to Watford.'

'But how did they know to follow the Porsche?' Marnie asked. 'That was a last minute change of plan.'

'Not difficult for a taxi to follow my old Beetle to Uxbridge. Then they waited around and watched for a car coming out of my street with Anne in it.'

'We did our best to lose them,' Anne said. 'But they just had to keep looking out for the Porsche. They didn't know we'd gone down the Mosel valley, but they knew where we were going. It was just a matter of waiting for us to show up.'

'So, coming back to my question,' Ralph said, 'Do you still think it's important for you to keep out of sight?'

'No point being complacent, but if they're looking for my Porsche in Germany and it doesn't show up anywhere, they may conclude that I'm dead.'

'And as they don't know who you are, anyway …' Marnie grinned.

Donovan permitted himself half a smile. 'Being unknown as well as being dead. Not bad cover.'

58
Confession

It was still dark on Monday morning when Marnie and Anne opened the office. By the time the postman called soon after eight-thirty, the sky was growing lighter and, looking out, Anne announced that more snow was on the way.

The first flakes were falling when the phone rang just after nine.

'Marnie, it's Angela. I just saw Sheila Stubbs in the shop. She said Anne had come back from a trip to Germany. Listen, I've got some news. Can I pop down to see you?'

Anne's forecast proved to be accurate and a heavy downfall of snow, accompanied by a gusting wind, preceded the arrival of the vicar. When she came into the office she was clutching her hat to keep it from blowing away.

'Blimey!' Marnie exclaimed. 'You look like a cross between Orphan Annie and Nanook of the North.'

Angela struggled out of her coat and flopped onto a chair. 'My goodness, it's wild out there. I've got the car stuck in a snowdrift, can't get it out, halfway down the track. Wheels just spin round.'

Marnie hung up the coat and looked through the window. 'We've got a tow-rope in the Discovery. I'll try to pull you out. But first, tell us your news.'

Angela took out a handkerchief and blew her nose. 'I got a letter from the bishop on Saturday. All clear for reburying Sarah. It can go ahead immediately. I've ordered a new coffin. Between ourselves, we had a generous donation from Celia Devere to pay for it.'

'So it's just a matter of waiting for the right conditions?'

'Yes. It should be some time –'

Angela broke off as her mobile began ringing. She apologised and took it out of her bag. When she disconnected, Angela was looking worried.

'Everything all right?'

'Not actually. That was Celia. She was frantic.'

'Really?' Marnie tried not to sound sceptical.

'She's in town, had a call from Mr Devere's butler. It seems that, knowing Celia was on her way home, he left Mr Devere sleeping while he went to the chemist's to collect his prescription.'

'Right.' Marnie was concentrating hard on this. 'You mean the old man's alone in the house?'

'Yes. Trouble is, Celia can't get back because the roads are too icy, and the butler's apparently stuck in Stony Stratford.'

Marnie snatched up her car keys and made for the door. 'Come on. We'd better get up there.'

'Will your car get through?'

'We'll soon find out.' Marnie grabbed her jacket from its hook. 'Anne, can you ring Donovan and get him to come and help. We may need to dig out the garage barn.'

Two minutes later Donovan was shovelling hard to clear a snowdrift that was blocking in the Discovery. He climbed aboard with the three women and they set off at a cautious pace up the field track. They willed the four-wheel-drive up the treacherous slope in conditions that resembled a blizzard, as its chunky tyres bit into the snow and ice.

'So far, so good,' Marnie murmured as they eased past Angela's abandoned car in the field.

They slithered through the field gates and out onto the high street. No other traffic was stirring as they took the road to Knightly Court. Visibility was worsening by the minute and the wind seemed to be gaining in force. The entrance to the Court loomed up ahead.

'Mind the gateposts, Marnie. They're very solid stone.'

Marnie suddenly turned to Angela. 'If the butler's out, how do we get in?'

Angela was aghast. 'Oh, lore. I hadn't thought of that.'

They parked by the front door and Angela trod carefully towards it. Inevitably, it was locked. Donovan walked round the side of the house and found a back entrance. Locked. He continued on his way and met Angela coming from the other direction. They took shelter from the elements in the lee of the conservatory.

'This is awful,' Angela said, raising her voice above the howling wind. 'There's no way of getting in. It's hopeless.'

Donovan pointed to an outbuilding. 'There's a ladder hanging on the wall over there. You go back to the car that way and see if there's a window open upstairs. I'll carry on round here.'

They met again by the front door and huddled in the porch. Marnie and Anne got out of the car to join them. Donovan indicated over his shoulder with a thumb.

'I think there's one window slightly open at the back on the first floor. I'll fetch the ladder and have a go at getting in, but you'll have to hold it to stop me blowing away.'

'Oh, Donovan, you can't do that,' Angela protested. 'It's too dangerous.'

Donovan spread his arms. 'Alternative suggestions gratefully received.'

'We'll all hold it firm,' Marnie said. 'Come on. Where is this ladder?'

With the three of them holding on tight, Donovan climbed gingerly to the window. Marnie tried to look up at him, but the snow whipped her face and she had to turn away. They felt the ladder shaking as Donovan struggled to raise the sash window high enough to climb in. The ladder became still and they heard his voice through the snowstorm.

'That's it. I'm through. I'll come down and let you in.'

'Can you see if Mr Devere's all right first,' Angela called up.

The women lowered the ladder to the ground and headed back to wait in the car. Minutes passed.

'Where is he?' Angela said.

'We know he's in there,' Marnie replied. 'Perhaps the old guy's in a bad way.'

'Something's happened.' Anne's tone filled the others with dread. 'Donovan wouldn't hang around for no reason.'

'Perhaps the window was on a landing,' Angela began. 'Perhaps he's fallen down the stairs or something.'

'No.' Anne pushed open the car door. 'I'm going to see.'

She was gone before anyone could stop her, rushing from window to window, peering in until she went out of sight round the side of the house. The snow was slashing at the windscreen, piling up against the glass like window-panes in a Victorian Christmas card. They waited, but Anne did not return.

Suddenly Marnie put a hand to her throat. 'Oh, no ... Anne!'

'What is it?' Angela looked alarmed.

'She'll try to climb up the ladder. I know she will. I've got to stop her.'

Marnie was out of the car, forcing her way against the blizzard, before Angela could react.

'*Oh Jesu*,' said the vicar, and leapt out in pursuit.

They found Anne battling to prop the ladder up against the partly open window. Marnie grabbed her arm.

'You can't do this, Anne.'

'I can if you'll hold the ladder,' she shouted.

'No. It's too risky. The conditions are getting worse. Come on, back to the car. If he's not out in five minutes, I'm going to call 999 for help.'

They half-dragged Anne back and climbed into the Discovery. Marnie turned the engine on to run the heater.

'There must be a reason why he hasn't come out.'

'That's what I was trying to find out,' Anne said calmly.

'What could be the reason?' Angela asked.

'God knows.' Marnie checked her watch. 'I don't like this.'

'How long is it now?' Angela again.

Anne replied. 'About ten minutes.'

Angela was wringing her hands. 'What can have happened?'

Marnie pulled out her mobile. 'We can't just sit here. We need back-up.'

She pressed three nines and raised the phone to her ear. As she heard the first ring, Angela put a hand on her arm.

'Listen, Marnie.'

Through the roaring of the wind they heard a siren wailing. Marnie pressed the red button on the mobile. The siren grew louder.

'It's getting nearer,' Angela swivelled to look out of the rear window. 'It must be coming here.'

Through the buffeting snow they saw lights, white and blue, as an ambulance beat its way through the gates and down the drive. It pulled up on the other side of the porch.

'There's Donovan!' Anne cried, pointing to the front door.

He stood holding the door open. Two men in green tunics leapt out of the ambulance, each carrying a bag, the word *Paramedic* emblazoned across their backs. They jogged into the house, quickly followed by Marnie, Anne and Angela.

Donovan led the paramedics up to the bedrooms and came down to find the others waiting at the foot of the stairs. His expression was grim.

'How is he?' Marnie said.

Donovan's mouth turned down. 'Not good.'

'But he's alive?'

'Maybe, hard to tell.'

'You've been trying to revive him?' Anne said.

'Not quite. Tell you about it later.'

One of the paramedics came down and walked briskly out through the front door. He returned carrying a bag the size of a rucksack and bounded up the stairs without a word.

The four of them stood in the hall, no one noticing the beautiful decor. While they waited, Anne's eyes drifted across to Donovan. He looked drained.

Ralph was becoming a dab hand at producing fortified coffee. As Marnie and the others were returning to Glebe Farm, she had phoned to let him know they were on their way back. They pushed open the door of the office barn to be greeted by the aroma of coffee and brandy.

They had been relieved of their duties not long after the paramedics arrived by the butler. With great presence of mind he had phoned Leonard Fletcher, the farmer, and asked if he could fetch him from Stony Stratford in the Land Rover. With nothing left for them to do, Marnie and the others had gone home.

Angela asked if she could make a phone call to tell Randall what had happened.

After she disconnected, Ralph said, 'You've had quite a morning.'

'But that's not everything, is it?' Anne said, looking at Donovan.

'No.'

'Are you going to tell us?' Marnie said. 'You were gone a long time.'

Donovan looked troubled. 'Confession is confidential, isn't it?'

'Confession?' Angela repeated. 'What confession?'

'To a priest, I mean. Isn't that kind of confession supposed to be secret?'

'Of course.'

'What if it isn't given to a priest, but to someone who's mistaken for a priest by someone who's too ill to know the difference?'

'Mistaken for a priest?'

They all looked at Donovan. He was wearing his usual black jeans and sweater with a white T-shirt visible round the neck. They understood what he meant.

Ralph said, 'I think you should tell us what happened, Donovan.'

'Okay. I will.'

Donovan managed to get the window open and slide into the house over the sill, lowering himself onto the floor in what was obviously a large bedroom. He called down to the others and heard Angela telling him to check Mr Devere before letting them in. As he turned to find the door in the darkened room, he realised that the bed protruding from the wall was occupied. He crept towards it and bent forward. Marcus Devere was lying on his back sleeping, his breath shallow and wheezing.

Satisfied that the old man was alive, he made his way across the room and was reaching for the door handle when he heard a faint voice behind him.

'Is that you, Robert?'

'No, sir.' Donovan walked quickly back to the bedside. 'No, it isn't. Can I get you something?'

Marcus Devere looked up from the pillow, his rheumy eyes trying to focus. 'Oh … it's you, father.' The voice was weak. 'Thank you for coming.'

'It's not –'

'I must tell you.' A hand reached out from the bedclothes and took hold of Donovan's wrist. 'You must hear my confession.'

'But I can't –'

'Before it's too late.'

Donovan knelt by the bed, his mind racing. What should he do? With the storm raging outside, it could be hours before Mr Devere's priest arrived. By then, perhaps the old man was right, it could be too late. What harm could it do to hear his confession, especially if he was dying? There couldn't be much to confess, and it might make him feel better.

Without waiting for a reply, Mr Devere spoke again. His first words sent a chill through Donovan's heart.

'The other body in the grave. It has weighed on me all my life. May I be forgiven for a mortal sin. All these years, living a lie. Bless me, father, for I have sinned, now at the hour of my death.' The quiet voice faded.

Donovan was breathing faster. 'What body … my son?' It seemed incongruous to address in that way a man old enough to be his great grandfather. 'Whose body was in the grave?'

'I knew he was a traitor. The things he said. The people he thought he fooled, but not me. Pretending to be loyal to the king, to his country. It had to be … had to be.' His head slumped on the pillow.

'Who was it, my son?'

The old man shook his head, breathing with difficulty, either too weary to speak any more or unwilling to go the whole way and finish his confession. Donovan felt desperate. The answer to all their searching may have been within reach, literally, of where he knelt. He hardened his heart.

'You have not confessed, my son. Nothing of what you've told me makes a confession. If you die, you will die unshriven.'

Marcus Devere swallowed and tried to clear his throat. Donovan tried to reach up to the bedside table to give him a glass of water, but the old man would not relax his grip.

'My father's butler.' The words were barely audible.

Yes! Donovan thought. It was logical. All that business about him going away to Scotland and getting killed in a bombing raid was a lie, a subterfuge. They had discovered that the butler was betraying his country to German Intelligence and they had killed him. Everything was clear now. The patriotic Deveres had taken drastic action rather than risk the tainting of the family name by association with an enemy agent. Worse, it would have made them look foolish, harbouring a Nazi spy in their midst.

'Who killed your father's butler?' Donovan asked.

'The Germans.' The voice was firm.

Donovan realised the old man was becoming confused. 'My son, who was it who killed the butler?' He spoke slowly and clearly.

'The Germans … bombed his home … Scotland.'

He must be sinking, Donovan thought. Perhaps there was time for one last effort.

'The body in the grave, my son. The butler. Who killed him?'

'Yes. He killed him. I was too weak …my asthma … too weak then.'

No, no, no, Donovan thought. Start again. 'The body in the grave. Tell me who it was.'

Marcus Devere breathed in and out. 'The traitor … my brother.'

'Your *brother*? But he was –'

'Brought dishonour on the family … thought Germany should be our allies … hated the communists … Russia the enemy … wanted the king to return … Edward … met Nazi sympathisers in Norway … contacted German Intelligence … our father's blue-eyed boy.'

You're telling me your brother Roland was buried in the grave?'

'My brother, yes. Fletcher helped bury him. Arthur … Fletcher.'

'Who killed him?'

'Butler … but my orders. My confession. Bless me, father …'

'What did you do?' Angela said. 'I mean, did you try to give him absolution?'

Donovan shook his head. 'He fell asleep, at least, I thought he did. I wondered if he was dead. I found a phone and called for an ambulance.'

'His brother,' Ralph said. 'He really did say the body in the grave was his brother?' He turned to Angela. 'He did have just the one brother, presumably?'

'Yes.'

'Good god. Who'd have thought it? The war hero was a traitor, his own brother.'

'It must've been unbearable,' Marnie said. 'The idea that one of the Deveres could betray his country. It was just too much.'

'Wait a minute,' Anne said. 'Who's buried in France, then?'

'I suspect we'll never know,' Ralph replied.

'The Deveres paid for that memorial in France, remember,' Angela said. 'Just as they paid for the memorial in our churchyard. Families like the Deveres have connections.'

'And they use them to cover up what they don't want to get out,' Donovan said.

'You mean like the remains being removed from Rosemary's lab?' It was Anne's turn to speak. 'Could they have done that, Ralph?'

'Connections,' Ralph said simply. 'It wouldn't surprise me. I'd like to discuss this with Guy Fellheimer and perhaps Henry Eustace.' He had a sudden afterthought and looked at Angela. 'Or would that be a breach of confidentiality?'

'In what way, Ralph?'

'Was Marcus Devere making his last confession? Should we respect it as such?'

'But I'm not a priest,' Donovan said. 'Surely it doesn't count.'

'Even so, if that was his impression, and you encouraged him to think of it in that way ...'

'We're dealing with the Nazis here.' Donovan's tone had hardened. 'Normal rules don't apply. Anyway, I've told all of you what he said, so it's hardly a secret now.'

'The question,' Ralph said quietly, 'is how far this should go.'

They fell silent as each of them considered the implications of what they had learnt that morning. Outside, the snow was falling, but the wind had dropped. Anne broke the silence.

'Do you realise?'

They all looked at her.

'What is it?' Marnie asked.

'It really was the butler who did it.'

59
Eustace

Guy Fellheimer was unavailable the next day, but Henry Eustace needed no second bidding to travel to Glebe Farm when approached by Ralph. Weather conditions had improved to the extent that it had stopped snowing and the wind had subsided, but Marnie advised Eustace to park in the high street from where she would collect him in the Discovery.

She provided the same shuttle service for Angela Hemingway and Randall Hughes, both of whom were anxious to resolve the final issues relating to the body in Sarah Anne's grave.

Donovan helped carry safari chairs through the spinney from *Sally Ann*, and they sat in a circle in the office with the phones switched to immediate answerphone, the barn doors shut tight and the door locked. Eustace found himself facing Marnie and Ralph, Anne and Donovan, Angela and Randall.

Donovan told his story, occasionally looking down at his notepad. He had decided to note every detail while the 'confession' was fresh in his mind. There was also the possibility that he might need to make a formal statement at some point to the police, and he wanted to be certain of his facts.

Eustace listened without interrupting. At the end of the narrative everyone turned their gaze from Donovan to look at him as he sat back and folded his arms.

'I think the facts are quite straightforward as presented. One or two questions. Donovan, was Mr Devere lucid as far as you could judge?'

'I don't think he was delirious.'

'You seem to have had some difficulty in understanding him.'

'Only because he was saying things I didn't expect to hear.'

'When he spoke of the butler in relation to the body in the grave, you mistook him to mean that the body was that of the butler?'

'Yes.'

'You're quite sure now, with hindsight, that he meant the butler was responsible for the body?'

'Yes. I got him to clarify that.'

'Because you pretended to be a priest and told him he would die unshriven.'

Donovan shifted in his seat. 'He mistook me for a priest.'

'Nevertheless, you exploited that mistake deliberately to induce his confession.'

'It may have been our only chance –'

Eustace raised a hand. 'I'm not criticising you. You showed great presence of mind. What you did may be regarded as somewhat ruthless, but I don't believe you intended it to be callous.'

'I gave him the chance to get things off his chest.'

'Quite. Why exactly did he think you were a priest?'

'I was dressed in black with a white T-shirt. It may have looked like a dog collar. The curtains were partly drawn in the bedroom.'

'This was all entirely by chance, your normal style of dress.'

Donovan nodded. 'I didn't know I was going to see Mr Devere.'

'Okay. Let's leave it there for the moment and return to the facts. We now know that the body in the grave was that of the older brother, Roland Devere, a Major serving in the Special Operations Executive, the SOE.'

'Was that a forerunner of the SAS?' Randall asked.

'No. The SAS had been in existence for a long time. The SOE operated behind enemy lines in world war two only. They were set up by Churchill to carry out sabotage and clandestine missions. The interesting point here is that Devere referred to Norway. The SOE had a lot of success in that country, including the destruction of a plant that was crucial to Hitler's nuclear weapons programme. When the invasion took place, SOE agents played a key role in disrupting German defences throughout France.'

'Including Normandy, then,' Randall said.

'Especially, but not exclusively, in Normandy.'

'You mentioned Norway as significant,' Ralph prompted.

'As an agent in Norway, Roland could have had contact with members or sympathisers of the Nasjonal Samling. That was the pro-German party that formed the puppet government. They were fanatically opposed to communism, and Roland may have sympathised with their anti-Soviet views. He wouldn't be the first member of the British upper classes to have done so.'

'Hence the reference to King Edward,' Ralph observed.

'Yes. I'm having to guess a lot here,' Eustace said, 'but it makes sense in light of what Marcus Devere told Donovan. Quite a few people of that class wanted Edward VIII to return to the throne and help create an anti-communist alliance to counter what they regarded as the red menace.'

'That's why he was killed,' Ralph said.

'Yes. He brought disgrace on a patriotic family who revered him as a war hero. It was too much to bear. A tragic story.'

'What about the tattoo?' Anne asked.

'Roland, remember, was operating behind German lines with the constant risk of capture. His tattoo was reasonable proof that he was not an enemy but an ally. More accurately, it might give a German commander reason to pause before having him shot. If he was taken, the tattoo number could be checked with German Military Intelligence and his story corroborated.'

'The Major Hallgarten link,' said Donovan.

'Correct.'

'So,' Ralph said, 'that seems to have resolved the outstanding issues. Presumably

Roland returned on leave after the Normandy invasion and told his family he believed they should side with the enemy against Soviet expansion. The family was outraged and Marcus took the decision to have him eliminated. Too feeble to deal with his highly-trained brother himself, he ordered others to do it for him.'

'How?' said Donovan.

'We'll never know.'

'We know he was strangled,' Marnie said. 'That broken bone in his neck.'

Ralph reflected. 'Perhaps some drug in a drink served by the butler to disable him beforehand?'

Nobody wanted to dwell on those details.

'What are we going to do about this?' Marnie asked the group. 'I mean, do we tell anyone, the police, the authorities, whoever they might be? Or should we keep Mr Devere's secret?'

Angela looked at Donovan. 'What do you think? You've played an important part in this. You've lost something very valuable that belonged to your father, nearly got yourself killed, heard the old man's confession. I think you have some rights in this decision.'

'I also threatened an old man on his deathbed.' Donovan glanced fleetingly at Eustace. 'That old man had taken a tougher decision than I've ever done. I have no sympathy with the murder victim in this case. I may not be eligible as father confessor, but Mr Devere spoke to me in confidence. If I have any say in the matter, I want to respect that confidence. Let it remain his secret.'

Marcus Devere took his secret to the grave. That afternoon, Randall paid a visit to Knightly Court and was met at the door by a tearful Celia. She told him that her father-in-law had not regained consciousness since the previous day and was now slipping away. Father Martin was expected at any time.

Randall went up to the bedroom where Celia left him to go in alone. He found Hugh sitting beside the bed.

Minutes later Randall came downstairs to tell Celia that her father-in-law had died peacefully in his sleep.

'What about his last confession?' Celia sobbed.

'I administered the last rites,' Randall said. 'He departed in peace with a clear conscience.'

60
Celia and Hugh

'Walker and Co, good morning.'

Marnie reached for the notepad and scoured the desk for a pencil. It was one week later. Life had returned to the Glebe Farm version of normality and, much to Anne's disgust, a spell of damp weather had settled in, bringing a thaw that scuppered her dreams of a white Christmas.

A familiar voice came on the line. 'Before this conversation goes any further, I want you to promise me no one will discover a body or anything else lugubrious while we're talking.'

'Hi, Beth. No probs. That's a dead certainty.'

Beth ignored her sister's attempt at humour. 'So how are you? Recovered?'

'Fighting fit. How's you?'

'Okay. We're thinking of going to see Mum and Dad in Spain over Christmas. Any chance of you coming?'

'Ralph and I are planning a quiet break at his cottage in Murton. It'll be empty. His tenants have returned to California.'

'Sounds good. What other news d'you have?'

'Am I allowed to mention bodies being put back in graves rather than being found in them?'

'Which ones? You seem to have collected so many over the summer.'

'Sarah. Sarah Anne Day. Angela's organising a small service for her in a few days' time. She's making it into the churchyard after 350 years outside.'

'The girl's a late developer, obviously. What about the others? Any more witches around?'

'Not that I know of. I'll check with Angela.'

'And the other one?'

'Sarah's uninvited guest?'

'That's the guy.'

'He's getting buried too, but not on the same day. He's getting his turn along with the two dead navvies some time in the new year.'

'It's nice to have a hobby.'

Shortly after lunchtime that same Monday, Anne was pouring the remains of a bottle of milk into Dolly's saucer in the kitchen while Donovan was unloading his clothes from the washing machine. Marnie was working on a design when she heard footsteps outside on the gravel. She looked up and her heart went into freefall. Passing the window were Celia and Hugh Devere. Was this to be a showdown?

They pushed open the door and entered, bringing with them a blast of chilly air that Marnie thought might not be entirely related to the winter weather. Advancing into the centre of the office, they stood side by side. Celia linked arms with her husband. They smiled. Anne thought that if they had been cats, they'd be purring. For Marnie, the words *lovey-dovey* came to mind.

'Hi.' Marnie hoped her smile did not look too artificial. 'This is a surprise.'

'It's been a day of surprises, Marnie.' Celia glanced briefly at Hugh. 'You tell her, darling.'

Hugh cleared his throat in the embarrassed manner of an Englishman of his class who is going to boast about something. Marnie had a flash of inspiration and guessed that she was about to be given a new commission: the design of a nursery at Knightly Court.

'This is after all the season for glad tidings,' Marnie said encouragingly. 'So you've got some good news.'

'That's right.' Hugh looked surprised. 'We had a letter this morning from the Ministry of Defence.'

'Congratu –' Marnie's turn to look surprised. 'The Ministry of Defence?' She repeated the name slowly.

'That's right. The MD wants to arrange a funeral with full military honours.'

'For whom?'

'For my father.'

'Isn't it wonderful, Marnie?' Celia joined in. 'They're going to send a guard of honour with pall-bearers, flags and everything.'

'Sorry to be thick, but I don't understand.' Marnie saw that Anne was equally baffled. Donovan was expressionless. 'I thought your *uncle*, Roland, had the distinguished military career.'

'Quite,' said Hugh. 'We always thought father's wartime service involved some kind of desk job in Whitehall, but no. Turns out he was one of the top people at Bletchley Park, you know, the code-breaking place, Enigma and all that. But he kept quiet about it all his life. It's only now that the story's coming out that people like him are getting recognition.'

'He's getting a posthumous medal for his contribution to the war effort,' Celia said, beaming a film star smile.

'So your father, Marcus,' Marnie began, 'was ...'

Hugh nodded. 'Yes. He was really important. It's amazing. We had *two* war heroes in the family all along. What d'you think of that?'

'Incredible,' Marnie said. She meant it.

Hugh and Celia looked at Anne and Donovan.

'Unbelievable,' said Anne. She meant it too.

Donovan shook his head, his face solemn.

'You shake your head in wonder,' Hugh said. 'It's people like my father and uncle who make you proud to be British, isn't it?'

Marnie bit her lip. Anne stared at Donovan. His reply was little more than a whisper.

'Absolutely.'

Marnie walked out with Celia and Hugh. It had been puzzling her why Celia was so buoyed up with the news that her father-in-law was going to be honoured by his country after his death. The truth was revealed when they reached the car. Celia turned to Marnie.

'Oh, one other thing.' She glanced across at her husband. He nodded. 'Between ourselves, Marnie, Hugh's been working on a major deal over the past few months, rather confidential sort of thing. Secrecy runs in the family, you might say. Anyway, he's won this contract for the company and got a *huge* bonus.'

Hugh coughed, as if partly to signal an indiscretion by his wife, partly to declare modesty at his achievement.

'The point is, Marnie,' Celia continued, 'I want to talk to you about another project.'

'You want to complete the redecoration of the Court?'

'What? Oh, yes, I suppose so, in due course. No, this is *much* more exciting. Hugh's said we can afford to build a *swimming pool*, an indoor one. I want you to do the interior design.'

'Right.' Marnie knew she had failed to sound enthusiastic.

'Oh, don't look so worried. I know you'll be up to it. It'll be something we can work on together, something for you to look forward to. Won't that be wonderful?'

Marnie's reply was little more than a whisper.

'Absolutely.'

Angela Hemingway arrived at four o'clock. Marnie was pleased to see her but wondered if she was ever going to get time to settle down to a solid block of work that day.

'Marnie, sorry to barge in like this, but I was passing and there was something I wanted to tell you.'

'Come in, Angela. This seems to be the day for sharing news, and actually there's something I wanted to ask you.'

'You go first, then.'

'My sister was on the phone this morning and the subject of witches came up.'

'You really should get out more, Marnie.'

'Thank you for that advice. Beth wondered if there might be any more buried out there and whether one ought to do anything about them.'

'Such as?'

Marnie shrugged. 'I dunno.'

'I don't believe in witches, Marnie, at least not harmful ones. That was all superstition in my view, born of ignorance, intolerance and probably misogyny. My sympathy's with those poor women. They were persecuted for no good reason.'

'That came from the heart!'

'You wouldn't believe how much prejudice there is against women priests. We get it from parishioners, male clergy, the media, you name it. We even get accused of being witches ourselves.'

Marnie was dumbfounded. 'I had no idea.'

Angela raised a hand. 'Don't get me started.'

'Okay. Fair enough. So you don't want to exorcise my field in case there are any more buried out there?'

'If there are any, let them rest in peace, Marnie. They're not doing anyone any harm.'

'Fine by me.' Marnie sensed that this was a matter to discuss further, but perhaps on some other occasion. It was time to change the subject. 'So, what was it you wanted to tell me?'

'Just that I've got a date for Sarah's funeral – that's what I'm calling it, rather than a reburial.'

'The first one didn't count?'

'Exactly.'

Marnie put the date in the diary.

'You're intending to come?' Angela sounded hesitant. 'I know church things aren't really your scene.'

'We'll all be there: Ralph, Anne and myself. Sarah's part of our lives.'

'That's wonderful.' The light was back in Angela's eyes. 'Did you know there's been a subscription in the village to raise money for a headstone? I'm not sure of the wording yet, but we've got time to decide on that.'

'Can I make a contribution?'

'That's kind of you, Marnie, but I think we've got the costs covered.'

'What about a brass plaque to go on the lid of the coffin?'

'That's a lovely idea.'

'I'll get it made.'

'What will you put on it?'

Marnie opened her notepad and wrote some words. 'Will that do?'

Angela read the inscription. 'It's perfect, Marnie. We'll use it for the headstone too. Couldn't be better.'

That night Anne had a phone call from Danny. She sounded more excited than usual.

'You won't believe what's happened to me.'

'Wanna bet?'

'No, I'm serious, Anne.'

'Go on, then. Tell all.'

'It's absolutely *incredible*. I met this boy …'

For the next twenty minutes Anne made all the right noises at all the right times and managed not to yawn or remind Danny of all the other boys she had met who had been incredible. Eventually Danny got round to one of her other favourite topics.

'Any news about Donovan?' Her tone was wheedling.

'Not much.'

'There must be something to tell.'

'Well ...'

'Oh go on, Anne.'

After a pause Anne said, 'He doesn't think the Nazis are really onto him. He thinks they probably don't know who he is. After the two men who were following us got killed when their car crashed and exploded, and Donovan's Porsche slid down the bank into the river Main, where it may not be discovered, he thinks they may have run out of clues about who he is, or was. Also, he thinks that if he lies low for long enough, the police may not after all have any way of linking him with the shooting of Garth Brandon last year, so they may not be likely to try to arrest him for murder.'

'Bloody hell!'

'Other than that, things have been fairly quiet round here since you left.'

Epilogue

A mid-week morning a few days before Christmas. Frost crunched under the feet of the congregation as they processed out of the church into the graveyard, following the coffin. Black-clad villagers against the light stone of the church. Angela had expected a handful of individuals to take part in the ceremony, but upwards of twenty people turned out. She gave a brief homily urging everyone present to think of themselves as supporters or witnesses rather than mourners, and there was an atmosphere close to joy among the participants. Sarah Anne Day was coming home to her final resting place.

There were tears in the eyes of the assembly, but these were brought on by the sharpness in the air. A chill wind hinted that a white Christmas might yet be in prospect.

Marnie, Anne and Ralph stood beside the open grave, where Angela gave a blessing, referring to Sarah as 'this innocent child, our sister in Christ.' The pall-bearers began lowering the coffin into place, sliding it gently down into the earth that had waited more than three centuries to receive her. Standing alone, slightly apart from the gathering, Celia stood in regal designer black, clasping her prayer-book with head bowed, the studied personification of elegance in grief.

Marnie found her mind wandering. She thought back over the past two years to all that Sarah had come to mean in their lives.

We therefore commit her body to the ground ...

Two vicars had been murdered and committed to the ground, victims of an age-old hatred. If Marnie had believed in prayer she would be asking for an end to all conflict in Knightly St John forever.

... earth to earth, ashes to ashes, dust to dust ...

Would there still be enmity in the village while they had a woman vicar? Perhaps the anxieties that Angela had expressed were only the faintest glimpse of antagonisms that would last for yet more centuries.

... in the sure and certain hope of the Resurrection to eternal life.

Perhaps Sarah had hoped that the sacrifice of her own claim to eternal life by a sinful death would cleanse the community of its bigotry and prejudice.

Marnie refrained from throwing soil into the grave, finding that custom somehow distasteful. She looked down at the fine oak coffin. The Deveres had done Sarah proud. On the lid the small brass plaque that Marnie had provided was shining faintly in daylight that would soon be taken from it for evermore. From where she stood, Marnie could just make out the inscription:

Sarah Anne Day (1622 – 1645)
Rest in Peace ***Amor vincit omnia***

Was it a forlorn hope or did love conquer everything in the end? Marnie hoped it might, for all their sakes. She turned, took Ralph and Anne by the hand and walked away from the grave.